While Love Stirs

Books by Lorna Seilstad

LAKE MANAWA SUMMERS

Making Waves

A Great Catch

The Ride of Her Life

THE GREGORY SISTERS

When Love Calls

While Love Stirs

The Gregory Sisters, Book 2

While Love Stirs

A Novel

Lorna Seilstad

a division of Baker Publishing Group
Grand Rapids, Michigan

Published by Revell
a division of Baker Publishing Group
P.O. Box 6287, Grand Rapids, MI 49516-6287
www.revellbooks.com

Printed in the United States of America

Library of Congress Cataloging-in-Publication Data
Seilstad, Lorna.
While love stirs : a novel / Lorna Seilstad.
pages cm. — (The Gregory sisters ; Book 2)
ISBN 978-0-8007-2182-4 (pbk.)
1. Sisters—Fiction. I. Title.
PS3619.E425W52 2013
813′.6—dc23 2013044755

Scripture quotations are from the King James Version of the Bible.

This book is a work of fiction. Names, characters, places, and incidents are the product of the author's imagination or are used fictitiously. Any resemblance to actual events, locales, or persons, living or dead, is coincidental.

Published in association with Books & Such Literary Agency, 52 Mission Circle, Suite 122, PMB 170, Santa Rosa, CA 94509-7953.

14 15 16 17 18 19 20 7 6 5 4 3 2 1

To Judy Miller, my "writing mom."
I treasure your friendship,
and I thank God
for bringing us together.

Now unto him that is able to do exceeding
abundantly above all that we ask or think.

Ephesians 3:20

1

Thursday, May 12, 1910

Charlotte Gregory stared at the elderly doorman. With his arm outstretched, he barred her access to Saint Paul's recently opened Million-Dollar Hotel.

"Sir, what is the meaning of this?" She fought the urge to shove past him and march inside. Creating a scene was not the way to make a good impression on the hotel's staff.

In front of her, the revolving door swished, and a stylish couple entered the establishment unimpeded.

Charlotte motioned her head in their direction. Perhaps the doorman would catch on.

He simply smiled.

She glanced down at her outfit. While not as fancy as that of the lady who'd been allowed inside, the cream-colored walking suit was one of her best, and her wide-brimmed hat was practically brand-new. Surely she looked good enough for a day visit to the prestigious hotel.

She tried to step around the man, but he moved to block her.

"Sir, I need to go inside. I'm here to apply for a position as the chef's assistant. Now, if you'll kindly let me pass—"

When he didn't drop his arm, she darted to the right. She'd come too far to let a portly little gray-haired doorman stop her.

For a portly, gray-haired man, he moved quickly.

"Miss." He dipped his head respectfully. "If you don't have a gentleman escorting you, you'll want to enter through the door on the side."

"Isn't this the public entrance?" She glanced at the curved front of the hotel and reread the signage.

"Yes, miss." He gave her a disarming smile. "But you lovely unescorted ladies enter through a separate door—for the protection of your reputation, of course."

"Of course." Charlotte's cheeks warmed. Why hadn't she remembered that? She'd read about this kind of hotel etiquette before, but it still seemed absurd—especially in 1910. "In that case, sir, where exactly do I find this ladies' entrance?"

"It's to your left, miss." He pointed his gloved white fingers to a door on the side. "It'll lead you directly into the lobby. The hotel's restaurant isn't open yet, but the roof garden and the Palm Room Café are. May I recommend a cup of tea to ward off the chill of this lovely spring morning?"

The doorman's deep, sonorous voice made it difficult to stay cross. Besides, he was simply doing his job. She only hoped this wasn't an indication of the rest of her day.

"Thank you. Perhaps I will have a cup of tea." *To celebrate when I get the position.* Charlotte nodded her head in thanks and slipped around the corner.

Unlike the grand entrance, the door for unescorted ladies sported no awning or fancy woodwork. But similar to the grand entrance doors, this one opened to the hotel's lobby. Square marble pillars rose from the floor toward the high ceiling. A large potted palm tree hung its fronds over a collection of leather-clad furnishings. The dining room was situated to the left of the check-in desk. Even this early, enticing scents wafted from its doors. Onion. Chicken. Garlic. Thyme. Was the chef making something like coq au vin?

She stepped inside the restaurant and her breath caught. From the arched wood panels on the walls to the rich crimson carpeting on the floor, everything spoke of exquisite taste. The tables, all draped in their starched white linens, were set with fine china and silver. Crystal chandeliers sparkled throughout the room.

A waiter looked up from polishing a glass. "Sorry, miss, we're not open for another ten minutes."

"I know. I'm not here to dine, but I would like to speak to the chef."

"The chef?" He rolled his eyes. "He doesn't like to be interrupted while he's *creating*."

The waiter said the last word in his best French accent, and Charlotte giggled. "If you'll direct me toward the kitchen, I'll take my chances."

He shrugged and pointed the goblet to the right. "Keep your head down if he starts waving pots around."

Charlotte followed the tantalizing aromas and clanging pots until she reached the swinging door of the kitchen. She paused, uttered a silent prayer, and licked her dry lips.

When she entered the kitchen, the bustle of the room came to an abrupt halt. The chef turned to face her.

"*Bonjour*, Chef." She approached him and held out her hand. "I am Charlotte Gregory, recent graduate of Fannie Farmer's School of Cookery. I'm here to apply for a position in your kitchen."

His brows furled. "My kitchen?"

"Yes. I have experience in various food preparation techniques, chafing dish cookery, and menu planning."

"But you are a woman!"

Charlotte frowned at the incredulity in his voice. "Women have been cooking for centuries. Did your own mother not cook in your family's kitchen? Were your first cooking lessons not at her table?"

"There will be no woman in the kitchen of Chef Boucher. Go." He dismissed her with a swish of his hand.

"Chef Boucher, you're making something akin to coq au vin, are you not?"

He dropped a handful of mushrooms into a sizzling skillet. "*Oui*."

"You look like you could use some extra hands in here. What if I volunteer to help you today? Then, if you like what you see, we can talk about me securing a permanent position."

The chef seemed to consider her offer, and Charlotte's heart skipped a beat. She crossed her fingers at her side and sent up another prayer.

"No." He shook his head. He raised his spoon in the air and swirled it around. "I will not have a woman cooking in my kitchen. Leave now. You are not welcome here."

A flurry of movement on the floor drew Charlotte's attention. She gasped. A mouse scurried up the leg of a preparation table and scampered across the work surface.

"Did you see that?" Charlotte's voice squeaked.

"Oui." The chef chuckled. "Apparently he wants you to leave as much as I."

"B-but this is a kitchen. Aren't you going to clean the table? Scald it?" She scanned the kitchen and, as if seeing it for the first time, noticed the grease-smeared stove and food-stained floor. "This place is filthy. What have you done to this brand-new, beautiful kitchen?"

The chef grabbed a butcher knife and marched toward her. "You insolent girl. You dare come into my kitchen and hurl insults?"

"Don't you care about your patrons' safety? How can you call yourself a chef?"

He waved the knife in the air, his face becoming as scarlet as tomato sauce. "You'll not work in my kitchen or any other kitchen in this hotel! I'll see to that personally."

Charlotte lifted her chin in the air. "I wouldn't work in your kitchen if I was starving."

"Get out!" the chef roared.

With a final defiant glare, she whirled and slammed open the swinging door, then zigzagged her way around the tables.

Noon patrons now began filing into the dining room. The poor souls had no idea they were taking their lives into their hands by eating here. Anger burned inside her. How could anyone who claimed to love the art of cooking serve customers from a dangerously dirty kitchen? The hotel had only opened in April. Was the management aware of the chef's lack of tidiness? She would inform them, but they'd probably do nothing as long as the restaurant's patrons were satisfied. After all, the famous French chef had been touted all over the city.

"You'll not work in any restaurant in the city!" the chef bellowed from the doorway.

Startled by his roar, Charlotte turned back. Her eyes widened as the knife he was still waving glimmered in the dining room's lamplight. Keeping her gaze on the knife, Charlotte quickly backed out of the dining room until she struck a man's solid chest.

She jumped and spun around. "I'm so sorry."

"Are you all right, miss?"

Charlotte's cheeks flamed as she tipped her face upward. Her breath caught at the depth of the man's bottle-green eyes. "I'm fine." She stepped away and glanced at the ranting chef. He continued to bellow his accusations across the room.

The green-eyed man followed her gaze. "Pardon me for asking, but are you stirring things up with the chef?"

"Let me put it this way. Do you value your digestive tract?"

His eyebrows drew close. "As a matter of fact, I do."

"In that case, sir"—Charlotte tugged one of her long sleeves back in place—"I suggest you find somewhere else to eat."

"Dr. Brooks?"

Joel halted at the sound of his name. Having just returned from lunch, he had yet to reach his office. "Is everything all right, Nurse Willard?"

"Harvey Richmond is having trouble breathing again, sir. You'd better hurry."

He raced down the hall behind the nurse, thinking of Harvey, a freckle-faced eight-year-old orphan with pericarditis brought on after a bout of rheumatic fever. Every day the boy grew weaker.

Joel entered the ward, greeted by Harvey's obstinate dry cough. Each episode racked his small frame. Joel slipped a hand behind the boy's back and waited while the nurse added another pillow. He lowered Harvey back on the pillow, withdrew his stethoscope from his coat pocket, and listened to Harvey's struggling heart.

"Nurse Willard, bring me the codeia, please."

"But Dr. Brooks, he's—"

Joel held up his hand to silence her. "I'll take care of it."

Since Joel had temporarily taken over two wards of City Hospital, money decisions had plagued him. He hoped to secure the position permanently and become the youngest assistant superintendent ever assigned to the task. He meticulously decided how to spend every penny he was allotted to give his patients the best care and to prove he could handle the job. Yet as much as it would mean to him for the temporary position to become permanent, this child meant more.

As an orphan, Harvey was a charity case, and hospital policy stated medication should be reserved for charity patients who had a hope of recovering, not those who required palliative care. Even if Joel had to pay for the medication himself, this little boy would be comfortable.

After ordering an ice bag, Joel administered the codeia and held Harvey's hand until the drug took effect.

"Hey, you want to play checkers tomorrow?" he asked.

The boy's heavy eyelids flickered. "Dunno if I'll be here."

"You'll be here." Joel brushed the ash-colored hair from Harvey's brow. "And if you need me, Nurse Willard will come get me right away."

Harvey didn't seem to hear the last words as sweet slumber claimed him. Joel tugged the blanket up to the boy's shoulders and met Nurse Willard's knowing eyes. Harvey had little time left for checkers or anything else.

Even though Joel had done everything he medically could, helplessness welled inside his chest. He shoved his stethoscope back into his pocket. "Come find me if there are any changes."

Charlotte hated hospitals.

The faint scent of alcohol stung her nose, reminding her of the awful days only two years ago that her parents lay dying. She shook her head. Time to put those sad thoughts aside. Today was a day to celebrate.

She quickened her pace as she walked down the corridor toward the maternity ward. The mews of newborn babies indicated she'd reached her destination. After stepping inside the sunny, semiprivate room, she scanned the two beds, and her gaze fell on her older sister. She barely restrained herself from racing toward the newest Gregory girl in Hannah's arms.

Hannah, still nearly as pale as the crisp white sheet covering her, beamed as Charlotte approached. Her younger sister Tessa rose from her chair to greet her with a warm embrace.

"I'm an aunt." Tessa giggled. "I can't believe it. It feels like a dream."

"I could pinch you so you'd know it was real." With a laugh, Charlotte released Tessa, then turned to the proud father.

Lincoln lifted the tiny bundle from Hannah. "Charlotte, are you ready to meet our Ellie?"

Charlotte eased her hands around the baby's soft blanket. "You named her after Momma?"

"Elizabeth Ruth Cole. Elizabeth for Momma, and Ruth for my favorite Bible story." Hannah shared a knowing glance with her husband. "But I think she looks like you."

Tucking the blanket away from Ellie's wrinkled face, Charlotte ran the back of her index finger along the babe's silky cheek. She touched the swath of brown hair with the same copper highlights all the Gregory sisters possessed. Ellie's eyes were dark blue, but

Charlotte had heard that could change. Would they turn hazel like those of the Gregory sisters, or would they end up gray-blue like her father's?

"She's the most beautiful baby I've ever seen." Charlotte pressed a kiss to Ellie's forehead. "Tessa told me she was perfect, and for once our little sister wasn't exaggerating. I'm sorry it took me awhile to get here. I was out seeking a position at the Saint Paul Hotel, and I didn't know she'd arrived until I got back to Aunt Sam's house."

Hannah sighed. "Guess she decided she wanted to surprise us and make her entrance early."

"I think she wanted to do things her way." Lincoln kissed his wife's cheek. "Like her momma."

Hannah smiled. "A true Gregory girl."

"But remember, this little princess is also my daughter. I'd like to think there's some Cole in her to balance things out." Lincoln reached for the baby, and Charlotte reluctantly gave her up. "But I'll be thrilled if she takes after her mother in every way."

"If that's the case, you'll end up very gray." Charlotte sat in the straight-back chair beside Hannah's bed and took her sister's hand. "Are you feeling all right?"

"I feel wonderful." Hannah pushed up in the bed, wincing at the movement. "Tell me about the position you were seeking. Did you get it?"

"I think it's safe to say I won't be working at the Saint Paul Hotel today or at any time in the near future, but that's fine with me. The cleanliness of the kitchen was far from satisfactory."

Lincoln chuckled. "And I suppose you made sure the chef knew you didn't approve."

Charlotte nodded. "I told the management too. I had to for the sake of the patrons eating there. The management was aghast and said they'd address the situation forthwith. Still, I was so hoping . . ."

Hannah squeezed Charlotte's hand. "You'll get your own restaurant someday, Charlotte. I know you will."

An apron-clad nurse bearing a dinner tray moved to the foot of Hannah's bed. "I have your dinner, Mrs. Cole."

"Oh, good. I'm starved."

"And you should be." Charlotte helped Hannah sit up in the bed and adjusted the pillows behind her before the nurse set the tray across Hannah's lap. "Delivering a baby is hard work. You'll need to eat well to build your strength back up."

Charlotte took the tray from the nurse, but its contents made her cringe. The bowl of grayish gruel and the cup of weak tea hardly seemed adequate. At Fannie's cooking school, she'd taken additional courses in feeding the ill and convalescent, and this food did not meet Miss Farmer's criteria. Equally disappointing was its presentation on chipped enamel dishes. Who could possibly want to eat this food?

"Ma'am," Charlotte said as the woman started to leave, "as a nursing mother, my sister needs better nutrition. She requires milk, vegetables, fruit, and proteids."

"Proteids?"

"Yes—meats, eggs, nuts."

The nurse shot her an apologetic look. "The doctor ordered the food, miss."

"But why this soft, bland diet? Hannah is feeling fine. She hasn't had any digestive issues. Most new mothers can handle a regular diet on the same day as delivery. At the very least, she could tolerate a meat-based soup or stew with some vegetables. It would be more substantial than this."

Hannah slipped her spoon into the gruel. "Charlotte, this will be fine."

"No it won't. How can you expect to provide for Ellie if you don't eat well?"

"Is there a problem here?"

Charlotte turned at the sound of the male voice, only to find the same green-eyed man she'd backed into this morning. "*You're* my sister's doctor?"

"As a matter of fact, I am." He scowled, disapproval turning down the edges of those bottle-green eyes. "And I see once again you're stirring things up."

2

Dr. Joel Brooks crossed his arms over his chest and stared down at the young woman. He didn't have time to deal with extra problems today, and this little spitfire had "troublemaker" written all over her pretty face.

"Well, someone needs to stir things up!" She pointed at his patient's food. "This is not enough nutrition for a nursing mother. My sister requires an adequate diet, and I intend to see she gets it."

Some women's faces looked pinched when they were fired up about something, but for some reason, anger looked good on this young woman. Maybe it was the way her hazel eyes flashed or her cheeks pinked in the light coming through the ward's windows. Still, no matter how attractive Miss Gregory was, her outbursts were drawing unwanted attention, and one look at the new mother in the bed told him his patient was overdoing it.

"Now, now, miss." He sighed. Dealing with family issues was his least favorite part of serving as one of the hospital's assistant superintendents, but it was part of his job. "Why don't you leave your sister's postnatal care to me? I don't presume to know how to make a fine dessert, so why should you presume to understand her nutritional needs?"

She folded her hands in front of her fabric-covered buttons. "For your information, I know a great deal about the care and feeding of the ill and convalescent. At Miss Farmer's School of Cookery we studied the caloric needs of men, women, and children. As a nursing mother . . ."

She prattled on, but he didn't listen. A cooking school? Did she seriously believe classes in food preparation made her an expert in a medical setting?

"Dr. Joel Brooks." Mrs. Cole's husband stood up. "May I introduce my two sisters-in-law, Miss Charlotte Gregory, whom you have apparently already met, and the youngest, Miss Tessa Gregory."

Charlotte. With her rich maple syrup–colored hair, her given name seemed to fit her. Earthy. Warm. At least until she opened her mouth.

Joel pressed a hand to Mrs. Cole's forehead. Good. No fever. Still, her eyelids drooped. "Miss." He looked directly at Miss Gregory. "I believe it's in Mrs. Cole's best interest for visiting hours to conclude for today."

She squared her shoulders, apparently not ready to give up her fight. "But what about her food? She'll be in here for at least a week, correct?"

He nodded.

"Am I to assume this is what she'll be eating every day? This bowl of unappetizing gruel contains less than one hundred and twenty calories. Surely you know a nursing mother needs at least two thousand calories a day to meet her and the baby's needs."

Hmm. Maybe Miss Spitfire did know more than he imagined.

The corner of his mouth hitched. "I'll be happy to meet with you tomorrow and discuss her diet." He motioned to the nurse to join them. "Meanwhile, Nurse Bryant will see you and your sister out, then she'll return and get Mrs. Cole a glass of milk to go with her dinner."

The nurse placed her hand on Miss Gregory's arm, but she pulled it free and turned back to him, her hands perched on her hips. "When?"

"I promise I'll get the milk when I get back to the ward, miss," Nurse Bryant assured her.

"No, Dr. Brooks, when do you want to meet?"

"Catch me when you come to visit." Joel lifted Mrs. Cole's wrist and pressed his fingers against the steady pulse. "I don't think we need to set a time."

"I disagree." The smile she clearly forced said she was not easily placated. "Two o'clock, then?"

Didn't this young lady know how busy he was? His patients needed him. His schedule was booked with people who truly *required* his attention.

He glanced down at Mrs. Cole, her eyelids growing heavier with added fatigue. She was his biggest concern right now, and he wanted her well-meaning sisters out of here so she could rest. He nodded toward Miss Charlotte Gregory. "Yes. Two o'clock is fine. Meet me in my office. Will fifteen minutes suffice?"

Tessa, the younger sister, smiled at him. "Doctor, Charlotte will just be getting warmed up in fifteen minutes."

Miss Gregory silenced her sister with a glare, then turned and dipped her head in his direction. "That will be fine. I look forward to an enlightening conversation."

Joel watched the nurse escort the sisters to the door. *Enlightening conversation?* Maybe so, but he had a feeling this little cooking school graduate intended to cook him and his hospital's food over her open spit.

3

Charlotte tapped the top of the fountain pen against her lip. What else did she want to mention to Dr. Brooks when she met with him tomorrow?

She glanced out the study's window. If she leaned to the left, she could get a glimpse of the tulips caught in a shaft of fading daylight. How blessed she was to be staying here at Aunt Sam's. And tonight Lincoln's aunt had opened her home up to Tessa as well. Given the birth of Hannah and Lincoln's new baby, Aunt Sam had insisted Tessa join her and Charlotte for at least a month or so, and she'd done everything she could to make Tessa feel at home.

Leaning back in the heavy leather chair, Charlotte smiled. Even though Aunt Sam was Lincoln's aunt and not her own, she'd come to think of this place as home. Aunt Sam had taken her in after her return from Fannie Farmer's School of Cookery and had treated her like the daughter she'd never had. The wealthy woman amazed her daily. Between her penchant for bloomers and her outspokenness, she certainly wasn't like any lady Charlotte had ever met.

"Are you still working on your presentation?" Aunt Sam set a cup of hot chocolate on the desk. "I thought you might like some nourishment. Don't worry. I didn't make it myself."

"Thank you." Charlotte wrapped her hands around the warm cup and watched the spry sixty-year-old perch herself on the corner of the desk.

"Tessa said it didn't go well at the hotel's restaurant today."

"You could say that." Charlotte sighed. "I'm beginning to wonder if God is trying to tell me something."

"Lottie, I don't want to hear you talk that way. God placed this dream in your heart for a reason." She slid off the edge of the desk as Tessa entered the room. "But keep in mind God may have a different way to carry out his plans than you do."

"There you are." Tessa sauntered in with a newspaper in hand and sat down in the chair opposite the mahogany desk. "I was afraid you two had taken off on some fun excursion and left me all alone to fend for myself in this big old house." She feigned distress by placing the back of her hand against her forehead.

Aunt Sam laughed. "Quite a dramatic display, young lady. I believe you have an untapped gift."

Charlotte set down her cup. "Oh, she taps it all right, but I wouldn't call it a gift."

"You shouldn't disagree with your elders, Charlotte." Tessa clutched the newspaper to her chest. "And if you aren't kind to me, I may keep the answer to all of your problems a secret."

"The answer to all of my problems is in that paper?" Charlotte dropped her pen on the blotter.

"That's what I said."

"And how does a newspaper secure me a position at a fine establishment? Is a restaurant seeking to hire a chef?"

She passed the folded paper to Aunt Sam. "No, it says there's going to be a cooking contest—and all you need to do, dear sister, is win."

"What kind of contest?" Aunt Sam snapped open the newspaper.

Charlotte rose from her chair and came around the desk. "You don't seriously think this is a good idea?"

"It bears investigation." Aunt Sam spread the paper on the desk and flipped through the pages. Charlotte leaned close to look.

Tessa wedged her way between them and pointed to the article on the third page. "It says, 'The Greater Northern Natural Gas

Company proudly announces a contest. All contestants will demonstrate their culinary skills by cooking on today's newest gas stoves, available in our fully equipped display room.'" She paused. "It starts on Monday."

Charlotte turned to her chair and pressed a hand to her beating heart. The idea of a contest was thrilling, and Miss Farmer had insisted all her students be well versed at cooking on gas stoves, but how could a cooking contest help her secure a position?

"It also says," Tessa continued, "there will be five rounds—layer cakes, pies, doughnuts, bread, and main dishes. A different category will be held each day, with the highest-scoring contestants advancing to the next round."

Aunt Sam lowered herself into one of the chairs opposite the desk. "What does it say the winner receives?"

"There are prizes for each day, with everything from a complete set of aluminum cooking utensils to a Bissell carpet sweeper. But the all-around winner will be awarded a brand-new Jewel gas range." She clasped her hands together. "Oh, Charlotte, you have to do this."

Charlotte laughed. "And what would I do with a new gas range?"

"Put it in your hope chest, dear." Aunt Sam grinned.

"That's a little large for a hope chest."

"I'm sure we could find some place to store it." Aunt Sam laid her hand on Charlotte's. "I think this is an opportunity you can't pass up. How could those chefs deny you a position once you've proved yourself over and over in a contest like this?"

"But it won't be that easy—"

Aunt Sam turned toward Tessa. "When does she need to sign up?"

Tessa ran her finger under the article. "Tomorrow morning at eight. Only the first twenty women who sign up can participate."

"I'll tell Henry to have the automobile ready at seven." Aunt Sam stood, her tone sealing the discussion.

Charlotte jumped to her feet. "Wait. A lot of women in this

city make wonderful cakes and pies. I'm not the only person who cooks well. What if I don't win?"

Aunt Sam chuckled. "And what if you do? God may have a whole new plan for you, dear. A whole new amazing and exciting plan."

Arriving late was not part of Charlotte's plan, and given the disapproving expression on Dr. Brooks's face upon her entrance, she didn't think it helped her cause one iota. After taking a seat across from the young doctor, she unfolded her list. The paper crackled and she winced.

She sat up straight and took in the man seated at the desk. For all his seriousness, Dr. Brooks was less than ten years her senior. His light brown hair, cropped short, was parted on the left, and the mole on his cheek added to his attractiveness rather than detracted from it. And those green eyes—

"Miss Gregory?" he said in a raspy baritone.

She blinked. Oh my. Had she been staring? Swallowing, she plunged in. "First, let me apologize for my tardiness." Even though the fact that Henry hadn't been able to get the automobile's engine to turn over would be a good excuse, she chose not to share it. Best for the doctor to know she took responsibility for her actions. "Shall we begin by discussing the hospital's meal plans?"

Dr. Brooks coughed into his fist. "The entire hospital's?"

"Of course." Without a second thought, she reached for a water pitcher on the corner of his desk and poured him a glass. "I imagine the whole system needs to be overhauled. We could start in the maternity ward and then address the other wards, floor by floor, of course."

Dr. Brooks held up his hand. "Wait a minute, Miss Gregory. I agreed to talk to you about your sister's nutritional needs, not those of all the patients in the hospital." He checked his pocket watch. "There are six hundred beds in this hospital. I don't think your remaining ten minutes will allow us to discuss quite that many patients, do you?"

"No, probably not." How foolish she had been to think he'd want to discuss overhauling the whole hospital! Miss Farmer had cautioned them to negotiate small changes whenever they could, not try for the large ones right away.

"Do you mind?" She pointed to the water pitcher.

"Not at all."

She poured herself a glass, took a long drink, and returned the glass to the desk. To her surprise, Dr. Brooks immediately moved it back to its original position. How odd.

Offering him her most agreeable smile, she stilled her hands in her lap and began again. "As you know, a nursing mother needs at least two thousand calories a day. What are your plans to see that my sister receives the nourishment she needs?"

"We have a set meal plan for the mothers in the maternity ward." Dr. Brooks turned the handle on the pitcher so it faced the right, as it had when she'd arrived.

Charlotte cocked her head to the side. "Which consists of what?"

"It consists of regular, nutritious meals that are easy for new mothers to digest and for the nursing staff to prepare."

"But I noticed today my sister was served cauliflower. Surely you of all people realize cauliflower can make a nursing baby gassy?"

"Is that why you were late?" He leaned forward. "Were you giving my nurses a difficult time about the meal?"

"No, of course not." Anger simmered inside her. How dare he accuse her of impropriety when it was *his* nurses who were in error? Charlotte squared her shoulders. "For your information, I said nothing to them, although I was sorely tempted. However, they do need to be educated. That would be your job, Dr. Brooks, would it not?"

Irritation flashed across his face. "Did you come here to insult me or discuss your sister's care, Miss Gregory?"

"I'm simply trying to make you see the need for proper nutrition for all the mothers in the hospital's care." She locked her gaze on his, then after a few seconds dropped it to the list in her lap. There was no way she was leaving until she knew Hannah would have everything she needed. As she read the items from her list, she ticked off each one on her fingers. "Will Hannah receive fresh fruit every day? Milk? Vegetables?"

"I can assure you her needs will be met." His words came out clipped, and he pushed back from the desk, apparently signaling their time was nearing an end.

"If you don't mind, I'd like some details. For example, how many grams of proteids are provided?" She looked up from her list to see Dr. Brooks scowling. "And are the mothers always served on the chipped enamelware I saw?"

Dr. Brooks rose to his feet, his lips pressed together in a thin line. "Miss Gregory, I'm afraid we don't have the money to serve the ladies on fine china. Any surplus we have tends to go for real needs—people without resources to pay, like orphaned children."

Charlotte's cheeks burned. "I know it's vital for the hospital to care for orphans, but these things are important too. If the ill and convalescent aren't well nourished, they won't recover."

He pressed his fists onto the desk blotter and leaned toward her. "We have the lowest mortality rate in the city—despite our chipped enamelware."

She stood and leaned on the desk too, displacing the inkwell. "But some people still die, and they might not if their nutritional needs were met by a caring medical staff."

"Miss Gregory." He put the inkwell back in place, but his jaw remained clenched tight. "Your time here is up."

The glass. The pitcher. The inkwell. Charlotte's breath caught as the pieces of the puzzle fell into place. "I see the problem now. You like everything to be in order, and I'm messing that up." She folded her list and slipped it back into the pocket of her skirt.

"Well, you'd better get used to things getting messy, because when I'm cooking something up, that's bound to happen."

Perhaps that hotel chef had a good reason to chase Miss Gregory out of his restaurant, brandishing a butcher knife. Joel stared at her as he considered doing the same with a scalpel. Who did she think she was, coming into his office, demanding changes in his hospital, insulting him and his staff, and moving things around on his desk?

Blood pumped in his ears. No one—not even a careless nurse—had made him so angry in such a short amount of time. Messy? What did she think a doctor did? If draining a boil didn't count, then nothing did.

The corners of her lips curved in a solicitous smile, and she nodded. "Until later then, Dr. Brooks."

"Until later." Why did he say that? He had no intentions of seeing her again, but he had to get her out of his office. "And I promise I will see to your sister's diet personally."

"Thank you, but I'd feel better if you'd let me prescribe it myself."

"I think we can manage without you, Miss Gregory." He shook his head. Prescribe it? Did her nerve never end? "Good day."

He watched her leave, surprised she'd let him have the last word, then dropped back into his chair and surveyed his desk. Sure, he liked items where they belonged. It made them easier to find when he needed them, but it didn't mean he was rigid and uncaring. Quite the contrary. He cared too much. Over and over, the older doctors had told him he needed to separate himself from his patients, but how could he? He knew suffering all too well.

He opened the ledger on his desk and sighed at the tight figures neatly aligned in the last column.

Chipped dishes were the least of his concern.

Nurse Willard tapped on his door. "Dr. Brooks, Harvey Richmond is having trouble breathing again. I thought you'd want to know right away."

What food would Miss Gregory prescribe to cure the inflamed heart of an eight-year-old? Would her soul ache as his did because every avenue had been exhausted?

Joel's footfalls echoed in the nearly empty corridor of Harvey's ward. His quickened his pace as he neared the boy's bed. Harvey's chest heaved as he fought for air. Joel knelt beside the boy, quickly administered codeia, and then took Harvey's hand. He swallowed hard. All he could do was make the boy more comfortable. It wouldn't be long now.

He prayed for the orphan who'd spent so much of his childhood without a parent's love and asked the Lord to welcome the child into his arms. Then he added a prayer of thanks that the only thing Miss Gregory had to worry about was chipped dishes.

4

Charlotte took stock of the white enameled Jewel gas range in front of her. With six gas burners, teardrop-shaped handles, a bread warmer, a large oven, and a broiler, it was a work of art. Why would anyone want to go back to cooking on a woodstove after using one of these beauties?

When she'd signed up the other day, she'd been told each of the twenty contestants would bake a layer cake and present it to the judging panel. Today, as soon as they'd all arrived, the twenty women had been divided into two groups and then paired within their groups with another contestant. Each pair would have a gas range to share. Glad to be in the first group, Charlotte laid her recipe on the worktable's surface and waited for the signal to begin.

"Don't crowd me when we start to bake." The young woman she'd been paired with plopped her basket on the worktable, then used her ample hips to nudge Charlotte to the right. The woman looked at the range and frowned. "It's hard enough to use a gas stove when I prefer coal, but I can't make a masterpiece if I don't have enough room to work."

Charlotte switched to the other side of the table. She needed room to work as well and didn't plan for anyone, including this bossy girl, to ruin her chance at becoming a chef. Two years ago she'd allowed someone else to dictate her actions, and she'd made a vow to never let that happen again. Even when it didn't feel natural to her, she'd be the one in charge from here on out—but in a nice way, of course.

She smiled at the newcomer. "I'll be sure not to interfere on your *half* of the table."

"Do you know anything about"—her partner flicked her hand in the direction of the range—"these?"

"Some." Charlotte picked up her own basket and set it on the table. "I'm Charlotte Gregory, and you are . . . ?"

"The one who is going to win." The girl laughed at her witty comment. "My name is Kathleen O'Grady, and I meant that last part. I don't do anything unless I can come out on top. Do you consider yourself a good cook?"

Charlotte smoothed her apron. "With God's help and a little creativity, I manage."

Kathleen filled her half of the table with ingredients from her basket. "I'm making a sunshine layer cake with orange cream frosting."

"It sounds delicious. Good luck." Charlotte picked up her recipe and slipped it into the pocket of her apron. No need to reveal her secrets too soon.

"And what are you making?"

"I'm making a layer cake." One didn't live with Tessa Gregory and not learn how to deal with prying questions. Excitement bubbled inside Charlotte, but she managed not to laugh.

After all, that would be rude.

A bespectacled man with a bulbous nose and a curling mustache stepped to the front of the room. "Welcome, ladies! My name is Stewart Johnson. I'm the vice president of the Greater Northern Natural Gas Company, and I'd like to personally thank each of you for entering our competition."

Those gathered applauded. Charlotte smiled at Tessa and Aunt Sam, who were seated with several other spectators in wooden folding chairs off to the side.

"As you've already been informed, you'll have either three hours this morning or three hours this afternoon, depending on the group you are in, to prepare a layer cake in one of our gas demonstration ovens. When your cake has been baked and frosted, you'll present it to our judges." Mr. Johnson motioned toward a separate table where two ladies were seated. Charlotte guessed the empty chair beside them belonged to Mr. Johnson himself since she'd seen him sitting there earlier. "Your cake will be scored on taste, texture, originality, and appearance."

Originality was good. The spiced ribbon cake with opera caramel frosting that Charlotte planned to prepare would most likely be something the judges hadn't tasted before. The apple jelly between the layers made it surprisingly delicious, and the nuts sprinkled on the top would make it even more attractive, but would that be enough? Maybe she should have gone with a more traditional cake and dressed it up with ornamental rosettes.

She shook her head. It was too late now. All of her ingredients sat packed in the basket, and Mr. Johnson would signal them to begin any minute.

"Please respect your partner's work space and share the oven, and remember, the five contestants with the lowest scores will not advance to tomorrow's pie round." Mr. Johnson took out his pocket watch and checked the time. "It's nine o'clock, ladies, and you may begin."

Charlotte glanced at Kathleen. "Did you want me to light the oven?"

"Well, I'm certainly not going to." Kathleen broke an egg into her mixing bowl. "But I'll need the oven first or my cake might fall."

"That will be fine. I'll start by making my frosting on the stove top." Charlotte opened the oven doors, struck a match, and turned the pilot light lever. Once the flame caught, she closed the doors and turned the gas lever all the way to the left. A familiar whoosh from inside the oven let her know the gas flame had caught.

Charlotte gathered a pan and added the brown sugar, light cream, and butter she needed for the opera caramel frosting. Once she set the flame beneath the pan, she stirred the mixture. Beating it until it reached a spreadable consistency made her arm ache. She noticed Kathleen wasted no time mixing the batter for her cake and pouring it into the pans she'd prepared. With so little time given to blending the ingredients, Charlotte feared Kathleen's cake would be heavy.

Kathleen cleared her throat. "I need to get these in."

Charlotte's frosting began to form a ball. "You might try asking me nicely to step out of the way."

"This is a contest." Kathleen elbowed Charlotte's side. "There's no room for niceties."

"But you haven't even checked the oven's temp—"

"Mind your own frosting." Kathleen let the door slam hard, and Charlotte's pot rattled. "Not that it will do you any good."

Charlotte steadied the pot with a towel and began whipping the contents in her bowl. It would serve Kathleen right if her cake did burn. Foolish girl. She didn't even take the time to put a teaspoon of flour in the oven to test the oven's temperature. Without determining how hot it was, how would Kathleen know when to remove the cake?

Charlotte pushed the thought aside. That was Kathleen's problem. When her frosting was spreadable, she nudged Kathleen's supplies back into her half of the work area and set out her own ingredients so she could get started on the cake. She picked up the metal measuring cup Miss Farmer had given her and balanced it in her hand. Like a plane in the hand of a woodworker, this measuring cup felt at home. She spooned it half full of butter.

"What is that cup for?" Kathleen asked. "A good cook doesn't have to measure. They know if they've put in enough by looking."

"I disagree." Charlotte emptied the cup into her bowl. "Measuring takes the guesswork out and ensures your food turns out well every time." She measured the first of the two cups of sugar, but when she went to pour it in the bowl, Kathleen bumped her arm and sugar went flying.

"Oh no. How will you ensure your cake turns out now?"

Charlotte shot Kathleen a glare. What kind of a person sabotaged someone's cake? Did she honestly think Charlotte couldn't handle a little spilled sugar?

Resisting the urge to give Kathleen a good tongue-lashing, she finished adding the ingredients for her cake and wiped up the spilled sugar. As soon as she'd finished filling the layer cake pans, she glanced at the oven.

"Uh, Kathleen, have you checked on your cake lately?"

Kathleen threw open the door and smoke wafted out. She grabbed a towel and yanked the pan from the rack. "You did this on purpose! You set the oven too high! Mr. Johnson! Mr. Johnson!" When the gas company's vice president arrived, Kathleen thrust a finger toward Charlotte. "She sabotaged my cake. She set the oven too high."

His brow furled. "Did you do that, Miss Gregory?"

"No, sir." Charlotte shook her head. "I started to tell her to check the temperature and she said to mind my own frosting."

"That's exactly what I heard as well." He twisted the ends of his mustache. "But ladies, do consider yourselves warned. If there are any more problems, I'll have no choice but to disqualify one of you."

Behind his back, Kathleen flashed a smug grin. Charlotte's blood came to a full boil, but she forced a lid on it. "Yes, sir. I'll do my best to help her in the future."

He glanced at the cake on the work surface. "Your cake doesn't appear ruined, Miss O'Grady. A little brown around the edges, maybe, but I think you can frost it and make it a fine entry." He nodded to Charlotte. "Good luck to both of you."

Charlotte set a pie tin with a teaspoon of flour on the middle rack and checked the clock. If the oven was sufficiently hot to brown the flour in five minutes, then the oven was the right temperature. She could turn the gas cock up or down if need be.

At the five-minute mark, she opened the door. Perfect. She set her layer cakes inside and closed the door.

"You think you're so smart." Kathleen plunked her ample frame on a stool. "But you're not smart enough to beat me. Remember that, Charlotte Gregory. I'm going to win this competition and get me a husband. You know what they say: 'The way to a man's heart . . .'"

Charlotte rolled her eyes. "The way to a man's heart isn't through his stomach. It's with a gentle and humble spirit. You give that a try. I'm sure it's something new for you."

Joel heaved a sigh. Nurse Watkins should know by now that Joel liked the morning reports on the left rather than the right side of his desk. Bone-weary, he deposited the stack in its correct position, leaned back in his chair, and closed his eyes. Fifteen minutes of shut-eye. That's all he needed.

A knock on the door jolted him awake. He relaxed when his sister, Nurse Mathilda Brooks, peeked in.

She set a cup of coffee in front of him and laid a hand on his shoulder. "I heard you lost Harvey Baker last night."

He nodded, not trusting the thickness in his throat. After a swig of the coffee, he glanced up at her and smiled. "I'm fine, Mattie."

She took a seat in the empty desk chair. "You stayed all night with him?"

"No one should die alone."

"Cathy Creston is a good nurse. She'd never let that happen."

He held up his hand. "I'm not attacking the nurses. I have the utmost admiration for all you do."

"That's good to hear." Mattie smoothed her apron. "Speaking of which, what happened with Mrs. Cole's sister? Charlotte Gregory, wasn't it?"

"And how did you hear about that?" He chuckled. "Never mind. I should know you've always had a way of learning about everything. And now I can tell by the way you're biting your lip you have something to say. Go ahead. You will eventually."

"I need to get back to work." She stood, walked to the door, then turned back to him. "Joel, that Miss Gregory has a valid point. New mothers do need adequate nutrition, and we nurses have been woefully trained in meeting those needs. We plan our menus based on what foods we have on hand, with little consideration for the nutritional requirements of the mothers. Maybe if she came to teach—"

"Mattie!" Joel mockingly thumped his fist on the desk. "You of all people know this hospital is in dire financial straits. Besides, we don't know if Miss Gregory could cook her way out of a paper bag."

"Aha. I saw that." She pointed a finger in his direction.

"What?"

"The way your eye twitches whenever something fascinates you." She tapped her finger against her jaw. "Is it the subject of nutrition or is it Miss Gregory herself?"

"Neither, and I have rounds." He slipped his stethoscope into his pocket and joined her at the door. "Things are fine as they are."

"You mean everything is in order. That doesn't mean they're good, Brother." She kissed his cheek. "And I think Miss Gregory may be the spice this place—and perhaps even you—could use."

Palms damp, Charlotte wiped her hands on her apron and took in the room of hopeful contestants gathered to await the results of the first round. She smiled at Tessa and Aunt Sam, seated with other spectators. Baked goods scented the air with vanilla and cinnamon, and Charlotte licked her lips. She glanced at the layer cakes displayed on a long oak table. With three slices taken from each confection, a myriad of frostings and fillings begged to be sampled.

Her own cake leaned a bit to the right. It hadn't baked as evenly as she would have liked. If she'd used that oven before, she would have known the right side baked hotter than the left and would have rotated her pans halfway through their cooking times. Her only hope now was the judges wouldn't notice or would decide it was so delicious they didn't care.

One little boy apparently could no longer resist the temptation of the decadent desserts. As soon as he thrust a finger toward the chocolate cake nearest him, his mother swatted his hand away.

Tessa slipped her hand into the crook of Charlotte's arm. "What happens to all these cakes? Do we get to at least take yours home?"

"Only if you buy it." Aunt Sam joined the two of them. "They're selling them and giving the funds to the orphanage."

"Oh." Disappointment rang in Tessa's voice. "But Charlotte, you can make one back at Aunt Sam's for us, right?"

"I'm a little tired today, but I promise I will soon."

"Look. There's Mr. Johnson." Tessa pointed to the rotund man as he made his way to the podium.

He twisted his mustache as he approached the podium and took his place. He paused for the room to quiet. "Ladies and gentlemen, what an exciting first round this has been. The judges were most impressed with the diversity of the cakes baked here today, and all of our contestants should be congratulated for their efforts."

The crowd applauded, and then Mr. Johnson continued. "I want to remind you that only the top fifteen contestants will continue on to tomorrow's pie round. In no particular order, I will now read those fifteen names." He glanced at the list. "Miss Kathleen O'Grady . . ."

Charlotte glanced at her partner from the morning, and Kathleen gave her an I-told-you-so smirk.

Charlotte rolled her eyes, but hope rose inside her like yeasty dough in a hot oven. If these judges advanced Kathleen's seemingly dry-as-sawdust cake into the next round, then perhaps Charlotte did indeed have a chance.

Tessa elbowed her. "You did it!"

"What?"

"Didn't you hear your name? You're moving on."

Joy surged through her. At least she had a chance. Now if only she could place.

When the next round of applause had settled, Mr. Johnson held an envelope in the air. "And now, what you've all been waiting for. Earning third place today is Miss Kathleen O'Grady with her sunshine cake. Second place goes to Miss Amelia Desmond with her chocolate almond cake."

Charlotte winced beneath Tessa's grip, but Aunt Sam gave her an encouraging smile. Charlotte prayed she would not disappoint either of them.

"And finally, first place today is awarded to . . ."

5

Joel's heart warmed as he approached Hannah Cole's bed. Her color was high and the baby in her arms had already put on weight—despite what Charlotte Gregory thought of the poor quality of the hospital's food. He'd be releasing Mrs. Cole tomorrow after only a week's stay.

Beside his patient's bed, his own sister sat on a stool. Young but wise beyond her years, Mattie seemed to bring a special kind of healing to every patient. He might heal a patient's body, but it was Mattie who healed their spirit. So it came as no surprise to find Mrs. Cole and Mattie laughing as if they were old friends. He'd expressed his concerns about Mrs. Cole's occasional crying spells but was pleased to find his sister had chased them away.

"Good morning, Mrs. Cole." He stopped at the foot of her bed. "It's good to see you in high spirits."

"I feel much better today." She smiled at Mattie. "Your sister has been a godsend."

"Nurse Brooks has her moments." He glanced at his sister and grinned. "And what, pray tell, were you discussing today?"

"Funny you should ask." Mattie offered him a newspaper. "Mrs. Cole's sister, Miss Charlotte Gregory, seems to have been quite successful in the gas company's cooking competition. She's won three out of the five rounds so far—layer cakes, breads, and pies. Today is the final round of main dishes."

"Is that so?" He snapped open the paper and scanned the article his sister pointed out, which highlighted Miss Gregory's accomplishments. He then folded the newspaper neatly and handed it to Mrs. Cole.

"No, keep it." She waved the paper away and readjusted the sleeping baby in her arms. "She truly is a wonderful cook, but I apologize for her behavior the other day. Since our parents' death, she's become rather passionate about the convalescent receiving proper nutrition. Somehow she's gotten it in her mind that if our parents had been fed better, they would have survived."

Joel brushed his hand across Mrs. Cole's forehead. No fever. Good. "And from what ailment did your parents die?"

"Influenza. They seemed to be getting better, but then . . ."

Her eyes filled with tears and Joel kicked himself. Just when the blues seemed to be passing, he'd let her dwell on a painful subject. The scowl on Mattie's face said his sister agreed.

"Let's not speak of that now." Joel slipped the baby girl from Mrs. Cole and passed her to Mattie. "You need your rest if you're to go home tomorrow."

Mrs. Cole's face lit up. "Home? Truly?"

"Yes, I think you and Miss Elizabeth here will do splendidly. Will Mr. Cole be in later, or would you like me to telephone him with the good news?"

"Oh, he'll be here. I can hardly keep him away."

"Good. Then I'm sure you'll be in good hands." He patted Mrs. Cole's shoulder and turned to leave.

"Dr. Brooks."

He turned back toward his patient. "Is something wrong?"

"No, I simply wanted to thank you. You've been kind, caring, and competent. If my parents had had a doctor like you, maybe—" She swallowed. "Anyway, I wanted to thank you and to ask you to consider my sister's ideas. I know she came across too strong—it's a family trait, I suppose—but I do believe her thoughts may hold some merit."

He caught the hesitance in her voice and chuckled. "You didn't like our food, Mrs. Cole?"

"It could stand a little improvement."

He nodded. "I can't make any promises, but I try to be open to change—even if the idea seems radical to me."

"I've found that the first step is often to change the way you look at something."

"You must be quite formidable in a courtroom." He grinned. "I'll have to give what you said a bit of thought."

He glanced at the newspaper in his hand. Final round, huh? Perhaps he should check out Miss Charlotte Gregory in action.

How Kathleen O'Grady had made it to the final round baffled Charlotte, but she refused to let the thought put a damper on the excitement simmering inside her. The gas company's display room crackled with energy as contestants and spectators waited for today's contest to begin. Charlotte only wished Aunt Sam could have come too. Of course, the suffrage rally had been planned weeks before.

Besides Kathleen and herself, only three other contestants remained. Charlotte gripped the handle on her own basket of utensils and spices and surveyed her competition while they awaited Mr. Johnson and his final directions.

Mrs. Inga Gustason was the oldest of the lot. Her recipes so far had been quite traditional but equally delicious. She'd taken second in the pie round and fourth in cakes, but she constantly expressed a desire for a good, old-fashioned wood oven.

Talkative Miss Dorothea McColley jabbered her way through every bread and dessert, and shy Miss Amelia Desmond second-guessed her every move but had placed second in the bread round and third in the pie round. Kathleen, it seemed, had the most creative flare, and her victory in the doughnut round told Charlotte the young woman had been a quick study on the use of a gas stove.

Charlotte breathed a quick prayer to do her best. She added a blessing for her competitors as well. It seemed like the right thing to do.

"Hello, ladies." Mr. Johnson splayed his thick hands on the oak podium. "Today is the final round, and you'll be making a main dish that will delight our judges. You will be judged, as you have been, on the dish's quality, the presentation, and the creativity used." His gaze swept over the contestants. "And remember, one of you lucky ladies will receive a brand-new Jewel gas range."

Oohs and aahs filled the room, and Charlotte sucked in her breath. This contest meant so much more to her than having a new stove. It was her chance to prove herself to the entire city and every chef therein.

"Ladies, you each have a chicken at your station, and there is a collection of pantry items available on the shelf for your use. You may also use any of the spices you brought with you." Mr. Johnson took out a pocket watch. "So, put on your aprons, pick up your spoons, and prepare the best meal you've ever made. And because we want everyone to know how quickly a meal can be prepared on a gas range, you have only an hour and a half to complete your dish."

Charlotte's stomach clamped like the lid on a Ball canning jar. An hour and a half? While the contestants had been told they'd be provided with a chicken for the main dish, no one had specified a time limit. All the other rounds had been three hours long, and Charlotte had thought this one would follow suit. Could she finish her chicken soufflé in time?

"Go!" Tessa pushed her toward her work space. "Bake. Broil. Braise. Whatever it is you do, be brilliant."

As soon as she reached her table, Charlotte took a calming breath. First order of business: gather her supplies and organize her work area. She may not need things as tidy as Dr. Joel Brooks, but a disorganized kitchen could lead to all kinds of catastrophes. The other contestants were already clamoring at the pantry shelf. Should she be as well? But what would she need? Milk, butter, flour, bread crumbs, eggs. There should be plenty of each of those. Mushrooms for her sauce? Surely no one would take those, would they?

First, she needed to cook the chicken. She'd never have time to cook the entire bird, so she cut off the breast and chopped it in small pieces before lighting the burner beneath the skillet. She added a bit of bacon grease and her chicken. When the pieces began to take on a golden color, she gave them a final stir, lowered the flame, and put the lid on. She smiled. Perfect so far. In ten minutes, her chicken would be ready for the soufflé.

After lighting the oven so it could be heating, she made her way to the pantry shelf. Only timid Amelia remained.

"Oh dear." Amelia dabbed at her eyes with a handkerchief. "What am I going to do?"

Charlotte touched her arm. "What's wrong?"

"I need a can of mushroom caps for my recipe and I can't find one anywhere."

Mushrooms? Charlotte's eyes immediately lit on the can behind some green beans on an upper shelf, but she needed those mushrooms as well. She scanned the shelf, but there were no other cans. What would her chicken soufflé taste like without the rich mushroom sauce to complete it?

Surely she could think of something else. Poor Amelia was already a bundle of nerves.

Before she lost her gumption, she grabbed the can and thrust it into Amelia's hands. "Here. Go get started."

Charlotte turned back to the shelf. She could do this. Miss Farmer always encouraged them to use the ingredients they had on hand in a creative way. A quick inventory of the remaining ingredients revealed they mostly consisted of raw vegetables—a couple of peppers, a few stalks of celery, asparagus spears, onions, and an eggplant. Of course the expected amounts of flour, milk, and butter were present too, but nothing that would replace mushrooms in sauce.

She asked God to help her see what she might be missing. Her gaze fell on a wheel of cheddar cheese on the top shelf. A thrill shot through her. She could certainly use the cheese. Paired with the asparagus, it would work well in the soufflé she planned. She added the asparagus and cheese, along with a loaf of bread, a quart of milk, and some butter, to her basket. She started to return to her station but then remembered the much-needed eggs. What if there weren't enough?

Four extra large eggs remained in the basket, and she needed only three. Hurrying back to her station, she lifted the lid on her chicken and her breath caught. Why was it still raw? Had the flame gone out?

No! It hadn't gone out—someone had turned it off. She looked up from the range only to see Kathleen quickly turn away. Her anger threatened to boil over. Any mention of this to Mr. Johnson would simply make her look like she was making an excuse for her own forgetfulness. Taking time to confront Kathleen would steal from her own precious remaining minutes.

Forcing her panic and anger to ebb, she struck a match. The chicken could cook while she mixed the other ingredients. She lit the flame again and then made quick work of chopping the asparagus, grating the cheese, and cubing the bread. On a different burner, she made a béchamel sauce of milk, butter, and flour. When it had thickened, she added the cheese, egg yolks, and bread cubes. Once she'd stirred in the chicken and asparagus, she started to clean up her work area so she could fill the pudding dish with the soufflé. She set her salt and pepper shakers back in her basket and spotted the nutmeg she'd thrown in on a whim.

Should she add it? It wasn't one of the expected ingredients, but somehow she thought it would work. She added a dash before beginning the arduous task of beating the egg whites until they formed soft peaks.

The motion of her egg beater and the familiar sound of the metal against the heavy pottery mixing bowl made her relax. This was going well. It might just work.

She folded in the chicken mixture, drew a circle in her soufflé to give it an attractive cap, placed the buttered pudding dish in the oven, and glanced at the wall clock. Forty-five minutes left. This would take at least thirty-five minutes to bake. What if it didn't cook fast enough? Was her oven hot enough? She hadn't had time to check it properly. Worst of all, what if the soufflé fell?

She scanned the room to see how her competitors were faring. Mrs. Gustason's fried chicken filled the air with a delicious aroma. Dorothea must have stuffed her chicken with something and had it in the oven already. Now the girl had found a spectator to hound with her incessant chatter. Amelia, on the other end of the room, struggled to get her chicken cut up. If only Charlotte could go help her.

Kathleen sashayed over to Charlotte's area with a heavy skillet in one hand and a dish towel in the other. "I see you got a soufflé in the oven. Courageous, don't you think?"

"I think all good cooks need to be a little adventurous." Charlotte set her mixing bowl in one of the room's two sinks. "What did you make, Kathleen?"

"My great-grandmother's famous chicken pot pie." She licked her lips. "Rumor has it she served it to the Indians and saved her family. No one has ever been able to resist it."

Pushing up her sleeves, Charlotte set to washing her dishes. "It must be delicious."

"Hmm. Speaking of delicious, look at the man who just walked in."

Charlotte lifted the heavy pottery mixing bowl from the water and followed Kathleen's gaze. She sucked in her breath. The bowl dropped from her hands, crashed to the floor, and shattered.

"Oh no! My soufflé!"

6

Joel pushed through the crowd and hurried toward Charlotte. He knelt beside her and took hold of her wrist. "Let me clean this up. Go check your food."

She blinked. "Why are you here? Are Hannah and the baby okay?"

"Of course, but I needed to see if you were as good as you claimed." He released her wrist and picked up the largest chunks of pottery. "Your sister has been singing your praises."

"It doesn't matter. I'm sure my soufflé fell because of the crash." She reached for some shards.

He took the shard from her hand, wrapped his fingers around hers, and pulled her to her feet. "Maybe it's fine. You might as well go find out."

She nodded. Her head hung a bit as she walked away. Cooking clearly meant a lot to her. He grabbed the other large pieces and deposited them in a trash bin before a man with a large mustache and an official-looking badge said he'd have one of his workers come sweep up the rest.

Joel leaned against the sink and watched Charlotte crack open the oven. A smile lit her face, relief flooding her features.

She turned her smile in his direction. He nodded and slipped back into the crowd. The last thing he wanted to do was give her the wrong impression of why he'd come here today. Curiosity alone had propelled him to come watch the finals of this contest.

He glanced her way again. He had to admit, she sure had a beautiful smile.

"Ladies and gentlemen . . ." The mustached man's voice rose over the din of the room. "Our contest ends shortly, so before they begin their final round of judging, I'd like to take this opportunity to introduce you to our esteemed judges." Three men entered from a room on the side. "Please show your appreciation for Mr. Edward Miller, representing the Saint Paul Bread Company, Chef Geoffrey Reisen from Carling's Restaurant, and last but certainly not least, Chef Boucher from the Saint Paul Hotel restaurant."

Wasn't he the same chef with whom Charlotte had had words?

He looked back in her section, but she was nowhere to be seen. Where was she? When he spotted her peering between tins of Baker's Best Cocoa and Nabisco biscuits on the pantry shelf, he bit back a chuckle.

Could the plucky Miss Gregory be hiding?

Charlotte held her breath and squeezed her eyes shut. If Chef Boucher spotted her, her chances of winning would be over. Why did he have to be one of the judges?

"Would you gentlemen like to say anything to our contestants?"

"*Oui.*" Chef Boucher stepped forward. "All you ladies will make your husbands exceedingly happy—and possibly quite fat."

Laughter rippled through the crowd, but his words kicked at Charlotte. How could he say something like that? No matter how well she did today, at least in Chef Boucher's eyes she would only be fit to serve food to her family in her own kitchen. If all the other restaurant owners and chefs felt the same way, would she ever realize her dream?

She glanced at Tessa and recalled the day she and her sisters pledged to support one another in achieving their dreams. Since then, Hannah had been able to finish her schooling and join the ranks of the few female attorneys in the country. Every time she stepped into the courtroom, she fought the prejudice of her peers.

But Hannah had always been a fighter. Standing up to life's injustices came easily to her. She'd often quoted their father, who once said, "If you don't like something, then you should either be quiet about it or be willing to do something to change it."

Was Charlotte truly prepared to do something to change this view of women? With another look at her younger sister, she stepped out of her hiding place. Even if it meant facing Chef Boucher again, she'd fight for her dreams. She'd fight because she wanted things to change. She'd fight so Tessa wouldn't have to fight so hard. She'd show Chef Boucher that he'd made a mistake in turning her down, and he'd soon see that someday she'd be in charge of the biggest restaurant in the city.

Chef Boucher turned her way. Like the whipped peaks of the egg whites in her soufflé, Charlotte froze. Did he recognize her?

Mr. Johnson returned to his place. "Now, if our judges will return to their room, our contestants can prepare their main dishes for the final round of scoring." When Chef Boucher paused, Mr. Johnson swept his arm toward the room. After the judges had gone, he took out his pocket watch and turned to the women. "Ladies, one of our volunteers will be around in five minutes to take your main dish in to the judges. You must have it ready to go as you'd like it served."

Charlotte bit her lip. Her soufflé needed every minute. The longer she left it in the oven, the better it would remain puffed, but she had to have it out before the five-minute mark.

She watched the clock tick by. Beside her, Kathleen bustled around, placing heaping servings on three plates. Across from her, Mrs. Gustason laid a piece of golden fried chicken on each plate beside a perfect mound of mashed potatoes ladled with creamy gravy. Was Charlotte's plan of serving the entire soufflé to the judges a mistake?

Unable to wait another second, she opened the oven door and a gust of warm air hit her face. Using two thick towels, she removed the soufflé from the oven and set it on her work counter.

"Time is up!" Mr. Johnson shouted. "Ladies, step away from your work area."

7

She'd won!

Tremors of joy coursed through Charlotte. If she wasn't carrying a trophy, a gift basket, and a Bissell carpet sweeper, she might skip her way to the motorcar. So much for being a queen.

"It wouldn't hurt you to carry the trophy a few minutes, Tessa."

"Be glad they aren't going to make you carry your new gas range home."

The spectators and other contestants crowded the sidewalk. The gas company's display room was more crowded than Charlotte had realized.

"Congratulations!" The judge from the baking company fell in step beside Charlotte. "Serving your soufflé in all its golden glory was a stroke of genius. I'm so glad you didn't put it on separate plates, and it was delicious, by the way. Chef Reisen was especially impressed."

A warm glow burned in Charlotte's chest. "Thank you."

It seemed as if everyone—that is, everyone except Kathleen—wished Charlotte well, and she responded with a sincere thank-you to each of them.

Tessa skipped ahead, then whirled to face her. "Aunt Sam sent her driver to pick us up. She said he'll be on the corner. Aren't you excited to get back and show her?"

Charlotte stopped to reposition her goods. "If I ever get there, I will be."

"Need some help?" Someone stepped up beside her and reached for the trophy.

"I can handle—" Charlotte sucked in her breath when she realized who was standing beside her. Dr. Joel Brooks gently tugged the trophy, and she released it, followed by the Bissell sweeper.

"Thank you. Some people aren't as inclined to lend a hand." She looked directly at Tessa.

Tessa shrugged. "You're the newly crowned queen of cookery, and no one said anything about me serving in your court."

"Yes, congratulations are in order." Dr. Brooks swung the trophy across his waist and bowed. "Well done, Your Highness."

Heat warmed Charlotte's face and neck. How different the doctor was now from when she'd met him in his office. Why? She couldn't place it at first, but it had to be the smile—an alarmingly dangerous smile.

She touched her collar. "I'm simply praying this win will open a door to cook at one of the city's fine restaurants."

"I saw the face of the Saint Paul Hotel's chef when you stepped forward." A teasing glint sparkled in Dr. Brooks's eye. "I don't think you're on his list of favorite people."

"No, I have a feeling he's still not interested in my services." Charlotte laughed. "I'm just lucky he wasn't holding a butcher knife." They reached Aunt Sam's automobile and the driver took her basket.

Dr. Brooks deposited the sweeper in the backseat. "I did a little checking, and apparently the hotel's management is watching the cleanliness of his kitchen much more closely now."

"You checked?"

"For the community's health."

"Of course." Charlotte tore her gaze away from his green eyes and his alarming smile.

Tessa hopped in the automobile and slammed her door. "Are you coming, Lottie? We've got news to share!"

Charlotte took the trophy from Dr. Brooks's arms. "Thank you for your help. I'm sure I'll see you at the hospital."

"Actually, your sister and your niece are going home tomorrow." His Adam's apple bobbed beneath a dimpled chin. "But I'm sure we'll run into one another."

"Yes, we still need to discuss the hospital's food service."

His back stiffened. "Good day, Miss Gregory, and congratulations on your win."

The driver opened her door as soon as the doctor turned to go. She pressed one shoe to the running board but stopped when she spotted Chef Reisen from Carling's Restaurant. Today would be the perfect day to speak to him about securing a position.

"I'll be right back," she told Tessa before scurrying past Dr. Brooks and crossing the street. She stepped in front of the contest judge, and he came to an abrupt halt. "Excuse me, Chef Reisen, but I was hoping to speak to you."

His smile widened. "Ah, you are the talented young homemaker who took the prize. Congratulations. Your soufflé was perfect—fluffy and delicious."

"I'm glad you feel that way, but sir, I am not a homemaker, nor do I wish to be one."

His eyes narrowed and his brows drew to a V. "No?"

"I was trained at Fannie Farmer's School of Cookery. We learned about scientific cookery and all its components, and in light of the contest today, I'm hoping you might be interested in my services in your kitchen."

He shook his head. "I'm afraid we have all the servers we need."

"I'm not interested in being a server. I would like a position in your kitchen—cooking."

"You want to cook in *my* kitchen?" His voice boomed against the brick and mortar building. A full-bellied laugh rumbled in his chest and rolled out. "Go home, little cook. Find a husband who will enjoy your soufflés, and make delicious cakes and cookies for your babies. You don't belong in a real kitchen. No woman does."

"But Chef Reisen, even New York's Women's Club has a female chef."

"A women's club?" He rolled his eyes, and with a dismissive wave of his hand he walked away.

Charlotte fought for a breath, but her corset seemed to tighten on its own. Hot tears filled her eyes. He was her last chance. If he could turn her down after tasting her food, how would she ever secure a position?

The sidewalk rippled before her and she pressed a hand to her chest. *Oh my.* Vapors? Now? For the first time in her life? She couldn't faint right here on the sidewalk. She leaned against the storefront and slid down onto the window ledge. *Breathe in. Breathe out.*

"Miss Gregory?"

She looked up into concerned green eyes. *Really, Lord, wasn't Chef Reisen's laughter enough? Do I need to be completely mortified?*

Dr. Joel Brooks knelt before her. "Miss Gregory, do you need to loosen your corset?"

Oh dear. Where was the nearest pickle barrel to crawl into?

Charlotte lay back on the davenport and tried to relax.

Why did Aunt Sam have to make such a fuss over her? Worse, why did Tessa insist on sharing everything that happened in vivid color?

"And then Dr. Handsome helped her all the way back to the automobile and told me to take her home and see to it she eats a good meal and rests the remainder of the day." Tessa feigned a swoon onto the back of the settee. "It was so romantic."

"Tessa, it was not romantic!" Charlotte yanked the cold cloth from her forehead and heaved it at her sister. "Besides, Aunt Sam doesn't want to know every detail."

"Quite the contrary. I'd like to hear all about it." Aunt Sam removed the pin from her suffrage sash, folded the wide ribbon, and set it on the marble-topped table beside her chair. Her eyebrow arched in Tessa's direction. "However, I'd like to hear about it from Charlotte. After all, it is her story to tell. I myself enjoyed a lovely morning in front of the capitol with my banner held high with my suffrage sisters." She glanced at the empty plates and cups on the coffee table. "It appears you've at least followed some of the good doctor's prescriptive. Now, tell me about the competition. Is that your trophy?"

Charlotte sat up and passed her the heavy silver cup. Aunt Sam grasped its heart-shaped handles. The trophy's reflection caught the light of the afternoon sun drenching the room.

"My, it's lovely." Aunt Sam rubbed a fingerprint from the cup's surface with her sleeve. "I'm so proud of you I'm about to burst. Soon the restaurants will be fighting over you."

"I wish that were true." Charlotte relayed the details of the day, from the burner being turned off by Kathleen, to the lack of mushrooms, to seeing Chef Boucher and fearing all was lost. She omitted the part about dropping the bowl and Dr. Brooks's sudden appearance. To her relief, Tessa didn't seem to notice the part she'd skipped in her retelling.

Tessa poured a cup of tea. "And after she won, a newspaperman interviewed her."

Aunt Sam set the trophy on the mantel. "But how did you come to meet up with Dr. Brooks?"

Tessa giggled. "He was there watching her the whole time."

Charlotte fired a glare at her sister. "He wasn't there watching *me*. He was there watching the conclusion of the competition."

"He made a point to congratulate you afterward, and he carried the trophy and the sweeper to the automobile for you. Think about it. Would a man carry your sweeper if he wasn't interested in you?"

"Tessa, your imagination knows no bounds." Aunt Sam poured

herself a cup of tea. "Did you grow faint on the way to the automobile?"

"Heavens, no." Charlotte felt heat creep up her neck. "Can we forget that even happened? It's so embarrassing. I simply skipped breakfast in all my excitement, and then with the interview and all, it was well past lunch."

"Was your corset too tight?" A glint sparkled in Tessa's eyes.

"No!"

Aunt Sam laughed. "Ignore her. Think about your victory."

Charlotte walked to the mantel. She laid her hand on the trophy. "But as wonderful as that is, I fear this win will not yield me a position." She explained how Chef Reisen had dismissed her without seriously considering her request. "He knows I can cook, but he still turned me down."

"But surely there are other fine establishments."

"I've exhausted nearly every one in this city. I could start contacting those in Minneapolis. Of course, I would have to move there if I were to find a placement." She turned toward Aunt Sam and forced a smile. "I'd hate to leave you, but I don't know what else to do."

Aunt Sam shook her head. "Let's not be too hasty. God may have another plan already in place."

"And Lottie . . ." Tessa giggled. "If you're lucky, maybe it'll involve Dr. Handsome."

After parking his Model T touring automobile, Joel removed his doctor's bag from the back, opened the clasp, and smiled. The children would be thrilled by *Anne of Green Gables* and the two picture books he'd picked up for their meager library. If only he could do more for these kids. He knew all too well what it was like to have less than everyone else.

He took the small orphanage's steps two at a time and knocked on the door.

Sweet, dimpled Alice Ann opened the door and wrapped her arms around his legs. "Dr. Joel!"

"Don't trip him, Alice. Let him in." Mrs. Goodwin patted the girl's blonde curls. "Your sister beat you today, Joel. She's already in the parlor, helping the older girls with their arithmetic."

"Sorry, I got held up at the hospital." He handed his bag to Mrs. Goodwin, who had been his mother's best friend, and shrugged out of his coat. Mrs. Goodwin used to be their neighbor, but when she lost her husband, she took on the orphanage. It was a perfect fit for the godly woman, and somehow being with her made him miss his own mother a little less.

"You don't have to apologize if you can't get here when you planned." She draped his coat on a hook by the door. "We know you're busy. We're blessed that you and your sister come visit us as often as you do. Your mother would be so proud of you."

"I wish I could do more." He scooped four-year-old Alice Ann up into his arms. "Now, let's go in the parlor. I have a couple of surprises in my bag to share."

"Gumdrops?" Alice licked her pink lips.

He bounced her as he carried her into the parlor. When had this child, the youngest in Mrs. Goodwin's care, stolen his heart? If only things had happened differently with Prudence, he might have been at a place to adopt Alice Ann. "Why do you always want gumdrops? Don't you think the licorice and the lemon drops feel left out?"

Alice Ann stuck her finger in her mouth, seeming to give the matter a great deal of thought. "I know. You could bring those too. Then they wouldn't get their feelings hurt."

He chuckled and set her down on the threadbare carpet. "Maybe I'll have to do that." A dozen children clamored around him, so he opened his bag and pulled out the sack of large gumdrops. He let one of the older girls pass out the treats while he sought out his sister.

From her seat at the long table, Mattie gave him a mock look of disapproval. "They'd love you even if you didn't bring them candy."

Lowering himself into a rickety wooden chair beside her, he clasped her hand. "But I don't possess your natural charm that so easily wins their favor."

"You have nearly every nurse in the hospital swooning over you. I think you have plenty of natural charm." She reached for the package he held under the table. "What are you hiding?"

He yanked it out of her reach. "It was for you to share with the older girls, but if you think *Anne of Green Gables* would spoil them—"

"*Anne*! The girls will adore it." She kissed his cheek.

"And I got a couple of picture books for the little ones."

"I wish you'd gotten one for him." She glanced at ten-year-old Jacob sitting in the corner by himself. "He's taking Harvey's passing badly. Mrs. Goodwin says he won't talk to anyone."

"Maybe I can get him to play some marbles with me. They've always been his favorite." He started to rise, but Mattie laid a hand on his arm.

"Wait. How did Miss Gregory do at the competition?"

"How did you—"

"You took a very long lunch. Besides, I knew you wouldn't be able to stay away." She flashed him a smile. "Well?"

"She won."

"And?" Her eyebrows arched, implying there was more to the story than he was telling.

"And what?" He kept his face devoid of expression, but pride swelled deep in his chest concerning Miss Gregory's accomplishment. He shoved those feelings away. She was not part of his plans for the future. The last time he got sidetracked by a woman was disastrous.

"Did you talk to her? Are you going to let her come speak to the nurses now?"

With no desire to go into the details about his conversations with Miss Gregory, he stood. "Mattie, now is not the time or place to discuss this."

"I don't want you to pass up this opportunity."

"An opportunity to spend money on something the hospital doesn't need? An opportunity to deal with a stubborn, know-it-all woman?" He gave her a wry chuckle. "Why in the world would I want to pass that up?"

"Because you're smart enough to know she has a point—and you're used to stubborn, know-it-all women." She grinned. "In fact, deep down, you like us very much."

8

Like a rash that wouldn't go away, Joel kept thinking about Charlotte Gregory. He turned the Model T onto Summit Avenue and passed the House of Hope Church. He could use a little hope right now—hope that this visit tonight would get Charlotte Gregory out of his mind once and for all.

He pressed the gas pedal and the car responded with an impressive thirty miles per hour. He shifted gears and sighed. Maybe he should turn around and go home, but Charlotte had looked awfully pale when he'd sent her home from the competition earlier today. Besides, if his sister learned he'd come this far and then hadn't spoken to Charlotte, she'd harass him for days.

Joel passed one stately columned house after another as he drove. What was he thinking? Going to Mrs. Samantha Phillips's fancy home without being summoned?

Not that he minded visiting Mrs. Phillips. She'd been an avid supporter of the hospital and was one of his first patients in the area. Even after he accepted the position at the hospital, she'd continued to retain him as her personal physician. He found her unconventional ways truly delightful, but even she might not appreciate the breach of etiquette.

Pulling to a stop at the corner of Chatsworth and Summit, he parked in front of the enormous brick mansion, picked up his medical bag, and bounded up the walk to the front porch. How many bedrooms would a house this size have? Seven? Eight? And fireplaces? From counting the chimneys, he guessed at least five or six. No wonder Mrs. Phillips had her two nieces living with her.

The porch's tiled floor caught his eye. His mother would have loved the rust-colored diamond pattern as much as the wicker furniture scattered along the porch's length. He rang the bell and waited. A half minute later, a butler answered.

He stepped aside and welcomed Joel inside. "Good evening, Dr. Brooks. I wasn't aware Mrs. Phillips summoned you. May I take your coat?"

Joel handed the man his coat and hat. "Actually, I came to check on Miss Gregory. When I saw her earlier today, she was feeling faint."

"Very well. I'll tell her you're here."

Joel shifted from foot to foot in the foyer. What was he doing here? No matter how down-to-earth the owner of this home might be, a man with his background shouldn't be calling uninvited. He glanced from the mahogany staircase with its hand-carved curlicues to the wide crown molding on the ceiling. All of the details in this home made it truly spectacular. Even the top of the newel post had been carved to resemble a lantern.

Unable to resist, he ran his hand along the banister's smooth finish.

"Sir." The butler stepped into the foyer again.

Joel yanked his hand away.

"Mrs. Phillips and Miss Gregory will see you in the drawing room." The butler opened a heavy mahogany door and motioned Joel inside.

Dressed in a brown-striped cycling costume, Mrs. Phillips stood as he entered and clapped her hands together. "Dr. Brooks, what a wonderful surprise! Have you had dinner?"

"No, ma'am, but I simply came to check on your niece." His gaze moved to Charlotte seated on the davenport in an apricot dress. Her cider-colored hair remained pinned up, but some curls had sprung free, framing her face. She no longer looked pale. In fact, from the blush of her cheeks and her uncharacteristic silence, he'd have to say his attention embarrassed her. "She looked quite peaked when I last saw her."

"As you can see, I'm much improved," Charlotte said. "You needn't have come." Mrs. Phillips pinned her with a stern look, and Charlotte cleared her throat. "But it was thoughtful of you to do so."

Mrs. Phillips laid a hand on his arm. "It certainly was, and you must stay for dinner."

He turned to gauge Charlotte's reaction, but she quickly looked down. Although he thought this might be the perfect time to talk to Charlotte about educating the nurses, if she didn't want him there, perhaps it was not. "I don't want to impose, Mrs. Phillips."

"It's not an imposition, and Charlotte made her specialty for dessert."

"Her specialty?"

Mrs. Phillips beamed. "Apple charlotte, of course."

So she hadn't followed his advice and rested this afternoon. That figured. He glanced at Charlotte again. As if she sensed what he was thinking, she gave him an I'll-do-what-I-please chuckle. Well, he could do as he pleased too.

He turned to Mrs. Phillips. "I'd be honored to join you."

"Perfect." She propelled him through French doors into the dining room. "And I want to hear all about how things are going at the hospital. How's Arthur doing? And is the new ambulance proving advantageous, as you thought it would?"

When her aunt wasn't looking, Charlotte glared at him. Apparently she'd wanted him to decline. Dining with him must not be on her list of favorite things. Oh well. It was too late to refuse now. Mrs. Phillips was much too powerful in the community to risk offending.

Charlotte took a seat across from him, and a few seconds later, the youngest Gregory sister bounded into the room. "I'm sorry. I was practicing my Puck—" She stopped short when she spotted Joel. "Oh. 'How now, spirit! Whither wander you?'"

"Tessa!" Charlotte hissed.

Tessa rolled her eyes and slid into her place. "Hello, Dr. Brooks." Her voice took on a hollow, grown-up sound. "I apologize. I wasn't aware you were joining us for dinner or I would have made an additional effort to arrive on time."

Mrs. Phillips smiled at the young woman, then patted Joel's arm. "Dr. Brooks, would you please say grace?"

"Certainly." Maybe it would give him a chance to show Charlotte he wasn't the ogre she'd made him out to be.

The prayer came easily to him. After he visited the orphanage, prayer always did. He asked God to help them be truly thankful for each and every blessing, for every morsel of food. "And Father, help us to be content in every situation."

As soon as he'd said amen, he looked at Charlotte. Something was brewing in those hazel eyes. He took a piece of roast beef from the platter and a generous helping of mashed potatoes. What had he said to upset her?

"Content?" The word almost burst from her lips. "Why should we be content in every situation? Some situations need to be changed. Children should not be working in factories. Men should be paid a decent wage for a day's work. Women should have the right to vote, and—"

"Charlotte." Mrs. Phillips spoke her name with firmness. "Shall we discuss this after dinner?"

"But—"

Mrs. Phillips hiked her eyebrows and Charlotte fell silent.

Tessa giggled.

"I didn't mean to upset you." Joel cleared his throat, then took a sip from his water glass. "I meant content in every situation as Paul commands us to be. Content with knowing God is in control. Personally, it's something I've always struggled with, Miss Gregory."

"Oh, call her Charlotte." Tessa speared a carrot. "Otherwise you might get the two of us confused. Right, Charlotte?"

She didn't answer, but if she felt familiar enough to argue with him over a prayer, he might as well call her by her given name. "Then all of you must call me Joel."

"Joel." Mrs. Phillips smiled. "It means 'Jehovah is the Lord,' doesn't it?"

"Yes, ma'am. Something my mother always said I was prone to forget."

Mrs. Phillips looked at Charlotte. "Something I think we all are prone to forget."

How could Joel sit there eating her apple charlotte with nary a care in the world? If she'd known he would be eating it, she'd have slipped him some of Garfield's laxative tea to go with it. It wouldn't kill him, but it would sure have made him uncomfortable.

Good grief. What was wrong with her? After her outburst—over a prayer of all things—he probably thought she was given to such explosions all the time. Why did he bring out the worst in her? One thing was for sure—if she wanted the policy at the hospital to change, she'd better start treating Dr. Joel Brooks with a little kindness.

"This is amazing, Charlotte." He slid the last bite into his mouth. "I don't know when I've had a dessert this good."

"Thank you." She forced a sweetness into her voice that made Tessa cock an eyebrow in her direction. "Would you like another piece?"

"No thank you. I couldn't eat another bite." He leaned back in his chair.

"Let's retire to the drawing room." Aunt Sam stood. "Unless, Charlotte, you and Joel would like to continue your earlier discussion outside." She inclined her head in the direction of the side door, which led from the dining room to the wraparound porch. "Or perhaps you'd care to stroll in the garden."

Stroll in the garden? With him?

"The fresh air would be good for you after your day." Aunt Sam nodded. "Yes, I think that's what the two of you should do. Do you mind escorting Charlotte on a walk in the garden, Joel?"

"Aunt Sam, he doesn't—"

Joel nodded slowly, deliberately. "Ma'am, it would be my pleasure. Charlotte, shall we?"

Charlotte released a long breath. His pleasure? Another strike against him. He lied well.

Once outside, wearing her spring coat, Charlotte walked beside the tall doctor. Tessa was right. He was handsome—and he was stuck in his ways. *Be kind. A gentle answer turns away wrath. Remember?*

The sun hung low in the sky and the air held the crispness of imminent nightfall. They couldn't remain out here long or it would be dark. Charlotte glanced at a group of sunny buttercups. They'd make a nice bouquet, but Tessa would be furious if she picked them. She stuffed her hands in her pockets. "Did you have a busy afternoon at the hospital after the cooking awards presentation?"

"It's always busy, but not more than usual. I had a delivery to make at one of the orphanages."

"Was one of the children ill?"

He waved his hand. "No, no. I took the children some books and some candy. The matron was a friend of my mother's. My sister and I like to help out when we can."

His statement caught her off guard. He and his sister helped at an orphanage? She hadn't thought of him doing something so benevolent. No one who took time for orphans could be all bad. "Which books did you take the children?"

He paused and turned to her. "*Anne of Green Gables* for the older girls. Have you read it?"

Charlotte stopped and looked up into his face. "Yes, I did. I rather fancied the thought of being like Anne, but I'm afraid Tessa would take that prize."

"I don't know." A wide grin spread across his face. "You certainly have Anne's spunk."

She started walking again and, without turning her head, cast a curious glance toward Joel. She liked *this* Joel. He was softer, more human. She never would have guessed that the man who wouldn't listen to her in his office took candy and books to orphans.

Joel broke the silence. "You've had quite a day."

"Yes, and I'm beginning to feel it now."

"So"—he motioned to a bench—"shall we sit down for a few minutes?"

"I'm fine, really. I didn't mean I'm unable to walk. I'm not feeling a bit faint anymore."

He chuckled. "I know that, but I wanted to speak with you."

"Oh." She lowered herself to the bench, but he remained standing.

He stopped in front of a lilac bush, its sweet scent filling the evening air. "My sister feels your ideas hold some merit."

"But you don't." Despite warnings to herself, her words came out clipped. A couple of years ago, Charlotte wouldn't have spoken up to any man, but not anymore. She might not be eloquent like Hannah or as adventurous as Tessa, but she did believe in what she was fighting for, and that emboldened her.

"I'm not convinced your plan is necessary." He propped one foot on the base of a large flower urn. "Contrary to your belief, I do have an understanding of the human body and its nutritional needs."

She held her hands out. "But there's so much new information of which I'm sure you are unaware."

"Charlotte, I assure you I keep abreast of all the newest medical developments."

She drew in a deep, lilac-scented breath. This was not going well. "Of course you do, but this information has yet to appear in medical journals. Please, let me explain. At Miss Farmer's cooking school—"

He pressed his lips together at the mention of the school, but she continued. "At the school, I attended and later taught a special course of study on the care and feeding of the ill and convalescent. Miss Farmer herself has spoken about the subject extensively. She was even asked to speak about it at Harvard Medical School."

His eyebrows lifted. "Go on."

Charlotte clasped her gloved hands. "She even wrote a book on the subject."

"All right." He brushed the dust off the tip of his shoe. "Miss Farmer has some credentials, and as her student, you have some as well, but I need you to understand something. That still doesn't mean we can implement the changes you suggested."

"You won't even try them? Any of them?" She swallowed hard. How could this be?

"I've looked at the hospital's financial records, and there simply isn't the money." His voice held a note of regret but hardened the more he spoke. "The figures don't add up, and I can't go to the superintendent and ask for more money based on your ideas."

Her neck muscles grew taut. "You can't, or you won't?"

"Charlotte, I'm being considered for a permanent position at the hospital as an assistant superintendent. If they make the position permanent, I'll be the youngest physician ever chosen to fill that post. I don't want to risk my position on experiments."

His eyes seemed to ask her to understand, but she couldn't give up so easily. This was too important. "Even if it means your patients will be better off?"

"You haven't proven that." He crossed his arms over his chest. "And I think I know what's best for my patients."

"Don't you mean what's best for you?" The pitch of her voice rose and anger burned in her throat. She stood and met his gaze. "You're afraid to rock the boat. You're content with the way things are and that's that. You won't look beyond what's in front of you to see how the situation can be different—how it could be better if you'd only give my suggestions a try."

"Wait a minute." He held up a hand. "I was trying to explain my decision to you, and now you're accusing me of being nearsighted.

What makes you so certain you have all the answers?" He spread his arms toward the mansion. "Look where you live. You've had everything in life handed to you. You don't know what it means to be content in a difficult situation. Do you even know what it's like to balance a budget?"

Tears pricked her eyes. Did she know? He had no idea how well she knew. How dare he make such assumptions? She and her sisters had struggled for every crumb after her parents' deaths. She'd made feasts out of beans. She'd taken odd jobs to have money for bread. She'd worn the same pair of shoes until the soles wore paper-thin.

But this man—this know-it-all, nearsighted man—didn't have the right to know those things about her. Not now or ever.

She pointed to the gate. "Get out."

9

Sunshine bathed the breakfast room in pale warmth. Charlotte glanced out the bay window and spotted Tessa working beside the gardener, tending the seedlings recently awakened by spring. She shook her head. If that girl couldn't get her hands dirty at least once a week, she went crazy.

Charlotte shared a knowing smile with Aunt Sam before tapping the shell of her soft-boiled egg. The ironstone eggcup, decorated with periwinkle blooms, held the egg upright. She scooped out the yolk with a rounded silver egg spoon. Two years ago, she wouldn't have known what an egg spoon was, let alone used one within the doors of a fine house on Summit Avenue.

Funny how fast things could change. If only her present predicament could change as quickly. No more ifs and wishes. She knew finding a position wouldn't be easy, but she would do it, and even if Joel never let her through the hospital doors, she'd be content as long as she could cook.

Content. Thanks to her discussion with Joel the other night, the last thing she felt this morning was content. Why did that man set her off like a teakettle every time they spoke?

She slipped a teaspoon of egg yolk through her lips and swallowed. Well, that shouldn't be a problem anymore. After that night, she doubted she'd ever see him again. Regret and anger mingled together inside her chest, but she shoved the strange emotions aside. Why did it all have to be so difficult?

Not only had she lost the opportunity to get Joel to realize the hospital needed to change its food service, but she'd also lost any glimmer of friendship. Had a friendship truly been a possibility between them anyway? He'd been so kind earlier in the day, but wasn't that a doctor's job?

"What are your plans today, Charlotte?" Aunt Sam sipped from her coffee cup. "Would you care to go cycling with me?"

"I'm afraid I can't. I think I'll head to Minneapolis today." She split a biscuit and spread a thick layer of raspberry jam on it. She'd spent the weekend considering her options and had decided this was her best one. Although getting a permanent position meant leaving Aunt Sam, it might be her only option. It would also get her away from any possibility of seeing Joel Brooks again.

Aunt Sam touched her napkin to her lips. "I don't want to sound like Brother Carstens in yesterday's sermon, but have you prayed about this?"

"I think God has better things to concern himself with than my situation."

"I doubt that."

Violet, the maid, stepped into the doorway. "There's a telephone call in the hallway for you, Miss Gregory."

She set down her biscuit. "For me?"

"Yes, miss."

Charlotte excused herself and hurried into the hall. She sat down on the tufted leather seat of the mahogany telephone table and picked up the candlestick phone. The line crackled. "Hello?"

A short while later, she returned to the breakfast room and dropped to her seat. Her heart thundered in her chest, and the egg she'd eaten earlier somersaulted in her stomach. "That was the Greater Northern Natural Gas Company."

Aunt Sam set her coffee cup back on its saucer. "Do they want to know where to deliver your new gas range?"

"No, they want to offer me a position teaching women how to cook with gas."

Removing a token from her pocketbook, Charlotte stepped onto the streetcar and smiled at the motorman. She dropped the token into the fare box and found a seat near the front. The bell clanged, and with a whoosh, the driver released the brakes. The fresh breeze through the open windows kissed her cheeks. Aunt Sam had offered her automobile and driver, but Charlotte had declined. She hadn't wanted to give the gas company the wrong impression.

The gas company was a short walk from the stop. The clerk in the front said they'd been expecting her and ushered her into Mr. Stewart Johnson's office.

He stood when she entered. "Please have a seat, Miss Gregory."

She obliged and folded her hands in her lap. "I have to admit your call caught me off guard. I have so many questions."

"And I'm here to answer them." Mr. Johnson's mustache waggled as he spoke. "And, of course, to ask a few of my own."

"Then, sir, perhaps you should go first."

He tapped his pencil on his paper. "First of all, is there anyone in your life who would be opposed to you traveling out of town? A father? Brother? Gentleman caller?"

"No, sir."

"Excellent." He looked up. "I apologize, that came out wrong."

"I understand. My family is supportive of my culinary aspirations, and I currently have no gentleman callers."

"Excuse me." He removed a handkerchief from his pocket and sneezed into it. "Let me give you the details concerning the position I'm offering you."

He went on to explain she'd be traveling to cities in southern Minnesota to give a series of lectures on cooking with gas. Each lecture circuit, he said, would take three to five days, so the job would mean traveling away from Saint Paul. She would be in each city a couple of days to speak to the ladies of the community about the outstanding benefits of cooking on a gas range. Along with that, she would be free to share her knowledge of nutrition, teach the ladies time-saving kitchen advice, and share recipes of all kinds with them.

"Most of the time, you'll travel for one week and then have the next off." He went over the pay and a few other details. "So, do we have a deal?"

Charlotte took a deep breath. Was this what she wanted? At Fannie Farmer's School of Cookery, she had taught under Miss Farmer and had loved doing so, but this was a far cry from working in the kitchen of a fine restaurant or owning her own establishment. How was she to know if this was what the Lord intended for her? Did it feel right?

"I'm sorry I can't give you more time, but I have to know today," Mr. Johnson said. "If you aren't interested, we'll approach the second-place winner."

She sat up straight and nodded. "Yes, Mr. Johnson, I'd be honored to represent your gas company."

Charlotte relaxed into the seat of the streetcar. A job. A position. Too good to be true. The trolley's clackety-clack beat in time with her jumbled thoughts. She couldn't believe she had accepted the position Mr. Johnson offered. It might not be in a fancy restaurant, but she would be cooking professionally.

Even though she was dying to share her news with Aunt Sam and Tessa, she had one stop to make first. Her sister Hannah deserved to hear the turn of events before anyone else. She had never forgotten Hannah's promise to help Charlotte and Tessa achieve their dreams. Every time Charlotte was tempted to give up, Hannah had been there to encourage her.

As Charlotte made the short walk from the streetcar line to Hannah and Lincoln's home, excitement bubbled inside her. The neighborhood where her sister now lived sported a lovely collection of homes, including several new square Craftsman houses with large porches. In front of some, purple irises added a spot of color against the brick and stucco facades.

When Charlotte arrived at Hannah's, she found her sister sitting on the front porch. Ellie, Hannah explained, was sleeping inside. She stood as Charlotte approached and clasped Charlotte's hands. "I'm so glad you came today. I want to hear all about the contest." She paused and tipped her head to the side. "Charlotte Gregory, you are positively glowing, and you look as if you're about to burst. What is going on? Did you find a position?"

"Yes!" A jolt of fresh exuberance shot through Charlotte. "Oh dear, you should be sitting down. You just got home from the hospital. Are you sure you should be out here? What if you catch a chill?"

Hannah sat down in a cushioned rattan chair. "I'm fine. The fresh air is good for me."

Charlotte shook out the soft wool blanket lying on the table and draped it over her sister's lap. "Where's Lincoln?"

"He's at work, but Mrs. Umdahl is here. She's in the kitchen, and she won't let me do a thing. Another reason I'm glad you're here." Hannah made a circular motion with her hand to hurry her along. "So don't make me wait. When do you start? What will you be doing?"

Charlotte sat down in the matching rattan chair on the other side of the small table. "I start next Monday working for the gas company."

"The gas company? Not a restaurant?"

Charlotte stiffened at Hannah's tone. She hurried to explain how she would be traveling to give lectures on the benefits of using the gas stove for cooking.

"I'm proud of you." Hannah reached over and squeezed her hand. "But I hope you won't wish you were working with a chef like you always wanted."

Emotion clogged Charlotte's throat. Was she settling for this position instead of pursuing her true dream? What if God had other plans for her? How was she to know the difference?

The screen door banged open and Mrs. Umdahl appeared with a tray laden with large glasses of milk and sandwiches cut in neat quarters. "I thought you could both use a snack."

Hannah's eyebrows rose. "Milk in the middle of the afternoon?"

"*Ja*, it's good for you and the baby." She set the tray on the table. "Are you warm enough?"

"Yes, thank you, Mrs. Umdahl."

"*Uff da*, I never heard of a mother out of bed so soon." She wagged her finger at Charlotte. "Don't let her get overtired. *Ja?*"

Charlotte nodded. "Yes, ma'am."

When the housekeeper had gone back inside, Hannah picked up a quarter of egg salad sandwich. "Your position sounds like a perfect fit for you in so many ways, but I must admit, I hate the idea of you traveling alone."

"I won't be." Charlotte removed her gloves, then set a sandwich on her luncheon plate. "The gas company has hired an older woman to be my traveling companion. They also plan to hire a singer who will perform before I speak to entice more women to attend the lectures. I suppose she will travel with us as well. The more women they can get interested in the benefits of the gas range, the more homes will start using gas. Not only will the gas company make money on gas range sales, but they'll get more gas subscribers."

"You'll have them all cooking with gas in no time."

"Some women who've lectured like this have gone on to have cookbooks published. Can you imagine?" Charlotte bit her lip. "I should slow down. I'm getting ahead of myself."

Hannah chuckled. "You're excited and you should be. And if you find it's not what you want, you can always return to looking for a placement with a chef."

That was true, but didn't Hannah understand how hard she'd already looked? Besides, working in a restaurant kitchen wasn't her only dream.

She could sit still no longer. She walked to the porch rail and looped her arm around a column. "Do you know one of the best parts? I can visit the hospitals in the various cities and speak to the staff about better nutrition for the patients."

"You'll be a regular crusader like Aunt Sam." Hannah picked up her glass of milk. "You're frowning. What's wrong?"

"I was simply thinking I hope I can get them to understand the importance of this matter better than I did Dr. Brooks."

"I told him he should listen to you."

She smiled. "I know you did. He came to the contest's final round to see if I was any good."

"And what did he say after you won?"

"Congratulations." She returned to her seat. It was true he'd congratulated her, but it was the sincere way he'd said it that touched her so.

"Maybe if some of the other hospitals in the area implement your ideas, he'll be more open to hearing what you have to say." Hannah returned her empty milk glass to the tray.

"Motherhood has made you optimistic." If only what Hannah said was true, but Charlotte had the distinct feeling Dr. Brooks was a long way from truly considering anything she had to offer.

"Tessa stopped by this morning. She calls him Dr. Handsome, and I'd have to agree. Wouldn't you?"

Charlotte's cheeks warmed as his face came to mind—the alarming smile and bottle-green eyes that could take anyone's breath away. And he carried himself in such a self-confident way. His hands had been a strange combination of strong and gentle as he'd assisted her back to the vehicle. She absentmindedly touched her elbow.

"Charlotte? Wouldn't you agree?"

She shook the image of Dr. Brooks from her thoughts. "Agree with what?"

"That Dr. Brooks is quite striking."

"I guess some might think so." Charlotte took a bite of her

sandwich. "But I think he's quite stuck in his ways too. He thinks he knows everything, and he's quite willing to tell anyone who'll listen what to do and how to do it. You and I both know that after what I've been through, that's the last thing I want."

Hannah smiled. "You've been thinking about him romantically?"

"No! It's just that Tessa brought it up." She tugged her gloves back on. "I only wish things had gone better for the hospital's sake. He came over to Aunt Sam's Friday night and things didn't end well."

"You'll figure out how to get through to him, and if not him, then someone else at the hospital."

"I certainly hope so."

"How's Tessa adjusting to living with Aunt Sam?" Hannah shifted the blanket on her lap. "I hope it wasn't a mistake to accept Aunt Sam's offer for Tessa to stay for the summer. While it's nice not to have to worry about anyone but Ellie, I do miss Tessa."

"I don't think she's suffering a bit. Aunt Sam spoils her, and she encourages Tessa's flair for the dramatic."

"Like Tessa needs any more encouragement in that arena. Next thing we know, she'll want to join a circus."

"Truthfully, her newest pursuit is the theater. She wants to capture the hearts of audiences across the globe as an actress."

"An actress? What happened to being a reporter, a photographer, and a librarian?"

"Well, you didn't think that last one was going to work, did you?"

Hannah laughed. "No, I guess not."

"Yesterday she told me if Lincoln won't teach her to drive his automobile, she wants to try her hand at acting."

Hannah's eyebrows rose. "Well, I certainly don't think Lincoln's planning on giving her any driving lessons, so I guess you'd better tell our little sister to start brushing up on her Shakespeare." She pointed to Charlotte. "And you'd better be brushing up on your speaking skills, Miss Gregory."

Her speaking skills. Not her cooking skills. Maybe Charlotte had made a mistake in saying yes to this position.

Hannah was the speaker, the attorney, and Tessa certainly knew how to use her mouth as well, but Charlotte had always planned to serve people. Would she be happy outside a kitchen?

10

"'O, look! Methinks I see my cousin's ghost seeking out Romeo, that did spit his body upon a rapier's point.'" Tessa held up her hand. "'Stay, Tybalt, stay!'"

"Tessa, what are you doing?" Charlotte looked up from her papers and cookbooks strewn across the desk in Aunt Sam's parlor.

Tessa clutched a perfume bottle to her chest. "'Romeo, I come! This do I drink to thee.'" She pretended to drink from the vial and collapsed backwards onto the sofa.

She waited. Where was the applause? Didn't her sister recognize the talent before her?

"Tessa, are you quite finished?"

Tessa sat up. "I have to practice. I start next week."

"You start working as a clerk in the theater's office." Charlotte wrote something on her paper. "Aunt Sam made it clear you would not be acting."

"She said 'yet' and you know it." Tessa clutched her book of Shakespearean works. Even the thought of stepping on the stage of Saint Paul's Metropolitan Opera House made every inch of her body tingle. "Once the director sees my natural talent, I'm sure he'll find a part for me."

"You'll be assisting the theater's manager, Mr. Jurgenson, in any way he asks. I doubt you'll even go backstage, let alone meet the director." Charlotte set her pen in the holder. "And Tessa, don't become a pest. It was very kind of Aunt Sam to arrange this opportunity. Mr. Jurgenson is an important man and her friend. Whatever you do at his theater will reflect on her, so I hope you won't do anything that might embarrass her."

"Me?" Tessa scowled. Why didn't her sisters trust her? They didn't understand this was important to her. Acting in the theater had consumed her every thought for at least ten days now. "I thought we promised to support one another's dreams."

"But you have a different dream every other week."

Tessa sat up straight, looking directly at Charlotte. "It's not my fault I have so many talents. It's impossible to pick only one thing to pursue."

"I imagine you have quite a dilemma." Charlotte chuckled and shook her head. She gathered up her papers and headed for the door.

"Where are you going? I wanted to show you my version of the balcony scene from *Romeo and Juliet*."

"You were going to do both parts?"

"I am unless you can breathe life into one of those gingerbread men you made."

"Sorry, Tess, I won't be able to witness your little dramatic foray. I need to go prepare these recipes that I plan to teach the ladies to make next week when I start my lectures. I have a real job to do."

Tessa glared at her. She'd show Charlotte, Hannah, and everyone else how serious she was. She'd get the director's attention, and she'd prove herself. When she took her place on the stage, they'd have to eat their words. Sooner or later, they'd realize Tessa Gregory could do anything she put her mind to.

Rubbing his eyes, Joel sat back in his chair. He'd spent an hour hovering over this antiquated microscope. His shoulder muscles bunched beneath his coat, and he fought the urge to toss the device and its scratched lens into the garbage.

He eased the slide he'd been examining from the stage and returned it to the box. Without better magnification, he'd never be able to determine if the cells from Mrs. Willadson's biopsy were normal or cancerous. A mistake in their identification could cost the forty-eight-year-old woman her life. What a way to begin the week.

That was ridiculous. Things might be tight at the hospital, but they shouldn't be so bad that a piece of equipment could cost a patient his or her life. He'd worked hard to keep his area within its budget, so Dr. Arthur Ancker was going to have to find pennies somewhere for a new microscope.

Recalling an earlier conversation with the hospital superintendent, Joel smiled. Arthur had promised Joel a share of the funds from the next Ladies' Guild fund-raiser. He remembered reading about the success of their event, which had brought in more than enough to make the microscope purchase.

After covering the brass microscope, he shoved his notes in a folder and marched out of the closet-size laboratory. He hurried down the stairs to the hospital superintendent's office, his heavy footfalls echoing in the tiled hallway. As he reached Dr. Ancker's office, Terrence Ruckman met him in the hallway.

"What brings you down here, Dr. Brooks?"

Joel eyed the hospital's officious bookkeeper. With his pristine suits and slicked-back hair, he always seemed as if he'd be more comfortable in a bank than a hospital. Joel disliked the way he acted like he owned the hospital when he actually held little power other than to pay the bills and keep the books.

"I've come to speak to Dr. Ancker about a new microscope for my ward." There was no need to keep that information to himself. This was an administrative decision, and Terrence would know all about it when he wrote the check.

"I'm afraid you missed him by about an hour." He exhaled through disapproving lips. "But I can already tell you there's no money for microscopes for you or anyone else."

"Thanks for the information, but I'll take this up with Arthur, if you don't mind."

Terrence shrugged. "Suit yourself, but the money isn't there."

"What do you mean? I know the Ladies' Guild raised three hundred dollars a couple of weeks ago, and it was earmarked for new equipment. Did he spend it already?"

Terrence coughed into his fist. "Trust me. That coffer is empty, Dr. Brooks. Maybe you should do some fund-raising yourself. With all the wealthy women who seem to patronize your women's ward, I'm sure you could charm a few dollars out of them."

"Fund-raising isn't my job." And neither was charming his patients. While some doctors gave the city's wealthy women extra attention, he had never been one of them and he never would be.

"But taking care of your patients is your job. If they need a microscope . . ." He let his words fall away. Then, with a brief nod of dismissal, the bookkeeper walked away.

Joel stared after him, trying to squelch the irritation the man inspired. Was he telling the truth about the money? Arthur had promised it to Joel, and it wasn't like him to go back on his word, but maybe something more urgent had come up. With a six-hundred-bed hospital, something was always coming up. He'd ask Arthur about it later. In the meantime, he'd better find a microscope in this hospital that worked better than his before he ended up performing an unnecessary surgery on poor Mrs. Willadson.

Black trim accentuated the long lines of Charlotte's copper-colored travel suit. Even though she'd been given appreciative nods from a few waiting passengers in the train depot, she still felt uneasy in the new clothes. She smoothed her narrow mohair skirt and glanced around the large space. The spiky pheasant feathers on her hat bobbed as she turned to take in the passengers at the ticket counter, those buzzing about, and those seated at the high-backed benches. How would she ever recognize the woman the gas company had hired to accompany her? She had hoped to meet her before boarding her train, but so far, no one seemed to meet Mr. Johnson's scant description of Mrs. Larkin.

She shivered against the cool of the morning and glanced out the window at the men loading a baggage car. Wasn't that her small trunk containing her new frocks? On Saturday's shopping trip, Aunt Sam had insisted Charlotte needed at least four new outfits for her lectures, including a duster. After the clerk pointed out that the sleeves on her current coat did not come to the fingertips as they should, Aunt Sam had added the coat to their order. Her new masculine-styled coat boasted a cape collar and a leather belt. Given the chill in the air and the steam rising from the locomotive's bowels, perhaps she should have worn the coat.

"All aboard the 310 from Saint Paul to White Bear Lake!" the conductor called from the doorway.

Charlotte drew in a deep breath and followed him out the door and onto the platform. She presented her ticket, boarded the train, and found a seat by the window. Peering out the pane, she searched for Mrs. Larkin.

"Is this seat taken, sugar?"

"No, ma'am." Charlotte turned to take in the older woman with the thick Southern accent. "I mean, not really. I was hoping to save it for my traveling companion, Mrs. Larkin."

The woman plunked down in the seat, and Charlotte stared at her wide-eyed. Perhaps the woman was hard of hearing and hadn't understood she wanted to save the seat.

"So, you must be our chef—Miss Charlotte Gregory?"

"You're Mrs. Larkin?"

"Yes indeed. The very same." She settled a large bag in front of her wide midriff. "But I declare, you need to call me Molly."

Could Charlotte allow herself to speak to an elder in such a familiar manner? As if the lady sensed her misgivings, she patted Charlotte's arm, a smile reaching her pale blue eyes. "We'll be together a great deal, you know."

"Yes, of course—Miss Molly." That seemed more appropriate. "Please call me Charlotte."

The whistle blew, and with a mighty whoosh the train pulled away from the station. Molly patted her gleaming white hair and checked the position of her hat. "Well, sugar, it looks like we're starting down a new track in life. It's as exciting as a cow in a cabbage patch."

Charlotte grinned. "I'm taking a guess, but I'd say you're not native to Minnesota."

"And whatever gave you that idea?" Laughter shook Molly's shoulders. "When my Oscar went on to his great reward, I moved in with my sister in Saint Paul." Molly shook her head. "My stubborn sister refused to move to the South, where it was warm, so I joined her up here in the land of blizzards."

Molly shared a bowlful of information with Charlotte. She'd never been blessed with children, so she'd helped her husband in his pharmacy for many years. She'd lived in Minnesota for three years now. "Living with Levinia isn't the easiest thing for a body to do. She's as tight as a corset on a fat lady and just as persnickety. I reckon my traveling will be good for both of us."

The elderly woman's ease in sharing opened the door for Charlotte to do likewise. She explained how her parents had died and how Hannah had left law school to take care of her and her younger sister, Tessa. "Hannah isn't a rule keeper, so working at the switchboard wasn't easy for her."

"And now?" Molly opened her bag and produced a large oatmeal cookie for each of them.

"She got a law degree and a husband. She married an attorney named Lincoln, and they recently had a baby girl named Ellie." Charlotte took a bite of the cookie. "This is delicious, Miss Molly. Maybe you should be teaching the classes."

"Heavens, no. I'm still attached to my old range. None of this newfangled gas stuff for me." She broke her cookie in half, and crumbs sprinkled across the tucking on her white shirtwaist. She brushed them away. "But I'll take good care of you and all the travel arrangements. You can be sure of that."

"I appreciate it." The quiet humming of the man behind them drew Charlotte's attention. "Miss Molly, do you know when the singer Mr. Johnson hired will join us?"

"Actually, at White Bear Lake—our first stop."

"It will be fun to have one more lady traveling with us. I do hope she can sing 'By the Light of the Silvery Moon.' It's one of my favorites. Aunt Sam has a wax cylinder for her phonograph with Miss Ada Jones singing that very tune."

"Aunt Sam?"

Oh dear. How would this elderly Southern lady view Aunt Sam and her penchant for men's britches? Not to mention her tireless suffrage work. Did Charlotte even want to broach controversial issues with Molly so soon?

"Aunt Sam is really Hannah's husband's aunt." Charlotte decided to stick to the facts. "She raised Lincoln after his parents died, and now she's sort of adopted Tessa and me—at least for the summer."

"That's mighty generous of her."

Charlotte dabbed her lips with a handkerchief. "Aunt Sam lives on Summit Avenue."

"Well, she must be high cotton. Your auntie can afford to be generous."

Heat warmed Charlotte's cheeks. "Yes, I suppose so."

"There's nothing to be bashful about, sugar. That's the way the good Lord has laid out your path. Count your blessings." Molly set her large bag on the floor, then slapped her gloved hands on her legs. "Now, honey, I want to hear more about you."

By the time they neared White Bear Lake, Molly had extracted a mass of information from Charlotte. As the train rattled and clacked along, Charlotte found herself answering all of Molly's questions without holding back anything. She shared her dream of someday owning a restaurant. She talked about her passion for improving the food served in hospitals, and even told Molly about her unsuccessful discussion of the matter with Dr. Brooks. "And then he showed up at the cooking competition just to see if I had any idea what I was talking about. Can you imagine?"

"The nerve of that man." Molly's blue eyes crinkled with amusement. "Perhaps he's more interested in chasing you than changing his hospital."

"Then he'd better look elsewhere. I've already had enough of bossy men to last a lifetime. I'm ready for a sweet man who doesn't care if I crusade."

"I see." The train's brakes squealed and Molly picked up her satchel. "You want a man who's as happy as a pig in a peach orchard."

Charlotte quirked an eyebrow at the older woman's odd saying, but the train came to a stop before she could inquire further. She drew in a deep breath.

Her journey was about to begin, and with Molly by her side, it should prove quite interesting.

11

"You're the singer?" Charlotte stared at the well-dressed, lanky young man who met them in the hotel's lobby.

"Yes, miss. Mr. Johnson said I'd be joining you two lovely ladies in your travels. I'm Lewis Mathis." He started to offer his hand but then drew it back and stuffed it in the pocket of his tweed trousers.

"A pleasure to meet you." Molly seemed to recover more quickly than Charlotte. "I'm Molly Larkin, and this is our speaker, Miss Charlotte Gregory. It'll be as sweet as pie to have a man to serenade us every day, not to mention escort us and carry our trunks."

Lewis, who had to be nearly the same age as Charlotte, didn't look like he'd be doing a lot of trunk lifting. He might manage a few satchels—if they didn't pack them too heavy and the wind didn't blow.

"I'll be happy to help you both any way I can." He pushed up his spectacles and tilted a nervous smile in Charlotte's direction. He tugged on his starched collar. "As soon as you ladies are settled in your rooms, perhaps we could take a look at the hardware store where the lecture is being held."

"That would be perfect." Molly passed Charlotte one of the room keys. "As soon as we freshen up a bit, we'll be down, and then you'll have to tell us all about yourself while we're setting up." Molly nudged Charlotte's arm. "Right, Charlotte?"

She forced her lips to curve upward to ease a bit of Lewis's discomfort. "Yes, of course. Give us half an hour."

A genuine smile graced his boyish face. "I'll be waiting in the café next door. I'm sure you're hungry after your journey."

Easing open the doors to the Metropolitan Opera House's auditorium, Tessa waited for her eyes to adjust to the black emptiness yawning back at her.

"Hello?" Her voice echoed. "Is anybody here?" The hair on the back of her neck prickled and she shivered. How could something so alive in the evening seem so dead at nine in the morning?

"Miss Gregory, there you are."

She whirled at the sound of a man's deep voice and heavy footfalls on the tiled floor. "I-I was looking for the office."

"Of course you were." The middle-aged man's lips curved in a welcoming smile. "It's a good thing I recognized you from your aunt's description. I'm Mr. Jurgenson, the manager of the Metropolitan Opera House." He motioned to the heavy mahogany doors. "And I see you found the theater."

"What little of it I could see."

Tessa stepped back and sized up Mr. Jurgenson. Time had not been kind to the poor man. More hair poked out of his ears and from his bushy eyebrows than grew on the top of his head, and deep wrinkles fanned his steel-gray eyes. Still, he seemed pleasant enough.

She hiked one shoulder. "It was as dark as an inkwell inside the theater. I couldn't see a thing."

"Yes, without the lights, it is rather ominous looking, isn't it?" Mr. Jurgenson tugged on the lapels of his plaid suit jacket. "Now, if you'll follow me, I'll show you to the office and get you started on your duties."

Tessa followed the manager across the Minton-tiled floor of the theater's foyer. She glanced at the arched doorways leading into the theater, each one adorned with crimson velvet curtains tied back at the sides. She passed the upholstered chairs and couldn't help but run her hand along their backs. Even though she'd been there before with Aunt Sam and her sisters, the lavish surroundings robbed her of breath. How did she get so lucky to work here?

She gripped the brass handrail as they climbed the stairs to the second floor, and then Mr. Jurgenson led her down another hallway and finally stopped in front of a room. He held open a door for her. "Welcome to the office of the Metropolitan Opera House, Miss Gregory."

By stark contrast, the office lacked any finery. One desk faced the doorway as they entered, and two others faced one another in the center of the room. Tall windows made the room bright and sunny, but nothing else added to the room's warmth. Tessa noted the absence of any pictures. Why wouldn't they have pictures of the actors and actresses hanging around the room?

A typewriter sat on each desk, as well as a lamp. Her gaze landed on a large stack of posters. She flexed her fingers. Were those playbills?

A prim-looking woman wearing a crisp white shirtwaist stood. "Good morning, Mr. Jurgenson."

"Miss Gregory, may I introduce you to Miss Walker. You'll be assisting her with filing and other general responsibilities."

"Filing?" She wrinkled her nose, then quickly covered her mouth with her hand. Why had she spoken it that way?

Mr. Jurgenson chuckled. "You didn't think you'd be working backstage, did you?"

She didn't dare admit she'd hoped she would. "No, sir. I'm sorry. I thought I heard you say something else and I wanted to clarify."

"Very well." He checked his pocket watch, then slipped it back into his vest pocket. "As you can see, my office is over there, so I'm sure you'll see me later today. Right now I have a meeting to get to, but Miss Walker will keep you busy."

As soon as the door shut behind the manager, Miss Walker turned to Tessa. "I run a smooth and orderly office. I'll do my best to make sure you understand the tasks assigned to you, and I'll expect you to complete them in a timely manner."

"Yes, ma'am." Tessa glanced at Miss Walker's crisp white shirtwaist. How did she keep it so wrinkle free?

"And if I happen to send you to the theater or backstage to deliver something to a member of the cast or a director, you are to return immediately. These actors can be of questionable character, and I won't be responsible for the degradation of a fine young lady such as yourself."

A little thrill shot through Tessa. She might be sent backstage after all. She'd bide her time here until she got her opportunity.

Look out, world. Here comes America's sweetheart, Miss Tessa Gregory.

Nearly thirty women crowded into the hardware store. Charlotte wiped her sweaty palms on her white apron and scanned the ladies who'd come. They'd turned out in their Sunday best. At least with her new shirtwaist with its well-shaped collar and three-quarter-length sleeves, she knew no one could fault her fashion. Her words? That was another thing altogether. Had she bitten off more than she could chew?

Her eyes widened. What was Kathleen O'Grady from the cooking contest doing here? She was bound to bring trouble. Charlotte drew in a deep breath. Well, if she could handle Kathleen's snide remarks, she could handle anything.

However, she had best manage the situation from the start. She strode over to greet the young woman. "Hello, Kathleen. What brings you here to White Bear Lake?"

"My brother Kelly had business here, so I decided to join him. Imagine my surprise when I discovered you were giving a cooking demonstration. I simply had to come and cheer you on."

Charlotte doubted that. "I appreciate your support, and I hope you enjoy the lecture."

Moving back to the stove, Charlotte waited for Lewis to perform. He stood off to the side. She'd been so busy getting her own things ready, she hadn't been able to ask him if he was nervous, but one look at him now told her he most certainly was.

The bell on the hardware store jingled, and Charlotte turned to see a man walk in. She gasped. Mr. Johnson? Had he come all the way from Saint Paul to check up on her? What if she didn't live up to his expectations? If Kathleen interfered with her lecture, her time with the gas company could be over before it began.

No. She wouldn't let that happen. She wanted this too much. She could do this.

Lewis stepped beside the hardware store owner. She gave him an encouraging smile. With his hair parted down the middle and slicked down on the sides, he looked even younger than he had yesterday. Could this tall, slender young man really croon?

Last night, Charlotte had discovered that Lewis was an agreeable fellow, quick to laugh and quick to lend a hand. The two of them worked side by side, unpacking her pots and pans. She'd set her lima beans to soaking while they talked. Meanwhile, Molly had taken Charlotte's list of groceries and made arrangements with the local mercantile and the butcher to have the necessary items delivered.

Now, as the hardware store owner stepped forward, Charlotte sent up a quick prayer for Lewis's performance and a longer one for her own success.

The owner inserted his thumb and pinky into his mouth and gave a shrill whistle. Immediately the room fell silent. "That's more like it." He glanced at Lewis. "Now, before I introduce our guest speaker, we have a special treat. Mr. Lewis Mathis, a bass from Stillwater, is going to perform for us."

Lewis moved to the front of the room. Could he be a bass? Truly? Not a tenor? Or a baritone?

"The first song I'm going to sing is one I believe you'll all recognize." All his nervousness seemed to vanish as he spoke to the crowd.

How odd. She hadn't noticed the deep timbre of his voice.

He smiled at the audience. "Here's my version of 'Shine On, Harvest Moon.'"

With no accompaniment, he began. His voice, strong and full, filled the room. Ladies smiled in appreciation and Charlotte blinked. Lanky Lewis Mathis could sing! News of that voice was sure to travel. By tomorrow, more women would surely attend. Would they be able to fit another twenty or thirty women in the hardware store?

After "Shine On, Harvest Moon," Lewis sang a fun rendition of "Good Evening, Caroline" and finished with "Then You'll Remember Me." By the end of that song, surely he'd won the hearts of nearly every lady who'd come to the lecture. He'd be a tough act to follow.

From the applause, Charlotte guessed the ladies would have liked to hear more, but Lewis bowed and the hardware store owner stepped forward to introduce her. Her stomach jiggled like unmolded gelatin as the man explained she was a graduate of Fannie Farmer's School of Cookery and would now delight them with her culinary skills, using the marvels of the gas range.

"Welcome, ladies. Thank you all for coming." Charlotte flashed her best smile to the crowd. "I know all of you work very hard. How would you like to have at least an hour of your day to do as you wish?"

The ladies murmured their agreement. Charlotte grinned. She had their attention, but a glance at Kathleen told her that girl was waiting for a moment to stir up trouble.

"Do you realize it takes at least an hour a day to care for your wood- or coal-burning stove—checking the flues, adding wood or coal, removing ashes, and blacking it? With the gas range, you can avoid all of that and save even more time during meal preparation."

She looked at Molly, who nodded her support.

Kathleen shoved her way to the front row and raised her hand. "But gas is so expensive."

"It can be if you don't use it economically." Charlotte stepped toward the table where her supplies lay arranged. “If used wisely, it’s the cleanest, cheapest, and most efficient fuel known—and best of all, it’s fast. It’s ready without delay at the touch of a match. No more waiting for the fire to get started.”

Charlotte paused until the murmuring between the ladies subsided. She explained a few aspects of scientific cookery and the need to use standard measures, then presented the menu for the day—cream of lima bean soup, graham muffins, broiled bass with sauce allemande, asparagus spears, and chocolate bread pudding with meringue. “And you’ll all be taking home a small recipe booklet compiled by the gas company as a token of our thanks for your attendance, so don’t fret if you miss something.”

This seemed to please her guests. Since the lima bean soup was made in a Dutch oven on the stove top and would take the most time, she started with that. After draining the beans, she had an audience member help her chop the celery and ham while she added salt, pepper, and water to the pot. Once it came to a boil, she covered it and explained she was letting it simmer.

“Simmering is a cooking technique that uses very little gas. The very low flame will cook the food slowly and is perfect to keep your food warm.”

She moved on to the chocolate bread pudding because it would take the most baking time. The ladies seemed delighted to know she used a day-old loaf from the local bakery, and she soon had it ready to go in the oven. She opened the oven door and struck a match. It didn’t light. She struck another, but it too wouldn’t light. She glanced at the wood. Why did it feel damp?

She swallowed hard. Kathleen! A wide grin split the woman’s round face. Somehow she’d found a way to sabotage Charlotte’s matches. Had she touched anything else?

“Here you go.” The hardware store owner handed Charlotte a fresh box of matches. The sun glinted off his bald head as he turned to the audience. “Our store always has plenty of matches on hand.”

The ladies twittered as if the advertisement had been done

purposefully. Charlotte struck another match and released the breath she was holding when the flame caught. "When lighting the oven, always open the oven door. Have the match ready and apply it at once to the pilot light." She touched the match flame to the pilot light and a tiny blue flame appeared. "Then turn on the oven burner."

She turned the lever beneath the oven door. "The perfect gas flame will be a blue flame with a purple tip. Too little air makes a yellow tip. This kind of flame will not be hot and will smudge your utensils. Too much air will make the burners pop and blow." She pointed to a cap on the end of the burner. "This cap allows you a perfect adjustment of air in the burner. Once you get it set, you'll seldom have to adjust it again."

She demonstrated how to determine the oven's temperature using a teaspoon of flour in a pie tin, then inserted her chocolate bread pudding. "Since we can make the fish in the broiler at the same time we are baking the muffins, we'll do that last. Now we're going to make our sauce and asparagus on the top of the stove."

"And exactly how do you think we can get that all done at once?" Kathleen didn't bother to raise her hand this time.

"That's a good question. As you know, timing a meal is one of the most difficult parts." Charlotte lit the pilot light on the stove top and turned on the burner. "It takes practice, but with a gas stove you have the option of using the warmer." She pointed to the small bread-warming oven on top. "And you can keep other items simmering on the burners until everything is ready."

When the chocolate bread pudding was done, she pulled it from the oven. The ladies moaned at the delicious scent that began to fill the room. "Would any of you lovely ladies like to join me in preparing the rest of the meal?"

Kathleen's hand shot up first. A couple of others also raised their hands but then lowered them when Kathleen shot each of them a glare.

Should Charlotte pick one of the other ladies? If she did, would

Mr. Johnson believe she still couldn't get along with Kathleen? Reluctantly, she motioned Kathleen forward.

To her surprise, Kathleen followed her directions to the letter in preparing the bass. Maybe this would turn out all right after all. She lifted a piece of paper on which she'd carefully written a recipe and handed it to Kathleen like an olive branch. "Clearly Miss O'Grady is an accomplished cook. I believe she can handle the recipe for the sauce allemande while I prepare the graham muffins."

Kathleen beamed and set to work. Even when Charlotte called over her shoulder to remember to measure each ingredient, Kathleen simply smiled and nodded.

After Charlotte had the graham muffins in the oven, Kathleen announced she was done. Charlotte tasted the sauce. "Excellent, Miss O'Grady. Thank you for your help."

Only one more thing to do and the meal would be complete. Charlotte added cream to the lima bean soup and tasted it. Good grief, how did it get so salty? Wait a minute. How had she been so stupid? She'd left Kathleen at the stove alone. Perspiration beaded on her forehead. She couldn't possibly serve soup like this.

"Is something wrong?" Kathleen's sugary voice rang out.

How could she quickly fix this? Charlotte spotted a bowl of potatoes Molly had picked up for tomorrow's demonstration on the work surface. She grabbed one and started peeling it.

"No, there's no problem." She returned the sugary smile to Kathleen. "The soup is a little saltier than I like. Does anyone know the trick to fix that?"

An older woman in a lavender hat raised her hand. "You add potatoes."

"Yes, ma'am. You are absolutely correct." Charlotte cut the potato into chunks and dropped it into the soup. By the time she'd removed the muffins and drizzled the sauce allemande over the fish, the potatoes had cooked and removed the saltiness.

She swept her arms toward the prepared food. "I believe our feast is ready for sampling."

Thank goodness the women had been instructed to bring their own forks! As they took turns coming up to the worktable to sample the goods, she answered their questions. Slowly the women trickled out of the hardware store with promises to return tomorrow.

Mr. Johnson joined her by the stove. "Well done, Miss Gregory, but be sure to sell the stoves and not just the food." He glanced at the table. "They didn't leave us much to eat."

"Never seen anything like it. Like pigs at the trough." Molly began to gather the empty plates. "I sure learned a thing or two, but smelling all that good food means now I'm starving."

"To be honest, I'm glad the first day is done." She glanced at Kathleen, who seemed to be prolonging her exit. "I'm sure it will be easier the next time."

Wiggling her fingers, Kathleen waved goodbye with a smug chuckle. "See you tomorrow, Charlotte."

Then again, maybe tomorrow would be even worse.

12

Like turtles basking in the sun, upturned rowboats lay on wooden racks along the edge of Raspberry Island. Joel jogged toward the Minnesota Boat Club's storage area and spotted his rowing partner, Dr. Knute Ostberg. Thinking about something other than the hospital or the way his discussion with Charlotte ended the other day was exactly what he needed. Nothing but hard work, a good friend, and lots of Minnesota sunshine.

"You beat me here." He joined Knute in lifting the boat off the rack. They carried it down to the end of the dock and set it in the water.

"Let's face it. I'm better at leaving when my shift is over." Knute climbed in the narrow boat and slid his oar into the oarlock. "And I was smart enough not to take a job as an assistant superintendent."

"Smart enough, huh?" Joel chuckled. Knute just didn't understand why the administrative position meant so much to him. How could he? Knute's father was one of the most respected men in the city, whereas Joel had spent half his life defending his father.

After easing into the spot behind Knute, Joel clipped his oar in place, slid his shoes into the foot plate, and strapped them in. "Ready?"

Without another word, the two of them worked in tandem to ease away from the dock and rowed toward the buoy that marked the beginning of their practice run. Spring had brought a high water level to the Mississippi River, and the current carried the boat away from their goal, but years of rowing together had taught them how to manage the motion.

"Let's take it easy on this first trip. Warm up slow." Bending his knees, Joel slid forward and lifted his oar from the water. "On your mark, Knute."

Knute gave the signal and set the pace as the two rowers took off. The familiar sequence of rowing—bunching muscles in his legs, back, and arms—released all of the cares Joel faced from the day. No more budgets or patients. Not even any irritating women who wanted him to serve food on pretty dishes. Just the steady dip and pull of the oars.

Joel matched Knute's pace stroke for stroke, remembering their first year on the college eight-man rowing team. The coach had rebuked Joel for showing off. "You'll only make your crew go slower. A crew is made up of individuals willing to sacrifice their personal goals for the team." The lesson had served him well both on the water and in life.

Seated with his back to their goal, Joel glanced at the shoreline to make sure they were keeping their course straight, then at Knute's back. Both of them reached the end of their pull, their backs at the thirty-degree point.

"Did you get to talk to Arthur about that microscope?" Knute asked, leaning forward into the next pull.

"I did. He said he didn't understand it either. He'd earmarked those funds for my wards, but they aren't there now. You know they were the ones from that charity fund-raiser your mother chaired." Joel slid his seat back at the end of his stroke and lifted his oar from the water. "He said he'd speak to Terrence Ruckman about it and try to get it ironed out."

"It sounds fishy. Do you think you should push a little harder? Maybe you're making it too easy for them to dismiss your concerns."

"It's a tough line to walk." As the youngest assistant superintendent, he wanted to prove he could handle the responsibilities he'd been given. He didn't want to make too much fuss about anything for fear his peers would think he was in over his head. At the same time, he didn't want his patients to suffer simply because he was trying to impress his superiors and not rock the boat. His time with the rowing crew may have taught him how to sacrifice for the team, but medical school had taught him that sometimes one had to be forceful to get ahead. How was he to know which skill to use now?

They reached the buoy that marked the three-mile point and took a moment to catch their breath.

"So, you still stewing about that microscope?" Knute stretched one arm across the front of his body, then the other.

"No, not really." Joel wiped his brow with the back of his hand.

Knute took hold of his oar, signaling it was time to turn the boat around. "Hey, I heard the nurses talking about some lady who came to the hospital and knows all about cooking for sick people. They said you talked to her."

"Yes, I did." Joel sighed. Charlotte seemed to haunt him everywhere he turned. "She has some lofty ideas. They're not very practical."

Knute shrugged. "That's not what your sister said. She thinks the nurses could use some education in the area of nutrition."

Joel readied his oar to begin the trek back. "Miss Gregory may know what she's talking about, but she doesn't know more than the doctors."

"But maybe she does know more than the nurses." Knute took a deep breath. "Now it's time to do some real work. On my mark."

Even though he couldn't see his face, Joel could hear the smile in his friend's voice. Knute set a grueling pace and Joel had no option but to match it. Good teams did that. Their strengths harmonized, and their rhythms, desires, talents, and blade work did as well.

Straining against the fast current, neither man had the ability to carry on a discussion. Joel's muscles burned. Even though they'd been out on the water since April when the ice had melted, they hadn't had enough training sessions yet this year to ease the strenuous workout.

Joel pushed past the pain and shoved the situation at the hospital out of his thoughts. Even when the rest of his life felt out of control, here on the water all went according to plan. No surprises. Only predictable, well-rehearsed strokes. Teammates working in tandem toward the same goal. Something he doubted Charlotte Gregory had ever done before in her life.

Good grief. He had to stop thinking about her.

The train rattled into the Stillwater station right on time. Charlotte followed Molly off the train and Lewis trailed behind. Without a word, each set to their tasks as if they'd been on the lecture circuit for years. While Molly arranged for the demonstration goods to be delivered to the city auditorium, Charlotte helped Lewis load their personal baggage into a waiting automobile his parents had sent.

"Are you certain your mother doesn't mind us staying at your home, Lewis?" Charlotte tried to shake the creases from her burnt-orange skirt.

"My parents are excited to meet the other gas company employees I'm traveling with. When they heard our second stop was Stillwater, they insisted you stay at our home."

Molly returned to join them. "Are you sure there's enough room? We won't be putting anyone out, will we?"

He grinned. "I think we can squeeze you both in."

How differently she'd come to see Lewis in the last few days. Yes, he was tall and lanky and his center-parted hair did nothing for his long face, but Charlotte found she didn't notice those things nearly as much now. Sweet and thoughtful, Lewis possessed an easy laugh that put them at ease even in difficult circumstances.

On the train, she'd laughed at the way he described the whole Kathleen O'Grady experience. "Molly put herself between you and Kathleen like a cow protecting her calf," he'd teased. "I thought Molly was going to charge if that girl made one more snide comment."

Molly had chuckled. "You got that right. I was ready to take that girl by the ear and show her a right proper way to exit a ladies' gathering."

Charlotte turned to watch the man loading their lecture supplies a few yards away. She counted the trunks—four in all—filled with utensils, spices, and dry goods. The man dropped one of the trunks, and she gasped.

"Do be careful with those!" Lewis called out. He turned to Molly. "Do you want me to go see to the trunks myself?"

"No, I packed them well. There are only a few breakables."

"In that case, ladies, may I?" He offered his hand to Molly to assist her into the waiting automobile.

After all three of them were situated, the driver started down the paved brick street. Charlotte fought a fog of sleepiness under the steady rumble of the engine as they drove.

Molly laid a hand on her arm. "You need a nap, sugar."

"I guess this morning's lecture took more out of me than I thought." She glanced out the window and watched a few colorful homes pass by—very large colorful homes. "Lewis, where do you live?"

"On Second. Off of Churchill. Are you familiar with Stillwater?"

She shook her head. "No, I'm not."

The automobile drew up in front of a huge three-story Queen Anne–style home with a steeply pitched roof, a wraparound porch, and scroll-saw detailing over the pediment.

"What did you say your father did?"

"I don't know that I told you."

"Well?" Molly laid her hands across her broad midsection. "Don't keep a body in suspense."

"He's in lumber."

Charlotte eyed the pretty white-iron fence surrounding the home and the carriage house out back. "As in he owns a lumber company?"

Lewis hopped out of the car. "Among other things."

13

"And you're a performer?" Charlotte stared at Lewis, who now stood in front of her and Molly. Again he'd surprised her. She needed to stop underestimating this man. Singing was hardly an occupation encouraged by the kind of men who worked in industries like lumber. "Weren't you expected to join the family business?"

"I'm the youngest of four brothers." He assisted both ladies to the ground. "My father tolerates my music and hardly notices when I'm not around." Two women, whom she guessed to be his mother and sister, threw open the front door and waved. Lewis rolled his eyes. "My mother, on the other hand, would keep me by her side every minute if she could."

As if she'd heard Lewis, his mother hurried down the stairs of the large home and drew Lewis into an embrace. "I've missed you terribly."

Lewis kissed her cheek. "Mother, I was gone for two days."

"Two days too many." She turned toward Charlotte and Molly. "And you must be the ladies giving the lectures and traveling with my Lewis."

She welcomed Molly and Charlotte with open arms and directed a maid to show them to their guest rooms. Charlotte's room sported pink carnation wallpaper. Each flower had a mesmerizing, fluid, blue-green stem. The coverlet on the brass bed bore the same rosy color as the wallpaper, but the curtains brought out the color of the stems.

Charlotte unpacked her small trunk and shook out the dress she planned to wear. So many wrinkles! She'd have to borrow an iron. After unpacking, she sat on the bed. The maid had pointed out that she and Molly shared a water closet, and she was tempted to go through it and knock on Molly's door. However, since there'd been no noise coming from her chaperone's room, she guessed the older woman might have chosen to take a nap.

Perhaps she should do the same. Charlotte slipped out of her jacket, kicked off her shoes, and lay down on the bed. It felt heavenly to close her weary eyes. She would never have imagined the amount of energy it took to be up in front of people for a couple of hours. Given Tessa's propensity for drama, she must be exhausted half the time.

Amid thoughts of Tessa, Hannah, and the new baby, Charlotte allowed herself to drift off. She never slept long, but a few minutes of rest might do her wonders.

Lewis rapped on her door. "Charlotte, I was wondering if you and Molly would like to go see a little of the area since we don't have a lecture until tomorrow afternoon."

Charlotte sat up in bed and rubbed her eyes. She glanced out her west-facing window and noticed the sun hadn't yet begun its descent, but how long had she slept?

She cleared her throat. "Have you asked Molly?"

"Yes, she'd like to, if you will."

"Thank you, Lewis." She crawled out of the bed. "I'll be down in a few minutes."

As soon as she'd freshened up, Charlotte hurried to meet her companions. Lewis led them to the automobile, insisting Molly sit in front. He and Charlotte settled in the backseat, and he directed the driver to take them to the mill. When they passed a child-size log cabin, Charlotte asked about it.

"Louis Bergeron built that for his children after they read about

Abraham Lincoln." Lewis draped his arm on the door of the motorcar. "Did you know Stillwater is the oldest city in Minnesota?"

"You don't say." Molly twisted sideways in her seat to give him a smile. "Are we going to your father's mill?"

Lewis looked down. "I need to stop for a minute and tell him I'm home. Then we can head down to the river for a picnic. I had the cook prepare a basket. The Saint Croix is beautiful in the spring when it's running high."

Lofty trees began to replace the homes in the landscape. Charlotte turned to Lewis. "Can we go through the mill?"

"Which one?"

"How many are there?"

"There's the sawmill and the planing mill. Oh, and there's the box factory." Lewis raked a hand through his hair. "I don't think Father would let you near the mill, but I can sneak you in the box factory. My brother Miles is in charge there."

Since they had some travel time in the automobile, Charlotte peppered Lewis with more questions about his family and their business. It didn't take long to learn he'd started piano lessons as a young man, and when he'd shown an early aptitude, his mother found the best teachers. He'd studied at Northwestern Conservatory of Music, but his father had insisted he also take business courses at a nearby business college.

"Every summer I worked in the mill office or the box factory. I can do the work, but I'm not a manager and I don't have a heart for the profession like my father or my brothers do." He sighed. "My father has basically written me off in that respect."

The pain in Lewis's eyes made Charlotte's heart ache for him. "You had a different dream than his, but it doesn't make you a failure."

"Somehow I don't think he'd agree with you." Lewis grew quiet a few minutes before speaking again. "There's the mill up ahead."

How different Lewis was from the men she'd known before. Back in high school, when she still lived in Iowa, she'd stepped out with a boy who wanted to change her. She'd vowed that would never happen again. Whenever the time came for someone to court her, he wasn't going to try to run her life or tell her what to do. No man would define her. She'd define herself.

Lewis had admitted he wasn't a manager, and she couldn't imagine him bossing anyone around either. On the other hand, Joel Brooks would probably boss around a toad if he had the chance—but he'd certainly look good doing so.

Where had thoughts of him come from? Wasn't she thinking about Lewis? Charlotte shook her head and strained to locate the mill amid the pines. The automobile rounded the bend in the road, and she spotted the three wooden buildings—one larger, two smaller. She guessed the largest of the three, the one closest to the river, to be the mill.

When the driver had parked the car, Lewis asked them to wait while he spoke to his father. The steam whistle shrieked and Charlotte startled. Lewis laughed. "I'll come back and show you around."

He returned five minutes later and opened Charlotte's and Molly's doors.

"Land sakes, I'm as creaky as an old bridge this afternoon." Molly pressed a hand to the small of her back. "Was your father pleased to see you, Lewis?"

"As much as ever. Are you ready for a brief tour?" He motioned them toward the mill and pointed to two men at the far end loading a log onto a steel rack. "When the logs reach us, they are already bucked and limbed."

"Bucked and limbed?" Molly raised an eyebrow. "You sure sound like you know what you're doing."

"*Bucked* means the logs are cut to length and *limbed* means the limbs have been removed." He led them closer to the river. "The logs have also been sorted and scaled according to quality. Those men are loading that one so it can be debarked. Inside, there's a huge head saw that will cut the logs into cants and flitches."

"You might as well be speaking Portuguese to me, and it's all hard to picture from out here," Molly said. "Are you sure we can't go inside and see?"

"The mill is powered by a steam engine." His voice rose with the whine of the saw blade. "Between the blades, belts, and boards, it's not the safest place."

Charlotte stiffened. "For a woman, you mean."

"No, for anyone." Lewis chuckled. "Don't see enemies where there are none, Charlotte."

They walked to the next building. Lewis explained it was the planing mill where the flitches, or unfinished boards, were planed, smoothed, and trimmed into lumber lengths. The faint scent of overheated oil filled the air, and Charlotte wrinkled her nose. Even from the outside of the building, the steady *kush-thunk* of the steam engine's massive pistons beat a rhythm.

"This is the box factory." He held open the door of the third shed. "Watch yourself, ladies."

Amid whooshes of different machines, men moved with practiced ease. In the center of the room stood piles of Premier Glove Company wooden boxes. Lewis's brother Miles greeted him and then introduced himself to Charlotte and Molly.

They moved to the far side of the room, and the stench of charred wood greeted them. Lewis held up a board bearing the Empire Sliced Dried Beef imprint. "This is where we brand the boards. Each company has a branding plate made of magnesium with their logo. This unit heats the branding plate and burns the impression in each board."

The worker at this station clamped the branding plate in place, set the guide plate for the boards to follow, and then dropped the cut sections of board in a tall guide on the table. He lowered the branding plate and, with a hiss, seared the image into the wood. When he raised the iron, another piece of wood slid into the slot.

"Can I try it?" Charlotte asked.

Lewis shrugged. "Sure, why not? You're used to hot ovens. This isn't too different."

The worker handed her a stack of the boards he was imprinting and she slid them into the slot. When the boards were ready, she moved to the branding part of the machine.

Lewis stepped behind her. "Now, move this lever." He reached around her and touched the lever with his hand. "Go ahead. I'm here if you need me."

He stood so close the skin on her neck prickled beneath his breath. She moved the lever and watched the branding iron begin its steady process of imprinting the boards. Lewis didn't step back but remained behind her. He was probably worried something might go wrong. Finally, the last board in the stack passed through and she shut the machine off. She turned, but Lewis had not yet stepped back.

She tried to move away, but he grabbed her arms. "Be careful of the branding iron, remember?"

Of course she remembered. She worked with hot pans every day. Still, his concern touched her. She glanced at him, and it seemed his concern had taken a whole new path.

"Y'all make a good team." Molly grinned at Charlotte. "Now, can we get on with the picnicking? I'm starved."

Lewis's cheeks colored and he released her. "Yes, of course."

Charlotte hurried to be the first out the door. Her cheeks felt as hot as the branding iron she'd used only minutes before. What was wrong with her? First thinking about Joel Brooks, and now this. But Lewis was only being helpful, wasn't he?

Why didn't Miss Walker understand that Tessa was only trying to be helpful? She could have delivered the message to the director a lot faster than prim Miss Walker with her perfect-size steps in her perfectly starched shirtwaist.

Tessa opened the ledger and sighed. When Miss Walker told her she'd be recording the box office receipts from the weekend, she made it sound like she was bestowing a great honor on Tessa. Rows of neat figures probably did thrill someone like Miss Walker, but they didn't do a thing for Tessa.

Oh well, sometimes one had to do the unpleasant jobs to get to the good ones—like getting a part in the production. Tessa glanced at the stack of playbills on the corner of Mr. Jurgenson's desk. *Rebecca of Sunnybrook Farm* lay on top. The dramatization of the book had appeared here at the Metropolitan Opera House last month. Aunt Sam had taken them all to see the production, and Tessa had fallen in love with the actress's portrayal of sweet Rebecca.

Laying her hand on the playbill, Tessa repeated Rebecca's last words in the play. "'God bless Aunt Miranda! God bless the brick house that was! God bless the brick house that is to be!'"

"Miss Gregory." Miss Walker let the door shut behind her. "What do you think you are doing?"

Tessa dropped her hands and grabbed her pencil. "I'm sorry. I'm afraid I was daydreaming."

"Daydreaming will not get those receipts entered. I suggest you put your imagination on hold and focus on the task at hand, young lady."

"Yes, ma'am." Tessa dropped her gaze. How could she do this tedious, mundane job?

A grin spread across her face. She could become an actress here too and pretend she was like Miss Walker in every way. Not only would it be excellent practice, but it was sure to win Miss Walker's trust. Once she had that, surely she'd get to make the deliveries backstage.

And then? She'd be one step closer to stepping onto the stage beneath the bright lights.

"Tessa?"

"Yes, ma'am?"

Miss Walker tapped the book in front of her, indicating Tessa needed to get busy.

Tessa sat up straight and pursed her lips like Miss Walker did when concentrating. She listed the first few numbers using her best Walker-ish penmanship. This wasn't so hard. She'd have the Miss Walker character down by lunch time.

That is, if those playbills stopped calling her name.

14

The Stillwater city auditorium held many more women than the hardware store in White Bear Lake. Gas lines had been laid to the auditorium especially for this occasion. Yesterday the seats had been two-thirds full, but apparently news had spread about the lectures for today, as there was standing room only. To Charlotte's relief, Kathleen was nowhere in sight.

Charlotte wished she had a Brownie camera to take a photo. Tessa would like seeing the crowd, and she'd love to share the images with Hannah and Aunt Sam. Today made for Charlotte's sixth day of travel, and she had to admit she was ready to head home. Had anything changed while she was away? How much had Ellie grown in the last week? How much trouble had Tessa gotten herself into? Had that stubborn doctor come to his senses yet?

Good grief. She had to stop thinking about that infuriating man.

Lewis sidled over to her. "Looks like the people of Stillwater love you."

"Why do you say that?"

"I think every lady in the city is here." He pointed to a row where several apron-clad nurses sat. "Your visit at the hospital yesterday must have gone well."

"It did. They'd like me to come back this afternoon and teach them more. I told them I'd do my best."

Lewis leaned closer and cupped his hand over his mouth.

"The woman with the peacock-feathered hat is Ida Nelson, and the woman beside her is her daughter Lillian. They live on West Chestnut, in the house with the gingerbread trim and the rounded stained-glass window you liked so much when we drove in."

"Lillian is very pretty. Is she married?"

"No." He shrugged. "And before you suggest anything, she's not my type."

"Your type?"

"I like ladies with a bit more creativity—and ones who can cook." He grinned at her before inclining his head to the other side of the room. "Nan Olson over there is a dressmaker. She and her sister Ellen, the milliner, must have closed down their shops for the day. And look at that."

"What?" She followed the direction of his gaze to two ladies standing in the back, wearing much plainer clothes than most of the women.

"The Bronsons sent their servants. That's really something."

Charlotte supposed she should feel honored, but the idea of having servants was still odd to her. Those in Aunt Sam's employ always felt more like family. She glanced at the clock and smiled at Lewis. "I think it's time to start."

Within minutes, Lewis had the women swooning over his melodies. And by the time it was Charlotte's turn to speak, the ladies already felt as if they'd had a treat. So when Charlotte announced the lecture today involved chafing dish cookery, the ladies applauded with enthusiasm.

"By using the gas stove to prepare your bread and side dishes ahead of time, you are free to prepare the remainder of the meal at the table in your chafing dish." Charlotte asked for volunteers to help her make savory rice, creamed carrots, and an apple spice cake with rum cream.

"Many of you already know a circular chafing dish is supplied with one lamp with an asbestos wick covered by fine netting." She held up the small metal lamp. "One regulates the flame by adjusting this screw. The lamp holds one gill of alcohol and burns for about one and one-half hours."

Charlotte explained that the ladies would want to serve seasonings and condiments in their pretty bowls, dainty jars, and odd-size pitchers for a chafing dish supper. "Unique pieces of china make the dinner a festive occasion."

She pointed to her aluminum measuring cup and her teaspoon and tablespoon. "Ladies, you must never forget that accurate measurements are essential for good results." She lifted a wooden spoon in the air. "And since chafing dish cookery should be as noiseless as possible, using a wooden spoon is important during preparation. A large spoon with an ebony handle is perfect for serving your creation."

Hands began to go up, and Charlotte did her best to answer questions. "No, you shouldn't mix at the table . . . Yes, you should have everything seasoned ahead of time if you can . . . No, chafing dishes are not appropriate for elegant dining, but they are perfect for entertaining friends."

By the time she was able to show them how to make the Vienna steaks, her own stomach was growling. Cinnamon laced the air from the apple cake in the oven, and she noticed the ladies in the audience licking their lips.

Charlotte sucked in a breath. There'd be no way for all of these ladies to sample the fare. What was she to do?

"Terrence, we need that microscope." Joel leaned over the man's desk. When he'd finally gotten to use another ward's microscope, he'd discovered Mrs. Willadson didn't have cancer after all. He shuddered to think she could have gone through an unnecessary surgery.

What if one of the other doctors had been in his place? One like Dr. Fitzsimmons? That man would never have gone the extra mile to check the slide somewhere else.

"I know Dr. Ancker earmarked money for my wards, and I won't endanger my patients again because of the lack of equipment."

Leaning back in his chair, Terrence Ruckman pushed up his wire-framed glasses. "And just where do you think I can get the money? Sorry, but I'm fresh out of rabbits' hats."

"You can start by finding out where the money went, and then you can get it back."

"I'm sure Dr. Ancker reallocated it to something more pressing. You can ask him about it yourself when he returns from his trip." Terrence steepled his fingers. "I realize you are young and inexperienced and your position is temporary, but those things do happen in a hospital of this size."

Joel clenched his jaw. "A lot of things can happen in a hospital of this size."

Terrence pushed his chair back. The rollers beneath it squeaked as he came to his feet. Standing several inches shorter than Joel, he had to turn his face upward to speak to him. "Perhaps you should watch your tone, before I have to suggest to Arthur that in his absence it became clear the stress of your responsibilities has begun wearing on you."

"The only stress wearing on me is you, Terrence, and my missing funds." Joel straightened and adjusted his morning coat. "Why don't you do your job and find the money?"

"A good assistant superintendent would figure out another way around this issue."

The words nicked Joel's pride, but he schooled his features. "I disagree. I think a good assistant superintendent would fight for his patients, and that's exactly what I plan to do. I don't care if you have to put the money back in from your own pockets, just make sure it's there by the time Arthur returns."

"Or what? You'll tell Daddy on me?"

"No, I'll turn you upside down and shake every cent out of your pockets each day until I have my money."

"You wouldn't dare."

Joel narrowed his eyes. "Try me."

Blood pumped through his veins with such force he could swear he felt it flowing. He marched into the hallway and let the door to Terrence's office slam behind him.

"Joel!"

He looked up to see his sister running toward him. "Mattie, what's wrong?"

"I've been looking all over for you. You had an emergency call."

"From outside the hospital? Who?"

"The call came in from Tessa Gregory." She thrust his bag into his hands. "Hurry! The ambulance is waiting."

Resisting the urge to lick the whipped cream from her fingertips, Charlotte reached for her napkin.

"Telling the guests they could only try one thing was brilliant, sugar." Molly set her fork down. "And I declare, this food is downright scrumptious."

"I feel a bit guilty there was enough left over for our dinner, but there was no way everyone could have tried all of the dishes."

Lewis patted his stomach. "And I'm personally grateful you made Vienna steaks just for us."

"You're welcome, but it doesn't take long in the chafing dish." Charlotte began to gather the soiled dishes.

Molly placed her hand on Charlotte's arm. "Lewis, why don't you walk Charlotte over to the hospital so she can talk to those nurses a little bit more?"

"But . . ." Charlotte allowed Molly to tug the dishes from her hands.

"No buts." Molly set the pile in a pail. "I aim to wash these up and get them packed away before you get back."

"You don't need to do that, Molly."

"This little bit of work is as easy as sliding off a greased log backwards." She shooed them with her hands. "Now, y'all get on out of here and let a lady do her work."

"You heard the lady." Lewis swept his arm toward the door.

Charlotte flashed him a smile and stepped out of the auditorium and into the bright Minnesota sunlight. All this beautiful day was missing was a lake and a picnic.

She glanced around at the patrons milling about the brick storefronts. "You don't have to accompany me to the hospital, Lewis. I doubt if you'll enjoy listening to me talk more."

He smiled at her, then swallowed. "At least I'll get to spend some time with you."

Heat crept up Charlotte's neck. The few comments Lewis had made like this left no doubt as to his intent, but she made no effort to encourage him. Since they traveled together, any exchange of affection would complicate matters. And even if they weren't part of the gas company's team, she wasn't sure she could feel that way about Lewis.

"Mr. Mathis!"

Lewis spun around and found a youth waving a telegraph. The boy jogged to meet them. "The lady in the auditorium said I could find Miss Charlotte Gregory with you. I've got a telegram for her."

Charlotte sucked in a breath and fought the rise of panic surging through her. A telegram meant bad news. What had happened back home? She stepped forward. "I'm Charlotte Gregory."

"Oh, good." The boy handed her the telegram. "It was marked urgent, so I wanted to get it to you right away."

Lewis tipped the young man and he jogged off. "Charlotte, you're white as your cooking apron. What is it?"

She reread the telegram. The print swam beneath her gaze in blurry images, but she already knew what it said. "I've got to get home right away. Something has happened to Aunt Sam."

15

The still figure lying in the bed made Joel's heart ache. Samantha Phillips had always been full of life. She was the last person he imagined he'd be attending for such an illness.

He looked over at Nurse Cora Pierce, the young lady he'd sent for soon after his arrival a couple of hours ago. In her starched apron and white cap, she was the epitome of efficiency, and because she was not easily dissuaded from her plans, she handled difficult patients well. She took Mrs. Phillips's pulse, then slipped the woman's hand back under the covers.

It was time for him to explain Mrs. Phillips's condition to her family. He sighed heavily. Although Tessa had been reluctant to leave her aunt at first, he'd persuaded her to go contact the rest of her family. He'd hoped by now he'd have more answers. By this point, the family had probably all gathered—including Charlotte. But where had she been earlier?

Her distressed face took shape in his mind, and he stood. He should get this over with. They'd waited too long already. "I'm going out to speak to the family. I'm sure they're worried. Come get me if anything changes."

She flashed him a smile. "Yes, Doctor."

In the drawing room, he found Hannah and Lincoln Cole seated on the leather sofa. Hannah held her sleeping baby in her arms, and Tessa, who'd been at the piano when he entered, scurried over to squeeze in beside her oldest sister.

Then his gaze fell on Charlotte, seated alone in an armchair. She wore a dusty traveling suit. Worry etched her features and she clutched her hands in her lap. Her hair had come loose from its pins and hung in curls about her face. She possessed a riveting, quiet type of beauty—the kind that only intensified the longer you looked. Too bad she was as stubborn as a bad case of gout.

Lincoln started to stand, but Joel motioned him to remain seated and then took the empty chair directly across from Charlotte. "I'm sorry to keep you all waiting so long."

"Is she dead?" Tessa blurted out.

"No. She's stable now." He turned to Lincoln. "I believe your aunt has suffered a cerebral thrombosis."

Charlotte gasped. "Apoplexy?"

He nodded. "It's too early to say how much damage has been done. It happens when a small clot blocks an artery in the brain. Some of my patients regain full use of their speech and their limbs. Others do not."

Lincoln raked his hand through his hair. "And Aunt Sam?"

"I know you want more details, and I can understand that. However, like I said, it's too early to tell. Right now the most important thing is for her to rest."

"She complained of a headache and feeling tired." Tessa's eyes brimmed with tears. "I should have realized how sick she was when she said she was going to lie down in the middle of the day. Aunt Sam never takes a nap. Maybe if I'd found her earlier—"

"Don't blame yourself, Tessa." Joel leaned forward and rested his elbows on his knees. "Once the cerebral thrombosis occurs, there is little anyone can do. I've given her glonoin to lower her blood pressure and to help her mental acuity."

"Shouldn't she be in the hospital?" Hannah asked.

Joel rubbed the back of his neck. "No. We've found patients

who suffer from apoplexy recover more quickly when surrounded by familiar people and things."

"Can we see her?" Charlotte's voice lacked its usual fire.

"One at a time, but don't wake her. She needs to rest." He stood. "You undoubtedly noticed I sent for a nurse. She'll be tending to your aunt's needs. It's important to have someone familiar with these types of cases as the recovery begins. She'll send for me if I'm needed."

Lincoln rose to his feet and offered the doctor his hand. "'Thank you' hardly seems adequate."

"I only wish I could do more." He looked at Charlotte. "All of you need to get some rest. It will be a long haul over the next few days, and you're the ones she needs now."

Charlotte wrapped her arms around herself and watched the rise and fall of Aunt Sam's chest. She was the last one to visit, having let the others go first. Hannah and Lincoln planned to stay in one of the guest rooms, and they promised to get Tessa off to bed as well.

She felt a hand on her shoulder and looked up to see Joel. "She's doing well. Why don't you go on to bed? You look tired."

"I'm fine." In truth, she was exhausted. The lecture she'd given that morning in Stillwater seemed like ages ago.

"Don't you mean you're stubborn. What if I make it doctor's orders?"

"I don't do well with orders."

"Now, there's a surprise." Teasing tinged his quiet words, and he flashed her that alarming smile.

"Are you staying all night?"

He shook his head, then gathered his medical bag. "I'll return if I'm needed, but otherwise I'll be back in the morning around nine." He offered her his hand.

Before she realized what she was doing, she slipped her hand into his and allowed him to pull her to her feet. “Let me see you out, Doctor.”

“I can find my way.”

“Now who’s being stubborn?”

With a chuckle, he followed her from the room and down the hall. They stopped in the foyer, where the butler presented Joel with his coat and hat. Joel slipped his long arms into the sleeves and buttoned the front before looking down at Charlotte. “I think this is a new record.”

“What’s that?”

“We’ve spent nearly half an hour together without coming to blows.”

He seemed pleased they’d not fought. She cocked her head to the side and grinned. “Well, there’s always tomorrow.”

“Good night, Charlotte.” He opened the door and stepped onto the porch.

“Joel.” Charlotte stopped the door from closing behind him. “Thank you.”

He tipped his hat. “You’re welcome, Charlotte, and get some rest. Doctor’s orders.”

“You just couldn’t resist that, could you?”

“Nope.” He kept on walking.

She watched him descend the stairs, and a new thought hit her. He might be an obstinate man, but he certainly was a good one too.

After a fitful night’s sleep, Charlotte woke early and dressed. She padded to Aunt Sam’s bedchamber and eased the door open. If Nurse Pierce was catching a bit of sleep, she didn’t want to wake her.

She tiptoed inside to find Aunt Sam alone. Charlotte pulled the chair close to her bed, sat down, and took Aunt Sam’s hand. To her surprise, her aunt’s eyes opened. Charlotte leaned close. “Welcome back.”

Aunt Sam's brow wrinkled. She seemed to try to speak, but no sound came out.

"Easy. You need to relax. You've had an apoplexy. Understand?" Charlotte turned when she heard someone approaching.

Nurse Pierce put a breakfast tray on the nightstand and jammed her fists onto her hips. "Exactly what do you think you're doing, Miss Gregory?"

"M-m-my aunt woke. She seemed confused so I was explaining what happened to her."

"She is to rest, not chat with you." Nurse Pierce slipped another pillow behind Aunt Sam's head. Then she picked up a bowl from the tray and sat down in the chair on the other side of the bed. "Ready for your breakfast, Mrs. Phillips?"

"Oatmeal!" Charlotte grabbed Nurse Pierce's wrist. "You cannot give her that. I forbid it."

Nurse Pierce jerked her hand out of Charlotte's grasp. "You forbid it? I'm afraid you don't have any say in the matter. In case you didn't realize it, I'm the one Dr. Brooks left in charge of her medical care."

Aunt Sam's eyes went from the nurse to Charlotte and back again. She clamped her lips shut so hard, Charlotte had to bite back a chuckle.

"Nurse Pierce, may I speak with you in the hall. I'd rather not upset Aunt Sam any further."

"Maybe you should have thought about that before your outburst."

Charlotte stood and motioned toward the door. "Nurse Pierce, please."

With a huff, the young nurse set the bowl on the tray and marched out of the bedroom. Charlotte directed her toward the top of the staircase at the end of the hall, away from those still sleeping.

She whirled toward Charlotte. "Let me make myself perfectly clear. I will not have the family of my patient interfering with her care."

"But you could kill her with that oatmeal."

"What are you talking about? It's oatmeal, not arsenic."

Anger simmered inside Charlotte's chest. This woman was a nurse. How could she not realize how dangerous that little bowl could be to someone in Aunt Sam's condition? This was exactly the kind of thing Charlotte could teach the nurses if given a chance, but of course, Dr. Brooks had squelched that idea.

She drew in a long breath. "When someone has an apoplectic fit, they sometimes lose the ability to swallow. If Aunt Sam is such a person, she could choke—or worse, she could aspirate on the oatmeal, which I'm sure you know could lead to pneumonia."

"That's ridiculous." Nurse Pierce tried to sidestep her.

Charlotte blocked her path. "No, it's a fact. The only thing Aunt Sam should be having today is liquids."

"All right, have it your way. We'll ask Dr. Brooks when he arrives."

Because she could see the staircase and it was to Nurse Pierce's back, Charlotte spotted the doctor approaching and smiled. "Yes, let's ask him."

"Ask me what?" Joel climbed the last three steps. "I heard you two squabbling all the way downstairs. Is there a problem, Nurse Pierce?"

Charlotte glowered at him. Why did he assume Charlotte had been the problem?

The nurse tipped her chin in the air. "I realize Miss Gregory is only expressing her concern, but she's interfering with her aunt's care."

"In what way?" His lips bowed downward and his brows scrunched.

"I was about to give Mrs. Phillips her breakfast, and she stopped me."

Charlotte crossed her arms over her chest and prayed that Joel understood as much as he claimed about feeding the ill. "Tell him *what* you were going to feed her."

"I don't know why that should matter."

Charlotte splayed her hands out in surrender. "You were going to give her oatmeal, and we don't even know if she can swallow it!"

Joel's eyebrows shot up. "Oatmeal?"

"We serve it at the hospital all the time." Nurse Pierce's voice held a strong defensive tone. "Besides, Doctor, you didn't leave any written orders regarding breakfast."

"I didn't realize I'd need to." One hard look from him, and the nurse seemed to lose all her bravado. He turned to Charlotte. "Thank you, Miss Gregory. I'll handle it from here."

"Not yet." Charlotte squared her shoulders. "I want to be in charge of my aunt's diet. I understand her needs better than Nurse Pierce, and I want your word she will adhere to whatever diet I set up."

"Don't you mean a diet *we* set up?"

"I believe I can handle it from here." She tapped her foot impatiently. "Well?"

He met her gaze, but Charlotte didn't back down. Finally, the corner of Joel's lip quirked upward. "Well, Miss Gregory does have experience in this area, and if it will put her mind at ease to prepare a menu for her aunt, then I think we will allow her to do so."

Ooooh. *Allow* her? This man could make her furious faster than anyone she knew.

The nurse's face flushed. "I am perfectly capable of—"

"Nurse Pierce." Joel's voice was firm. "I said Miss Gregory would make up the menus, and I expect you to adhere to them."

"Yes, Doctor." Her words came out clipped. "I will go see to my patient now."

Charlotte stepped out of her way. "And I'll bring you up a fresh breakfast tray, but feel free to have the oatmeal yourself."

The nurse shot her a glare, then strode down the hall.

Joel didn't speak until the woman was out of earshot. "She's a good nurse, Charlotte."

Charlotte ran her hand along the smooth wood of the railing and tried to envision her anger sliding down the banister. What had Aunt Sam warned her about? Being so passionate about this issue that Joel Brooks could misinterpret her zeal as not making a sound decision? This situation was a clear indication the nurses needed more education, and she needed to approach Joel with logic, step by step.

"I'm sure she's competent in many areas, but Joel, this could have killed Aunt Sam. What if she had aspirated on the oatmeal?"

He rubbed his chin. "You're right. In this area, Nurse Pierce erred. But remember, she's a competent nurse or I wouldn't have her tending your aunt. Go get the broth, and I'll check her swallowing ability myself."

"Thank you." Charlotte stepped toward the staircase but turned back toward him. "I had no intention of interfering with her care when I woke up this morning."

"I doubt you ever intend to interfere. Stirring things up just seems to be your way." His eyes crinkled around the edges. "And this time it was a good thing. You may have saved your aunt's life."

There was a bounce in Charlotte's steps she couldn't explain as she departed. She refused to admit Joel's words had anything to do with it. She was happy because Aunt Sam was awake and alert. That was all.

But if that was true, why couldn't she wipe the smile from her face?

16

Something was wrong. Joel could sense it. He eyed his desk, then scanned the room. What was out of place?

His books! He hurried to his bookcase and trailed his finger over the spines of the leather volumes. Only one person would do this.

The door creaked open and he heard giggling on the other side.

"Mathilda Imogene Brooks, get in here and explain yourself."

His sister eased the door open. With feigned innocence, she stepped into the room wearing her blue nurse's uniform covered in a crisp white apron. Her nurse's cap, slightly askew, gave her heart-shaped face an impish look. "You called?"

"I did." He motioned his hand toward the shelves. "What's the meaning of this?"

"What's wrong with your books?" She kept her face devoid of expression.

"You know exactly what's wrong with them. They're not in alphabetical order."

"Oh, and that's a problem?" Apparently unable to control herself any longer, she erupted in a fit of giggles and sat down in the chair opposite his desk. "They're only books, Joel. Besides, it serves you right."

He started to rearrange the books. He should have made Mattie do it, but she'd probably put them in reverse order to annoy him even further. All his life, she'd loved to shift something out of place, first in his bedroom and now in his office.

To her it was a game. To him it was annoying, but he'd long since gotten over being too riled by it. He moved Lorenzo Lockard's *Tuberculosis of the Nose and Throat* to its rightful place beside Franklin Mall's *A Study of the Causes Underlying the Origin of Human Monsters*. "It serves me right for what?"

"For not asking for me to take care of Samantha Phillips instead of Cora Pierce." She picked up his letter opener and toyed with it. "You know I'm a better nurse, and I like the Gregory sisters."

He shoved the last volume in an empty slot and returned to his desk. "You are a better nurse, but that's why I didn't ask for you. We need you too much here."

She set the letter opener back down on the wrong side of the desk. "That's very sweet of you to say, but you have to admit you had ulterior motives too."

"And what, pray tell, would those be?" He moved the letter opener to its original position.

"Nurse Pierce has been carrying a candle for you for months. I'm thinking you figured this would be a good way to avoid her batting eyelashes and infernal sighs every time you appear."

"She does not sigh every time she sees me."

"Really?" She clasped her hands in front of her like a soprano in the choir, struck a pose, and batted her eyelashes. "'Would you like some help with that, Dr. Brooks?' *Sigh*. 'Can I bring you a dinner plate, Dr. Brooks?' *Sigh*. 'You are so brilliant, Dr. Brooks.' *Sigh*." She giggled and dropped her hands to her lap. "Swear to me you haven't noticed."

Joel shrugged and picked up a chart from his blotter. "Once or twice, maybe, but I would never allow an inferior nurse to tend to Char—Mrs. Phillips."

"You were about to say Charlotte's aunt, weren't you?" Mattie's lips curled in a smile. "Oh, I knew she'd caught your eye."

"More like she caught my ire," he mumbled as he reached for his pen. Every time he'd visited in the last four days, they'd had words of some kind. Why did she have such an uncanny knack of getting under his skin? "Don't you have work to do, *Nurse*?"

"Yes, *Doctor*." She came round the desk, hugged him, then made her way toward the door. She stopped in front of his bookcase. "By the way, how is Mrs. Phillips?"

"I'm very optimistic. Her speech is only slightly slurred and her mind seems sharp. Her left foot doesn't seem to be cooperating well, but her hand doesn't appear affected. She still needs her rest, but I think she'll make a good recovery."

She picked up one of his rowing trophies and dusted its base before setting it back down. "And is Charlotte Gregory overseeing her meals?"

"Every single bite."

"I bet Nurse Pierce doesn't like that one bit." Seeming to be deep in thought, she slowly ran her hand along the length of the bookcase. "Hmm. I hadn't thought about this before, but you and Cora Pierce might make a good pair after all, since you both like to have control so much."

He jerked his head up to make a retort but only saw Mattie's retreating figure, which was followed by the definitive click of the door.

Releasing a huff, he walked over to the bookcase and moved the trophy over two inches to the right. He did not have to be in control. It simply made sense for everything to be in its place. It was less messy that way.

And a cluttered life meant a cluttered mind, which would not get him where he wanted to be in life.

Charlotte removed the tarts from the oven and set them on a rack to cool. The whole house seemed to fill with the sweet scent of lemon. She smiled. Any minute, Lincoln, Hannah, and baby

Ellie would arrive for a visit with Aunt Sam. While Lincoln had been over to visit each day, Hannah had waited until Aunt Sam was stronger to bring Ellie in to visit.

It was a good thing they were coming. Aunt Sam had already tired of remaining bedridden and was growing petulant. This visit would surely lift her spirits.

Thanking Mrs. Agle for again sharing the kitchen, Charlotte untied her apron and hung it on the hook. The older cook never seemed the least bit possessive of the kitchen, but Charlotte didn't want the woman to think she was intruding.

Too bad it wasn't so easy to appease Nurse Pierce. Ever since Joel had directed Nurse Pierce to adhere to the menu Charlotte made for Aunt Sam, things had been tense. No matter what Charlotte did to make amends, the young nurse seemed intent on holding a grudge.

Even Joel had noticed. He took Charlotte aside and mentioned that any disharmony might have ill effects on Aunt Sam's recovery, then suggested she do her best to make the situation work with the nurse.

Taken aback, Charlotte tried to explain she'd not done anything to irritate the nurse, but Joel didn't seem to believe her. After he left that day, Nurse Pierce seemed more determined than ever to treat Charlotte badly—refusing her entry on more than one occasion, ignoring her concerns about Aunt Sam's spirits, and talking about her to the staff. Tessa was tolerated only slightly better. Still, the nurse was incredibly kind to Aunt Sam. She'd not left her side, and she'd treated Aunt Sam with unbelievable gentleness. Charlotte had overheard her encouraging words on more than one occasion, assuring Aunt Sam not to fret, that she'd recover in time. Charlotte could deal with the nurse as long as Aunt Sam's needs were met.

The brass knocker rapped soundly against the front door, and Charlotte hurried in the direction of the foyer. Even though the butler would answer the door, she was so eager to hold the baby she couldn't resist the urge to rush.

Dressed in a frothy moss-colored hat and wearing a matching dress, Hannah entered first. A swaddled Ellie lay nestled in her arms.

Lincoln passed the butler his hat and kissed Charlotte's cheek. "How is Aunt Sam today?"

"If I say she's as sweet as pecan pie, would you believe me?"

He chuckled. "No, I'm afraid I wouldn't."

Charlotte hugged her sister, then relieved her of her precious bundle. "I want a few minutes with my niece before I have to share her with Aunt Sam. I'm sure it will do Aunt Sam wonders to see all three of you, especially Ellie."

Hannah followed Charlotte into the drawing room and sat down on the divan beside her. "How long did Dr. Brooks say Aunt Sam was to remain bedridden?"

"Another three days." Peeling back Ellie's blanket, Charlotte gushed over the baby's tiny smocked gown and delicately crocheted booties. Hannah seemed delighted to show off her firstborn, and Lincoln's chest puffed with pride. "Do you want me to rewrap her?"

"No, I think she'll be warm enough. Here, I'll take her. You don't have to carry her up."

"I don't mind a bit." Charlotte climbed the stairs, mindful of the sweet baby in her arms. Hannah and Lincoln followed behind her. She tapped on the door to Aunt Sam's bedchamber and waited for Nurse Pierce to greet them.

The young nurse opened the door, saw them waiting, and scowled. Without speaking, she stepped out of the room and closed the door behind her. She frowned at Charlotte. "Why are you bringing a baby up here?"

"This is Aunt Sam's grandniece." Charlotte slipped her finger into Ellie's tiny fist and cooed at the baby. "I think Aunt Sam would love to see you. Wouldn't she, Ellie?"

Nurse Pierce propped her hands on her hips. "Even though you aren't a trained medical professional, I would think you'd know children carry all sorts of diseases."

"She's a newborn baby. She doesn't carry anything but sweetness," Hannah said.

"Mrs. Cole, your daughter is darling, but I'm afraid there will be no children visiting Mrs. Phillips." She turned to Charlotte. "Miss Gregory, please take that child away."

That child? As if Ellie were some street urchin? Anger surged through Charlotte. How dare this woman try to keep them from seeing Aunt Sam?

Lincoln laid his hand on Charlotte's shoulder. "We'll wait to bring Ellie to see Aunt Sam, but what if Charlotte takes Ellie downstairs while Hannah and I visit?"

"Your aunt should be resting." Nurse Pierce blocked the doorway. "She doesn't need a bunch of visitors."

"But I've been here to visit her every other day." Lincoln rubbed his collarbone.

"You were here alone, Mr. Cole. Not with your wife."

Charlotte stepped forward. "I see no harm—"

"Of course you don't. You're not Mrs. Phillips's nurse, but I am." She folded her hands in front of her. "Now, I need to get back to my patient."

"Wait." Lincoln's voice was mica-hard. "I will see my aunt. Charlotte said her spirits were low, and I want to speak with her myself. If she's asleep I won't wake her, but I won't leave without speaking with her at some point today."

"Of course, Mr. Cole."

Hannah laid her hand on his arm. "If Nurse Pierce doesn't think it's wise for me to visit right now, I'll wait."

Lincoln kissed his wife's cheek. "I'm sorry."

After Lincoln and Nurse Pierce slipped into the room, Hannah took hold of Charlotte's arm, pulled her into one of the empty bedrooms, and closed the door. "What have you done to get on her bad side?"

"Nothing," Charlotte snapped. "I swear nothing has happened except for our disagreement about Aunt Sam's menu."

Ellie began to fuss at the raised voices, and Charlotte shifted the baby to her shoulder and patted her back.

Hannah drew in a deep breath. "I'm sorry. Insulting my baby must have brought out the worst in me."

Ellie began to fuss more so Charlotte passed her to her mother. Once Hannah was situated in the rocking chair to nurse, Charlotte took a seat on the bed. She picked at a nubby thread on the coverlet. Maybe she hadn't started well with Nurse Piece, but why was Hannah being ostracized too? Maybe she should march up there and demand Nurse Pierce let her sister in.

"Charlotte, has she been treating you badly all week?"

"She's a good nurse." Charlotte stood and walked to the window. She pressed her hand against the cool frame. "She won't be here long."

"You should speak to Dr. Brooks. He'd put her in her place."

Charlotte wrinkled her nose. "I can take care of my problems. I don't need a man to fight my battles for me."

"You sound like me now." Hannah laughed.

"Besides, he thinks I'm the one always stirring things up."

Hannah sat Ellie up and patted her back. "Well, you are the current lady of this house. Aunt Sam has made it clear you're in charge. You can dismiss her and hire a new nurse if you like."

"I've considered it, but Dr. Brooks asked for her by name. If he has faith in her, then I think we should as well. Besides, you should see how devoted she's been to Aunt Sam. She scarcely steps away from her side. She does seem unnerved by our family, though. I asked her about her own, and she didn't answer. Perhaps she doesn't have any."

"Well, maybe you'd better start buttering her up with some of that delicious-smelling dessert downstairs."

Charlotte shook her head. "They're lemon custard tarts, and when it comes to me, I think she's already sour enough."

Smoothing the sides of her tight bun, Tessa smiled to herself. Stepping into her prim Miss Walker–like character each morning had become second nature, and on this sunny Friday morning, her plan to win the woman over seemed to be working. The real Miss Walker seemed to warm to her more each day and had begun to trust her with more tasks. Now if only she'd let her get near the stage.

Tessa closed the filing cabinet with a thud. "All finished. Anything else?"

Miss Walker looked up and smiled. "You've come a long way in a short period of time, Tessa. I must say I'm delighted with your progress. You may have a career in the theater after all—behind the scenes, of course." She glanced at the wall clock and back at the paper in her hands before taking a deep breath. "On your way out, can I trust you to deliver this contract to the show's director without creating a scene?"

The director? An electrical charge surged through Tessa and threatened to explode on her face in a broad smile. At the last second, she managed to remain in her Miss Walker character and gracefully stood. "Would you like me to go now?"

"Yes, I think that should work out well." Miss Walker handed her the papers. "Be sure you don't dawdle. Remember, the director is an important man, and we should not bother him in any way."

Unwilling to risk Miss Walker changing her mind, Tessa walked with great decorum from the office. Once outside, she released a little whoop and scurried away. This was exactly what she'd been praying for—a chance to get on the stage.

Should she go backstage to find the director, Mr. Frohman, or should she look first in the auditorium? It simply wouldn't do to look like she didn't know what she was doing, even if that was the truth. But if she came in through the backstage, she might get a glimpse of the actors. That would be an added bonus.

Having already poked around after her regular hours, she located the hallway leading to the backstage door. At the end, she slipped inside and stood there for a minute. It even smelled richer. Could the air smell rich with opportunities?

Heavy ropes hung to the hardwood floor to move settings and close curtains. A few props lay scattered around—a throne, a kerosene lamp, and chairs in various sizes. Voices from onstage told her the actors were in the midst of practicing. Perhaps she should go around to the auditorium after all.

"There you are." A man wearing a patterned vest waved at her.

"Me?"

"Well, who else would I be talking to?" He thrust a script in her direction. "I've marked your lines. You don't have much time to learn them, but there are only a few, so it shouldn't be too difficult."

"But—"

He stepped behind her and gave her a little shove. "Get on out there. Stage left. You're by the door. We don't want to keep Mr. Frohman waiting."

Tessa swallowed hard and stepped out on the stage. Was this really happening? Electric lights at the foot of the stage blinded her for a second, and she looked back at the man she guessed to be the stage manager. With a flick of the wrist, he waved for her to hurry to her place.

Three beds sat in the middle of the stage. A man lay on the floor near the last bed.

"Take it from the top of scene five," the director called out from his seat in the auditorium. She glanced down at her script, which was open to the scene, and noted the lines of Liza were starred. She closed her eyes. Who was Liza in *Peter Pan*?

Wait a minute. She'd read enough of the reviews in the office upstairs to know. *Peter Pan* was J. M. Barrie's whimsical tale of a boy who refused to grow up. Peter took the Darling children to Neverland. Liza, the Darlings' maid, was in charge of watching over the children while they slept, but she failed to stop the children from leaving the nursery with Peter Pan.

The man lying on the floor raised his head and scowled. "That's your cue."

She looked down at the script in her hand and then up at the director.

It was now or never.

17

A ruckus offstage caused the play practice to come to a halt. Tessa continued delivering her line, then craned her neck to the side to see what was happening.

A tall, middle-aged woman pointed her finger in Tessa's direction. "Who is she? I'm the actress who's supposed to take over Liza's part!"

Tessa slinked behind the prop door. If only she had some pixie dust right now to make herself invisible.

"What's going on back there?" Mr. Frohman bellowed.

The stage manager walked out onstage and the disgruntled actress followed. "Apparently we have two actresses here to play the role of Liza."

"How did that happen?"

The stage manager shook his head. "I don't know. When Miss Gerard had to leave because of her family emergency, I sent the telegram you asked me to." He turned to the actress. "This is Maude Gilroy. She said she came from Minneapolis and was sent by your friend."

Mr. Frohman climbed the stairs to the stage and crossed his arms over his chest. "Then who's the girl?"

The stage manager motioned Tessa forward. "Go ahead. Tell Mr. Frohman your story."

A boulder settled in Tessa's stomach. She wiped her damp palms on her skirt and stepped forward. "I'm Tessa Gregory."

"Did Harstad send you from the Orpheum in Minneapolis?"

"No, sir. I came to deliver this contract to you." She swallowed hard, pulled the paper from her pocket, and passed him the contract she was to deliver earlier. "I believe the stage manager mistook me for the actress he was expecting."

Mr. Frohman's eyebrows rose. "You're not an actress?"

Heat singed her cheeks, and she lowered her gaze. "I'd like to be, but no, I'm not. I work in the office here at the theater. I'm very sorry."

He waved off her attempt to rectify the situation. "You." He pointed to the new arrival. "Stand by the girl."

The woman stomped over to Tessa's side, sulking. Mr. Frohman walked across the stage in front of the two of them, rubbing his bearded chin, and stopped in front of Miss Gilroy. "You can return to Minneapolis. You're too old and too tall for the role of Liza. This girl will be fine."

Her mouth fell open. "But she has no experience."

"She's already shown us she can handle the role. Thank you for coming, Miss Gilroy. Tell Harstad hello for me." He turned and started for his seat. "Let's pick up from where we left off."

"Well, I never—" Miss Gilroy stomped off the stage.

The stage manager nudged Tessa's arm. "I think you'd better get to your place before he changes his mind."

As if she were Peter Pan, Tessa felt like she could fly to her spot on stage. She'd done it. God had answered her prayers, and she was an actress in a real play. She fiddled with her script, and it fell open to a phrase someone had jotted in the margin. "All the world is made of faith, and trust, and pixie dust."

Right now, Tessa must surely be sparkling with all three.

The front door banged open in the foyer. Startled, Charlotte dropped her fork and it clattered against her plate. She looked at

Hannah and Lincoln, who'd come for dinner. Who would enter Aunt Sam's house and make such a ruckus?

"Stay here." Lincoln set his napkin beside his plate. "I'll see what's going on."

Before he stood, Tessa flung open the dining room's French doors and burst inside. "You'll never believe what happened. Not in a million, billion, trillion years."

"Tessa, breathe." Hannah patted the chair beside her. "Come sit down and tell us what you're talking about."

"I can't sit. I'm too excited." She clasped her hands under her chin and bounced on her toes.

Charlotte chuckled at her sister. "Don't hold us in suspense any longer. What are you so excited about?"

"I got a part in the play at the Metropolitan!" she squealed.

Lincoln cleared his throat. "What? How?"

His words were drowned out, however, when Hannah and Charlotte both jumped to their feet and surrounded their little sister, hugging and congratulating her.

"Shhh!" Nurse Pierce stood between the French doors with her finger pressed to her lips. "I could hear your yammering all the way upstairs. Have you no consideration? It's not good for Mrs. Phillips's delicate condition."

Charlotte whirled toward the nurse. "I don't think our little celebration would upset Aunt Sam one bit. In fact, I think she'd be delighted. Tessa, why don't you go up and share the news with her right now?"

"Absolutely not." Nurse Pierce spread her arms wide to bar Tessa from leaving but kept her gaze locked on Charlotte. "She's eating the exact dinner you, Miss Gregory, planned for her—although I think it's much too rich. When she's done, she needs her rest. She's hardly slept all day, and I'm concerned about her."

"But she was fine when I left her." Lincoln set down his water goblet. "I think a little visit from Tessa while she eats would help, not hinder, my aunt's recovery."

Nurse Pierce lowered her arms and folded her hands in front of her. "Very well, sir. I'll not go against your wishes. If you'd like the girl to visit, then so be it. But remember, I am not responsible if your aunt relapses."

Tessa hung her head. "I don't want her to get sicker. I can talk to her in the morning, and I'm sorry for making such a fuss."

The nurse nodded. "And I apologize for being so abrupt. Enjoy your dinner."

Everyone returned to their places, and Hannah began to pepper Tessa with questions. Charlotte wanted to join in, but her thoughts turned to the nurse. She looked down at the congealed gravy on top of her mashed potatoes, now cold and unappetizing. It was just as well. Another conflict with Nurse Pierce had soured her stomach.

What would happen come Monday when she had to leave on another lecture tour? Would Nurse Pierce follow the diet she prescribed? Worse, would she continue to keep Aunt Sam from seeing her family?

Accidentally eavesdropping on patients happened, but this time Joel stood at Mrs. Phillips's bedchamber door and listened to Charlotte speaking with her aunt. By scooting to the right, he could see the two women chatting. Mrs. Phillips sat upright in bed, propped against a mountain of pillows. Charlotte sat on the edge of the bed, her hair hanging loose down her back like a russet river. Nurse Pierce, to his surprise, was nowhere in sight.

Since he was much later than usual, they probably didn't think he'd stop by tonight. He'd been drawn to the house. But why? Mrs. Phillips was on the mend, and visiting her could have easily waited until morning. Still, he'd learned not to ignore the Lord's prodding.

"If I have to stay in this bed one more day, I think I'll scream." Mrs. Phillips banged shut the book she was holding. "And why is

Cora so mean to you? I'm sure Dr. Brooks would request a different nurse if we asked."

"Do you like her?"

"Yes, I do, but I don't like how she treats you."

Joel shifted his weight to his other foot. Funny, Charlotte hadn't mentioned Nurse Pierce giving her any problems. Then again, maybe Charlotte had done something to upset the nurse. She did have that ability. On the other hand, he imagined Nurse Pierce liked things her way.

"She's a good nurse, and so far she's managed to make you follow the doctor's orders. I can handle her attitude toward me as long as she treats you well." Charlotte stood and rearranged some flowers in a tall pink vase. "You seem in better spirits tonight."

"And you could tell that from my complaining?" She laughed. "If my spirits seem better, it's from those delicious meals you planned for me."

"You really believe they are helping?"

"Absolutely. When the tray comes with flowers or ribbons, with food on those pretty dishes, I do feel better just looking at it. Like someone cares. Then, when I'm able to feed myself the foods on it, it lifts my spirits. It makes me feel like I'm not an invalid. I know you planned all that and made sure it was tasty to boot."

"I only wish Dr. Brooks could hear you say that. It's important for patients to be able to do things for themselves."

"And hearing Tessa's news was exactly the medicine I needed. Thank you for sneaking her in while Nurse Pierce was resting. Tessa is still so excited. I want to see her in that production, which is another reason why I need to get out of this bed and get to working on this uncooperative foot."

Sneak Tessa in? Why would Charlotte have to do that? He'd put no limitations on visitors.

"Dr. Brooks, thank you for waiting for me," Nurse Pierce said from behind him.

He turned to find her eyelashes flapping like bat wings. "Uh, yes, shall we see to our patient?"

"Certainly, Doctor. She is so lucky to have such a dedicated and talented physician."

Joel groaned inwardly and motioned for her to precede him into the room. "Hello, Mrs. Phillips. You're looking well this evening."

Charlotte moved to stand beside the bed.

"Miss Gregory." He nodded.

"Remember, call her Charlotte." Aunt Sam pressed her hand to the bow at the neck of her gown. "And I'll have you know I will be getting out of this bed tomorrow, with or without your blessing."

"Aunt Sam—"

"Dr. Brooks and I will take it from here, Miss Gregory." Nurse Pierce picked up Aunt Sam's wrist and pressed her fingers to her pulse. "I'm sure you have other matters that need your attention."

Charlotte gave a tight smile. "Yes, I'll be in the kitchen if you need me."

Nurse Pierce didn't look up. "We'll be fine. Won't we, Doctor?"

A twinge of anger made Joel's temple throb. It had been a long day, and now the tension in this room was palpable. Charlotte kept her gaze averted as she slipped from the room. He sighed. He'd ask Charlotte about the problem between her and Nurse Pierce before he left. It wasn't good for his patient.

Following his examination, Joel gathered his bag and hurried downstairs to give Charlotte the good news that her aunt was indeed ready to become ambulatory. He'd bring a cane by tomorrow after church services if they didn't have one in the house.

As he approached the kitchen, he could hear Charlotte singing a hymn in a soft, sweet voice. Good. Maybe she had put the affairs from upstairs aside. If he was lucky, perhaps she'd offer him a piece of whatever she was cooking. It smelled delicious. Fresh bread? No, who would bake bread this late at night? Besides, it sounded like she was chopping something.

He stepped into the room. Apparently deep in thought, she didn't look up. He cleared his throat. "Hi, Charlotte."

Charlotte jolted. The knife slipped and sliced deep into her index finger.

18

"Ow!" Charlotte dropped the knife and it clattered onto the chopping board. Grabbing the tea towel beside her, she wrapped it around her throbbing finger.

Joel dropped his bag on the table and took hold of her wrist. "Let me take a look."

"It's only a cut." She tried to pull away, but he held fast. "You shouldn't sneak up on a person holding a knife."

He eased the towel off, took a quick look, and covered it back up. He pressed the towel firmly over the wound.

Pain jolted through her finger, and Charlotte sucked in her breath.

"Sorry. The pressure will stop the bleeding." He scanned her face. "Do you need to sit down? You're not dizzy, are you?"

"I cut up chickens for a living. I don't faint at the sight of blood." *Except you're standing so close to me I can hardly breathe.* She drew air into her lungs, catching a 100 percent masculine whiff—an earthy blend of soap, spices, and cedar. "I can keep pressure on this by myself."

"That's okay. I've got it." His gaze darted to the chopping board. "What were you making?"

"I was cutting up an onion to fry with my steak." Charlotte ordered her heart to quiet its erratic beat. He was a good doctor—of that she had no doubt—and he was simply trying to take her mind off the cut. Nothing more.

He cocked his head to the side. "Steak is an odd late-night snack."

"I didn't eat much dinner."

"Why?" His voice filled with concern. "Were you ill?"

"Two words." Even if he treated all his patients with this much attention, she might as well use this time to her advantage. "Nurse Pierce."

He started to speak but seemed to think twice about it. "I'm sorry I startled you, Charlotte."

Those bottle-green eyes met hers, and she nearly forgot the drumming in her finger. She swallowed hard. "I should've been more careful."

Slipping his free hand around her back, he urged her toward the sink. "Let's wash this off and see what we've got." Without releasing her, he turned on the tap, then removed the stained towel and tucked her arm beneath his. "This is going to sting."

He placed her hand in the flow of cold water and she gasped. Instead of thinking about the cut—or the fact that she was pressed against Joel's side—she watched the pink swirls of water in the bottom of the porcelain sink circle the drain. Mesmerized, she leaned into him.

"Charlotte? Are you sure you're not dizzy?"

"Uh, yes." Heat infused her cheeks and she straightened. Good grief. What had she been doing? She needed to put some distance between them. "Can you bandage the cut and then be on your way?"

"Sorry, I'm afraid you're going to need some sutures in this."

"Really? Are you sure?"

"'Fraid so. Remember, I cut up people for a living." He flashed her a smile that almost took the pain away, then pressed a bar of soap into her palm. "You wash it and I'll get my bag." He returned a few seconds later. "Where are the fresh towels?"

Charlotte let her hands drip dry over the sink. "I'll get them."

"You sit." He pointed to a stool by the table and then began opening one drawer after another until he found what he sought. He tossed a towel toward her and spread another on the table, where he placed the instruments he withdrew from his bag.

Charlotte's stomach knotted when he opened a small case revealing a hypodermic needle. "I don't think you'll need that."

"I can put the sutures in without the anesthesia, but I promise you, you'll like it a whole lot better if you let me give you the injection." He placed a pan of water on the stove to heat.

She jumped up. "My popovers!"

"Relax. I've got them." He opened the oven door and removed the shallow pan holding six small baking dishes, each with a mounded, slightly brown popover. "See? Still good."

"They're overdone."

"Then you won't mind sharing them with me when we're finished."

When the water came to a boil, he lowered his instruments into the pot. Once he'd shucked his coat and rolled up his sleeves, he washed his hands, transferred the instruments to the towel, and assembled the syringe and filled it. "Ready?"

Charlotte wrinkled her nose. "If I say no, will you go away?"

"Not a chance." He chuckled. "Take a deep breath and this will all be over before you know it."

If only that were true. It came as no surprise that Joel's sutures were painstakingly perfect, but the way his gaze bore into hers every time he looked up caught her completely off guard.

This man was not the same one she'd been sparring with since their first meeting. He was kind and sympathetic—and much too handsome tonight with his hair tousled and his guard down. He leaned over her hand until he was so close she could see his hair ruffle every time she exhaled. Only the slight tug of the needle told her he'd made the first stitch.

While he worked, he explained he'd come to tell her that Aunt Sam could get out of bed now and offered to bring over a cane.

Charlotte assured him she was certain Aunt Sam's husband had probably owned a cane, but if not, she'd go get one.

"She's already made an exceptional recovery." He clipped the silk with a pair of scissors. "When I told her that, she sang your praises for the menu you prepared."

"Aunt Sam doesn't miss an opportunity to speak her mind." But what did he think about the menu? Charlotte worried her bottom lip. Did she dare ask his opinion? Right now wasn't exactly the best time to get him riled.

He set the scissors down and lifted his gaze. "I think your meal plan was beneficial to her. That's what you're wondering, isn't it?"

She nodded.

"Your aunt mentioned you chose foods she could feed herself. Those who suffer apoplexy often become melancholy because of their loss of independence. Did Fannie Farmer teach you that?"

"Among other things." She shifted on the stool. "Miss Farmer's course specifically addressed five areas the patient requires—sense of sight, sense of taste, digestibility, nutritive value, and economy."

He looked up from his work. "What food is easiest for a patient to absorb?"

"Are you testing me?"

"Maybe."

"Sugar is completely absorbed by the patient. Starches hold second place. All but three percent of proteids are absorbed."

"Impressive. There. All done." Joel dabbed iodine onto the cut. "Take a look at my handiwork."

Charlotte examined the neat row of tiny stitches on her orange-tinted finger. "If you ever decide to change occupations, you could always become a tailor."

"Believe me, there are days I'd consider it." He reached for her hand and wrapped the finger in a gauze bandage. "You're going to have to keep this clean and dry."

"For how long?"

He grabbed her hand to hold her still. "Five days or so."

"But how am I going to lecture?"

"You seem to do fine giving lectures." He tied off the ends of the bandage. "You've never needed your finger to give me one, anyway."

She leveled her gaze at him and then proceeded to fill him in on her position with the gas company. Explaining how she was to leave on Monday for her next series of lectures around the Lake Minnetonka area, she held up her bandaged finger. "So how am I supposed to cook with this?"

"We'll think of something." Joel set his instruments back into the boiling water, then reached for the coffeepot on the stove. "Can I get you a cup too?"

"Thanks, but I can do it."

"Are you always stubborn?"

"No, just with you."

He pressed his hand to his chest. "I feel so honored." He filled two coffee cups and handed her one, then gathered a popover for each of them. "Is there butter in the icebox?"

"And honey's in the pantry." She pointed to a door at the end of the kitchen.

Once he'd retrieved both items, he sat down at the table across from her. Charlotte broke open her popover. Even though it had been out of the oven for some time, steam escaped from the pastry, making her mouth water.

Joel slathered his with butter and honey and took a bite. "Delicious. You really are a good cook, aren't you?"

"I think so." She smiled and drizzled honey on her popover. The first bite melted on her tongue. She licked the honey from her lips and took a sip of the hot coffee. The warmth seemed to wash away the stress of the last hour. "You know, there are a lot of things I could show your nurses if you'd let me."

He grinned. "I've seen how well you get along with my nurses."

A stone thudded in Charlotte's stomach. "What do you mean by that?"

"You and Nurse Pierce. I could tell upstairs you two haven't been playing nice."

"And you think that's my fault?"

He hiked an eyebrow. "Isn't it? That seems to be your pattern."

"Ooooh." She plopped down her coffee cup and some of the liquid splashed out. "Just when I'm beginning to like you, you have to go and judge me again. I'll have you know—"

"So you like me?" A wide grin spread across his face.

Her neck and face infused with heat. "I didn't . . . I don't . . ."

When was she ever going to learn to keep her mouth closed?

19

The sight of Charlotte's blushing cheeks and her flustered words made heat pool in Joel's chest. It shouldn't have, but it did. He must be more tired than he realized.

"Easy. One case of apoplexy per household, please." Grabbing his napkin, he wiped up her spilled coffee. "Charlotte, I was only teasing you."

Using her bandaged hand, she shoved a mass of loose auburn curls from her shoulder. Her hazel eyes flashed with golden flecks. "You don't think I've been through enough tonight?"

"You certainly have, and I'm sorry." He withdrew his instruments from the water, dried them, and placed each in its spot in his bag. He needed to get home before he got himself in trouble. "By the way, I saw how Nurse Pierce was acting upstairs. I knew she didn't like that I told her to follow your menu, but I'd hoped she'd warm to the idea."

"She has. Like a snowman warms to an igloo. And now that I'm leaving for a week, I fear she'll completely ignore any menu I make for Aunt Sam."

"I'll speak to her." He clasped his bag shut and slipped his coat back on. "She won't like it, but your aunt is doing so well I don't want to risk changing a thing. I'll tell her to follow whatever directions you leave to the letter."

Charlotte walked behind him to the front door and sheepishly held up her bandaged hand. “Thank you.”

“You’re welcome.” That sounded odd to him, though saying “my pleasure” would hardly be appropriate. She looked nearly as tired as he felt, but an irrepressible light shone in her eyes. A tenderness for this vivacious woman tugged at his heart, and he had to tuck his hand under his armpit to keep from reaching out and cupping her cheek. “Get some rest.”

“Doctor’s orders?”

“A suggestion. I seem to recall you don’t like orders.”

“And I didn’t think you ever truly listened.” Her mouth widened, the corners lifting heavenward.

“I always listen, but I don’t always agree.” Her words stung, but he probably deserved them. He’d not taken her ideas seriously, and now, even though he saw some merit in them, he still wasn’t willing to go out on a limb and embrace them. Still, he did enjoy her company—at least when they weren’t fighting. Couldn’t they at least enjoy some kind of friendship?

He reached for the doorknob but then turned back toward her. “Charlotte?”

“Yes?”

“I’m beginning to like you too.”

He left her standing speechless in the foyer, cheeks rosy and mouth agape.

Yes, with a friend like Charlotte Gregory, things would never be dull.

The throbbing in Charlotte’s finger had grown to a dull ache by Monday morning. With her trunks packed, she and Tessa stood in the foyer waiting for Henry to bring the motorcar around. Charlotte would have him drop Tessa off at the theater before taking her to the railroad station.

“I wish you were going with me.” Charlotte adjusted Tessa’s

collar. Her sister smelled of the orange she'd eaten for breakfast. "I worry about you being here alone."

Tessa swatted her hand away. "Hannah said she and Lincoln would be here every evening. I'll hardly be alone. Besides, Aunt Sam will be here, and the household staff. And how could I forget the delightful Nurse Pierce?"

"Tessa, be kind to her, and please, try not to get into trouble."

"How much trouble could I get into in six days?"

"I don't even want to imagine." Charlotte removed a folded piece of paper from her purse. "This is my itinerary. I left another copy on Aunt Sam's desk with a contact name in each location. We'll spend two days in Minnetonka, two in Excelsior, and two in Deephaven. I've listed the location where I'll be giving the lectures in each city on this paper too. Don't hesitate to send a telegram if I'm needed back here."

"Relax, Charlotte." Tessa tossed the paper onto the hall table. "Aunt Sam is on the mend, and I'll be so busy rehearsing I won't even know you're gone."

The driver opened the door and collected the first of Charlotte's trunks. Tessa scampered out behind him, but Charlotte hurried into the study to collect a recipe she'd copied from a book last night. She heard the door open again. "I'll be right there, Henry."

She startled when she spotted Joel and sucked in her breath. He was framed by the morning sun shining through the front door windows.

He nodded toward her. "Good morning, Charlotte."

"I thought you were Henry." She ran her hand down the side of her traveling suit. "I didn't realize you were coming to check on Aunt Sam this morning."

In a couple of easy strides, he was in front of her. "I'm not here to check on her. I'm here to bring you something."

"Me?"

"Yes, you're leaving for your lecture this morning, right? I told you I'd think of something to protect your finger while you cooked."

He held out his palm. In it was a rubber nipple from a baby bottle. "Give me your good hand. I'll show you how it works."

When she didn't move right away, he took her uninjured hand in his and lifted it to his chest. He eased the rubber nipple over her index finger, then clasped her hand. "See? You can put it over your stitches when you take the bandage off."

"When did you think of this?"

"It came to me in the night." He swallowed, his Adam's apple bobbing like a child playing hopscotch.

He'd been thinking of her? The thought warmed her more than she wanted to admit, but there was no need to romanticize this. He was a doctor and he was simply taking care of his patient. Besides, nothing could ever come of her and Joel. They reacted to one another like vinegar and baking soda.

She smiled. "Thank you, Joel. It will help a lot."

"You'll have to rebandage your finger, of course, when you're not cooking." He removed a roll of gauze from his pocket and handed it to her as well. "I'll take the stitches out when you get back Saturday."

"It will be late when I get home."

"I don't mind." He eyed her other trunk. "Can I carry this for you?"

"Henry will get it."

"Dr. Brooks, you're here early." Nurse Pierce descended the stairs with the brightest smile Charlotte had seen on the woman in days, but it was directed at Joel and not at her. "What a wonderful way to start the week. Mrs. Phillips will be delighted."

He glanced at Charlotte. "I wasn't here to see Mrs. Phillips, but I guess I can—"

"She's already taken her first steps. I think you'll be impressed. The exercises and stretches I've been doing with her have apparently worked wonders." Nurse Pierce batted her eyelashes. "Shall we?"

He set his doctor's bag down on the hall table. "I'll join you in a minute."

"But Mrs. Phillips may tire if you delay."

"I'll be right along. I'd like to speak to Charlotte a minute before she leaves." He waited, and finally Nurse Pierce departed with a scowl on her face.

The driver returned for the final trunk and told her he was ready to leave when she was. Charlotte slipped the rubber bottle nipple into her purse and pulled on her gloves. "Was there something else?"

He shifted his weight to his other foot. "About what I said the other night."

"Yes." She sucked in a breath. Her heart skipped a beat. What was happening? He'd been thinking of her during the night, and he'd come here to see her off. What would she say if he asked her to step out with him?

"We're friends, right?" He cleared his throat. "Just friends."

The air whooshed from her lips, but she managed a tremulous smile. "Friends, Joel."

He dipped his head and turned toward the staircase.

As she walked to the automobile, she mused over the encounter. She'd not honestly fancied anything else developing between her and the doctor, and at least they'd grown from being sworn enemies to friends, but still she felt an odd loss at his need to emphasize friendship.

She should be happy. She'd had her fill of men like Joel when she was a teenager back in Iowa. Like Joel, George had been a strong and masculine fellow. He'd been the star of the baseball team, and he'd wanted her to be his girl. He'd grown more and more demanding of her—of what she said and how she acted—and she'd tried so hard to become what he wanted that she'd lost herself.

It was probably better she and Joel draw the line at friendship. Like George, he had a strong personality, and she'd promised herself she'd never become involved with anyone like that again.

Henry helped her inside the automobile and she took a seat beside Tessa. Glancing back to the house, she spotted Joel waving goodbye. She wiggled her gloved fingertips in his direction and sighed. "Goodbye, my friend."

If she kept doing her work without drawing any attention to herself, Tessa wondered how long it would be before Miss Walker learned of her foray into the theater. As she walked to the office, she imagined an assortment of scenarios she might face. If the pedantic Miss Walker had no idea of what transpired, she would greet Tessa with a smile on her prim face and utter a proper "good morning" before assigning the day's tasks. If she'd learned about the part, her reception might be considerably cooler. Would she go so far as to dismiss her?

Although Tessa wouldn't be heartbroken to be released from the office responsibilities, she'd hate for her work to reflect badly on Aunt Sam. Would Miss Walker and Mr. Jurgenson understand she hadn't intentionally asked for the part? Would they believe she'd literally stepped into it?

If Miss Walker didn't know, how long could she keep the information from her? Since the rehearsals in no way interfered with her office work, and since Miss Walker never ventured beyond the office to interact with the questionable actors, would it be possible to keep her role a secret?

A tiny seed took root in Tessa's mind and she smiled to herself. If Miss Walker and Mr. Jurgenson didn't yet know of her role in *Peter Pan*, she was certain she could keep it from them until opening night. After all, that was just over two weeks away.

And she was exceptionally good at keeping secrets.

20

Lake Minnetonka spread out like an ocean before them. On the streetcar, the conductor had said the lake boasted 110 miles of shoreline. Charlotte stepped out of the streetcar pavilion and drew in a deep breath. She relished the taste of the tangy air on her lips and tipped her face to the sun before turning to Molly and Lewis to see if they, too, found the surroundings as welcoming as she.

Maybe here she'd forget the worries that kept plaguing her—Aunt Sam's illness, Lewis's obvious budding affection, and the growing sense she still was not doing what was intended for her.

"I declare, this sun is a welcome sight after yesterday's rain. That was a real frog wash." Molly rubbed her arm. "My body was aching somethin' fierce. But the rain sure didn't keep those folks from coming to hear you, did it?"

"I think it was Charlotte's promise to prepare all desserts." Lewis chuckled.

"Either way, I'm glad to finally be here," Charlotte said. While her lecture yesterday and the day before in the city of Minnetonka had gone well, she was itching to spend the rest of the week closer to the lake. Molly couldn't get over why a city that shared its name with this massive body of water would barely touch it. She wanted to be on the water, not near it.

"I'll go arrange for the cooking supply trunk to be delivered to the Excelsior City Hall and our traveling trunks to be delivered to the hotel. Y'all don't leave without me." Molly grinned and waddled back inside the station.

"I can't wait to show you some of the sights." Lewis took out his pocket watch and checked the time. "What do you say we start with lunch?"

As if the mention of food reminded her stomach it was empty, it growled. She pressed her hand to her midsection and smiled. "That would be delightful."

Charlotte's gaze swept over the choppy water and the waiting passenger steamer painted the same sunny yellow as the streetcars. No wonder she'd heard some people call the steamers *streetcar boats*. This one bore the name *Minnehaha* in red block script on its stern.

She spotted lovely homes lining the shore and recalled Lewis explaining that many of the upper class from the Twin Cities had summer homes here. Unfortunately, Aunt Sam was not among them, so Charlotte, Molly, and Lewis would be staying at the Excelsior Bay Hotel. Lewis, she'd learned, had spent last summer with a local family. He'd be visiting them after the second lecture in Deephaven.

When Molly returned, the three of them decided to walk into Excelsior for lunch. Following a delicious lunch at Newell's Bazaar Café on Water Street, Molly directed them to Axel Nordstrom's gas company. He'd been the one to request that Charlotte present in the area and had arranged the lectures at the city hall.

Mr. Nordstrom, a robust man with high cheekbones and an angular jaw, greeted them warmly and offered to take them to the city hall. Charlotte found everything in order there, except the trunk had yet to be delivered. Mr. Nordstrom promised to send word to the hotel when the supplies arrived.

Once they'd reached the Excelsior Bay Hotel, Charlotte pushed back the curtains of the room she and Molly shared and stared out at the lake. With the window slightly ajar, a delicious breath of fir pine wafted in on the breeze.

She should feel so blessed to be here, enjoying these lovely accommodations provided by the gas company. Instead, uneasiness churned inside her. Why couldn't she be content? She wanted to be in charge of her own kitchen, but instead she had a different, perfectly wonderful position. Had she traded one dream for another?

Molly repinned her white hair in a tidy bun. "Sugar, you might want to get yourself dolled up before Lewis comes to fetch us. That young man is as sweet on you as maple syrup on a stack of hotcakes, or maybe you didn't notice."

"I noticed, but honestly, Molly, I've done nothing to encourage it."

"For goodness' sake, why not?" Molly mumbled the words through the pins in her mouth. She plopped her hat on her head, removed the pins, and jabbed them in place. "He's a perfectly fine young man—wealthy too. You ought to be tickled he's showing an interest in you."

Charlotte let the curtains swing back in place. "It is flattering."

"I hear a 'but' coming." Molly dropped into a chair and sighed. "Well, spit it out. Won't do any good to keep it bottled up inside."

She sat down on the bed across from Molly and clasped her hands in her lap. "When I was in high school, I was courted by a fellow who seemed nice at first but turned out to be controlling. He got angry when I didn't do what he liked, and he tried to change me. He even talked me out of going to cooking school." The memory burned in Charlotte's chest. She went to the water pitcher, poured herself a glass, and passed one to Molly. "I vowed I'd never let anyone control me like that again."

"And well you should." Molly took a long drink. "Do you think Lewis is the kind of fella to do something like that?"

Charlotte shook her head. "Not really, but I didn't think George was either."

"There are no guarantees, sugar. Sometimes faith means taking a chance."

Charlotte rubbed her thumb over her bandaged finger. "But what if he's not the right one?"

"And what if he is?" Molly reached over and covered her hand. "Spend some time with him and see what happens—unless, of course, there's someone else tugging on your heartstrings."

"No. No, there's no one else." Charlotte patted her hand and stood. Thoughts of Joel wormed their way into her mind, but she pushed them aside. "Thank you. I'd better get ready before Lewis comes."

Charlotte handed the purser her ticket and carefully made her way onto the streetcar company's steamer, the *Hopkins*, a sister ship to the *Minnehaha* they'd seen earlier. Lewis followed and pointed to an empty seat. Since Molly had decided to skip the amusement park, citing a sudden headache, Charlotte and Lewis would be spending the remainder of the day alone. Charlotte slid in toward the window, and Lewis folded his long legs into the place next to her.

Besides the yellow paint on the outside of the boat, which had split cane seats and large windows, the inside of the boat resembled its streetcar cousin. She glanced at the other passengers all headed to the Big Island Amusement Park. Two seats in front of her, a little girl with blonde ringlets turned around and timidly smiled at her. Charlotte winked back and the little girl whipped around, only to turn again and begin an impromptu game of hide-and-seek.

Lewis nudged Charlotte's side. "You appear to have a new fan. People seem drawn to you."

The little girl bobbed down behind the back of the seat, and Charlotte laughed. "Or I make them want to run and hide."

He leaned closer. "No one could ever want to run from you."

His breath tickled her ear. "Don't speak too soon. By the end of the day, I might surprise you."

Thankfully, Charlotte had been able to shake off her earlier concerns. Lewis was a nice young man, and perhaps God had put him in her life for a reason. In any case, there'd been far too few days like this in her life, and she had no intention of wasting this one on worries. She'd accept it as a blessing and enjoy it.

"Let's go to the top deck." She turned toward the wood stairs in the center of the steamer.

"It might be windy."

"I won't blow away."

Lewis jumped up and held out his hand to assist her. She had to hold on to the brass handrails to climb the steep staircase, and it felt odd to have Lewis walking so close behind her. Up top, she and Lewis sat in one of the bench seats beneath the red-and-white-striped canopy. An American flag flapped in the wind off the stern, and Charlotte had to hold her hat on.

Since only a few passengers had decided to brave the wind today on the second deck, she and Lewis found themselves mostly alone. She feared their time would grow awkward, but instead he kept up a steady flow of information about things he'd learned last summer. The streetcar boats could carry 120 passengers, and with their unique torpedo stern, they were designed to travel twelve miles an hour. Charlotte also learned the friend he'd be visiting at the lake was an old school chum from the Northwestern Conservatory of Music.

"I'm sure you and Molly would be welcome to join me. The house is massive." He pointed to the shoreline in the far distance. "Their estate is over there in Carson's Bay by Deephaven. One of their neighbors, the Burtons, calls their estate Chimo. Have you heard of it? They hold a lawn tennis tournament every year there in the Cow Bowl."

"Cow Bowl?"

"That's what they call the area where the tournament is played. Folks from all over come to watch. It's a big deal. Do you play tennis?"

"I've tried a couple of times, but I wouldn't say I accomplished it."

"Me either, but Reggie likes to play, so I'm sure he'll talk me into it." He looked down at her hand. "How's the finger?"

"Fine."

"You said the doctor was there visiting your aunt when you cut it? That was sure lucky."

Lucky? If it wasn't for Joel, she wouldn't have cut it in the first place. Why did he have to creep into her thoughts at every turn? He was making it very hard to simply enjoy herself. She looked up at the approaching island. "Oh my, this is amazing."

Spanish Colonial Revival–style arches greeted them at the entrance to the Big Island Amusement Park. Even though it was still spring, pink, yellow, and purple flowers exploded from planters. Charlotte watched the crowd mill about and her stomach clenched. So many couples!

Calliope music spilled out into the mall area. Lewis ushered her inside the gates, and they paused by a water fountain. "What would you like to do first?"

"What are my options?"

"There's the arcade, the Old Mill Ride, the Scenic Ride to Yellowstone, the roller coaster, and the carousel, among other things." He turned. "On that side is the music hall. It has fifteen hundred seats, and mostly local bands play there."

Charlotte tapped her finger against her lips. "Let's start with the Old Mill Ride. It sounds a little more sedate than the roller coaster."

"Good choice."

On the way, Lewis treated Charlotte to warm peanuts and ice-cold lemonade. He suggested they stop and play a few arcade games. They each took a turn at tossing pennies in a dish and then watched a man move a ball beneath three cups. No matter how many tries Charlotte was given, she never picked the correct cup. Lewis, on the other hand, chose right every time. In her honor, he selected a porcelain vase and tucked it in his jacket pocket.

The line for the Old Mill Ride wound around the corner of the building. After they took their place at the end, Lewis smiled down at her. "I've heard that some couples have found true love inside the mill."

Charlotte didn't miss the hope in his eyes. While she enjoyed his company, she'd yet to feel stirred by him. *Just enjoy the day.* "I imagine those couples were well on their way before they got on this ride."

Three other patrons joined them at the end of the line—a middle-aged couple sporting wedding rings, and an older woman who Charlotte guessed was probably the mother of either the husband or the wife.

The elderly woman's eyes crinkled when she smiled. "Two young folks headed into the dark mill. I know what that means. How long have you two been courting?"

"Lewis and I are friends." Charlotte glanced at him to confirm her words. "We work together."

"It's fine to take things slow." The woman laid a wrinkled hand on Charlotte's arm. "You can't rush affairs of the heart."

Rushing in without being sure? That was the story of Charlotte's life.

"Mother." The middle-aged man blotted his face with a handkerchief as the line moved forward. "Don't bother the young people."

"She's not bothering us." Lewis offered the man his hand. "I'm Lewis Mathis, and this is Charlotte Gregory. We work for the gas company, and Charlotte will be doing a cooking demonstration in Excelsior tomorrow."

The man's wife brightened. "I saw that advertisement. You must be quite a cook."

"She is." Lewis beamed.

"I'd love to own my own kitchen someday," Charlotte said.

The older woman chuckled and glanced at Lewis. "I have a feeling you'll have your own kitchen sooner than you think."

"Yes." The gentleman flashed a knowing smile at his wife. "When you get married, you'll certainly have a kitchen of your own."

Charlotte's face warmed. "That's not what I meant. I enjoy cooking for others, so I expect my life may take a different course."

The elderly woman laughed again. "Oh, sweetheart, most of our pleasures come when we least expect them."

"That's true." Lewis grinned. "Thank you, ma'am." They stepped to the front of the line. "I think it's our turn. I hope you're not afraid of the dark. I wouldn't want you holding on to me for dear life or anything."

His teasing words relaxed her, and she slipped into the boat beside him without a second thought. They were friends, and even riding through a dark tunnel wouldn't change that.

Lewis, as she had suspected, remained the perfect gentleman. He didn't try to sneak a kiss in the tunnel, but he did hold her hand. When they finished at the mill, they laughed their way through the roller coaster and the scenic railway. Once the sun set, the lights came on, turning the park into a constellation. Charlotte asked about the electric beacon mounted on a tower in the park's center.

"It's nearly two hundred feet high, and the light can be seen for miles." Lewis took her elbow and ushered her around a group who'd come to a stop. "We can go to the music hall or have dinner. Your choice."

"Why don't you choose this time? You've let me make the decisions all day."

"As well you should." He slowed his long stride when she couldn't keep up. "But if you insist, I have to admit I'm starved."

After dinner, as they walked back toward the streetcar boats, Charlotte couldn't help but think how romantic this setting was. Lewis had been so sweet all day. He'd been the perfect companion, and they'd enjoyed good conversation.

If God had placed him in her life, shouldn't she feel something special for him? Even when he'd captured her hand in the dark tunnel of the mill ride, no thrill shot through her. Would those feelings come in time?

She touched the bandage on her finger. The jolt of Joel's tender touch fired through her. But that made no sense. Lewis was the kind of man she'd been praying for. He treated her like a queen. He made no efforts to push her into anything. Most of the time, Joel, on the other hand, treated her like a bad itch that wouldn't go away.

They boarded the *Minnehaha* and took a seat on the first level. As the boat picked up speed, Lewis offered her his coat since the air had grown chilly. She declined. She welcomed the bite of the breeze on her warm cheeks.

She glanced again at Lewis—young, intelligent, talented, and sweet. Why couldn't she make herself like him in a romantic way? Maybe she was destined to make poor choices when it came to men.

Never again, she'd vowed, would a man control her and try to change her. Lewis wouldn't do that, but Joel certainly might.

Her pulse raced and she made a decision. She had to stand firm. No matter how many sparks Joel Brooks fired through her, she needed to be ready to douse every one.

21

Saturday took forever to arrive. Joel grabbed his swimsuit out of a dresser drawer and shoved it into his doctor's bag before putting on his coat and leaving home. He and Knute hadn't had as much rowing practice as he'd have liked, but he hoped they could do well in the Lake Minnetonka Yacht Club's regatta. Even if they didn't win, the trip would be worth it if he ran into Charlotte.

What was he thinking? If he had any brains in his head, he'd paddle down another stream altogether. He didn't need to complicate his life with a relationship, but he couldn't stop himself either.

Again he'd felt that prodding.

But God didn't seem to be divulging why he'd been nudging Joel in Charlotte's direction.

One by one, the rest of the Saint Paul Boat Club's rowing team arrived at the station and boarded a streetcar. They switched to another line south of Minneapolis that would take them all the way to Lake Minnetonka. He could have driven, but why would he when the bright yellow streetcars traveled almost a mile a minute and could make the trip much more quickly and more economically than his motorcar? A one-way trip for a quarter suited him fine.

He slid into a seat by the window, and Knute scooted in beside him. As the sun awoke over the horizon, the streetcar skimmed along Lake Calhoun's edge and plunged into a wooded area.

Knute covered his mouth with his fist and yawned. "I hate these early morning heats. Why isn't there a rule that rowing regattas should start after noon?"

"And go on past sunset?" Joel raised his eyebrows. "No thank you." He had no intention of being on the water after dark. He had other plans.

He removed the note with Charlotte's itinerary from his coat pocket, and guilt pricked him. He shouldn't have taken it from the hall table at Mrs. Phillips's house after Charlotte left the other day. She'd obviously left it for Tessa, but if anything happened to Mrs. Phillips, he'd be the first to know. And should the need arise, he wanted to be the one to contact Charlotte.

"What's that?" Knute leaned over to read the note.

Joel folded the note in half, the paper crinkling in his palm. "Just the schedule of a friend who's going to be at the lake."

Knute's dark eyebrows arched. "A male or female friend?"

Joel stared out the window, his mouth clamped shut.

"Your silence tells me it's a woman."

"Silence is seldom equated with women." Joel chuckled. "And in this case, *silent* is not a word I'd use to describe my friend."

"So it is a lady friend. Tell me about her. Is she pretty?"

Joel shot him a scowl. The last thing he needed was Knute making this into more than it was.

"Or maybe she's dreadful. Ugly as a cartload of—"

Joel's elbow found its mark in Knute's side.

His friend grunted. "What was that for? I was going to say, 'Ugly as a cartload of corn cobs.' Apparently you're a little touchy about this lady friend of yours. So, will I get to meet her?"

Joel shrugged. "I haven't yet decided if I'm going to see her myself."

"Trust me. You will."

"And why is that?"

"No one has made you act like this since Prudence Townsend."

"And that ended so well." Sarcasm drenched his words.

"Hey, buddy." Knute lowered his voice. "I know how much it

must have hurt when you caught her kissing Goodwin Nyland of all people, but you've got to take a chance again someday."

"And what would you know about taking chances?" The streetcar rounded a curve then plunged into a valley.

"Back in college, I picked you for my team, didn't I?" Laughter rumbled in Knute's chest. "Biggest chance I ever took."

Joel sighed and gazed out the window. Did Knute have a point? Thinking about the moment when he'd caught his fiancée, the woman he'd loved, in the arms of another man still stung like it had happened yesterday. Was it time to take a chance again on someone new?

One thing was for sure, if that person were Charlotte Gregory, it would certainly be the biggest chance he ever took.

After slipping the apron over her neck, Charlotte tied the strings in a neat bow. Since this was lake country, she decided on easy-to-prepare summer fare. The newest special sandwich called a French dip was sure to be a hit with the ladies. They'd be surprised to learn how easily a beef roast could be placed in the gas oven before heading out for a day at the lake. Without the need to stoke any fires, the lady of the house could enjoy her day and return to find her meat ready to serve. Accompanied by broiled tomatoes and a puff pastry basket, the meal would appear as if it had taken hours to prepare. Only the cook herself would know the truth.

Everything on Charlotte's demonstration table was in order, with the ingredients lined up like toy soldiers. Joel would approve of the table's tidy appearance.

Her finger! She withdrew the rubber nipple from her pocket and rolled it over the tip of her index finger. A perfect fit.

"Charlotte." Lewis laid his hand on her arm. "Since I'll be leaving before you finish your lecture, I wanted to come say goodbye now."

"That's very thoughtful of you, Lewis."

He stuffed his hands into the pockets of his trousers. "I also wanted to tell you how much I've enjoyed every moment I've been with you these last few days—the time at the amusement park, the walk by the lake, and dancing with you last night."

Heat warmed Charlotte's cheeks. They had spent a great deal of time together the last three days. Talking with Lewis was pleasant, and she found his sweet nature a delightful contrast to George's. She could see his feelings were budding, and even though she wasn't sure she felt the same way, she'd accepted when he'd asked her to dance after dinner at the Excelsior Bay Hotel.

Dancing came as easily to him as music, but when the song was over, she'd not yearned to be in his arms any longer. Maybe, like Molly said, that would come in time. Maybe she wasn't giving Lewis a fair chance to win her heart.

He removed one hand from his pocket and covered hers. His Adam's apple bobbed. "Charlotte, I wanted to ask you if it would be all right to call on you when we're back in Saint Paul."

Oh dear. She wasn't ready for that question. What would Joel say if he came and saw Lewis there?

Joel? Good grief. He even argued with her in her thoughts now.

She looked at Lewis worrying his lower lip and forced a smile. "I'm not sure this is the proper time, with my aunt being ill."

His eyes widened and he pulled his hand from hers. "Oh, I hadn't thought of that. Of course, you're right. May I at least telephone you to see how she is faring?"

His concern touched her, and a telephone call should be of no harm. "That would be most kind."

"Then, I'll be thinking of you until our next lecture circuit begins." He dipped his head before taking his place in front of the crowd.

Charlotte leaned against the worktable as he began to sing. His deep bass voice almost made the room throb. Many of the ladies were clearly moved by his crooning, and one young lady in the front row appeared ready to swoon.

It was odd how much more handsome the lanky young man

had grown to be in the few short weeks they'd known each other. Instead of seeing a man who seemed all awkward limbs, she now saw a kind, thoughtful soul. A friend. But no more than that.

Whenever he stepped in front of the crowd, he became someone else—confident and almost flirty. He glanced her way and smiled as he sang, "Cuddle up a little closer, lovey mine."

Oh my. Could she imagine ever cuddling with him?

Turning away, she pretended to examine her notes. Lewis didn't make her heart soar, but he was a good, godly man, and she didn't want to end up alone. Yet she didn't want to rush into anything either. Look what had happened when she'd quickly given her heart to George. She'd promised herself there would be no repeats of her earlier behavior. No, this time she wouldn't let her heart rule her head.

After referring to Charlotte's itinerary, Joel didn't take long to locate the large brick hardware store in Deephaven where she was scheduled to speak. Inside the store's display room, he was surprised to find standing room only. He moved along the back row until he found a spot where he could see Charlotte if he craned his neck to the right.

As soon as he saw her, he felt a prickle of sweat on the back of his neck. She had on a pretty blue striped dress covered with a ruffled white apron. Her hair was pulled up, but she wore no hat or cap. Had it been a mistake to come here? It wasn't too late to sneak back out. She'd never even know.

He froze when she glanced in his direction. Had she seen him? No. There was no recognition on her face, only a bright smile she apparently reserved for the public and not for him.

She opened the door of a shiny gas oven and removed a golden-brown loaf of bread. Its scent permeated the room and his stomach growled. He'd been in a hurry to get here after they'd won their first heat. His 5:00 a.m. breakfast wasn't going to hold him over much longer. He drew in a lungful of air. Something else smelled delicious. Apples? Had she made a pie? Or that scrumptious apple charlotte from the other day?

Charlotte explained each step as she worked. She added in time-saving tidbits and ideas they could use at home. He marveled at how she simplified complicated concepts about nutrition.

Maybe she should speak to the nurses and hospital cooks.

Unfortunately, how well his patients ate was not his greatest concern. Before he left work yesterday, one of the nurses had broken the sphygmomanometer. He'd spoken to Dr. Ancker about it and was told he'd pass on the request to Terrence Ruckman. Although Arthur said Joel should be able to order one right away, he had his doubts.

"Now, ladies, before we open the table up for your sampling pleasure, I want to leave you with one thought." Charlotte stood in front of the table with her hands folded. "My mentor, Miss Fannie Farmer, once said, 'Progress in civilization has been accompanied by progress in cookery.'" She motioned to the oven behind her, and Joel spotted the baby bottle nipple on her finger. He smiled to himself. Good. At least the beautiful, stubborn lady was using it.

"This gas oven is indeed progress," she said. "It is progress in cookery, but as Miss Farmer said, it is also progress in civilization. Because of this appliance, you ladies will no longer be a slave to your kitchens. You can enjoy the art and science of cookery, and you can serve your family better and more healthy food than ever before. Join me in a step forward for women everywhere and insist you have a gas stove in your home."

Joel joined in the well-deserved applause Charlotte garnered. As the women lined up with their forks in hand, he slipped behind a shelf full of bins holding nuts and bolts. He waited while she spoke to each of the ladies as they came up to take their choice of forkfuls. With so many ladies, the plates emptied quickly, dashing any hopes he had of snagging a snack.

When the last of the ladies had departed, Charlotte began to gather her empty bowls and utensils. She was so involved in a conversation with the older lady beside her that she didn't see him slip from his place behind the shelf and approach the table.

"Charlotte."

The spoon in her hand clattered to the floor.

"I need to stop sneaking up on you in the kitchen." He laughed, scooped up the spoon, and passed it to her, his fingers brushing hers in the process.

She sucked in her breath at the contact.

He looked into her eyes, golden flecks awash in hazel sea foam, and felt his heart rate quicken.

Yes, this had been a mistake.

But it was too late now.

"What are you doing here?" Her cheeks colored, and she tucked a strand of hair behind her ear.

He slipped a finger into the collar of his shirt. "Seeing how hot things can get in your kitchen."

22

What was Joel really doing here in Deephaven? And how did he know where to find her? She couldn't imagine he'd happened upon this particular hardware store.

Charlotte glanced at Molly and the older woman smiled. "Charlotte, you're all flushed. He's right. It is warm in here."

It was. Now. Since he came.

Wrapping an arm around Charlotte's waist, Molly tugged her close. "Sugar, how long do I have to stand here before you introduce me to this handsome fella?"

Joel ducked his head to hide a grin.

"Miss Molly Larkin, this is Dr. Joel Brooks. He's treating my Aunt Sam."

Wait a minute. Was that why he'd come? Fear constricted her chest and threatened to buckle her knees. She leaned into Molly's side. "What's happened to Aunt Sam?"

"Nothing, Charlotte. She's fine."

"Are you certain?" Her shaky voice betrayed her fear.

"Absolutely. She's getting better every day." He swept his hand over the dishes. "Why don't you rest, and I'll help Miss Larkin clean up?"

"If that don't beat all. A man offering to do women's work. Bless your heart." Molly pointed to a shelf across the room. "First, call me Molly, and second, bring that washtub from over yonder and we'll put all these here dishes in it. The owner's offered to have these dishes done up, so once they're gathered, we'll go have us some lunch. You're coming with us, aren't you, sugar?"

Joel dropped the washtub on the table with a resounding clang. He flashed Molly that take-your-breath-away smile of his. "Actually, I was hoping to treat you both." He eyed the dish in Molly's hand. "That is, if I can have those last three bites of apple charlotte."

She slid the pan toward him along with a large cooking spoon. "Eat up. It's our Charlotte's specialty, you know."

He looked over the dessert-filled spoon at Charlotte and met her gaze. "It's only one of her many specialties."

"Oh? What are some of the others?" Molly set a bread pan in the washtub.

"She's good at . . . making her point."

Charlotte tossed an aluminum measuring cup in with the other dirty dishes. "He means I'm good at arguing."

"Is that a fact?" Molly's ample chest shook with laughter. "Well, Dr. Joel, as we in the kitchen would say, life is pretty boring without a pinch of spice every now and again."

"Miss Molly, I think you may have a point." Joel deposited his empty pan and spoon with the other dishes before turning to Charlotte. He swept his arm toward the door. "Ladies, shall we?"

Grabbing her hat, Charlotte followed Molly out. Joel pulled the hardware store's door shut behind them.

"I thought we could eat here in Deephaven, if that's all right with both of you." Joel led them down the street to a café.

Questions filled Charlotte's mind. He seemed familiar with the area. Did he come to Lake Minnetonka often? Or perhaps Joel was from one of the towns surrounding Lake Minnetonka? He had yet to disclose why he'd shown up at her cooking demonstration. Despite what he said, she doubted he'd come there simply to see her.

After they had ordered, they fell into easy conversation. Joel again assured Charlotte her aunt was fine and Nurse Pierce had followed the menu plan she'd left. He'd checked every day. He asked about her speaking engagements at Excelsior, and she explained they'd gone well once the missing trunk had been located.

"Tessa is bursting with excitement about the *Peter Pan* premiere in a couple of weeks." Joel scooped his last bite of mashed potatoes onto his fork. "And your aunt is determined to be present for the occasion."

Charlotte dabbed her lips with her napkin. This could be a problem. If Aunt Sam wanted something, deterring her was next to impossible. "What do you think her chances are of attending?"

"Like I told her, if she'd use a wheelchair, I think her chances are excellent."

"And if not?" Charlotte couldn't imagine Aunt Sam agreeing to that.

"I fear it would be too much walking for her in her present condition." He set down his fork. "By the way, how's your finger?"

"Healing nicely."

"Let me see." He held out his hand, palm facing upward, clearly expecting her to place her hand in his.

She tucked her hand in her lap. "It's your day off. You don't need to bother with my silly injury."

He wiggled his fingers. "It's no bother. I rather like taking care of you."

Her insides coiled with pleasure. How did he do that? Make her face feel like it was on fire with a look or a few words?

Molly nudged her. "Go on, sugar."

She placed her hand in his and sucked in her breath as tingles shot up her arm at his touch. His long fingers closed around her palm, his thumb absently stroking a circle as he peered at the stitches.

"It looks great. Who took the stitches out?"

"I had Molly do it this morning."

"Hope you don't mind, Doc. I've had plenty of practice over the years pulling threads." Molly chuckled and her ample belly shook.

"Not at all." He gave Charlotte's hand a subtle squeeze and released it.

Once the waitress had cleared their empty plates, Joel pulled out his watch. "I hate to rush, but I'm afraid I have to leave. I have to be back at the yacht club by one thirty."

"Is someone ill there?" Charlotte folded her napkin and set it on the gingham tablecloth. "Is that why you're here at the lake?"

Joel squared his shoulders. "No, I'm competing."

She studied his suit. While he looked handsome in his tan tweed suit and creased homburg hat, it didn't look like the sporting clothes worn by the smartly dressed, wealthy yacht owners she'd seen since her arrival. "You have a yacht?"

"Me?" Sputtering like an old faucet, he laughed hard.

She bristled. "What else was I to think?"

"Charlotte, I'm not laughing at you. Honest. I'm laughing at the idea of me having the money to own a yacht. I'm an oarsman on a rowboat. I compete with a partner in men's doubles." He inhaled and sobered. "I was hoping the two of you would come watch our final heats."

Joel was an oarsman. It figured. Steady, regular, stay-the-course Joel. There would be few surprises in a rowboat. Still, she found the idea of watching him compete rather exciting—and he had specifically invited them.

"I declare, that would be positively delightful!" Molly gushed. "Charlotte, don't you agree?"

She looked at him and thought she saw expectant hope reflected in his eyes. Even if she wanted to, which she didn't, she could not have told this man no right now.

Her lips curled in a smile. "Yes, I'd like to see that very much indeed."

Spectators continued to thicken on the Minnetonka Yacht Club's pier and on the nearby shore. The water glittered in the sunlight, and Charlotte couldn't imagine a more perfect day for a regatta.

As they walked along the boardwalk, she admitted she knew

little of rowing and sculling. Molly, too, claimed no knowledge of the sport, so Joel gave them a brief introduction. He explained rowing events are head-to-head races. There could be teams of two to eight, depending on the event. "Teams with eight rowers also have a coxswain who sits in the stern and steers the boat and directs the crew."

Molly snapped open her fan and flicked it back and forth. "Some of the fellas in the boats have two oars and some have one. That hardly seems fair."

Joel's chest shook in a silent laugh. "Men on sculling boats have an oar in each hand. On rowboats, each oarsman has only one. You'll be watching the final heats. All of these boats won in their first semifinal heat, so every race this afternoon determines a winner."

He led them to the far end of the pier. "This would be a good place for you to watch. You'll have a good view of the finish from here." He paused and cleared his throat before meeting Charlotte's gaze. "And while we're still on the subject of winners, I have a question to ask you."

"All right."

"There's a celebratory dinner planned for this evening at the yacht club for all of the winners." He looked down, picked up a rock off the pier, and tossed it into the bay. "If I win, would you, and Molly, of course, attend with me?"

"Count me out, sugar. I have to get home to my sister. She gets meaner than a crippled snake if I don't come home when I said I would. Since we're traveling by streetcar, there's no problem leaving separately." Molly winked at Charlotte. "Besides, you'll have more fun if I'm not there."

"Molly, I haven't agreed to go yet."

"But you should, sugar. You should have some fun while you're here."

Joel grinned at Molly. "Listen to the smart lady, Charlotte."

"You're forgetting you haven't won yet, aren't you?"

"If you say you'll join me, I will win." He raised his eyebrows. "And if I don't, we'll go somewhere else for dinner. Maybe the Hotel Del Otero's dining room. Unless you're afraid to be alone with me."

"Of course not, we've been alone before—"

"Oh?" Molly put on a good show of looking prim, then chuckled. "Sugar, say yes to the poor man. I'm sure he needs all the help he can get to win this. Look at those spindly arms and narrow shoulders."

Joel straightened his broad shoulders and placed his fists on his hips. No, there was nothing spindly about this man. But a whole afternoon and evening with Joel if he won?

She took a deep breath. "All right, I'll stay."

"And one more thing." He tapped her nose. "It has to be a fight-free evening."

"He's upping the stakes now, sugar."

She tipped her head to the side. "And if you lose, what do I get?"

"You can start any discussion you like."

"Even talk about the food served at the hospital?"

"Even that."

Her pulse raced and her stomach fluttered. She drew in a deep breath, tasting the lake breeze on her lips. What would one fight-free night hurt? And could they truly not fight that long?

Finally she nodded. "It's a deal."

Joel's stunning smile widened. "Good. I've got to go get ready for my heat. See you afterward."

She watched him jog off, feeling a little thrill of expectation.

Molly nudged her arm and pointed to a row of boats lining up in the bay. "Look, the scullery boats must be next."

"I think they're called sculls, Molly. Those must be what Joel said were quadruple ones."

The five competing sculls, each holding four men with a set of oars locked in place for each man, made quick work of the course. With no idea who to root for, Charlotte cheered for the scull in front and joined the crowd in applauding it when it took the prize.

A few minutes later, she caught a glimpse of Joel readying his boat, now wearing a dark blue, sleeveless bathing suit cut low beneath each arm. Like his partner's, his suit was trimmed in light blue. Yet it wasn't his suit that made heat pool in her stomach, but what it revealed. Narrow shoulders and spindly arms? Heavens, no. Muscles rippled across his shoulders and arms. Even his legs seemed as if they belonged in one of Michelangelo's paintings. Her cheeks warmed and she forced herself to turn away.

Molly leaned closer. "That doctor's finer than a frog's hair split four ways."

"Molly!"

"Don't try to pretend you didn't notice. I saw those pink cheeks of yours. What's going on with y'all? Are the two of you sparkin'?"

"We're friends—at best."

"Friends? Sugar, I may be old but I'm not blind. That man is considering some serious sparkin' with the cook."

"I doubt that. Every time we're within a few yards of each other, we end up having words."

"Uh-huh."

She watched Joel and his partner row their boat out to the starting area. "He can be very stubborn. Closed minded too. He won't even consider my ideas about the need for better nutrition in his hospital."

"Uh-huh."

"And you should see what he's like in his office. Every object has to be in a certain spot. Not a fraction of an inch off. It's very odd." Charlotte's pulse raced as she waited for the heat to begin. "And he sure knows how he thinks things should be. Safe. Nothing out of place."

"And yet he came to find you." Molly caught Charlotte's eye. "Wonder why that is?"

The gun went off and the rowers dug their oars into the water. Facing backwards, they headed for the end of the course. How could Joel and his partner tell where they were going? The two of them took an early lead, but one of the other teams seemed to be closing the distance.

"Why are y'all letting the other team catch up?" Molly shouted, waving her handkerchief in the air. "Hurry, sugar! Hurry!"

Charlotte bit her lip. "They seem to be slowing. Perhaps they're tired already."

The gentleman beside her cleared his throat and stuck his thumbs in his vest pockets. "Ladies, allow me to explain. Rowing depends on a combination of immense strength and stamina. Each team must set a pace that will give them the most speed and distance from every stroke, yet retain enough energy for a strong finish."

"Then they're all right." Charlotte didn't take her eyes from the race but bounced on her toes as excitement coursed through her. "Thank you, sir."

"You're most welcome." The man tipped his hat.

The other boat was now neck and neck with Joel's. They still had half a course to cover. Would Joel and his partner have the stamina to finish strong?

As they neared the last third of the course, Joel and his partner nosed ahead by half a boat. The other team soon joined them. The two boats seesawed back and forth, first one in the lead and then the other. Charlotte shouted along with the rest of the roaring crowd. With only a few lengths left, she could almost feel Joel and his partner push harder, the steady rhythm of their oars digging into the water with increased intensity.

She held her breath. Their boat lunged forward.

Joel had won!

"He did it!" She whirled toward Molly.

Her traveling companion pressed her hand to her chest. "And he gave my poor little ol' heart palpitations in the process. Goodness gracious. That's too much excitement for an old lady."

They had been on their feet for quite a while and were feeling fatigued. "Let's find a place to sit," Charlotte said.

They secured a bench, and Molly eyed Charlotte. "You ready for a night on the town, sugar?"

That was right. His win meant she'd be staying and Molly would be going. How could she have forgotten already? Now who was having heart palpitations?

She glanced up to see Joel approaching, his alarming smile glinting. Her chest heaved as if she'd been the one rowing. She should never have made that agreement.

He stopped in front of her. "I think you, Miss Gregory, owe me one fight-free evening."

"Do you honestly think we can do that?"

He shrugged, but his eyes bore into hers. "I'm willing to give it a try if you are."

She looked from Joel to Molly and back to Joel. Her pulse pounded in her ears. Could she refrain from arguing with him for a whole evening? Only time would tell.

23

Being an aunt still seemed odd to Tessa. With her fussy niece in her arms, she swayed back and forth as she'd seen Hannah do. How long would Hannah and Lincoln stay upstairs with Aunt Sam? Didn't they realize she was not experienced in the care of an infant?

When she'd protested about them leaving Ellie alone with her, Hannah had assured her she'd do fine. "You play a maid, don't you?"

"One who lets the children fly out the window," Tessa called, but her sister kept on climbing the staircase as if she'd not heard her.

That had been half an hour ago.

"Ellie, sweetie, if you keep crying, they're going to think I'm not up to the task of caring for you." She switched the infant to her shoulder and patted her back. "And while we both know that's true, perhaps you could pretend it isn't so." She sat down in a chair and held Ellie at arm's length so she could look into her eyes. "I pretend all the time. You'll find it's easier the more practice you get."

The baby quieted, so she went on in a singsong voice. "Would you like to hear a little Shakespeare?"

Ellie's tiny mouth quirked in a bit of a smile.

"Am I holding a budding thespian?" She smiled at the baby. "You've been acting upset with me all this time when in fact, you like me. Isn't that right, my sweet little niece? So, let's see, how about some lines from *Macbeth*? No, that's a bit much for a baby.

Hamlet? Too depressing. *Romeo and Juliet*? We'll talk about that when you're older." Ellie's eyes drooped a little, so Tessa cradled her against her side but kept talking. "I know the perfect lines. They're from *The Tempest*. One of my favorites."

The baby's eyes drooped further.

"In *The Tempest*, the heroine is strong. In his comedies, all of Shakespeare's heroines are strong. He probably thought the idea of a strong woman was funny, because in his tragedies, things seldom go so well for the ladies. We'll read *The Tempest* together someday, you and I." Tessa's voice grew soft as Ellie's eyes closed. "'We are such stuff as dreams are made on, and our little life is rounded with a sleep.'"

The steady rise and fall of Ellie's tiny chest told Tessa she'd done it. She'd gotten the baby to sleep. The act, while simple, left her with the most satisfying feeling. Was that what it meant to be an aunt?

Hannah joined her in the parlor and smiled. "You did it. You conquered the mighty Ellie."

"I think she conquered me." Tessa stroked her niece's milkweed-soft cheek. "'Though she be but little, she is fierce.'"

"*Much Ado About Nothing*?"

"*A Midsummer Night's Dream*. Act two, scene three." She rolled her eyes. Apparently it would be up to her to educate her niece in life's most important matters. "Don't worry, Ellie, Aunt Tessa will teach you everything you need to know."

For a minute, Joel feared Charlotte would change her mind and refuse to accompany him to the dinner that evening. To his relief, she kept her word.

He wasn't sure why he felt so strongly about her remaining with him at the lake today. He'd spent hours praying about it last night. The only answer God seemed to press on his heart was he needed her to stay.

After the Minnetonka Yacht Club's awards ceremony, he'd

helped the two women pack up their supplies and arrange the shipment of their trunks. He waited with Charlotte until Molly boarded the streetcar back to the city, then suggested they take a tour of the lake on one of the streetcar boats before dinner.

Once he'd purchased the tickets, he and Charlotte boarded the *Stillwater*. Since Charlotte preferred the seating on the top deck, he followed her to the indoor staircase. "Careful."

"I'll be fine."

And she was.

Too bad. He rather liked the idea of having to catch her.

The only seats available were in a row where a man sat with his arms outstretched, taking up at least three spaces. Charlotte stood at the end of the bench. "Sir, would you mind moving down a bit so we can share your bench?"

The man huffed and moved about a foot to his right.

Charlotte glanced at Joel and whispered, "Maybe we should sit down below."

"The boat is for everyone." He kept his voice low. "Go ahead and have a seat. I'm sure he'll move on down."

Charlotte slid in, but the man didn't budge an inch. Joel sat down beside her and placed his doctor's bag beneath the bench. He leaned around Charlotte to speak with the man. "Sir, would you mind giving the lady a few more inches?"

The man crossed his arms over his chest. "She sat here. I'm done moving."

Joel's jaw clenched, and Charlotte laid a hand on his arm. "It's okay. It's not a long ride."

He lifted his arm over her head to rest on the bench and pulled her toward his side. "I hope you don't mind, but I'd rather you be next to me than next to him."

Her cheeks colored. "Thank you. You do realize we've gone several hours now without a cross word. That's twice now."

"If you hadn't stopped me, I might have had a few cross words for Mr. Friendly there." He smiled at her. "But the night's not over."

The wind began to pick up and he glanced upward. Where the sun had been only a half hour ago, clouds now moved swiftly across the sky. The air felt heavy. Were they in for a thunderstorm?

He'd planned on the two of them riding to Spring Park to catch a glimpse of the famed Hotel Del Otero and then returning to Deephaven, but maybe they'd make an early departure to be on the safe side.

"I think we're in for a storm. Let's get off at Excelsior. We'll get back on when the storm passes."

"But you'll be late for your dinner."

"I'd rather miss it altogether than let you get hurt. Being on the water during a thunderstorm is dangerous."

"The wind is picking up." She pressed a hand to her hat and smiled at him. "I guess I won't argue."

He winked at her. "About time."

By the time they reached Excelsior, rain had begun to fall. The boat's steward told everyone the boat would remain docked there until after the storm, so they should all seek shelter on the shore. While Charlotte didn't relish the thought of making a dash in the rain, she also didn't like the lightning that had begun to flash in the sky.

Joel grabbed his medical bag, then pulled her to her feet. A thunderclap broke the stillness and she jolted. "We'll be off here in a few minutes."

Behind her, the rude man pushed his way through. She fell against Joel's chest. If not for his strong arms steeling her, she might have pitched right into the water.

Joel's eyes grew fierce. "Someone needs to teach him a lesson. What kind of man doesn't let a lady go first?" A lightning bolt cracked the sky. "Sorry. Let's get going."

The choices of where to seek shelter appeared limited. Most of the people headed toward the Excelsior Bay Hotel, but it seemed the parlor couldn't handle the influx and some were left standing on the porch.

"Over there." Joel pointed to Steton's Blue Line Café.

She, Molly, and Lewis had eaten breakfast there. Had that only been this morning? The run to the café would take longer, but they'd be assured a spot. A gust of wind tore her hat from her head and she gasped.

"Let's go." Joel locked his hand around hers, and they fled into the sheeting rain.

With her skirts hiked high, they ran down the boardwalk toward the restaurant. The sky darkened to a gray-green color. A tree branch cracked and gave way. Charlotte stumbled and Joel caught her about the waist.

"We're almost there!" Joel urged her forward.

When she turned the door handle, the wind whipped the door from her grasp. It banged against the wooden building. She heard what sounded like a train and spun around. The roping tail of a tornado reached toward the earth. A scream died on her lips as Joel heaved her inside.

"Get under the table!" he ordered.

She fell to her knees, and he covered her with his body.

The train's roar grew louder. Women screamed. Her body convulsed with fear.

Was she going to die in the arms of Joel Brooks?

24

Silence now reigned over the chaos, and sunlight filtered in through the open doorway. Joel eased away from Charlotte and sucked in a breath to calm his racing heart.

Charlotte didn't move. Fear coursed through him again. "Charlotte? Charlotte, are you hurt? Look at me."

"I'm okay." Her voice didn't sound convincing, and when she scooted out from under the table, tears trailed down her cheeks. She swiped them away. "Sorry. I was saying an important thank-you."

He glanced around the café. A few other customers emerged from hiding beneath the tables, and a man who appeared to be the owner came out of the back room and asked, "Is everyone all right in here?"

"Looks that way." Joel climbed to his feet, dusted off his trousers, and helped Charlotte stand. "You sure you're okay?"

"Yes, but did the tornado hit anything?"

"I'll go check." He stepped into the doorway. A sense of dread pooled in his stomach. Uprooted trees lay toppled like felled giants. While the hotel remained standing, there was damage to the porch. Two other buildings lay in unrecognizable heaps.

"How bad is it?" Charlotte placed her hands on his shoulders and tried to peek over them at the damage. "Joel, we have to go help. What if someone is trapped in one of those buildings? And remember how many people from the boat were on that porch." She tried to shove past him. "We need to go help those people."

He turned and gripped her arms. "*I* need to go, and I need you to stay here."

"I am not going to stay here like some society girl who can't keep her wits about her in an emergency."

"Charlotte, listen to me, please. I can't help those people if I'm worrying about your safety."

"I can take care of myself."

"Remember your promise? One night without arguing."

"But—"

"Charlotte, please."

She scowled but clamped her mouth shut. Even windblown and tear-streaked, she was beautiful. He couldn't let her go out there. Who knew what he might find in the rubble. *Lord, help me figure this out.* How could she help without causing him worry?

He glanced toward the kitchen. "We're going to need food and coffee. Lots of it. Some of these people are going to be in shock, and the workers who come to help will need to keep their strength up. I need to know I can count on you here."

She sighed, picked up his medical bag, and handed it to him none too gently. "Be careful."

"And you'll stay here?"

"I'll do my best."

It wasn't a guarantee, but it was most likely the best he'd get from her given the circumstances. And for that he was grateful.

With the porch damaged, the hotel wouldn't be able to provide food or beverages for the workers or injured. On every floor, windows had been shattered as well. Charlotte watched Joel jog in that direction. How many injured might there be? And who could say what lay beneath the two toppled buildings?

Other customers pushed by her to get a look at the damage.

She stepped aside and wrapped her arms around herself. The sun would be setting and it would get chilly soon. They might need blankets too. It was time to get to work.

She marched toward the kitchen. "Sir, I'm Charlotte Gregory and I work for the gas company giving cooking demonstrations. I'll be happy to help you make food and hot beverages for the injured and the workers if you'll acquaint me with your kitchen."

"And who's going to pay for this food?"

"This is an emergency. We all need to do our part."

"Like I said, who's going to pay for it?"

Aunt Sam would be willing to foot the bill, but it would be presumptuous to offer that.

Wait a minute. Charlotte made an income now from the gas company. What better way to use her money?

"Sir, I will personally guarantee you'll be paid for any food we use."

"You?"

"I told you I work for the gas company." She found a pencil and a piece of paper and scribbled her information. "Here's my name and address."

He read it and whistled. "Summit Avenue, huh? Guess you can afford the food, or at least your parents can. Come on. Let's get cooking."

She didn't bother to correct his assumptions but instead followed him into the kitchen. He pointed out the basics—the pantry shelf, the pots and pans, the icebox—then turned to leave.

"Where are you going?" Charlotte reached for an apron from a hook on the wall.

"I have a family I need to go check on. You can handle making coffee, right?"

"Of course I can make coffee." She slipped the apron over her head and tied its strings.

"Then you ought to be fine while I'm gone." He swept his arm around the kitchen. "She's all yours."

Charlotte took a few moments after he left to gather her thoughts. *Lord, help me know what I need to do first.*

An answer permeated her thoughts. *Get some help.*

She hurried into the dining room. Several female customers sat at the tables, stunned, their husbands having gone to help outside. One woman tried to console her crying infant while another seemed to have her head bowed in prayer.

"Attention, ladies!" They all jerked. "I need some volunteers in the kitchen to help me prepare food and warm beverages for the victims and workers."

"I'll help." The praying woman jumped to her feet.

"Me too." A tall lady with a deep voice came to the counter.

Soon nearly every woman had volunteered. One older woman, who said she wasn't up to standing in a kitchen, offered to hold the baby so the baby's mother could help out.

Charlotte directed two ladies to make sandwiches with the bread the man had on hand, another woman volunteered to make biscuits since the bread wouldn't last long, and a couple of others set about preparing coffee and tea. Charlotte recruited the tall lady, who she learned was named Fern, to help her make no-bake mud pie cookies on the stove.

"Charlotte!" Joel called from the dining room.

She hurried out and watched him lower the rude man from the boat into a chair. "What's wrong with him?"

"Shock, mostly. Can you bring him something warm to drink? Is there any chance of finding a blanket?" He caught her arm. "Is everything still all right here?"

"Fine." She rummaged through the shelves behind the counter and found some tablecloths. She brought a cup of coffee for the man and one for Joel, then she draped the man's shoulders with the blue gingham. "Don't worry. I'll take care of him."

"I know you will." He paused and seemed to be studying her. "I don't know how many, but there will be more."

"We'll be ready."

And when additional storm victims arrived, the ladies were prepared. Over the next couple of hours, workers brought in ten victims in various states of shock and injury. A few had been hastily bandaged and might require stitches. Joel had set one man's broken arm, which seemed to be the worst injury so far.

As her ladies passed around the warm biscuits and cookies, Charlotte stepped outside for a breath of air. Joel's celebratory dinner at the yacht club would be over by now if there'd been no damage at Deephaven. She had no way of knowing yet, but perhaps she'd soon learn since one worker said the express boats were running again.

Beneath her hand, her stomach protested the lack of dinner. She tried to find Joel in the diminishing light. He'd worked tirelessly for several hours. He had to be starving too, and he wasn't alone. Some of the other workers hadn't taken a break from digging through the rubble of those two buildings either.

With a new task in mind, she went to the kitchen to find a basket to fill with sandwiches and cookies. Only Fern remained in the kitchen. After hearing Charlotte's plan, Fern offered to join her, as it appeared Steton's Blue Line Café was out of gas.

"Fern, will you hand me those enameled cups?" She pointed to a shelf.

The tall woman had no problem reaching the shelf. She started to hand the cups to Charlotte and swayed. She reached for the countertop with one hand and pressed the other to her head. "I have the worst headache, and I'm so dizzy all of a sudden. Maybe the fresh air will help me keep my eyes open."

Charlotte took her arm. "How long have you felt like this?"

"The last half hour or so."

Something was off. The air in the room felt stale, heavy. Charlotte's head throbbed too.

Headaches. Dizziness. And the stove was out of gas.

Alarm bells sounded in Charlotte's mind. "Fern, we have to get everyone out of this café now!"

25

Sweat trickled down Joel's back and seeped under his waistband. He straightened and stretched his arms over his head. They'd been at this pile of rubble for the last hour but thankfully had found no one buried in it.

"Doc." Ollie, one of the men who'd been working side by side with him, tossed a board on the pile. "Why don't you go to the café and see about tending those folks? If we find anyone else, we'll come get you."

"That's probably a good idea. I should go check on them." He grabbed his coat, long since tossed aside, and draped it over his arm. Once he'd located his doctor's bag, he trudged toward the café. The lake lapped at the shore as if nothing had happened. The air had grown chilly, and with the sun losing its hold on the day, the temperature was bound to grow even colder.

At least Charlotte was safe and comfortable inside the café. Thank goodness she'd remained there like he'd asked. From what he'd seen, she'd taken control of the place and made it into a wonderful place of warmth and healing for the unfortunate lake guests who had fallen victim to the storm.

Shadowy figures dotted the area outside the café. How odd. In the waning light, he couldn't tell who or how many, but he could see some of the people wore skirts. What were women doing outside with the air cooling? Had the café run out of room?

He drew closer and spoke to the first man he saw. "What's going on?"

"The lady in charge thinks there's a gas leak." The man clearly didn't believe there was a problem.

Joel's chest tightened. "Where is she?"

"Still inside. Helping some man who didn't know up from down."

"And you left her there?" Joel didn't wait to hear the man's response. He ignored the voices that called for him to stay out and raced inside. Without being able to light a lamp, he found it hard to see in the dim dining room. His eyes took a minute to adjust. "Charlotte?"

"Over here."

He spotted her supporting the disoriented man from the boat. Sliding the man's arm over his shoulder, he relieved her of her burden. "Go! I've got him."

She didn't immediately release the man. "First you tell me to stay, and now you're telling me to go."

He huffed and dragged the man to the door. Once outside, he deposited the man several yards from the café and whirled toward her. "How did you know there was a gas leak? Are you sure?"

"The stove was suddenly out of gas. Fern had a headache. She complained about being dizzy and tired. After that storm, I figured—"

"How about you? Do you have a headache?"

"It's getting better now." She paused. "And before you launch into a tirade about putting myself in danger, you might want to consider if I'd have stayed inside the restaurant where you told me to, I would have died. Still, I'm very thankful I was there. I think it was part of God's plan all along."

Hannah's pacing was driving Tessa insane.

"Would you please sit down?" Tessa gripped her sister's wrist and attempted to draw her down to the davenport. "You're making me tired looking at you."

Hannah pulled her hand away. "I'm glad you called us, Tessa, but I don't understand why Charlotte isn't home by now. I spoke to that sweet Molly she travels with, and she was certain Dr. Brooks would bring Charlotte home by nine or ten, and it's almost midnight."

"She's with a doctor. *Your* doctor. Nothing is going to happen to her that he can't fix." Tessa shot Hannah's husband a pleading look. "You tell her."

Lincoln rose and pulled Hannah into his arms. "I'm sure she's fine."

"But the storm—"

"Sweetheart, you aren't going to like hearing this, but Tessa is right." He stepped back far enough to see Hannah's face, then kissed her lips.

Tessa moaned. If those two were going to make dove eyes at each other all night long, she wished Hannah would go back to pacing.

Electric lights lined the streetcar route back to the city. Charlotte had never seen what was referred to as the Great White Way, but she knew now why so many people spoke about it. The blur of the lights had a hypnotic effect, and she struggled to keep her weary eyes open.

"I feel like I've lived five years in one day." She sighed. "And you must be even more exhausted."

"I have to admit I was happy to see some help arrive to care for the victims, but I think you saved more lives than I did."

His words warmed her. She hadn't thought of that, but it was true. The man who arrived from the gas company had confirmed her suspicion of a leak. When the owner was contacted, he was so grateful she'd discovered the leak and had kept the place from exploding, he'd said the food and drinks would be his treat.

If only she'd thought to eat at some point.

Too spent for conversation, they rode in silence. Charlotte thought about how the day had begun with Lewis asking to call on her and how it had ended with Joel sitting beside her. How different the two men were. A twinge of guilt pulled at her. She hadn't even thought about Lewis until they stepped on the streetcar tonight. Was he safe? She'd asked the conductor if he'd heard of any more damage at the lake other than what had occurred in Excelsior. To her relief, he'd said no.

Her head bobbed. She jerked and glanced at Joel to see if he'd noticed.

Without a word, he slipped out of his coat and patted his shoulder. "Charlotte, use me as your pillow."

"What will people say?"

"You'll argue with me at the drop of a hat, but you're worried about what people you'll never see again will say?"

"I see your point, but—"

"Charlotte, no arguing today, remember?"

"Yes, but I'm planning a crackerjack of a fight for tomorrow." Her lips curled as she tentatively laid her head against the solid muscles of his shoulder.

"I'm looking forward to it." He draped his coat around her and tucked it in place.

She burrowed into its warmth and closed her eyes. Joel's soap and wood scent lingered in its folds. If Lewis was as sweet as cobbler, what was Joel? She'd figure it out tomorrow. Right now she wanted to give in and sleep.

Was she dreaming, or had she felt a kiss on the top of her head?

26

All Charlotte wanted to do was wash her face, crawl into a warm bed, and sleep for a year. But when she opened the front door, she found herself surrounded by family members with more questions than a curious six-year-old.

While still standing in the foyer, she gave them a brief explanation of the evening's events, which only seemed to fuel more inquiries.

"I think Charlotte would rather answer all your questions in the morning." Joel glanced down at her. "It's been a long day for both of us."

"And it's getting longer and longer and longer." Tessa yawned.

"I think Dr. Brooks is right." Lincoln wrapped an arm around his wife's shoulders. "You can come back in the morning to cross-examine your sister."

Hannah nodded. "At least let me help her get to bed."

"You want to tuck her in?" Tessa rolled her eyes.

Even a well-honed glare from Hannah didn't stop her youngest sister from giggling.

"I'm going up right now to draw her bath." Hannah paused at the doorway. "Coming, Tessa?"

"Good night, gentlemen. Looks like I'm on lullaby duty." Tessa took Charlotte's hand. "Time for beddy-bye, Lottie love."

Charlotte cleared her throat.

"Oh." Exaggerated realization exploded on Tessa's face. "You want to tell Dr. Brooks goodbye without an audience. Don't be shy. Just tell Lincoln. He'll understand."

Lincoln came to the rescue. "I think she wants us *both* to leave." He pressed his hand to Tessa's back and led the grumbling girl out of the foyer.

Charlotte looked up into Joel's dark-rimmed eyes. Exhaustion etched his dirt-smudged face. His white shirt, with the sleeves still rolled up to his elbows, was beyond repair.

She slipped his coat off and handed it to him. "Thank you—for everything."

"As strange as this may sound, Charlotte, I truly enjoyed our day together." For the first time since she'd met him, his voice lacked its usual air of authority. It sounded almost vulnerable.

"Up until the tornado?"

"After it too." He held her gaze for several seconds, then said good night, closing the door behind him.

Charlotte leaned against the hall table and waited for her pulse to stop hammering. Her emotions swirled. She felt so safe with him, but was she again falling for a man who would want to make decisions for her?

She drew in a deep breath and pressed a hand to her chest. That tornado had done more than strike a couple of buildings. It had stirred things up inside—feelings that scared her witless.

Bubbles surrounded her. Charlotte leaned back, closed her eyes, and let the warm water ease her aching muscles. Ah, heaven.

She felt someone staring at her. Opening her eyes, she found Tessa sitting on a stool with her elbows propped on her knees. "What was worse—the tornado or being stuck with Dr. Brooks all night?"

"Tessa!" Charlotte sat up, splashing water out of the tub. "Joel was a perfect gentleman."

"Joel?" Hannah stepped into the bathroom and placed a fresh nightgown on the hook behind the door. "You're on a first-name basis? I wasn't aware you and the doctor had become friendly."

"I wouldn't say they're friendly." Tessa sat back. "They fight like Grant and Lee."

"She's exaggerating, Hannah." Charlotte scrubbed her face with a washcloth. "Dr. Brooks and I have talked a little. That's all. And for your information, Tessa, except for the tornado, we had a pleasant evening." Charlotte flicked suds at the youngest Gregory girl's cheek.

"You know this means war." Tessa scooped up a handful of suds and let them fly in Charlotte's direction. She fired another handful at Hannah.

"Hey, what was that for?" Hannah held her hands out in shock.

"Payback." Tessa giggled.

"For what?"

"Pacing insufferably until Charlotte came home."

"Why, you little—" Hannah gathered a handful of suds and aimed them at Tessa. The suds war was on.

Puffs of white flew back and forth in the soapy exchange of volleys. Within minutes, all three sisters were drenched. Hannah and Tessa sat on the floor with their knees pulled up to their chins, and Charlotte settled back in the bath.

Hannah sighed. "I'm sure glad you're home safe, Lottie."

Tears suddenly pricked Charlotte's eyes. Her heart swelled with an indescribable love for her sisters. Tonight she'd come much too close to never seeing either of them again. She swallowed the lump in her throat. "I love both of you. With all my heart. I need you to know that because you never know when you might not get the chance to say it again."

"Enough sappy stuff." Hannah held out a towel. "You're getting all pruney in there, and Dr. Brooks will never fall in love with a pruney, wrinkly woman."

"Fall in love?" Tessa stood up. "She'll be lucky if they can fall in *like*. When there aren't any tornadoes around to spin them silly, they can't be in a room together without a war breaking out."

Charlotte toweled dry and slipped into the fresh gown. Tessa had a point. Tonight wasn't a regular situation. Tomorrow, when the real world returned, would she and Joel go back to mixing like oil and vinegar? And what should she do about dear, sweet Lewis?

Why did babies always have to arrive in the middle of the night? Joel stretched his arms over his head and pushed his palms toward the hospital's ceiling. He should be grateful Mrs. Anderson hadn't delivered on Saturday night after he'd gotten home from Lake Minnetonka. At least this baby waited until early Monday morning to make an appearance.

Very early.

He sat down at his desk and opened Mrs. Anderson's file. He'd make his notes and then head home to catch a few more hours of sleep.

The words blurred on the page before him. A few minutes of rest was all he needed to reenergize. He leaned back in his chair, folded his hands behind his head, and closed his eyes. Was Charlotte recovering from their ordeal any better than he?

After church services on Sunday, he'd checked on Knute to make sure he'd gotten home safely, and then he'd telephoned Charlotte to see if she was all right. Tessa said her sister decided to take a nap right after Sunday services. Too bad he hadn't followed her example. He wished he'd been able to talk to her in person, but he wasn't sure what he'd say right now.

This morning the preacher had talked about how God's plans were often quite different from those of man. What verse had he quoted? Something from Proverbs? "A man's heart deviseth his way: but the Lord directeth his steps."

With a prayer on his lips, he felt sleep begin to claim him. *Lord, my heart hasn't made the best plans in the past, so I need you to establish my steps.*

Was someone in her room? Charlotte thought she'd heard a floorboard creak, but she didn't want to open her eyes to find out. Finally she lifted one eyelid.

"'Bout time you woke up." Tessa spread the curtains wide, and sunlight spilled into the room. "You'd better hurry up and get dressed. We have work to do. I've got everything planned."

Charlotte rolled onto her back and moaned. Whenever Tessa planned something, there was bound to be trouble. "What's going on?"

"Aunt Sam wants to come downstairs and sit in the garden or even the parlor, but that awful Nurse Pierce won't let her." She placed her hands on the footboard and leaned over it. "However, Nurse Pierce is going to visit her family this morning, so we're going to spring Aunt Sam from her bedroom prison."

Tossing back the covers, Charlotte sat up and swung her legs out of the bed. "If Nurse Pierce doesn't think Aunt Sam is ready for the stairs, then maybe she isn't."

Tessa rolled her eyes and propped her tiny hands on her hips. "Think about it. As long as Aunt Sam is kept in that room, she needs a nurse to care for her. I tell you, this is all part of that woman's plan to keep her job. Can you think of a better job than caring for a not terribly sick woman who lives in a house like this? Besides, what harm could there be in Aunt Sam coming down the stairs?"

Charlotte slid her feet into slippers and tossed on a wrapper. "Go. Let me get dressed and have some coffee. Then maybe—and I mean maybe—I'll consider your covert operation."

Half an hour later, Charlotte met Tessa upstairs. She found Aunt Sam, dressed in a lavender morning dress, sitting in a comfortable armchair.

"Lottie, come on in." Tessa motioned her close. "See? Aunt Sam is ready to go. She even wore a dress in case of callers."

"Aunt Sam, was this your idea or Tessa's?"

The older woman squeezed Tessa's hand. "I believe we worked it out together. I am quite tired of staring at these four walls, and when Tessa began telling me about the lilacs and tulips blooming in the garden, I decided it was time for a change." She frowned. "And before you start saying we should wait to speak with Dr. Brooks, may I remind you I've been up here for more than two weeks now."

Charlotte looked from Tessa to Aunt Sam. If something happened to Aunt Sam, she'd never forgive herself, but two weeks was a long time. And if Aunt Sam wanted to do something, she'd find a way with or without their help.

She sighed. "Oh, all right, but on one condition—you have to let Tessa and me help you."

"If you must." Aunt Sam moved forward in her chair. "Let's get moving, ladies."

With Tessa on one side and Charlotte on the other, they walked beside Aunt Sam to the stairs. Aunt Sam's left foot still dragged a bit, but nothing like it had even a week ago.

Aunt Sam stopped. "I think you'd better let me hold on to the banister."

"Oh yes. That makes sense." Tessa released her.

"Tessa, you go down right in front of us and be ready to help if we need it." Charlotte gripped Aunt Sam's arm. "Easy, now. Nice and slow."

Aunt Sam lowered her bad leg first. Once it was firmly planted, she stepped down. Charlotte bore as much of the weight as she could. Painfully slow, together they made it halfway down before Charlotte noticed a sheen on Aunt Sam's forehead.

"Are you all right? Do you need to rest?"

"Resting isn't actually a possibility at this point, dear." Aunt Sam drew in a deep breath. "Sometimes you have to keep moving once you're committed."

When there were only five steps left, Charlotte sent Tessa for the butler, all the while assuring Aunt Sam it was only a precaution. "You're almost there."

Aunt Sam leaned more heavily on Charlotte but said nothing. If it was this hard for her to get down the staircase, how would they ever get her back up?

Someone clacked the brass knocker on the front door. Callers? Possibly. Word had gotten out about Aunt Sam's illness and that she was feeling much better.

Another step.

Three to go.

Footsteps in the foyer. Good. Tessa had found Geoffrey.

Nurse Pierce's voice bounced off the walls of the foyer. "Miss Gregory, what do you think you're doing?"

27

Charlotte glanced up to see Nurse Pierce standing in the foyer with a wheelchair in hand. Oh, how Aunt Sam loathed the idea of using such a contraption.

As if the appearance of the wheelchair spurred her forward, Aunt Sam made the last three steps with aplomb. "I decided it was time to venture beyond my bedroom. Charlotte and Tessa were kind enough to help."

Nurse Pierce pushed the wheelchair into the room. "Please sit down before you fall."

Aunt Sam's eyebrows shot upward. "In that?"

"Many apoplexy patients require one, Mrs. Phillips. You'll find it much easier to get around in while you're recovering. I stopped by the hospital to borrow it. I hoped it would be a welcome surprise."

"You may return it." She patted Charlotte's arm. "Shall we retire to the parlor?"

Charlotte did as she was asked with Nurse Pierce trailing behind. "Miss Gregory, Dr. Brooks will not like this."

Of that, Charlotte had no doubt. She didn't like it herself. But what had Aunt Sam said? "Sometimes you have to keep moving once you're committed." She guessed this was one of those times, and hopefully she could make Joel understand.

Anger churned inside Joel like a festering wound. Ever since Nurse Pierce had telephoned him to tell him what Charlotte had done, he'd been livid. Did Charlotte honestly think she knew better than he did?

This was not the way he wanted to speak to Charlotte when he first saw her again. He rather hoped he could ask her to accompany him out for a drive, but he should have known better. She couldn't go more than a couple of days without causing some pot to boil over.

He marched up the walkway to Mrs. Phillips's home and banged the brass knocker with far more strength than necessary.

The door swung open, bringing him face-to-face with Tessa. She stepped aside to let him enter.

"Where's your sister?" He pushed past the youngest Gregory sister.

"It wasn't her idea. It was mine."

"Yours?" Without slowing his pace, he headed directly for the drawing room. Maybe it wasn't Charlotte's idea, but she should have known better. Tessa practically lived in a fantasy world.

Tessa stepped in front of him and put a hand on his chest. "Stop! I said this wasn't Charlotte's fault."

Charlotte stepped into the foyer and put her hand on her sister's shoulder. "Tessa, thank you, but you may go on to the theater now. I need to speak to Dr. Brooks alone."

"Don't be mean to her, understand?" Tessa poked his chest with her finger, gave him a final glare, then departed.

"Well?" He crossed his arms over his chest and stared down at Charlotte.

"I admit allowing Aunt Sam to attempt the stairs was a bit premature."

"A bit? What do you know about whether she should be trying that?" His mica-hard voice made her wince, but he pressed on. "Are you a doctor? Are you a nurse?" He didn't wait for an answer. "What could possibly possess you to do this?"

She looked at him stonily. "Aunt Sam was determined, and

frankly, if anyone is to blame, it's Nurse Pierce. She's the one who kept insisting Aunt Sam stay in that bedroom."

"Because I issued the order for her not to try the stairs!"

"Then I guess you're to blame." She lifted her chin. "She did make it down, you know."

"What would you have done if she had collapsed? You couldn't have possibly handled her weight, and then you both would have fallen." He needed to calm down, but every time he tried, he thought of something else he needed to say. He rubbed the back of his neck, his heart pounding. "Not letting her attempt the stairs was for her safety and the safety of anyone who was helping her. Can't you understand that?"

"I didn't think—"

"That's certainly obvious."

"Joel Brooks, I won't stand here and be bullied." She glared at him. "I did not make the decision to help Aunt Sam lightly. I realize now that I may have acted prematurely and I may have put myself and Aunt Sam in danger. I would have never forgiven myself if she'd fallen and been hurt." Her eyes filled with tears and her lip trembled. "So you can stop your lecture, because you aren't saying anything I haven't already told myself a hundred times today."

His heart sank. He'd been a heel and made her cry. "Where is she now?"

"In the parlor."

"May I go in and see her?" He softened his tone.

"You don't need my permission—although apparently I needed yours." She stood rigid, her shoulders pulled back.

Tears or not, she could still fight. He admired her passion more than he could say, even when it was misguided. "Will you join me?"

"I'd rather not."

"Very well." He left her standing alone in the foyer but could feel the heat of her glare as he walked away.

She fascinated and infuriated him like no one else ever had. He should apologize for being so harsh, but the words wouldn't come. Anger still had hold of his tongue—but he feared Charlotte Gregory might have hold of his heart.

Charlotte picked up the section of dough farthest from her and folded it toward her body before giving it a solid push. Kneading bread cured anger like nothing else. Given how she felt right now, she might have to make a dozen loaves before the day was out.

After giving the dough a quarter of a turn, she repeated the process, putting all of her weight behind the push. Sure, she had made a slight error in judgment, but Joel had blown it out of proportion. He'd made it sound like she'd acted foolishly and without thought, but she had weighed the dangers in taking Aunt Sam down the stairs before making her decision.

She thrust her hand forward into the spongy dough. Maybe she'd let Tessa and Aunt Sam persuade her in some ways, but she honestly believed this was the right thing to do. How stir-crazy could they let her aunt become? Joel Brooks might be content to live in a static world, but Aunt Sam certainly was not.

Perspiration beaded on her forehead, so she swiped her brow with the back of her hand. And even if her judgment was in error, he didn't need to speak to her so harshly. What had happened to the kind man she'd been with at the lake?

Prodding the dough into the shape of a ball, she placed it in a greased bowl, smooth side up, and covered it with a damp kitchen towel. She set it on the back of the stove to rise. Once it did, she'd punch it down—like she was doing with her hopes of a relationship with Joel Brooks.

For all his huffing, Joel had to admit Mrs. Phillips seemed rather exuberant today. Her color was excellent and she seemed to have more vigor. He asked her to walk across the room and was impressed by the improvement in her gait since last week. Truth be told, he may have freed her for the staircase had she not already attempted it.

Mrs. Phillips returned to her seat, requested that Nurse Pierce ask Charlotte to join them at her earliest convenience, and then freed the nurse to enjoy a walk in the garden. Once the nurse had departed, she turned toward Joel. "I heard you and Charlotte speaking in the foyer."

"It was a hard day at the hospital. Some pieces of equipment have broken lately, and I can't seem to find the funds to purchase replacements." He tucked his stethoscope into his bag. "I apologize. I fear I may have overreacted a little."

"Perhaps, but I should not have put Tessa and Charlotte in that position." She patted his arm. "But that is not what I want to speak with you about right now. Charlotte said you attended one of her cooking lectures at Lake Minnetonka. What did you think?"

"She did an excellent job. I was quite impressed."

"She's very knowledgeable, yes?"

"Yes, ma'am. I learned a great deal."

"So, are you ready to consider her ideas about improving the hospital's food services? I believe she has a great deal to offer the hospital."

He sighed. "I do too, but I simply don't have the funds to change anything. As I said, there's hardly enough money for the supplies and equipment we need to have, let alone any luxuries."

Aunt Sam took a sip from her teacup. "I've had a great deal of time to think lately, and I believe I have the solution to the lack of funds needed for this experiment."

"Experiment?"

"Well, you are a man of science, aren't you?" She glanced at the doorway. "Charlotte, do come in and have a seat. I have a proposition for you and Dr. Brooks."

Charlotte glanced at Joel. Her gaze fell to the spot beside him on the davenport, but she quickly selected the chair farthest from him.

"During my convalescence, I've seen firsthand what a difference proper food can make in one's recovery. I've come up with a wonderful idea I believe will allow Charlotte to help the hospital's food services and will also address your budget concerns, Dr. Brooks."

Joel sat up straighter. Mrs. Phillips was a wealthy woman, but even she couldn't financially support something of this magnitude.

"Aunt Sam, I won't let you pay for this. It's too much."

The older woman smiled. "Yes, dear, it would be too much for me alone. However, if you will only listen to my plan, I think you will see it is quite manageable."

Joel glanced at Charlotte. "Go on. We're listening."

"Never before have I lent my name to a specific charity function, but I propose we hold the first Phillips Charity Ball." She laughed. "Of course, with my name attached, no one in the upper society should dare miss it. I'll start things off with a generous donation. The others, not to be outdone, will undoubtedly contribute as well."

"But you're not up to planning a charity ball, Mrs. Phillips."

"No, I'm not." Her eyes crinkled. "However, you and Charlotte are. If the two of you can stop squabbling with one another long enough to plan this event, I shall provide the funds to get it going."

He glanced at Charlotte again. She had her knuckle pressed against her lips. Was she considering this crazy idea?

28

A charity ball? Charlotte stared at her aunt in disbelief. What made her think Charlotte could plan a ball—especially with Joel Brooks?

Aunt Sam set down her teacup. "I believe a successful charity ball should not only yield sufficient funds for a change in the hospital's nutritional services, but would also pay for those pieces of medical equipment you mentioned you needed."

Joel stood and walked to the mantel. "I don't have any experience in planning an event, let alone a ball."

"And Aunt Sam, you know that I don't either," Charlotte said.

"You don't?" Joel's voice raised a notch.

"Why would I?"

"Well, I assumed if you lived here, then you grew up attending functions like this."

"I grew up on an Iowa farm." She stared at him blankly as pieces began falling together in her mind. "Aunt Sam is Lincoln's aunt by blood. Not mine. She is letting Tessa and me stay here out of the goodness of her heart. You didn't know that?"

He shook his head. "I assumed you were Mrs. Phillips's niece."

"And she is in every way that matters to me." Aunt Sam squeezed her hand. "I always wanted to have some girls to spoil, and thank goodness Lincoln had the sense to find me some. Now, back to the subject of the ball. First, I think we need to set a date."

"Wait a minute." Joel held up his hand. "If neither of us knows anything about charity balls, then how could we possibly put one together?"

Like a patient schoolteacher, Aunt Sam folded her hands in her lap. "You are both intelligent and resourceful. I'm sure you can manage. Of course, I will advise you as necessary. Now, about the date."

Didn't Aunt Sam see how unwise this idea was? Charlotte rubbed her temple. "I wouldn't know where to start."

"I do." Aunt Sam tapped her finger against her open palm. "First, we need to set a date."

Charlotte locked her gaze with Joel's. He tilted his head to the side and shrugged.

Could they do this? An hour ago, she'd have chopped Joel into little pieces with her meat cleaver, given the opportunity. Now she was considering working side by side with him to plan an event well beyond the abilities of either of them.

Of late, she'd prayed so much about knowing when to wait on the Lord for an answer and when to act. This seemed like one of those defining moments. *Lord, what would you have me do?*

Pressing a hand to her churning stomach, she bit her lip. Joel nodded in silent agreement, or so she hoped. "Aunt Sam, what do you think about the second Saturday of July?"

Shutting the door softly, as Miss Walker had instructed her to do, Tessa slipped into the theater's office a few minutes late.

Miss Walker looked at the wall clock. "Promptness is a virtue, Miss Gregory. In the future, please try harder to be on time."

"Yes, ma'am." Tessa sighed inwardly. Did this rigid woman have any idea how much she'd rather be somewhere else this morning?

"I have a surprise for you today." Miss Walker held out a cash box. "Though I have my doubts, Mr. Jurgenson believes you're ready to enter the cash receipts from the Friday and Saturday night performances."

Oh, goody. Tessa took the cash box and forced her lips to curl upward.

"You may work in Mr. Jurgenson's office, as he does not like the account ledgers removed from his desk." Miss Walker returned to her seat. "This is quite an honor, but of course I'll want to check your work, so please let me know when you are finished."

Tessa rolled her eyes after Miss Walker returned to her typing and trudged to Mr. Jurgenson's office. She sat down at his desk, located the ledger, and began to count the bills inside the cash box. Was there anything less entertaining than this?

Perhaps if she imagined she was a queen's treasurer in charge of the castle's gold, the job would seem less tedious. She lost count as her mind wandered to court jesters and beautiful dresses.

She flipped open the ledger and located the column where the receipts were to be listed. Thank goodness she'd already taken bookkeeping in school. The numbers Miss Walker had listed from previous entries lined up in neat rows in her perfect script. Even if Tessa used her best penmanship, the ledger would be marred forever when she wrote down a single entry.

Glancing at the top of the desk, she had an idea. If she used pencil, then Miss Walker could more easily correct her figures if need be.

She counted the bills into piles, added the figures, and jotted down the ticket sales total for Friday night. Studying previous weekends, she noticed the figures were lower. Probably because it was almost time for a new show. Would the receipts from *Peter Pan*'s premiere next weekend do better?

What did the theater do with the money it made? She couldn't resist flipping to the other half of the ledger. Here she recognized Mr. Jurgenson's writing, heavier and more angular. She ran her finger down the row and read the list to which the theater manager paid out money: the gas and light company, the performance company, salaries, supplies, and repairs. Then, in a column all his own, a Mr. K. O. was listed. He received weekly sums with the amounts varying little.

She tapped the pencil against her chin. That was odd. She'd never met a Mr. K. O., and why was he referred to with initials rather than a name like everyone else?

Perhaps Mr. Jurgenson committed murder and this Mr. K. O. was extorting money from him in exchange for his silence. Or maybe Mr. Jurgenson had a wife at an insane asylum and money was sent to Mr. K. O. for her care. Or maybe he was paying Mr. K. O. to court Miss Walker.

She giggled to herself. That was the only way Miss Walker would find someone.

Jumping at the sound of Miss Walker's footsteps outside the office, she hurried to turn back to the correct page and then picked up the money from Saturday night.

"Do you have any questions?" Miss Walker asked from the doorway.

Only one, but she couldn't ask it. *Who's Mr. K. O.?*

Questions pummeled Joel's mind as he approached Mrs. Phillips's home in his Model T. If he hadn't had to get back to the hospital right after Mrs. Phillips had surprised them with her charity ball idea, he might have gotten some answers then. Delivering a baby had kept him from returning that evening, so another day had passed since Mrs. Phillips had presented her idea, and there'd been no opportunity to speak with Charlotte about the plans either.

Was Charlotte still upset with him? That question loomed above the others. And a close second was the question of whether the two of them could work on something without killing one another. He wasn't sure how to ask either of those.

He parked the motorcar and started up the walk. After patting his jacket pocket for the list he'd made last night, he rapped the brass knocker. The butler greeted him and directed him to the kitchen, where he found Charlotte seated at a table with papers strewn haphazardly around her. How could anyone work in this clutter?

She looked up as he entered. "What have we gotten ourselves into?"

"Hey, you're the one who told her yes."

"But I didn't hear you correcting me." She pushed a paper in his direction. "Sit down and we'll get started."

He pulled out a chair across from her and examined the sheet. She'd written a cursory to-do list in eloquent, flowing handwriting.

Charlotte went to the stove, poured a cup of coffee, and brought it to him at the table. "Have you had dinner?"

He took the warm cup in his hand. "I'll make a sandwich when I get home."

"I'll make you something here." She didn't wait for him to answer but instead took a small round skillet off a hook on the wall. "What do you like in your omelet? Cheese? Ham? Peppers?"

"Really, Charlotte, you don't need to bother."

"It's no bother." She dropped a pat of butter in the skillet and turned toward him, spoon in hand. "You'd better tell me what you want in this, or I might get creative."

"Ham and cheese."

Once she'd gathered the ingredients from the icebox, she cracked three eggs into a bowl and whipped them with a fork.

He found himself spellbound by the way she moved around the kitchen. She cut, mixed, and poured with a surgeon's precision—and she made it all look so easy. He'd always been drawn to a woman's hands, and Charlotte's long, tapered fingers danced as she worked.

Pulling his gaze away from her, he went back to the notes. He tried to concentrate, but the scattered papers on the table begged to be straightened. While Charlotte finished making his omelet, surely he could help her out here on the table. It took him only a few seconds to make a neat stack. He held it vertically and tapped the stack on its end to line up the sheets.

Charlotte set a plate down in front of him with a clatter. "What do you think you're doing?"

"Helping you organize these."

"They were organized—my way." She scowled at him and sat down. "I knew exactly where everything was."

"Well, let me put it all back." He laid the pile on the table and scattered the contents with his hand. "There. Everything is back where it was."

"Joel Brooks! I can't believe you did that. You're supposed to be logical—not full of surprises."

He grinned at her. "I like order, but that doesn't mean I won't surprise you."

"For the record, I like my surprises in the form of chocolate." She began sorting the papers into jumbled piles. "Eat up. We have a lot of work to do."

He stilled her hand with his own. "Will you pray with me?"

She blinked and looked down at his hand on hers, then nodded. "That's an excellent idea. I think we're going to need a lot of prayer."

"Of course we need flowers." Charlotte stared at Joel sitting across from her at the kitchen table. She couldn't believe he would even suggest flowers weren't a requirement. "What kind of ball would it be without floral arrangements?"

"All I'm saying is floral arrangements might be an area where we could cut costs." He rubbed the back of his neck. "Mrs. Phillips gave us a set amount to work with, and I want to make sure we stay within our budget."

She jammed her fists onto her hips. "We'll have to cut somewhere else, because flowers are nonnegotiable."

Joel sighed and picked up a sheet of paper. "Well, what about all this food? Is there anything you could cut from the menu?"

Charlotte yanked the list from his hands, frowned, then tossed the paper back. "I guess we could eliminate the olives."

"The olives?" Laughter shook Joel's chest. He pushed back from the table and stood. "We need a break. Does Mrs. Phillips have a billiards room?"

"Yes, but you want to play billiards now? Right in the middle of our work session?"

He pulled Charlotte to her feet. "I do and so do you. Come on. It'll be a nice diversion."

"Joel, I don't know how to play billiards."

"I'll teach you." He placed his hand on her back and propelled her from the room. "Lead the way."

The billiards room was in the back of the house. Since it was Aunt Sam's husband who'd played billiards, the room was kept closed and unheated. However, Aunt Sam kept it dusted for the occasional times Lincoln decided to use it when he was over.

Charlotte opened the large double doors and a gust of cool, stale air struck her. She stepped inside and eyed the billiards table in the center of the room, daring her to come closer. "It's chilly in here."

"I'll start a fire." Joel knelt before the marble fireplace and soon had a small blaze glowing. "Ready to play?"

She stood before the fireplace, rubbing her arms. "It might be better if I simply watch you."

"Hey, if I have to plan a charity ball, you can learn to play billiards." He passed her a cue stick before gathering up all the colored and striped balls inside a wooden triangle. He put the black eight ball in the center. "The white ball is the cue ball. You have to strike that ball and make it hit the other ones."

"I have watched the game before." Her voice held a tinge of sarcasm.

"Good." He removed the triangle. "Okay, you can break them."

"What?" The image of breaking eggs popped into her mind, but she was certain he didn't intend for her to crack the balls in that manner.

He motioned her to the end of the table. "Come stand down here and I'll show you." Charlotte joined him and he moved beside her. "First you have to align your body with the shot. Now take the cue stick in your left hand like this." He demonstrated the hold on his own cue with his thumbs pointed downward. "And then you need to, well, bend at the hips."

She leaned over and put her left hand on the table like she'd observed others doing. "Is this right?"

"Sort of." He wrapped his arms around her and placed his hands on top of hers.

She sucked in her breath as a delightful warmth spread through her body. If only he were holding her for a different reason. But she mustn't let herself give in to those feelings. Joel was not the kind of man she needed—not after George.

His mouth was so close to her cheek she could feel his breath. "Make a bridge with your left hand like this." He manipulated her fingers into place, then squeezed her right hand on the cue stick with his own. "Now, we're going to give it a firm strike. Ready? One, two, three."

Together they hit the cue ball. It struck the colored balls and scattered them.

"Look at that." Joel stepped away from her. "My turn. Red ball in the corner pocket." He pointed to the ball and then the pocket with his cue stick. The ball easily fell into the pocket with a thunk. Moving around the table, he pointed to a yellow ball. "The number one ball in the side pocket."

"Wait a minute. Don't I get a turn?"

"As soon as I miss."

"That hardly seems fair."

"Life is not always fair, Charlotte." He sank another ball, then missed. "You're up."

"Show-off."

"Me?" He pressed a hand to his chest. "You get the striped balls. Which one do you want?"

"I have no idea. Let's go for that blue one." She positioned herself on the side of the table nearest the striped number ten ball.

"Where are you going to put it?"

"Probably through the window."

Chuckling, he stepped behind her again and slid his arms around her. "How do you think we should do this?"

With his chest pressed against her back, she could scarcely breathe, let alone think. "I'm not sure."

"This one will require a gentle touch. Easy."

His breath against her ear sent chills coursing through her. Did he feel her tremor? She let him pull her hand back with his and lead her in tapping the white ball. It hit the striped ball, which landed perfectly in the side pocket.

Nurse Pierce cleared her throat from the doorway. "Well, aren't you two cozy?"

Charlotte startled, but Joel didn't move from his position. Her face grew warm under the nurse's intense gaze.

"Do you need something, Nurse Pierce?" Joel finally stepped back but kept himself between Charlotte and the nurse.

"I heard noise down here and didn't want it to interrupt Mrs. Phillips's rest, Doctor." She spoke in a syrupy-sweet tone that turned Charlotte's stomach.

Charlotte tapped the end of her cue stick against the floor. "But her room is on the other side of the house."

"Nevertheless, your aunt stirred." Her smile boarded on a smirk. "Sound travels, Miss Gregory."

"She has a point, Charlotte. We don't want to wake Tessa or your aunt." Joel took her cue stick and returned it to the stand.

Charlotte fought the pinprick of disappointment. He was right, of course, but she hadn't wanted the game to end.

Nurse Pierce seized the opportunity to fire a glare in Charlotte's direction while Joel's back was turned. But why? Besides the menu situation, she'd done nothing to Nurse Pierce. And recently she'd even thought they'd made a little headway with some civil discussions. Did this woman have her starched white cap set for Dr. Brooks?

"Let's leave the balls in place. We'll pick up our game later." He nodded toward the nurse. "Thank you. That will be all."

"Yes, Doctor." She paused. "I know there are a lot of patients counting on you tomorrow. I do hope you get some sleep soon."

He nodded. "I will be going home directly. Thank you for your concern."

Concern, my foot! Charlotte had guessed correctly. The nurse was doing whatever she could to keep Charlotte and Joel away from each other. Even though there was nothing between them, the idea was irksome.

Nurse Pierce gave the doctor a brief nod and departed.

Joel banked the fire, then stood. "Nurse Pierce was right. I do have a lot of patients to see tomorrow. I'd better be going."

"I'll walk you out."

They padded down the hallway in silence and stopped in the foyer. She smiled up at him. "I'll take the olives off the list."

"No. Leave them. If you think they're important, then they are. We'll take a fresh look at it all tomorrow." He grabbed his hat from the hook on the hall tree. "If you're out and about, why don't you come by my office around lunch time? We can work on some things while we eat. I'll cook."

"You?"

His lips curled. "Sure. I know all the best places to eat near the hospital."

She laughed. How quickly things could change between the two of them. One minute they were ranting at each other and the next they were laughing together and having fun. She opened the front door. "You'd better go. Patients, remember?"

"Yeah, I guess I should. Good night, Charlotte."

"Good night." She pushed the door shut behind him and watched him walk down the sidewalk to his automobile, broad shoulders held erect and sure.

As he walked away, she recalled how he'd stepped between her and Nurse Pierce. And if she closed her eyes, she could still remember the feel of his arms around her.

Joel might make her crazy sometimes, but with him she always felt safe. Since her father had died, she'd lost the feeling of security. She'd had no one's arms to run to with life's scrapes.

She sighed. Joel would be that kind of man to someone.

But it couldn't be her. Joel liked control, and she couldn't risk letting him control her.

29

With morning rounds complete, Joel headed downstairs to speak once again with Arthur about funds for new equipment. He'd waited nearly a week to allow the superintendent time to speak with Terrence Ruckman about the supposed missing money. Given Dr. Ancker's way of dealing with things, he'd most likely sorted everything out and given Ruckman a well-deserved sermon.

"Morning, Joel." Arthur pointed to an empty chair. "What can I do for you?"

"It's about that equipment I need for my wards. Remember we spoke about it earlier?"

"Ah yes." The superintendent pressed his fingertips together. "A new microscope."

"And a sphygmomanometer. One of the nurses dropped it and shattered the glass. Mercury everywhere."

"I spoke to Mr. Ruckman. He says you've used up your allotted supply of funds already."

Joel narrowed his eyes. "Listen, Arthur, something is going on here. You told me I was supposed to get some of the money donated by Mrs. Ostberg's women's club, but when I went to claim it for the microscope, Terrence said it was no longer there. I understand unexpected expenses can come up in a hospital, but I want to know where that money went if it didn't go to my patients."

Arthur leaned forward. "Are you accusing Mr. Ruckman of foul play?"

"I don't know." Joel raked his hand through his hair. "I don't like the man, but that doesn't mean he's doing anything crooked."

"He says you're too inexperienced to handle your wards."

"Is that what you think?"

"If I thought that, you wouldn't have the position you do, even temporarily." He drew in a deep breath. "Be careful of him, Joel. He's friends with several board members. Hospital politics, I'm afraid, are the ugly side of medicine, and you need those votes if you want to make your position permanent."

"Am I the only one complaining?"

"Frankly, yes. At least right now." Arthur stood up. "But that doesn't mean something isn't awry. You've always had an uncanny sixth sense, and I've always encouraged you to trust that." He laid his hand on Joel's shoulder. "You're on a good career path right now, and I don't want to see you mess that up because of a little microscope."

Joel released a long breath. "Don't worry. I'll step carefully."

Charlotte glanced around Joel's office. Everything was in perfect order. What would Joel do if she moved something? Would he notice?

She shifted the water pitcher on his desk over an inch and snickered. Tapping her lip with her finger, she looked for other items to move. She tipped his pencils upside down in the holder so all the points faced the ceiling. Such a small thing, but she imagined he'd see it.

What else could she do? Ah, his letter opener faced to the right on his desk. She picked it up.

The door opened and she jumped.

"Joel, what time do you—" A nurse stopped in the open doorway. "Oh, hello. I didn't realize Joel wasn't in. I'm Mattie Brooks, Joel's sister. And you are . . . ?"

"Charlotte Gregory."

Mattie eyed the letter opener in Charlotte's hand. Her gaze traveled to the pencils. "And you were moving my brother's things around, weren't you?"

Charlotte reached for the pencils. "I can put them back."

"Don't you dare." Mattie giggled and closed the door. "This is one of my favorite things to do. Let me show you what really bugs him." She moved to his bookcase. "See how they are all in alphabetical order? I like to move one or two out of place and see how long it takes him to notice." She grabbed a volume and switched it with another.

"How long does it take?"

"Usually less than a minute." She turned to her. "Nice work with the water pitcher too."

Charlotte studied the trophies on top of the bookcase. "Did he win all of these rowing?"

"Yes, he loves it. Go ahead. I know you want to move one."

"I do." She laughed. "But how did you know?"

"Because I want to do it every time I get a chance."

Charlotte rotated one of the trophies ninety degrees. "There."

"Miss Gregory, you're a gem." Mattie sat down in one of the chairs.

"Please call me Charlotte." She sat down in the chair beside her. "Will all this make him angry?"

"Angry? Heavens, no. He knows it's weird to act like this. He'll give us a mock glare and start setting things to rights."

When Mattie's lips curved upward, Charlotte saw that she shared Joel's same stunning smile. But unlike Joel, Mattie seemed much less controlling.

"How long has Joel been obsessed with order?"

"He's always been a little bit this way. Aren't we all? But he started becoming obsessed with *his things* in college. It seemed like the harder he worked in his classes, the more order he needed other places."

"Interesting. So is he like this anywhere else?"

"Well, a hospital is a pretty orderly place, but no, he doesn't expect others to keep their things in perfect order. He might straighten a crooked picture every now and then, but nothing else." She pressed a finger to her lips. "I think I hear him coming. Thirty seconds from door to pencils."

Mattie turned and plastered on an innocent look. As Joel entered, Charlotte did likewise.

"Hello, ladies." He crossed the room to his desk and came to a halt. Reaching for the pencils, he scrunched his brow in Mattie's direction, then flipped them over and reinserted them. "What have you been teaching Charlotte?"

"Actually, I caught her doing that." Mattie stood and smoothed her white apron. "Of course, I applauded her efforts."

He rolled his eyes and turned the letter opener the other direction. "Now I'm going to have to deal with two of you messing with my things?"

Mattie laid her hand on the doorknob. "Yes, dear brother. You are one lucky man."

He chuckled as Mattie left, then turned to Charlotte. "She's the only one who's ever done that—until now. Did you enjoy yourself?"

She grinned. "Immensely."

"I'd better get you out of here before you do any more damage." He moved the water pitcher back to its original spot, then came around the desk. He stopped at the bookcase and moaned. "Give me a minute, will you? Mattie loves to mess with this."

Charlotte bit back a chuckle as he righted the trophy and replaced the books. Should she tell him she'd been the one to twist the trophy? No, he'd taken the teasing in stride, which genuinely impressed her.

For a man who liked everything in order, Joel Brooks was also full of surprises.

Greeted by the tantalizing scents of today's special of seared steak, Joel held the door to his favorite café for Charlotte. It might not be up to her standards, but they made a great T-bone. She'd been unusually quiet on their walk to the restaurant. With her chin tucked and her lips tight, this charity ball clearly had her concerned.

After they both ordered food from the waitress, Joel pointed to the tablet Charlotte carried. "Well, tell me what's got you so worried."

"I'm not worried."

"Charlotte, you can always be honest with me." He raised his eyebrows. "So, how bad is it?"

Charlotte set the tablet on the table. "I think we are in way over our heads. I met with Aunt Sam this morning and she went over the details. Do you know how many details go into a ball?"

"Honestly? No. I can name all the bones, organs, and nerves of the body, but I can't tell you a thing about balls."

"Besides the theme, decorations, orchestra, and food"—she pointed to each item on her sheet as she spoke—"we need a reception committee of men to greet the guests, with badges of distinction."

"Naturally," he teased.

She glared at him. "And we'll need a candy booth, a lemonade booth, and a fancywork booth."

"Fancywork?"

"Since this is a fund-raiser, Aunt Sam said women are often willing to donate tatted doilies and embroidered handkerchiefs and dresser scarves they've made." She pointed to the next item on her list. "We'll need to organize a grand march and decide who's to lead it. That person is usually the chairman of the floor, with the lady he's escorting."

"And what does the chairman of the floor do?"

"Select the music, I think." She looked up at him. "I think you should do the honor on this one."

"Me?" He leaned back in his chair. "Do you have any acquaintances with a background in music who could help me pick the songs?"

She started to say something and stopped. That was odd. Why did she look guilty?

"We'll think of someone." She forced a smile. "And then there are the dance cards that need to be designed and the presentation of the debutantes, and—"

"Charlotte, breathe." He covered her hand with his, drawing a circle with his thumb over her soft skin. "We can do this."

"There's so much to do." She seemed to notice his hand on hers and froze.

"But you're not alone. I'll help, and I'm sure your sisters will too." He withdrew his hand. "And I bet you've recruited my sister and you didn't even realize it."

"You think Mattie will help?"

"I doubt if you could stop her. She'll probably round up the other nurses to pitch in too."

The waitress delivered their food. Joel offered grace, then Charlotte placed her napkin in her lap. "Joel, is Mattie your only sibling?"

He nodded, slicing into the thick steak. "I think my mother would have liked more children, but that didn't happen."

"So she put all her hopes and dreams on you."

"More than you realize." He mentally kicked himself. Why did he mumble that? Knowing Charlotte, she'd want more information, and he didn't want to get into his family history here and now.

"What did you say?"

"Never mind." He speared a green bean. "Now, about the ball. Where do you think we should start?"

She paused for a moment as if she were considering whether to pursue his remark or let him off the hook. Finally she nodded and picked up her tablet. "We need to decide on a theme. I have two ideas—a garden scene with butterflies and flowers or a Mother Goose theme. All of the committee members could come as characters from nursery rhymes like Little Bo Peep and Old King Cole."

"Would I be one of those committee members you'd expect to dress up?"

"Absolutely."

"I can't believe I'm going to say this out loud, but in that case"—he rolled his eyes—"I like the butterflies."

Butterflies collided inside Charlotte's stomach every time she was with Joel. After leaving the café, she boarded a streetcar that would take her to Hannah's. She slid into the seat and pressed a hand to her stomach.

It wasn't the way he'd touched her hand, which certainly made her shiver. It was the way he'd looked at her while they stood waiting for the streetcar to arrive. Sometimes it was like he could see inside her emotions like the heroes did in one of Hannah's books. Other times it was as if he were seeing her for the first time. She'd never be able to explain it to anyone, but it was in those seconds the butterflies took flight inside her.

She stared out the window at the passing businesses and reminded herself those were simply feelings. "Feelings," her mother had often said, "can change as fast as Iowa weather. Snow one day and a heat wave the next." And then she'd cautioned Charlotte against making decisions based on feelings alone. "Use the brain God gave you, not just your heart."

If only she could talk to her mother now. Would she be able to explain how Lewis was a much more sensible choice, but every time she was with Joel, her heart pounded an erratic rhythm all its own?

The trolley clacked down the street and passed beneath the Sibley tunnel. When it came to her stop, she stepped onto the curb. Before she got to Hannah's, she needed to put both men out of her thoughts. Her attorney sister was a bloodhound when it came to romantic inclinations, and she wasn't ready for Hannah to put her heart on trial.

That was strange.

Tessa spotted the accounts ledger lying open on Mr. Jurgenson's desk, but she could have sworn the receipt total had been different the other day. Could she have miscounted?

She glanced at the door to see if anyone was coming, then spun the book around for a better look.

That wasn't her handwriting. Someone had erased some of her numbers and changed them. But who? Mr. Jurgenson? Miss Walker? And why?

Picking up the ledger, she studied the handwriting. She'd recognize that neat script anywhere, even with only a few faint numbers.

She flipped to the payouts section, searching for any more references to the mysterious Mr. K. O. Her gaze lit on the last entry and her breath caught. It was for the same amount deducted from the receipts. Coincidence?

Miss Walker stepped into the office. "Miss Gregory, what exactly are you doing?"

30

Tessa jumped. Why hadn't she heard Miss Walker approaching? "I, uh, I was—"

"You were looking at Mr. Jurgenson's books." She crossed the room, grabbed the ledger, and slammed it shut. "What do you have to say for yourself?"

"I'm sorry, Miss Walker."

"You do realize we cannot keep you here under the circumstances. We will not have any theater employees who cannot be trusted." Her brow remained furled as she sat down at the man's desk.

This couldn't be happening. What would Aunt Sam say? What would her sisters say? She could see their disappointed faces already. And what would happen if the director found out?

"Miss Walker, I noticed a discrepancy in the books. My figures had been changed. I need to tell Mr. Jurgenson right away."

"I changed the figures. You simply counted wrong."

"No, I counted correctly, I'm sure of it. I counted twice. Do you know what happened to the money?"

Miss Walker jerked her gaze upward, eyes wide.

Uh-oh. The look on Miss Walker's face frightened her.

Miss Walker tapped the desk with her finger. "If I let you keep this position, will you remain silent?"

"I don't think I can."

The clerk's eyes narrowed. "Yes, I suppose your aunt wouldn't take kindly to this little operation, given she's such a patron of the arts." She leaned forward and laid her folded hands on the desk. "However, I must admit I didn't think you'd care about keeping your position in this office when you seemed to have secured a part in the play."

Tessa froze. Perspiration beaded on her upper lip.

"Did you honestly believe you could keep it a secret from me? I know everything that happens inside this theater. I don't think Mr. Jurgenson would appreciate knowing how you got that part, and I doubt he'd let you keep it."

Lose her part! Tessa's heart plummeted. The opening was just over a week away.

What could she say? Her mind went blank. Only a few lines from Shakespeare's *Julius Caesar* took the stage inside her head. "'There is a tide in the affairs of men, which, taken at the flood, leads on to fortune; omitted, all the voyage of their life is bound in shallows and in miseries.'" She blurted the lines out without thinking.

"I see you grasp my situation well." Miss Walker gave her a wry laugh. "All right, Miss Gregory. We'll exchange silence. I'll say nothing of your part in the play, and you'll keep my occasional dalliances to yourself. Understood?"

Even as Tessa nodded, guilt tugged at her conscience.

"Good. I believe you have a play practice to get to."

Stunned, Tessa left the office and walked down the stairs. The heels of her shoes clicked against the tile. How strange it was that the theater suddenly felt cold and blighted, not the home of fairies and boys who could fly.

What was Miss Walker really up to? Did the mysterious Mr. K. O. have anything to do with it, or was the matching sum simply a coincidence? Like a flame to kindling, her curiosity about what was going on flared. She'd get to the bottom of this. She simply had to.

Fresh excitement bubbled inside her. Maybe instead of becoming an actress, she should become a Pinkerton agent.

Charlotte needed to hurry or she wouldn't be ready before Joel arrived. She'd stayed too long at Hannah's, and now she was running behind.

She threw on a soft lemon-colored tailored suit and jabbed pins into her loose curls. She smoothed her hands down the suit's slender silhouette and then quickly added an ostrich-plumed hat with a dark green satin bow before heading downstairs to meet him.

At lunch, he'd asked if she'd like to meet the rest of his family. When she'd pressed for more details, he explained they'd not be visiting his real family, but he would not elaborate. He must have sensed her reservations because he added that Mattie would be present.

She'd accepted the invitation partly out of curiosity, partly out of wanting to speak with Mattie, and partly because she found herself enjoying her time with Joel more and more.

"Miss Charlotte," one of the maids called from the door. "You have a gentleman caller."

Charlotte hopped around as she tried to get her second shoe on. "Please show him to the parlor and tell him I'll be right down."

A few minutes later, she walked into the parlor and came to a halt. "Lewis."

He stood. "It's good to see you, Charlotte. You're looking lovely as always." He glanced at her wrap. "In fact, you look as if you're ready to go out for the evening. Am I interrupting something?"

With her heart still torn, she didn't want to tell Lewis about Joel, and vice versa. Still, she couldn't lie.

She smiled and indicated he should sit down. She sat in the chair beside him. "I have a meeting with a friend soon, but we can talk for a few minutes. What brings you here?"

"I spoke to Molly and learned you were still at the lake the night of the tornado, and I wanted to see how you were."

"You came all the way from Stillwater to check on me?"

"I was hoping to persuade you to join me for a ride in my dad's motorcar. I wanted to surprise you." He looked down at his shoes. "I should have telephoned, but don't look so fretful. I have friends here in the city I can visit. Tell me, what happened at the lake? Are you truly all right?"

"It was scary, but I'm fine. Was there any damage at your friend's estate?"

Lewis explained how they'd taken shelter in a root cellar and were delighted to find only tree limbs down when they emerged. "If I had known you were still at the lake, I would have come and found you. I'm sorry you went through that alone."

"I was with a friend." She patted his arm. "But thank you for your thoughtfulness."

"I'd better go." He stood. "I'll see you next week in Red Wing."

"Yes. I think it will be a great trip." Charlotte tried to glance at the front window. Was Joel here yet? How would she explain Lewis's presence if he was?

She walked with Lewis to the front door. "Thank you for coming."

As he departed, she spotted Joel's Model T parked at the curb, but he wasn't inside the car or walking up to the house. Where was he? Had he decided to speak to a neighbor?

Nurse Pierce descended the stairs about the same time she closed the front door behind Lewis.

"Have you seen Dr. Brooks?" Charlotte asked.

"I thought that was him. That's why I came down."

"That was my friend Lewis. He's the singer who travels with Molly and me." She smiled. "Tessa is in the garden. Perhaps she's seen him, or maybe a neighbor called him over."

Charlotte slipped through the back door and spotted Tessa kneeling in front of a cluster of pansies, wearing a broad-brimmed straw hat with a wide yellow ribbon.

"Tessa, have you seen Joel?"

Her sister glanced up and smiled.

"Look behind you."

She recognized the familiar deep voice and whirled around. "Joel. What are you doing out here?"

He handed her a forget-me-not. "I heard someone in the garden after I parked. I found Tessa out here and thought maybe I should brush up on my flowers and butterflies before the ball."

"Ball?" Tessa stood up and wiped her dirty gloves together. Clumps of dirt fell to the ground. "Have I missed something?"

Charlotte filled her in.

"Will I get to go? I'll need a new dress. When can we go shopping? And speaking of shopping, Aunt Sam wants to know what you're wearing to the play next Friday. It is a premiere, after all."

Joel leaned against a garden urn and met her gaze. "Yes, Charlotte, what are you wearing?"

Something in his eyes made her breath hitch. "I-I don't know yet."

He grinned. "I know what I'm wearing."

"You're going?" Her voice squeaked when she spoke.

"I am. With you—and the rest of your family. Your aunt invited me. She said she wants her doctor close by and her nurse as far away as possible." He straightened. "Shall we leave Tessa to her flowers?"

They walked around the outside of the house and down the sidewalk to the Model T.

Joel glanced at her. "You do realize we haven't fought all day."

She giggled. "Ah, but the day isn't over yet."

He opened the door for her and then went around front to crank the engine. Once it was running, they putt-putted down Summit Hill. To her great relief, Joel said nothing about Lewis or the car Lewis had been driving. Perhaps he thought it belonged to a neighbor, or maybe he was simply waiting to see if she explained.

If that were the case, he'd be waiting a long time.

It didn't take long to reach their destination. Along the way, Charlotte hadn't prodded Joel with questions as to their destination. She seemed to have taken his promise to introduce her to his "other" family at face value.

She'd been quiet on the way, but it hadn't been an uncomfortable silence. It was more like the kind of peacefulness between people who don't feel compelled to maintain a steady flow of conversation.

At least that's what he hoped was going on. Maybe he should have asked if everything was all right.

He parked the automobile in front of the orphanage and went around to her side of the motorcar to open the door. As he helped her out, he flashed her an encouraging smile. He couldn't wait. The girls in the orphanage were going to love her. He pulled a package off the floorboard and handed it to her before grabbing his doctor's bag. "You can give them this."

"What is it?"

"I'm not going to tell. It would ruin the surprise for all of you."

As soon as Charlotte entered with him, all activity came to a stop and the children stared wide-eyed at her. She pulled off her gloves, smiled at them, and looked around the tidy but worn dwelling. Little Alice Ann grabbed onto Joel's legs and peeked around.

Charlotte knelt in front of her. "Hello. Aren't you a pretty thing. I'm Charlotte. What's your name?"

Alice Ann didn't say a word.

"Oh, you want to play a guessing game. All right." She placed her finger on her cheek. "Let me see. You must be Polly Puddinghead."

The four-year-old shook her head.

"Mary Mouse? Tillie Tea Leaves?"

Alice smiled at each new name, her blonde curls bobbing as she shook her head.

"One more try, okay?" She waited for Alice to respond. "I'm absolutely, positively sure your name must be Lucky Lucy Lemondrop."

The little girl giggled. "No, I'm Alice Ann."

"I should have known. Now that you've told me, I can see you are indeed an Alice Ann." She held out her hand. "Nice to meet you, Miss Alice Ann. I'm Miss Charlotte. Would you like to help me open this package?"

Offering the girl the brown paper package tied with string, Charlotte smiled. Alice Ann tugged the ends of the string and then helped Charlotte peel away the paper.

Charlotte looked down at the Hershey's chocolate bars in her hand, then beamed at Joel. "You remembered?"

"I believe you said it was your favorite kind of surprise."

The children lined up to be introduced and to get their chocolate bar. Charlotte treated each of them as if they were a little prince or princess.

"And this"—he turned to Mrs. Goodwin, who was cutting up a chicken—"is the queen herself, Mrs. Goodwin. She makes this orphanage a home."

Mrs. Goodwin gave him a sidelong glance. "I'm no queen, but I'm pleased as punch you have a lady friend. Sorry, I'm up to my elbows in chicken or I'd welcome you proper."

"Is that an apron?" Charlotte pointed to a white frock on a peg.

"Yes, miss, it sure is."

Charlotte snagged it and slipped it over her head. "Put me to work, Mrs. Goodwin. In fact, I'd love to treat you and the others to dinner tonight. You could go sit down and let Joel and me make dinner."

Mrs. Goodwin cut through a chicken joint. "I couldn't do that. A fine lady like you cooking in my humble kitchen."

"I'm not a fine lady. I'm a farm girl from Iowa, and Joel, don't you think she deserves a rest?" Charlotte glanced around the bare-bones kitchen. "I can assure you I'm a good cook, so I won't ruin supper."

Joel joined them and laid his hands on Mrs. Goodwin's shoulders. "If anyone deserves a rest, it's you. Let us treat the whole family to something special. Charlotte travels all over Minnesota teaching cooking classes—and she's as stubborn as you."

"Well, in that case, I'll take you up on it. Tommy's been feeling poorly, and I reckon he could use a little attention from me."

"He's sick?" Joel glanced at Charlotte. It would be rude to leave her to go check on Tommy, but if the boy needed medical attention, that should come first before he helped her make supper.

"Go." She picked up a knife and smiled. "I believe I can manage without a doctor present."

"Send Mattie up when she gets here."

"Yes, Doctor." She flashed him a cheeky grin.

Joel couldn't curb the smile on his face as he followed Mrs. Goodwin up to Tommy's room. He knew how much Charlotte could stir things up, but he was only beginning to understand how well she blended love into everything she did.

"Mrs. Goodwin needs a new stove." Charlotte climbed into the Model T and waited for Joel to take his place. With the top down, she could keep speaking as he went to the front to crank the engine. She stood up and placed her hands on the brass edge of the windshield. "With all those children to tend to, a gas stove would save her so much time."

He gave the crank a solid turn and the engine came to life. Coming around to the driver's side, he mounted the running board and stepped inside the motorcar. "I'm sure you're right, but there's barely enough money to feed the kids at the orphanage. I'm afraid there's no money for things like stoves." He put the car in gear and pulled onto the street.

"I can get her one."

He stopped at an intersection. "Charlotte, I didn't bring you here so you can spend your income buying things for the orphanage. I wanted you to meet them. That's all."

"I know, but I have a stove I can't use." She twisted in her seat so she could look at him as he drove. "Remember when I won the cooking contest? The prize was a brand-new Jewel gas range, but since I had nowhere to put it, the gas company said they'd keep it and I could have one anytime I was ready."

"But you won that. You should get to use it in your own home."

"I might not have my own home for years. Mrs. Goodwin and the children need it now." Joy bubbled inside her, and she clasped her hands together against her chest. She could picture Mrs. Goodwin's face as the stove was delivered. "Do you think Mrs. Goodwin will let me come over and show her how to use it?"

He turned onto Summit Avenue. "Slow down a minute, Charlotte. First of all, we need to see if she wants a gas range, and second, we have to find out if the orphanage's finances can handle a gas charge."

"Yes, Mr. Practical. Why can't you be happy I found a solution to her problem?"

"Her problem? What if she doesn't think she has a problem?" He parked the car. "Mrs. Goodwin may be perfectly happy with her coal burner. She may not want your gas stove. Don't you think she should have a say in it?"

"Of course she should, but I know this would help her out if she'll only give it a try."

"The orphanage is fine." He hit the steering wheel with his palm. "Why do you have to stick your nose into things wherever you go?"

Charlotte winced as if she'd picked up a hot skillet with a bare hand, and then a heavy silence invaded the motorcar.

Joel tipped his head back, his chest heaving.

Apparently his opinion of her hadn't changed a bit. He still saw her as a busybody, or at the very least, he thought she was intrusive. Was she? Had she let her excitement over giving Mrs. Goodwin the stove outweigh being sensible about it? Those children had so little. She'd only wanted to do something for all of them.

Tears pricked her eyes. She stepped out of the motorcar and hurried toward the house. She couldn't stay with Joel one minute longer.

31

"Charlotte, wait!" Joel bolted out of the car and raced up the sidewalk. He had to stop her before she went inside the house.

Halting at the bottom of the wraparound porch steps, he saw her place her hand on the doorknob. "Please, don't go in yet. Charlotte, I need to apologize."

She sniffed and slowly faced him. Was she crying?

"You don't need to apologize." Her voice hitched. "You're right. I did rush into this without thinking—again."

"Oh, Charlotte." He took the stairs two at a time and pulled her into his arms. Relief washed over him when she didn't resist. "I didn't mean what I said. You have to believe me. Your generosity tonight deeply touched me." He pulled back enough to see her face and tipped her chin toward him. "As soon as you went into that orphanage today, the place came alive. Every person there loved you. You didn't just serve them dinner. You served them love."

"But I—"

He pressed his finger against her lips. "Let me finish."

His heart raced. He swallowed, attempting to wet his chalk-dry mouth. Could he do this? Now? It didn't make sense and he hadn't planned it, but deep inside he knew he couldn't stop himself.

"Charlotte, when you said you didn't see a need for the gas range in your near future, it was like someone punched me."

"Why?" Her eyes widened and she sucked in her breath. "Oh."

"I was hoping the day would arrive when we might discuss where that stove could end up someday. You know, in a kitchen of *our* own. So I said those things because I was upset, and I'm sorry."

"What are you saying?"

"I'd like to court you."

"Truly?"

"Yes." His lips curled. "Now, may I kiss the cook?"

She gave him the tiniest of nods, but it was enough. He cupped her cheek and lowered his lips to hers. The spicy scent of her perfume and the softness of her lips dared him to deepen the kiss, but he refrained. He was determined to hold on to this moment, so passionate and yet so innocent, and etch it into her memory forever.

Raising her trembling fingers to her lips, Charlotte leaned against the massive oak door in the foyer and closed her eyes. Had Joel really kissed her? Asked to court her? Had he truly been thinking of marriage? Or would she wake any minute from this delicious dream?

"Why do you have such a goofy grin on your face?"

Charlotte opened her eyes to see Tessa staring at her, head cocked at an angle. Hannah stood next to her with a sleeping Ellie in her arms.

A slow smile spread across Hannah's features. "I believe our sister has had a rather enjoyable evening."

Tessa's eyes narrowed. "How enjoyable? Did you go someplace special? Without me?"

"Oh, I don't think it would have been nearly as special if you'd have been there." Hannah giggled. "Right, Charlotte?"

"No, not nearly as special." Her words came out with a dreamy quality.

Tessa crossed her arms over her chest. "What are you two talking about? And why do I always miss out on the good stuff?"

"You're a little young for this discussion." Hannah draped her arm around Tessa's shoulder. "Why don't you let Charlotte and me go into the parlor alone for a while before Lincoln gets here to pick me up?"

"I'm sixteen, almost seventeen. I'm not too young for any discussion. I know about the birds and the bees, after all." She looked at Charlotte, her eyes growing round. "Oh my goodness, Dr. Brooks kissed you, didn't he?"

Charlotte glanced up the staircase and saw Nurse Pierce peek her head around the corner. Oh no. The last thing she wanted was for the nurse to hear about her evening. She pressed her finger to her lips. "Shhh. Let's go in the parlor and talk."

As soon as they'd closed the parlor doors, Tessa held out her hands. "Well? Did he kiss you or what?"

"Yes!" Charlotte squealed.

Within seconds, she was enveloped in sister hugs. Tessa took her hand. "Sit down and tell me all about it. Don't leave out a single detail. And before you say I'm too young, I can assure you that I'm not. Besides, you'll never sleep unless you tell someone, and we're the only ones available."

Charlotte did her best to comply with Tessa's request for details, but some things were private and for her alone to cherish.

All her life she'd been a little invisible. With an outspoken older sister like Hannah and a dramatic younger sister like Tessa, it was easy to be overlooked. Tonight Joel had seen her for who she truly was. He'd seen the good and the bad, and yet he'd taken her into his arms and mentioned a future together.

If she ever got to sleep tonight, her dreams would indeed be spun-sugar sweet.

What a difference one week could make. Joel tossed his white coat on a hook and hurried out of his office. A week ago, he might have stayed late even if he didn't need to, but not now. Since he'd kissed Charlotte two days ago, things had changed both inside of him and for the two of them.

With a bounce in his step, he walked down the hall. Tonight he'd head over to see her after a round of rowing practice with Knute.

Inside the boat club, he spotted Knute speaking to some other club members—a few of whom Joel doubted had been in a boat in years. Knute saw him and said his goodbyes before Joel had to go pull his friend away. One thing was certain about Knute—he had never met a stranger.

They walked down to the boat rack and carried their boat to the water.

"Okay, buddy, what's going on? My friend Joel reserves a grin like that for near-miraculous recoveries. Did Dr. Ancker make your position permanent?"

"I wish." Joel picked up the oars.

"It's her, isn't it? The lady friend you visited at Lake Minnetonka." He clapped Joel on the shoulder. "Well, good for you."

Joel climbed into the boat. "I didn't confirm your suspicions."

"You didn't deny them either." Knute seated himself in the bow. "So I suppose the rumors of you planning some charity ball are true."

"Charlotte's aunt is sponsoring the whole affair. I'm helping Charlotte plan it." They rowed away from the dock out into the river.

Knute chuckled. "Never thought I'd see you planning a dance."

"The hospital needs the funds for equipment. You know that."

Knute set an easy warm-up pace. "Yeah, I do. Need some help?"

"Do you know anything about music or building garden arches?"

"No, but I could set up tables and such." Knute pushed them a little harder. "And I'm good with numbers. I could help with collecting the money that night."

"Thanks. We'll need someone we can trust with that. Someone who will keep Terrence Ruckman away from the funds."

"He's coming?"

"Yeah. He asked me about it yesterday." Joel took a deep breath as sweat began to bead on his forehead. "Let's get moving. I have places to be."

Crystal goblets sparkled on the dining room table. The Haviland china, with its gold-scalloped edges and pink and lavender lilies, marked each place setting. Charlotte glanced at the bouquet of purple irises Tessa had arranged and then looked around the table, where her family and Joel had gathered for the celebration.

With Aunt Sam on his arm, Lincoln entered the dining room and helped her to her chair. She set her blue cut-glass-topped walking stick in the corner and smiled at her family.

Lincoln remained standing. "Before I offer grace, I want to thank Dr. Brooks for his care of my aunt. I'm glad you can be with us to celebrate her recovery. It seems like a long time since we could all dine together, and we are grateful that you used your God-given gifts to tend Aunt Sam."

Under the table, Joel took her hand as Lincoln began the prayer. Lincoln's words brought tears to Charlotte's eyes, reminding her it was only by God's grace that Aunt Sam was among them, with a little help from Aunt Sam's stubbornness.

Guilt jabbed Charlotte hard. Nurse Pierce probably deserved credit for it all too. Besides assisting Aunt Sam with exercises, she'd provided her aunt with added incentive to recover quickly. Understandably, Aunt Sam was growing weary of the woman. Still, they should have invited Nurse Pierce to join their celebration. It was probably too late to set another place.

Seldom did Aunt Sam request a full-course dinner, but tonight was an exception. Her cook, Mrs. Agle, had asked Charlotte for a menu but had insisted she not help in the meal preparations.

Mrs. Agle did not disappoint. Conversation continued round the table as the food was served. The watercress and stilton soup was delicious, the salmon poached to perfection, and the asparagus, roasted and drenched in butter, nearly melted in her mouth.

Joel leaned close. "You're enjoying this, aren't you?"

"Absolutely. Aren't you?"

"I am, but not nearly as much as I'm enjoying watching you."

By the time the lamb and mint sauce was served, talk had moved on to the ball. Charlotte explained the Saint Paul Orchestra had agreed to play, and with Aunt Sam's help, she was able to secure the Saint Paul Hotel's ballroom, which could accommodate up to three hundred guests.

She turned to Joel and smiled. "Joel has started recruiting some volunteers."

"And I called the Golden Rule to set up an appointment for new gowns," Tessa announced. "Don't look at me like that, Hannah. Aunt Sam told me to."

Aunt Sam dabbed her lips with her napkin. "Indeed I did. You will all need to be turned out in something new."

"I wish I were a debutante." Tessa's tone turned pouty.

"You're lucky you get to attend, young lady." Hannah buttered a slice of bread. "You haven't yet come out, but I'm sure Charlotte will find somewhere you can be of use."

Tessa turned to Charlotte. "Can we go look at gowns tomorrow?"

"I can't." Charlotte's cheeks warmed. "I have plans."

"I'm afraid I'm stealing her away for the day, Tessa." Joel flashed Charlotte a smile. "Before she leaves for Red Wing on Monday."

"You're going to Red Wing?" Lincoln's brows drew close. "I read there was some trouble there concerning the gas company."

Joel set down his fork. "Trouble?"

"Nothing serious. Some of the townsfolk were upset the gas company shut off the streetlamps because the city hadn't paid its bills." Using his knife and fork with expert manners, he sliced a piece of lamb and dipped it in the mint sauce. "The article said a protest was planned, so it might affect your turnout."

"Mr. Johnson already spoke to me about the unrest, but he expects my lectures to be the key to solving the problem. He said the gas company is counting on my lecture series to help smooth the situation over and mend the rift." Charlotte smiled. "So I have to go."

Joel drew in a deep breath. "But we don't have to like it."

Nurse Pierce appeared at the door. "Excuse me, Mrs. Phillips, but it's time for your evening exercises."

"Tonight?" The word burst from Charlotte's mouth before she could stop herself. "But we've not yet had dessert."

Nurse Pierce crossed her arms over her chest. "It's important we stick to a schedule. Right, Doctor?"

Charlotte laid her hand on Joel's arm. "Surely it won't make a difference if she does her exercises fifteen minutes from now."

"No, I don't think fifteen minutes will make a significant difference in her recovery. Do you, Nurse Pierce?" He turned toward the woman. "But I do appreciate your attention to detail. We'll help Mrs. Phillips upstairs when dinner is over. She can do her exercises then."

"Yes, Doctor." She glared at Charlotte, spun around, and marched from the room.

Charlotte took a bite of her plum pudding, but the smooth texture did little to calm her. She hadn't meant to upset the nurse, but she feared she'd once again ruffled her feathers. "I don't think I made any friends there."

"I'm not sure Nurse Pierce has made many friends anywhere." Aunt Sam took a bite of her pudding. "But you, my dear, make them wherever you go. I wouldn't worry about it."

"If she's becoming more difficult, I could replace her," Joel said.

"No, we'll manage." Charlotte shook her head. It wouldn't be fair to send her away now. She'd done her job well, and as long as she provided excellent care to Aunt Sam, Charlotte would tolerate the nurse's attitude toward her. After all, what could she do to hurt her?

32

"Good morning, Nurse Pierce, Aunt Sam." Charlotte set a bouquet of powder room–pink peonies on the mantel in the drawing room and sniffed their sweet fragrance. Given Nurse Pierce's look of disdain last night, Charlotte had awakened determined to improve her relationship with the nurse.

Aunt Sam grunted as Charlotte turned. "How are the exercises going?"

Seated in an armchair, Aunt Sam struggled to lift her left leg at the knee. "Nurse Pierce is a slave driver."

Charlotte smiled at the nurse and kissed her aunt's cheek. "She's only doing what's best for you, and I, for one, appreciate it."

Nurse Pierce's eyes widened before her lips curled in a smile. "Thank you."

"You're especially chipper today, Charlotte, and I must say you look rather lovely." Aunt Sam smiled. "I think the good doctor will approve."

The nurse quickly averted her gaze. At least she was keeping her opinions in check. Charlotte glanced at the chevron-shaped wall mirror. Small flowers painted in muted shades crowned its frame. She studied her own appearance. She'd hoped the periwinkle-blue dress, with its embroidered flowers and crocheted cap sleeves, would make her appear soft and gentle rather than argumentative, but perhaps it wasn't the best choice for a park outing.

"Charlotte, did you hear me?" Aunt Sam asked.

She turned. "I'm sorry. No, I didn't."

"I asked when you're expecting Dr. Brooks."

"Within the hour. I have to go pack the picnic basket before he arrives." She pinned her matching hat in place and adjusted the white rose on its side.

Aunt Sam stood, and Nurse Pierce turned her chair around so the older woman could grasp the back. She proceeded to begin her leg lifts. "Did you awake early enough to make food for a lunch?"

"She certainly did." Nurse Pierce crossed her arms. "Didn't you hear her banging pots around in the kitchen?"

"I did have a rather unfortunate spill involving a couple of pans. I'm sorry if I woke you." The telephone rang in the foyer and Charlotte glanced at Aunt Sam. "Would you like me to get that?"

"No, Geoffrey can. Will you pass me my cane? It's time for a break before my morning walk."

"You've worked hard today. You've certainly earned a break." Nurse Pierce passed Aunt Sam her cane. "You won't require this at all if you continue your hard work, ma'am. I predict you'll be cane-free by Christmas."

"Christmas? Young lady, I intend to rid myself of that walking stick by the end of the month and return to my cycling before fall."

"Let's not get ahead of ourselves." Nurse Pierce glanced at Charlotte, her eyes pleading for help in the matter.

Charlotte chuckled. "I have every confidence that under Nurse Pierce's care you'll make great strides."

"Miss Charlotte." Geoffrey stood in the doorway of the drawing room. "There's a call for you from a Mr. Lewis Mathis."

"Thank you, Geoffrey. I'll be right there." She squeezed Aunt Sam's hand. "Don't give Nurse Pierce too much grief while I'm gone."

After she expressed her surprise at Lewis's call, he explained he'd have to meet them in Red Wing. He wouldn't be able to travel with her and Molly there. Already aware of this, Charlotte asked a few questions about his well-being but tried to keep the conversation short. It wouldn't do for Joel to arrive and find her on the phone with another man.

"Charlotte." Lewis paused and cleared his throat. "The real reason I called is because I miss you."

Her breath stilled. The candlestick phone base felt heavy in her hands. What was she supposed to say? She needed to set Lewis straight, but she didn't want to hurt him over the telephone. It seemed so cold. Besides, courting was new with her and Joel. What if they didn't work out?

"That's sweet of you to say, Lewis." She kept her voice light and friendly. "I'll see you and Molly on Monday. Goodbye."

As she hung up the earpiece on the receiver, her stomach churned and a sense of dread filled her. Now she'd have to sit down with Lewis and make sure he understood they were simply friends. It would not be a pleasant way to start the week.

Once they'd crossed the Marshall Street Bridge, Joel took Hiawatha Avenue toward Minnehaha Park. Charlotte's picnic basket sat behind her seat. What goodies had she packed?

As far as he was concerned, she could have packed a can of beans and he'd have been happy simply because he was with her. She looked like an angel in her delicate pale-blue dress. He smiled to himself. An avenging angel at times, but still an angel.

Charlotte was a passionate woman. Whatever she believed in, she believed in with her whole heart. However, he still saw a hesitance—almost a fear—when she was with him. It was as if she was afraid she'd say or do the wrong thing, and everything happening with the two of them would vanish like the steam from one of her pots. He wasn't sure who or what had instilled that fear in her, but today he had one goal. He wanted to erase it. She needed to know that even when their tempers exploded, he was not going anywhere.

"And Hannah and Tessa will work on making the butterflies while I'm gone."

He sucked in his cheeks to keep from grinning. Whatever she'd said in the last few minutes had been lost on his musings, but he didn't want her to know that. "I'm sure they'll turn out great."

Once they reached their destination, Joel parked the motorcar and helped Charlotte out. "We'll come back and drive to the upper part for our picnic." Side by side, they began the descent into the gorge. They followed the path, and he carefully helped her down the damp steps that led to the base of Minnehaha Falls. To his delight, Charlotte said she'd not seen it before. They headed down the path into the lower glen, a densely wooded area. For a Saturday, the crowd was considerably light.

Charlotte looked up at the canopy of tree branches. "Being here brings Longfellow's poem alive, doesn't it?" She took a deep breath. "'All day long roved Hiawatha in that melancholy forest, through the shadow of whose thickets, in the pleasant day of Summer.'"

"Do you know the whole poem?"

"Heavens, no. Just bits and pieces." She smiled. "But I remember *Minnehaha* means 'falling water,' not 'laughing water.' Still, the poem seems to fit this area perfectly." She paused and swept her gaze over the area. "'And the streamlets laughed and glistened, and the air was full of fragrance, and the lovely Laughing Water said with voice that did not tremble, "I will follow you, my husband!"'" She stopped and her cheeks turned a lovely shade of crimson. "Do you remember any parts of the poem?"

"A lot less than you." He laughed. "Let me see. Isn't there a line that says something about famine and fever?"

"Naturally you remember the part of the fever. His beloved was dying."

"What I remember most is she heard the Falls of Minnehaha calling her to the Islands of the Blessed, and when Hiawatha returned, he found his love had died. I believe he didn't move for seven days." He drew in a deep breath. "When I read that in high school, I don't think I fathomed the pain of that kind of loss."

"And now?"

"I've seen it. I've seen it on the faces of men who lost their wives in childbirth." There were parts of his medical work he'd love to shield her from, but if she was to be part of his life, she'd have to understand. "But I've never loved anyone like Hiawatha loved her." He pointed to a walking bridge that crossed the Minnehaha creek. "Enough melancholy. Don't you want to talk about Hiawatha's bravery or his wisdom or how much he was like me?"

She smiled at him, a twinkle in her eyes, and he had to fight the urge to kiss her then and there. He directed her toward a rustic foot bridge that spanned the stream. "I should make you close your eyes."

"If you do, you might have to pull me out of the water."

As they moved forward, Minnehaha Falls came into full view. Water tumbled over a fifty-foot-high cliff and plunged into a pool below with a mighty roar.

Charlotte gasped. "Oh, Joel, it's breathtaking."

But the falls weren't the only thing that took his breath away. It was the way her face lit up. She placed her hand on the rustic bridge's tree limb railing, and he covered it with his own. Leaning into his arm, she sighed. Together they stood at the base of the falls, spray hitting their faces, in awe of God's wonder.

There was no need for words.

Some moments were beyond them.

Shetland ponies bearing boys and girls trotted in a circle around the ring. Charlotte laughed when one boy pointed his "finger gun" in the air and fired a make-believe shot.

It had been hard to tear herself away from the falls, but Joel had wanted to show her the rest of the park, so she'd relented.

"Did you come here as a boy?" Charlotte looked up at him.

"Once or twice, but we didn't get to ride the ponies. It cost too much. We did go to the Longfellow Gardens Zoo, though." He stepped away from the fence that surrounded the pony rides and started walking down the path. "Did you want to go to the zoo? Fish has quite a menagerie."

She fell in step beside him. "Fish?"

"Fish Jones. He has lions, jaguars, leopards, bears, camels, and a whole herd of sacred cattle from the Holy Land. My dad said he used to keep them on the third floor of his building on Hennepin."

"Inside?"

"Well, he staked the bear outside to draw customers."

She frowned. "That sounds cruel."

"I agree, but I bet it worked." He pressed his hand to her back as they turned a corner.

"Joel, tell me about your parents."

He stiffened beside her.

What was wrong? Things had been going so well. Had she made a mistake in bringing up the subject?

33

"Charlotte." Joel touched her arm. "Don't look so frightened. You don't need to be scared to ask me anything. I want to tell you about my parents, but you caught me off guard for a minute."

A familiar anchor tugged on his soul. If she judged him for his father's problems like so many others had done, this could be the end of their relationship. But Charlotte wasn't like that.

"Are your parents still alive?" Her honey-smooth voice broke through his thoughts.

"No." He rubbed his chin and watched a squirrel stop in the middle of the path, then skitter away. "My father died while I was in high school. My mother passed while I was in college."

"I'm sorry." She took a deep breath and fingered the silver beads of her necklace. "What did your father do?"

"Not much."

"Excuse me?"

They walked in silence for a minute before he could answer. "When I was about seven, my dad hurt his back on the railroad. The pain was debilitating. Sometimes he'd work awhile, but then he'd have to quit. He couldn't keep a regular job."

"How did your family make ends meet?"

"My mom was a housekeeper for a woman on Summit Avenue. She took in sewing too." He scooped up a rock and tossed it into the woods. "While my dad medicated himself."

"Medicated himself?"

"He drank, Charlotte." He wiped his hands on his handkerchief. "But it's not what you think. I promise the pain was real. He didn't have any other way to deal with it, so he numbed it with liquor."

"I believe you."

He released a long breath. "Thanks."

"There's more to this story, isn't there?" She pointed to a bench along the path. "Let's sit, and you can tell me everything you're not saying."

He sat down beside her. "I think one of the reasons I went into medicine is that I saw my dad suffering so much. I wanted to find answers that would help him and people like him."

"It had to be hard to watch him suffer year after year. Couldn't the doctors do anything for him?"

"They tried, but there's still not much we can do for chronic, severe lumbago even today. My mom spent a fortune on quack pills like Dr. Sheldon's Gin Pills." Anger at the mere thought made the muscle in his jaw tick. "Sometimes my dad would be doubled over in pain. He said it was like someone stuck a knife up his spine. That's when he drank." Joel clenched his fists. "It made me feel helpless, and I hated that feeling."

"So you fought for control in other areas." Her words barely rose above a whisper.

"I suppose so." He leaned forward so his elbows were resting on his knees. "That wasn't the worst of it. Some of our neighbors didn't understand how much pain he was in. They thought he was using his back injury as an excuse."

"That's ridiculous. Did they say that to you?"

He turned toward her. "One time the boy down the street told me he wasn't allowed to play with me because his mother said I'd never amount to anything. She told him I'd turn out exactly like my dad." He took a deep breath and stood up. "That day I decided I'd make something of myself. I'd do what it took to succeed."

"And you have." She accepted the hand he offered. "Your parents would be proud of you. I only wish we could find that boy's mother and let her know what kind of man you've become."

"You've met her."

"I have?"

"The Lord got ahold of her since then." He picked up the picnic basket and pressed his hand to her back to indicate they should begin walking again. "The neighbor was Mrs. Goodwin."

"As in the orphanage's Mrs. Goodwin?"

"The very same." He chuckled. "Except Jesus changed her. My mother shared the gospel with her, and she became my mother's best friend. Mrs. Goodwin has apologized many times for her remark, and I've forgiven her, but deep down I knew she only voiced what a lot of people were thinking."

"That's why making your temporary job as an assistant superintendent into something permanent is so important to you." Her eyes widened. "And it's why you haven't brought my food service ideas to the superintendent."

"Charlotte, I'm sorry. It's just—"

"I understand, Joel. Really, I do."

She'd responded too quickly. The truth still had hurt her.

"I need you to understand." He stopped, turned toward her, and took her hand. "In the beginning, I wasn't willing to stir up any trouble and risk my position when I wasn't sure I believed in your ideas myself. And now that I've seen their value, and once we have the funds from the ball, it will be a lot easier to bring your proposal to Dr. Ancker. He'll see what I've seen. I promise I'll talk to him."

She smiled up at him, faith evident in her hazel eyes. "I know you will."

Despite the sting she must have felt only moments before, he could see she'd managed to forgive him for his selfishness.

His heart swelled. Charlotte Gregory was truly amazing.

He didn't release her hand. Instead, they walked down the path between two rows of crab apple trees exploding with white and pink blossoms. A sweetness filled the air—and his heart. He'd confided in her and she'd accepted him, weaknesses and all.

Joel directed her off the path and selected a spot in the shade for their picnic. "Is this okay?" She nodded, so he took the blanket from beneath the basket's handle and shook it out. The blanket floated down onto the grass.

She opened the picnic basket and withdrew two bottles of Coca-Cola. Along with a bottle opener, she passed the Cokes to Joel while she took out the chicken salad sandwiches and the enameled plates.

He popped the top off the Cokes, passed her one, and then reached for the lid of the basket. "What else do you have in there?"

She swatted his hand away. "It's a secret."

He grinned and prayed aloud, thanking God for bringing her into his life. "So what's this secret you cooked up?"

She peeled the waxed paper off and offered him first choice of sandwiches. "I intend to show you so you can see why I love feeding people."

"I figured it was because you and your mom used to cook together." He bit into his sandwich.

"We did all the time, and I do feel close to her when I'm in the kitchen. Sometimes it's almost like she's there with me."

"You miss her?"

"Every day, but that's not the only reason I'm passionate about food." She used her fork to pick up a bite of the chicken salad that had escaped the thick slabs of bread. "Eating is about using our senses—all of our senses—at the same time. Smell, sight, taste, touch—"

"Hearing? Not unless you slurp your food."

"Yes, hearing. When was the last time you bit into an apple and didn't hear a satisfying crunch?" She smiled. "No other activity involves all the senses at the same time like eating does."

Joel could think of one. Kissing Charlotte.

"I want to make a game of it. I want you to close your eyes and try to guess what you're eating."

"If my eyes are closed, how will I feed myself?"

"I'll feed you." Her cheeks bloomed with color. She cocked her head to the side. "Do you think you can handle not being the one in control for half an hour?"

He chuckled. Not only could he handle it, but he thought he'd enjoy it a great deal. He squeezed his eyes shut. "Okay, I'm ready."

Charlotte first fed him a spicy cheese straw and followed it with smooth, creamy custard laced with a hint of nutmeg.

"Is there more?" Lying on his side, he propped himself up on his elbow and tipped his face toward her, eyes closed.

"Yes. I think you'll like this." Digging into the basket, Charlotte located the small rectangle of waxed paper she'd packed. She unfolded it, broke off a piece, and lifted the square of the baked good. "Are you ready? Here it is."

He opened his mouth and she laid a bite of the brownie on his tongue.

Pleasure rippled across his face and he moaned. "I think I've died and gone to heaven. I know I've never had anything like this or I'd remember it."

"It's a brownie. I used Fannie's recipe, but I added an extra egg to make it more dense. As I said before, chocolate is the best and most delicious surprise there is."

A teasing glint sparked in his now-open eyes. "I can think of a few other delicious surprises. I'll show you one later."

She giggled and handed him the rest of the brownie before taking one for herself.

"You really do enjoy feeding people, don't you?"

"It's probably hard for you to understand, but cooking is a way I can express myself—like an artist does on canvas. Someday I'd love to have my own kitchen. The biggest one in the city. It's my dream."

He sat up and took her hand. "From what I've seen, I doubt if you'll let anything stop you." Reaching for the basket, he laid his hand on the lid to claim it. "My turn."

"But I already know what's inside."

"Ah, but not in what order I'm going to give it to you. Go on. Close your eyes."

When he shifted beside her, she heard the dishes in the basket rattle. She felt his arm against her hip. He was so close and she fought to keep her eyes closed. He touched her lips with his finger. Her tongue darted out to taste what was there. Honey.

"Open your mouth."

She felt his breath on her cheek. She parted her lips and he pressed something against them. A strawberry. She could smell it. Her tongue wrapped around it and she bit into the honey-drenched fruit. The explosion of flavor sweetened by the honey stole her breath. Her first strawberry of the season!

Juice trickled from a corner of her mouth and Joel dabbed it away with his thumb.

"Keep your eyes closed." His voice, husky and gentle, stirred her. "I have to finish my own strawberry before . . ."

"Before what?"

"This." He tilted her face toward him and pressed his lips against hers.

At first the kiss was as soft as fresh bread, but it deepened like warm, rich fudge. He tasted of honey and strawberries, overwhelming her senses. Heat pooled inside her like she'd never known, exploding with all the ripeness of summer.

34

Would there be a problem tomorrow? Even the clerk at the Saint James Hotel seemed to think so. He'd told Charlotte he was surprised she was still coming, given the city's current attitude about the gas company.

Charlotte picked up a gray butter crock from the shop's shelf and examined the red wing design on its front. The community of Red Wing, home to the Red Wing Union Stoneware Company, sported these pieces of pottery throughout the town in various stores. Clearly the people of this town were proud of its wares and of the town itself.

"Molly, I think the fact that the city is refusing to let the gas company use the city auditorium for this set of lectures is a bad sign."

"You've spoken at a gas company showroom before. We'll be fine, sugar." Molly bent to examine a larger crock with the number fifty printed above the wing design. "I don't reckon I've ever seen a crock this size. What do you think a body would put in it?"

"A lot of pickles?"

"Fifty gallons of them?"

A woman from the store approached them. "Did you know every crock is hand-turned on a pottery wheel?"

Molly cocked her head. "Even this big one?"

The shopkeeper smiled. "Yes, ma'am. Are you interested in making a purchase?"

"I don't think I could carry that, let alone buy it."

"But I would like these." Charlotte handed the shopkeeper a set of heavy mixing bowls. They would be a perfect addition to her baking supplies.

Once Charlotte had paid for the bowls, the woman offered to have the purchase delivered to the hotel so Charlotte wouldn't have to tote it around with her. Charlotte thanked her, then she and Molly headed for the butcher shop to place a meat order.

Nestled beneath the level-crested Barn Bluff, Red Wing appeared to be a thriving, charming community. Brick buildings with molded facades lined the streets. Charlotte stopped in front of a millinery and examined the hats in the display window. Maybe she should get a new hat. There was a green one that was almost the color of Joel's eyes.

"So, you gonna tell me what's got you looking happier than a june bug in a lamp store, or are you gonna make me guess?" Molly asked. "'Cause if I had to guess, I'd say it might have something to do with that nice young doctor who came to see you in Deephaven."

Charlotte gave her a cheeky grin. "It might."

"Well?"

"He asked to court me. We've been stepping out together."

"Has he kissed you?"

"Molly!"

"Sugar, I was married for thirty years. I know what love does to folks."

Love? Charlotte hadn't said a word about love. She hadn't even thought about it. Her feelings for Joel had been growing, but did she love him?

Molly nudged her arm. "And before you go denying it, I know what love looks like too."

"But we haven't known each other long enough for that kind of attachment to form." Charlotte moved past the millinery and began walking down the sidewalk again.

"I don't think your heart is wearing a watch, sugar." Molly

puffed at Charlotte's grueling pace. "And could you please walk a little slower for those of us whose legs are not a mile long?"

"You're in luck. Here's the butcher's." Charlotte held the door for her friend.

Inside the shop, Charlotte looked around at the carcasses hanging on hooks. Even the window sported a rack of beef. A bald man with a white apron tied around his waist approached the counter from a butcher's block, where he'd been cutting up a side of beef. "May I help you ladies?"

"Yes, sir." Charlotte pulled out her list. "I'm in town to give a cooking demonstration."

The man narrowed his eyes. "The one with the gas company?"

She nodded. "I'll need eight pork chops for tomorrow and a five-pound beef roast, sliced very thin, for Wednesday."

"Sorry, miss, I can't help you."

"You're out of pork chops and beef roasts?" She glanced around the room. Could all of this meat be spoken for? "Well, I guess I can change my plans. I'll take two chickens and a leg of mutton."

"Miss, it's not that I'm out. I can't help you because you work for that thieving gas company." He draped a thick arm over the top of a large meat grinder and leaned against it. "I'm sure you're real sweet, so don't take this personally."

"But the gas company shut the streetlights off because the city didn't pay its bills. That's hardly the gas company's fault."

"Listen, miss. The town's lady folk weren't too happy when they shut the lights off. They said it made our streets dangerous. And when the lady folk aren't happy, then we menfolk suffer." He scratched his cheek. "I can't help you 'cause if my wife found out, I'd be eating boiled peanut sandwiches for a week."

"But how am I going to get the supplies I need? Is there another butcher?"

"By now, probably everyone in town knows you're here. I doubt if you'll get meat from any of the butcher shops."

Molly took hold of her arm. “Come on, sugar. This fella is about as helpful as a back pocket on a Sunday shirt.”

But the butcher had been right. The town’s two other butchers refused them service, as did the two grocers.

Back in their hotel room, Charlotte stared at her notes, tears pricking her eyes. She didn’t have enough food for a demonstration. They’d only brought a few things on this trip because they’d planned to purchase the rest upon arrival. Maybe she could come up with a new menu, but it would hardly demonstrate the superior abilities of the gas range. What was she going to do?

Fanning herself in a wicker chair, Molly released an exasperated breath. “Sugar, we need to have a heart-to-heart talk about empty vessels.”

“What? I think all of our vessels are looking pretty empty right now.”

The older woman smiled. “I declare, Charlotte, did you hear a word I said in the last ten minutes?”

“I’m sorry. I wasn’t listening.”

She snapped her fan shut and laid it on her lap. “I was asking if you remember the story of the widow who approached Elisha. She owed a great debt after her husband died, and she came to Elisha to get help.”

“I sort of remember the story. Didn’t he ask her what she had in her house? And she said all she had was a little bit of oil.”

“That’s right.” Molly pushed herself out of the chair with a grunt. “Then Elisha told her to collect all the empty vessels she could from her neighbors.”

“You want me to go beg for meat from the neighbors?” Charlotte paced the room.

“Heavens, no.” Molly sat down on the bed and patted the spot beside her.

“I need practically everything.” Charlotte plopped down. “Flour, yeast, sugar. The only thing I have enough of is spices.”

“No, sugar, you’re missing the point. God can always open a way for his children when they’re in trouble.”

"I didn't even think to pray." Charlotte looked down at the rug on the floor, then back up. "It's too late, though. We don't have anything."

"What you have is enough for God. You've got some spices, you've got a smart head on your shoulders, and you've got friends." Molly laughed. "Think about it. All Moses had was a rod when he approached Pharaoh, David faced a giant with a handful of rocks, and Samson used the jawbone of a donkey to slay a thousand Philistines. And remember, Jesus fed multitudes with five loaves of bread and two fish."

"I don't even have that."

Molly chuckled and lifted Charlotte's chin. "God's teaching us a lesson here, sugar. How little we have doesn't matter. He can take what little we have and use it in a big way, but we have to bring him our empty vessels so he can fill them."

"I know you don't mean you want me to set my empty bowls out on the table."

"Sugar, I want you to ask God to show you what to do." Molly stood up. "I'm going downstairs to one of the restaurants to see if I can rustle us up a couple of lemonades. I'll take them out back to the veranda and wait for you. After you've had a chat with the Lord, you can join me."

"I don't know what to ask for."

"Then sit tight and listen. Sometimes that's better anyway."

Charlotte rushed onto the veranda and found Molly in a rocking chair, head tipped back and eyes closed. Perspiration dotted the older woman's upper lip. Poor Molly. Today was warm, but it was a far cry from July and August temperatures. Molly would be miserable by then.

Two glasses of lemonade sat on the table beside her. Charlotte could hear the rush of the Mississippi River about a half mile away. With the breeze from the water, this was a peaceful place for a nap.

Too bad she needed to wake her traveling companion. But God had pressed an answer on Charlotte's heart, and they needed to get going if they were to fill those "vessels."

She laid her hand on Molly's shoulder, but Molly didn't stir. My, she was sleeping soundly. Giving her shoulder a little shake, Charlotte waited. When Molly didn't respond, she shook her harder. "Molly! Are you all right?"

Molly opened her eyes. "Goodness gracious, Charlotte. You trying to send me to meet my maker?"

"You weren't waking. You scared me to death." She drew in a deep breath. "Are you sure you're okay?"

"Well, of course I am." She stretched. "Sit down and have your lemonade. You look a mite peaked."

Charlotte sank into the chair and grabbed the glass. A few sips of the cold, tart beverage relaxed her. "I came to tell you I got my answer. I asked God what I could do with what little I had. I got to thinking about what you said about having a mind and friends, and then I had my answer, but we're going to have to act fast."

Less than a half hour later, Charlotte located the Western Union office while Molly headed to the hardware store to start setting up for tomorrow's lecture.

Inside, Charlotte eyed the boxed telephone area and then looked at the long list in her hand. If she telephoned, things would move more quickly, but with the quality of the telephone lines and the length of her list, placing a call was a risk. She would need all of the ingredients she asked for delivered.

The telegraph operator approached the counter and asked if he could help her. Charlotte passed him the list. "I'll need this sent."

The operator's eyes widened. "You want me to send all of this, miss?"

"Yes, sir, and right away."

"Are you sure? You realize a telegram is a penny per word, right? This is going to cost you a fortune."

"Will fifty cents be enough for you to do it quickly?" She held out a coin. While she was certain she could have billed the gas company considering the circumstance, she didn't dare reveal her connection to them to the operator.

"That ought to cover it." He took her money and deposited it in his cash register before pushing a lined telegram form in her direction. "Once you fill this out, I'll get started."

"I might need two of those." She took the second one he offered and began to copy her list, the pencil scratching across the paper as she scribbled the ingredients on the form.

Lord, please let this telegram get to him on time.

35

The train rumbled into the station right on time. Charlotte stood on the platform waiting to see if her vessels would be full tomorrow. Her stomach churned. Had her telegram gotten through on time?

Passengers exited one after another, but she didn't recognize any faces. Finally, a familiar lanky figure emerged. Lewis glanced around, spotted her, and started walking in her direction.

"Did you get my message?" The words burst from her lips.

His eyebrows scrunched together. "What message?"

A lump of dough dropped in Charlotte's stomach. What would she do now?

"Sorry, I'm teasing you." He chuckled. "Yes, I got your telegram, and I have everything you need. It's probably being unloaded as we speak."

She threw her arms around his neck. "How can I ever thank you?"

"Have dinner with me?" He stepped back and took hold of her hands. "That's how you can thank me."

Charlotte's corset suddenly felt too tight at the look of hope in his eyes. After all he'd done, she couldn't dash his hopes right now. "Molly is waiting for us at the hardware store, and she's made plans for us all to eat together at the hotel."

"Then promise me you'll go to the show with me after dinner."

She gave him a slight smile. Taking in a picture show would be the least she could do to say thank you. "As long as we come right back. I have a big day tomorrow. I'm speaking at the hospital in the morning, and then there's the lecture in the afternoon."

"It's a deal." He released her hands. "Now, let's go get your food."

How empty Mrs. Phillips's home seemed without Charlotte.

The butler told Joel that Mrs. Phillips and her nurse were in the garden, so he wound his way through the halls and stepped out on the veranda. Mrs. Phillips leaned heavily on her cane as she walked beside Nurse Pierce. He admired the elderly lady's fierce determination to walk again without a cane, but he wondered if it would ever happen.

He grinned. Charlotte might not be her blood niece, but they were certainly both strong women, so Mrs. Phillips would probably be running footraces soon.

"Psst."

Turning to his right, he spotted Tessa kneeling by a rosebush. "Don't look at me."

He quickly averted his gaze. "Okay. What's going on?"

"I need your advice, but I don't want Aunt Sam to see us talking or she might ask you what we were talking about. Then you'd have to lie to her."

"Why would I lie to your aunt?" His brows arched.

"Because I'm about to swear you to secrecy."

He crossed his arms over his chest. This was not looking good. "Tessa, are you in some kind of trouble?"

"Yes. I think so." She hesitated. "Remember, you're sworn to secrecy. Agreed?"

"Maybe you should talk to Charlotte or Hannah about this." He glanced her way.

"I told you not to look at me. For a doctor, you don't have a very good memory." A spade scraped against dirt. "I can't tell my sisters because they'll think I'm making this up. I can't tell Aunt Sam because her friend might be involved."

Taking a seat on a bench to the side of the rosebushes, he finally agreed to her vow of silence. "This is starting to sound serious."

For the next several minutes, she explained how she'd discovered strange things in the theater's bookkeeping ledgers, like payments made to a Mr. K. O. and deposits that had been changed after she'd entered them. "Then when I was snooping around—"

He fired her a stern look.

"I know, I know." She sighed. "Anyway, when I was snooping around, Miss Walker, who's the most prim woman you've ever met, walked in. I was scared to death. When I mentioned someone had changed the figures, she tried to get me to believe I'd counted wrong, but I told her I didn't and that I thought Mr. Jurgenson should know about the discrepancy. Lo and behold, she basically confessed to taking the money."

"The office stenographer is embezzling funds? Tessa, you need to go to the manager."

"I can't."

"I'll go with you, or you can talk to Lincoln, or something." He heard scissors clip something.

"Mr. Jurgenson may be in on it too." There was a long pause. "If I say anything, Miss Walker said she'd make sure I lost my role in *Peter Pan*. I just have to stay quiet until the end of the week, but I wanted to tell someone in case something happened to me."

"What's going to happen to you?"

"You know criminals." *Snip snip*—she sliced through the air with her garden shears. "They might have to do away with me to keep their secret safe."

At first Joel wanted to chuckle, but then his gut tightened. What if Tessa were in danger? This was probably her overactive imagination, but did he dare take that chance? If Charlotte found out he'd kept this kind of secret from her and her family, she wouldn't be happy.

"Tessa, has this Miss Walker said anything to you since that day—like threaten you?"

"No. She watches me like a hawk, but she's back to being the model of efficiency."

"And this Mr. Jurgenson?"

"He seems clueless."

Joel risked a glance behind him. "Tessa, you need to tell someone."

"After this weekend. Remember, you're sworn to secrecy until then."

Why did he have the feeling he'd been hoodwinked into a Tessa-size scheme?

Charlotte couldn't sleep. In the twin bed beside hers, Molly lay snoring—a snort followed by a faint whistle. Lying on her side, Charlotte stared at the window. A soft breeze made the curtains billow and sigh in the moonlight.

Accompanying Lewis to the picture show had been a mistake. Although he was a perfect gentleman and she'd insisted on paying for her own ticket, Charlotte sensed he wanted more than friendship to grow between them. The triple feature included Mary Pickford in two different shows, as well as a poor adaptation of Mary Shelley's *Frankenstein*, produced by the Edison Company. She'd nearly screamed during *Frankenstein*, and she'd wished Joel had been there so she could grab hold of his hand. Instead, she had to press her knuckles against her lips to keep from crying out.

Since each film lasted less than fifteen minutes, the sun had not yet set when they returned to the hotel. She had started to tell Lewis about Joel, but the words simply wouldn't come, and guilt knifed through her. Her reasons for not telling him the truth were selfish.

Joel. She flopped onto her back and stared at the ceiling. Thinking about him sent warmth radiating through her limbs. Everything in her wanted to enjoy these feelings, but every time she started to relish them, doubt dampened her thoughts like rain on a picnic.

Joel was strong, yet he didn't make her feel like she couldn't be herself when she was with him. In fact, she was almost more herself than ever. He brought out parts of her she dared not show anyone else. Still, would he change in a few weeks? A month? If only she could learn to trust her own judgment again.

She glanced at Molly. What would her wise traveling companion tell her to do? Most likely she'd say Charlotte should pray about it. Drawing in a deep breath, Charlotte felt her eyes begin to droop.

She'd talk to God about everything in the morning.

The nurses at Red Wing's small hospital listened intently to Charlotte's words. She explained the caloric needs of various patients to the ladies, gave them some simple ways to cut costs, showed them how to make trays more attractive, and even introduced them to a list of common ailments and food that worked well for patients suffering from those illnesses.

"And one more thing—cold foods are often the best way to entice a sick person with little appetite." She held up a tin can and a crock. "You can buy a miniature ice cream freezer that makes a pint of ice cream at a time, or you can make your own freezer by placing a smaller can inside a larger crock. You'll need to stir the contents of the can every three to five minutes, and the ice cream in your smaller freezer won't be quite as smooth, but it will still be quite popular with your patients. Cold puddings and custards work well too." Charlotte set down the tin can and crock, turned to face the audience, and clasped her hands in front of her. "Does anyone have a question before I go?"

Several nurses raised their hands. She answered questions until she finally had to excuse herself for her lecture. After inviting them all to join her and receiving several promises from those who planned to attend, she said goodbye and hurried to the hardware store.

She came to a halt a block from the door. Outside the hardware store, about ten demonstrators lined the walk. Four women held a fabric banner on which someone had painted the words, "Go home, gas lady. It's lights out for your company."

At least they were creative.

When she considered the effect this would have on attendance at her lectures, she shuddered. She'd have to make a note to Mr. Johnson so he'd understand the sharp decline here in Red Wing when she turned in her reports. Even so, since he was counting on her, she'd do her best to mend the situation.

Taking a deep breath, she squared her shoulders and marched forward. "Hello, everyone." She flashed them a gracious smile. "I'm Charlotte Gregory, the gas company employee who is giving the cooking lecture today." She extended her hand to the lady in front, but the woman simply stared at it. "It's a pleasure to meet you all. I want you to know I respect your right to express your dissatisfaction, and I'll be sure to relay it to the gas company."

"They don't care!" a man in the back shouted.

"Why don't you go home?" another joined in. "You're not wanted!"

Charlotte took a step back. Kindness wasn't winning them over.

"You may not wish to attend the lectures, but others in your fine city may. All I ask is that you let them pass without incident." She locked eyes with the woman in front. "Agreed?"

"This is a peaceful demonstration." The woman emphasized the word *peaceful* loud enough for all to hear. "You'll have no problems from us."

Charlotte nodded. "Thank you."

Reluctantly the group parted to admit her, but her stomach knotted at the thought of any guests attempting to breach the line.

"There you are!" Molly set a bunch of carrots on the worktable.

"I think everything is ready except for getting the meat out of the icebox."

"Thank you, Molly." She slipped into her apron. "But I'm not sure anyone will come as long as those protestors are out there."

Lewis joined her. "They'll come. You'll see."

Half an hour later, no one had stepped through the doors. Charlotte glanced up from the chicken she was cutting to the clock on the wall. Five minutes. Still no guests.

"Charlotte, look. You must have made quite an impression earlier today."

A smile bloomed on her face as a row of nurses, still wearing their blue dresses, white starched aprons, and white caps marched down the street. The group outside parted to admit them, and once they entered, a few other ladies followed their ranks. The crowd was small—the smallest yet—but she'd give them the best lecture she possibly could.

Then, maybe tomorrow, news would spread and this whole protest affair would be over.

Even though he no longer needed to check on Mrs. Phillips every day, Joel still made his daily trek to the mansion. Today he was coming much later than usual. His stomach growled in protest as he parked his motorcar. Too bad Charlotte was away or he'd sneak into the kitchen in hopes of nabbing some of her delicious concoctions.

He found Mrs. Phillips in the drawing room at her desk, and Tessa sat curled on the divan, rehearsing her lines.

Mrs. Phillips looked up from her work. "Good evening, Doctor. I didn't think you were coming."

"I apologize for being so late. It was a busy day." He set his medical bag down on a table, opened it, and removed his stethoscope. "How are you feeling?"

"Excellent. Which is good, since Tessa's play is only a few days away."

"And you don't want to use a wheelchair to attend, right?"

"That, sir, is a fact."

He pressed the stethoscope's diaphragm against her chest and listened to the steady drumming of her heart. "I worry you may tire."

"I'll be fine." She shook her finger in his direction. "And if anyone is tired around here, it's you. Have you looked in a mirror lately?"

"I'm afraid I was up late last night delivering a set of twins, and before you ask, the mother and babies are doing well. Here. Squeeze my fingers." He held up two fingers on each hand and she gripped them. The strength of her left hand had nearly reached that of the right. "Mrs. Phillips, I do believe you're right. You are in excellent condition considering all you've been through."

She lowered her voice to a whisper. "So perhaps it's time to dismiss Nurse Pierce."

He grinned. "Not quite yet."

A long sigh escaped her lips. "Very well. I shall endure."

"There's the spirit." He dropped his stethoscope back into his bag.

Tessa set down her script. "Aren't you going to let him see the telegram from Charlotte?"

The bag's latch clicked. Fear slid up his spine. Why would she send a telegram? "Is there a problem?"

"No, she sent the telegram because I asked her to, given the gas company's situation in Red Wing." She handed over the half sheet of paper with "Western Union Telegraph Company" printed in block letters across the top.

All is well. Gas co. protestors block meeting. Few attendees.

His fear ebbed, but unease still plagued his thoughts. Even though she'd said, "All is well," he was certain she'd been disappointed by the low turnout to her demonstration. He'd seen her previous crowds, and having only a handful attend would irritate her. And if she'd been rankled, he predicted she'd have no problem approaching the protestors and asking them to leave.

He'd seen patients in the hospital who'd been present at a strike when things got out of hand—both men and women. Surely Charlotte had enough sense to stay out of that kind of fray.

Then again, this was Charlotte, and trouble seemed drawn to the Gregory sisters like chicken pox to a five-year-old.

Given his tenuous position at the hospital, he really shouldn't take tomorrow off and go see her, but maybe if he called in a few favors, he could get someone to cover for him.

"Enough is enough!" Charlotte tossed her spoon down on the worktable as the last bit of a splattered tomato slid down the window of the hardware store door—a rotten tomato, no doubt. Why were they acting like this now when yesterday there'd been no trouble?

She turned to her audience of fifteen women, half of whom were nurses. "I'm sorry, but I need to go speak to our outside visitors for a moment."

"You'll do no such thing." Molly held up her hands and shooed her back. "Y'all keep cookin', and I'll take care of the hooligans."

Charlotte motioned for Lewis to go with Molly while she continued with the demonstration.

She pulled the roasted potatoes from the oven and poked them with a fork. When the fork came out of the potato wedges easily, she declared them done and scooped them onto a waiting platter. "Ladies, notice how easy the cleanup is with the gas stove. A simple wipedown is all the enameled surface will require. No more blacking a stove or removing ashes."

The hardware store's door swung open and Lewis stuck his head inside. "Charlotte, come quick! It's Molly!"

Her heart grabbed. She raced through the smattering of chairs and burst through the door. She found Molly on the ground, leaning against a light pole, a hand clutching her chest. Rushing to Molly's side, she knelt beside her companion. Molly's face was pale, and sweat beaded on her upper lip.

"Molly, what's wrong? What is it?" She turned to call for a nurse and gasped. "Joel, where did you come from?"

"I just arrived. I was worried about you." He squatted beside Molly, whipped open his medical bag, and withdrew his stethoscope.

Relief flooded over Charlotte as she reached for Molly's hand.

"Miss Molly, take slow, deep breaths." Joel listened for only a short time before grabbing a small vial from his bag. "I'm going to put this under your tongue. It will ease the pain."

One of the nurses from inside knelt beside them. Joel turned to her. "I'm Dr. Joel Brooks from Saint Paul. Does this city have an ambulance?"

"Yes, Doctor. I'll send for it right away."

Charlotte studied Molly, and the anger that had been churning inside her all day poured out. She jumped to her feet and faced the crowd. "Are you happy now? Look what you've done. We're not responsible for your city's problems with the gas company. Why don't you speak with your mayor and leave us alone?"

Something struck the back of her head, and red-hot pain exploded inside her. It lasted for only a second before the crowd of protestors in front of her became a dizzy blur and her legs gave out.

36

Joel caught a glimpse of a youth from the corner of his eye only seconds before the boy threw the stone. "Charlotte!"

Powerless, he watched as the stone hit Charlotte's head. Thank goodness the man beside Charlotte caught her as she fell. Everything in him wanted to rush to her side, but his duty was to the patient who needed him most, and right now that was Miss Molly.

"Is she bleeding?" he called out to the gangly young man holding Charlotte.

"No, but there's a big lump on her head."

"Go." Miss Molly touched his arm. "I'm not going anywhere at the moment."

"I'll be right back." He nodded to the nurse beside him and hurried to Charlotte. The young man stepped aside, and Joel knelt beside her.

Charlotte's eyelashes fluttered. "Joel?"

Horses pounded up the street, pulling the ambulance wagon. She started to sit up, but Joel pressed her back. "Easy. Lie still."

"What happened? And why are you here?"

"What do you remember?"

Her eyes widened and she struggled to sit up. "Molly!"

Against his better judgment, he helped her to an upright position. She moaned and gingerly probed her head.

"Charlotte." He held her shoulders. "I need to get back to Molly, but I need you to promise you won't get up and move around yet. This man is going to stay with you until I can get the nurse over here."

She followed his line of sight. "Lewis?"

Joel didn't have time to ask who Lewis was and how she knew him, but he could see the concern in the young man's eyes, so he was certain he and Charlotte were acquainted in some way. Cousins, maybe?

Leaving Charlotte propped against the young man's chest, he returned to help get Molly in the ambulance. Once she was loaded onto a stretcher, the driver and a volunteer from the crowd carried her to the ambulance, where the doctor who'd come from the hospital began to assess her condition.

"Do you want us to come back for her?" the driver asked, nodding his head toward Charlotte.

Joel shook his head as he hurried away. "No, I've got my motorcar. I'll bring her." When he reached Charlotte, he again squatted before her. "Your turn."

"For what?" Her brow scrunched.

He cupped her cheek. Confusion was to be expected following a concussion. "You're going to the hospital."

"I am not. I have food in the oven."

He chuckled and scooped her into his arms. "Someone else can take it out."

"I don't like to be bossed around, you know." Her head fell against his shoulder.

"In the future, I'll try to remember that."

"You'd better."

"Charlotte," the lanky young man called after her, "I'll be there as soon as I can."

Jealousy pricking him, Joel frowned and set Charlotte down on the front seat of his Model T.

He turned toward the young man. "Molly and Charlotte will

need their rest tonight. Why don't you wait to see the ladies until the morning?"

There, that ought to handle him—cousin or not.

Opening her eyes, Charlotte startled. Where was she?

Moonlight drenched the white sheets and blankets on her bed. Beside her, Joel sat in a straight-back chair with his arms crossed and his head drooping against his chest. Her heart swelled.

"Joel?" She reached out and her fingertips brushed the stubble on his cheek.

He lifted his head and rubbed his eyes like a sleepy toddler. "Hey, you're awake." He kept his voice low. "Are you in pain?"

"Dull ache."

"That's to be expected." He smoothed her mussed hair, his touch heartbreakingly tender.

"How's Molly?" She shifted, trying to lift her head.

He pointed to the bed next to her. "She's resting comfortably."

"Will she be all right?"

"Yes, you both will." He took her hand in his own and squeezed it. "She'll need to rest more often and carry some of those pills I gave her. I'm not sure she can continue to travel with you. I'm sorry."

"As long as she's okay." Tears clouded her eyes. "I'm glad you came when you did."

"So am I." His thumb traced circles on the back of her hand.

"You should go find a bed. This hospital has nurses." Her words came out slurred, and her heavy lids closed against her will. Sleep began to reel her in. "You didn't need to stay with me."

He kissed her forehead. "I couldn't leave the woman I love."

Warmth swept from her head to her toes. She tried to open her eyes but couldn't break sleep's hold. If this was another one of those delicious dreams, it was the best one yet.

Today was the day all her dreams came true. Tessa almost bounced up the stairs to the theater office. Well, maybe it wasn't all of her dreams, especially since it was only a full dress rehearsal, but it was very close to the real thing.

Tomorrow night she'd step onto the stage, and Miss Walker would have nothing to hold over her head any longer. Tessa still didn't have a plan as to how she'd handle the whole embezzlement situation, but hopefully Dr. Brooks had come up with some ideas for her. Tapping into his brain was a stroke of genius. When Hannah and Charlotte inevitably found out about this whole affair, she'd be able to say she did speak with an adult about it. Sure, it might get Dr. Brooks in a bit of trouble with Charlotte, but with a gift of a few chocolates and some flowers, she'd soon forgive him.

With a skip in her step, she whistled as she walked. Nothing could possibly ruin this day.

She opened the office door and paused. Where was Miss Walker? Tessa glanced at the wall clock and saw it was five past nine. In the time she'd been working here, Miss Walker did not deviate from her morning routine—she was at her desk by 9:00, went to lunch at 11:30, took a break at 2:45, and left for home by 5:00. Perhaps she was ill?

"Ah, Miss Gregory, there you are." Mr. Jurgenson set a pile of papers on the desk. "Miss Walker phoned in sick today. She said you could handle everything."

Tessa grinned. This day just kept getting better.

"But that means you'll have to stay until five o'clock. She said that shouldn't be a problem for you. Will it?"

Ooooh, Miss Walker knew very well it was a problem. Had she done this on purpose? There was no way Tessa could be late to the dress rehearsal, but it started at three o'clock. If she told Mr. Jurgenson she couldn't stay until five, he'd most likely want to know why, and she certainly couldn't tell him.

She bit her lip. Her appearance in the play was brief. If she took her lunch late, maybe she could time it to be in the theater for her scenes and still be back in the office to finish the day, with no one the wiser. It would require some quick changes, but with a little luck and a lot of prayer, she could pull it off. Besides, being alone in the office would give her an opportunity to practice her newly acquired detective skills.

Offering him her warmest smile, she walked to Miss Walker's desk. "I've got it all covered, Mr. Jurgenson. Don't worry about a thing."

37

Freshly shaven and wearing a clean shirt, Joel entered the hospital ward. Both Charlotte and Molly were seated upright in their beds with breakfast trays on their laps. A long braid of maple syrup–colored hair lay draped over Charlotte's left shoulder. He wished the nurse would have left Charlotte's hair loose. He'd enjoyed seeing it down more than he should have.

"Good morning, Doctor." One of the nurses who'd helped yesterday stood beside Charlotte's bed. "Miss Gregory seems to be improving quickly."

"Is she now?" Joel glanced at her breakfast tray laden with coddled eggs, toast triangles, jelly, orange slices, and cocoa—all served on pieces of china. There was even a vase with a purple coneflower. The nurse had outdone herself.

"Are you enjoying your pretty little breakfast?" He flashed Charlotte a knowing grin.

"I am. The nurses here are excellent students." She glanced at the nurse. "Thank you again, Maeve."

"My pleasure." She turned to Joel. "Do you need anything, Doctor? Coffee, perhaps?"

"That would be wonderful. Thank you, Nurse." After the nurse had gone, he stepped closer to Charlotte's bed. "How's the headache?"

She took a tiny bite of toast. "Barely there."

He tipped her chin up so he could see her eyes. "Liar."

"Molly is the one with the heart problem. Why don't you go bother her?"

"Ah, but irritating you is my specialty." He squeezed her hand, then noticed the tall young man from yesterday enter the ward. "It looks like you have company."

She turned her head toward the door, and her face paled. Her lips tight, she caught Molly's gaze, then smiled at the young man when he stopped at the foot of her bed. "Hello, Lewis."

Joel crossed his arms over his chest. What an odd reaction. Had this young man been bothering Charlotte in some way?

"Oh, let me introduce you two. Dr. Joel Brooks, this is Lewis Mathis." Charlotte pushed her coddled egg around on her plate. "He's the musician who performs before the lectures."

A man? Well, she'd not shared that little bit of information. Joel hiked an eyebrow. "Is he now?"

"He sure is, and he does a mighty fine job." Molly poked her fork at him. "Even if he says howdy to all y'all first and not to me."

Lewis's cheeks flamed. "Pardon me, Miss Molly." His deep voice rumbled. "You look much better today."

"Fit as a fiddle. Bet they'll be kickin' me out before day's end."

"I'm afraid not, Miss Molly. You're looking at five days here, at least." Joel thumbed through the chart the nurse had left on Charlotte's table. "You, however, should be able to go home tomorrow afternoon."

"Tomorrow?" She coughed and grabbed her juice glass. "I have to go home today. Tomorrow is Tessa's play."

"Charlotte, you have a concussion. You need to rest."

"I can do that at home."

"I can't let you go home alone." Joel set the chart down. "And Miss Molly is certainly not ready to be discharged. Don't you want to stay here with her?"

"But you said Molly was going to be all right. Besides, you know I can't let Tessa down."

"I can escort you." Lewis tugged on the lapels of his suit coat.

"I had the maid pack up your things this morning and sent word to the gas company that we'd not be going to Hastings today."

Well, he was certainly taking charge of the situation. Trying to impress Charlotte, no doubt. When Charlotte glanced at Molly and rubbed her temples, Joel realized he needed to put an end to this, but before he could say anything, Molly spoke.

"That's sweet of you, Lewis, but Charlotte should be heading home with the doctor—especially given her condition. Dr. Joel, if you're staying here on my account, I don't reckon that's necessary. This hospital has doctors who can tend me just fine, don't they?"

"Yes, but—"

"No buts about it." Seemingly spent, Molly leaned back on her pillow. "You're taking Charlotte home so she can see her sister's play. Lewis can stay in town with me a day or so if he likes or head on home."

Joel studied Charlotte. Medically, she was recovering well, but he had yet to shake the feeling of helplessness he'd had when he saw her crumple last night. She hadn't been unconscious long, and it wasn't like she'd be running races when she got home. If she were anyone else, would he hesitate to release her? Was he being overprotective? If so, he imagined she'd soon tell him exactly how she felt about that.

He sighed. "Charlotte, I suppose we could leave this afternoon if you promise to take it easy until then."

"Thank you." She beamed at him.

"In that case, I'll see that your bags are brought here. I'll speak to the nurse about where they can be stored until you're ready to go." Lewis dipped his head. "I'll check back on you—I mean both of you—a little later."

Joel waited until Lewis was gone before he turned to speak to Charlotte. He had a lot of questions he wanted answered about that young man—for starters, why she'd never mentioned Lewis, and why Lewis was quite willing to volunteer as her escort. But one look at Charlotte's droopy eyes and he held his tongue. They'd have plenty of time for questions on the way back to Saint Paul.

If Tessa didn't eat soon, her ribs might rub together hard enough to start a fire.

She carried a stack of invoices to the filing cabinet. The wooden drawer stuck and she yanked it. It gave and she nearly lost her balance. Wouldn't Miss Walker have a conniption if she came back to an upturned drawer in the center of the room?

Thumbing through the files, she searched for the maintenance folder. The invoice in her hand was for electrical repairs. She slid the slip of paper in place and glanced at the clock. The dress rehearsal was starting promptly at three, so she'd sneak downstairs at a quarter till and change into her maid costume in one of the dressing rooms.

Since she had lines only in the first act, she should be able to race backstage, put on her regular attire, and hurry back upstairs before Mr. Jurgenson returned from his meeting. He'd been gone most of the afternoon, which had allowed her to snoop at will. Unfortunately, she'd found little to tell her who Mr. K. O. was or if Mr. Jurgenson was in cahoots with Miss Walker. If he, too, was a criminal, she certainly didn't want to confide in him. She needed to work carefully and not raise any suspicions if she wanted to complete her investigation.

Tessa filed the remainder of the stack, sat down at her desk, and picked up her newly acquired copy of Allan Pinkerton's *Professional Thieves and the Detective*. Finding the book in Aunt Sam's library had been a stroke of luck. Perhaps Aunt Sam's husband had been interested in the famed detective or his work with the railroad.

According to the book, she needed to keep a strict watch on Mr. Jurgenson's movements and not let him out of her sight. Unfortunately, she'd have to start her surveillance after he returned, and of course, she couldn't follow him home—or could she?

Tessa placed a note on her desk, explaining she was leaving for lunch, then hurried to the dressing room and donned the heavy black maid's dress, apron, and mobcap for her role of Liza. She made it on stage in time. The thrill of seeing everyone in costume with the set behind them made her giddy, but she managed to stay in character and say her lines.

But things did not go as smoothly for Peter. When the rope that lowered him into the nursery jammed, he missed his cue, and Mr. Frohman ordered them to take the whole act from the top. When her part was over, Tessa exited stage left.

"Miss Gregory." The stage manager stepped in front of her. "Where are you going?"

"I have to change and get back upstairs."

"But you need to remain in costume for the curtain call. We'll be practicing that at the end." He stuck a pencil behind his ear. "Mr. Frohman won't be happy if you're not back in time."

"Don't worry. I will be."

Even though she preferred to stay and watch, she traipsed offstage. In the dressing room she whipped off her apron and mobcap. Since her practice had gone later than she'd planned, she skipped changing the black dress. Men seldom noticed such things anyway.

She hurried upstairs and into the office. Her chair squeaked loudly as she sat down, and she winced.

Just as she feared, Mr. Jurgenson came out of his office. "There you are. I was beginning to wonder how long your lunch would be. You must have taken it much later than usual, but honestly, Miss Gregory, I'm sure Miss Walker doesn't expect you to accomplish everything she usually does." He cocked his head to the side. "Were you wearing a black dress this morning? I was certain you had on a white shirtwaist."

"Sir?"

"Oh, never mind." He passed her a handwritten letter. "I need this typed up right away."

"Typed?"

"Yes. I know you're not as fast as Miss Walker, but as long as you finish it before you go, it ought to be fine."

Not as fast? Her typing instructor had called her Tessa the Turtle in class.

"Please bring it into my office when you're finished." He gave her a parting smile and went back to his office. "Remember, I need it today."

Tessa picked up the paper bearing Mr. Jurgenson's barely decipherable scratches. Her stomach knotted. She'd never get this typed up in time to make the curtain call. Should she sneak out in about an hour, or could she simply tell Mr. Jurgenson the truth about her part in the play?

Miss Walker had made it sound like he wouldn't approve. What if he still wouldn't let her leave, or worse, what if he got her fired from the cast?

Too bad she didn't have a little bit of that fairy dust right now.

38

After dressing behind a screen, Charlotte gathered her suitcase and walked to Molly's hospital bed. "I hate leaving you."

"Nonsense, sugar. I'll be right as rain by Sunday." She shifted in her bed. "And the nurses here are as sweet as your apple charlotte—except that one. Did you see her? She has her nose so high in the air she could drown in a rainstorm."

Charlotte laughed. "I agree, but if you're nice to her, maybe she'll be nice in return."

"Speaking of being nice, when are you going to explain to Lewis about the doctor?"

"I should have told him already, but he's so kind, and I don't want to upset him."

Molly laid a hand on Charlotte's arm. "Sugar, what's the Lord putting on your heart about this?"

Emotion clogged Charlotte's throat. "I'll tell Lewis about Joel the next time I have the chance."

Molly reached for her hand. "And don't you worry. Lewis might be hurt, but you won't lose his friendship. I reckon deep down he already knows the truth." She chuckled. "Anyone in the room with you and Dr. Joel for more than a few minutes can feel the spark between you two, and it tickles me to no end."

"That makes you happy? I thought you'd be on Lewis's side."

"If I was any happier, I'd be twins." She pushed herself up in the bed so she was sitting straighter. "Sugar, Lewis didn't stir you. If you'd picked him, you'd have been settling, but God doesn't want us to settle for what's in front of our face. He wants to bless us with things beyond our imagination."

Charlotte grinned. "Thank you."

"You're welcome. Only remember, sugar, bring your empty vessels to the Lord to fill them. Not to any man." Molly glanced toward the doorway. "Lookie there, here comes your blessing right now."

Joel crossed the room and picked up Charlotte's suitcase. "Looks like you're ready to go. Miss Molly, I'll keep in contact with Dr. Bomgars. He'll take good care of you. When you're ready to be released, I'll come get you."

"That'd be mighty nice of you."

"Now, we'd better get going." He glanced at Charlotte. "Ready?"

She hugged Molly goodbye, then made her way to Joel's waiting Model T, where he helped her inside. He went to the front to crank the engine. It roared to life, and she leaned back into the leather seat.

A nice, peaceful ride home would be the perfect medicine for what remained of her headache.

The steady clack of the typewriter beneath her fingertips did nothing to soothe Tessa's growing anxiety. Why did Mr. Jurgenson insist on having this letter today? She glanced up at the wall clock and moaned. The curtain call would be any minute now and she had another paragraph to type, but she needed to get down there.

She pushed back from the desk. One quick trip wouldn't hurt.

"Ah, you're finished," Mr. Jurgenson said as he rounded the corner from his office. "Good. I can go post it."

Like a child caught with her hand in the cookie jar, Tessa jumped back from the door.

Mr. Jurgenson's brow furled. "Miss Gregory, were you going somewhere without finishing my letter?"

"Uh . . ." What was she going to do now?

Joel impatiently tapped the steering wheel as Charlotte kept up a steady stream of discussion concerning the ball. He had questions he wanted to ask her before they reached Saint Paul, but he wasn't sure how to bring the subject up.

"And Lewis agreed to help you with music selections, if that's all right with you. His knowledge of music is excellent. He studied at the Northwestern Conservatory of Music in Saint Paul."

At the mention of Lewis's name, Joel's lips puckered as if he'd eaten a lemon. "You seem to know a lot about Lewis."

Charlotte stiffened. "What do you mean by that?"

"Nothing." He tried to shrug nonchalantly. "You two travel together. Of course you know about him. Why haven't you mentioned him before?"

"I told you I traveled with a singer."

"Not a *male* singer." He gripped the steering wheel until his knuckles whitened, hating the doubts forming in his mind. But the facts were undeniable. Lewis had been too considerate, too eager to tend to Charlotte's needs. And she was clearly nervous about his attention.

"You never asked."

"So why did you keep it a secret?"

"I didn't. The subject didn't come up." Charlotte's voice rose. "Joel, there's nothing but friendship between Lewis and me. Can't you see that?"

He couldn't very well admit he'd only been watching Lewis's reaction to her.

The image of his former fiancée in the arms of his friend filled his mind, and his chest constricted. Perhaps he was overly sensitive about such matters after what had happened with Prudence.

They hit a bump and Charlotte moaned. Joel mentally kicked himself. What was he doing pummeling her with questions in her condition? She was still recovering and didn't need this pressure.

"Charlotte, I'm sorry. I didn't mean to upset you." He massaged the knotted muscles in the back of her neck. "Lay your head back and try to close your eyes for a while."

She gave him a sidelong glance. "Are you telling me what to do again?"

"I wouldn't dream of it." He chuckled. "Now, get some rest."

Tessa's mind whirled. She had to get out of the office and downstairs for the curtain call. But now that Mr. Jurgenson had caught her trying to leave before she was finished with his letter, she was trapped.

"I was, uh . . . uh . . ."

Mr. Jurgenson's cheeks colored, and he averted his gaze. "Oh, of course, Miss Gregory. How insensitive of me. Take your powder room break. The letter can wait."

She hid her smile and scurried away, thankful for Mr. Jurgenson's fortuitous assumption. Her quick steps echoed on the Minton tile as she crossed the theater's foyer, but she didn't dare slow.

Flinging the backstage door open, she paused to let her eyes adjust. What scene were they on? Had she made it in time?

"Miss Gregory, you're next." The stage manager dragged her to the curtain. "You go on after the pirates."

"What do I do?"

"Step to the center, curtsy, and then step back." He nudged her arm. "Go!"

She did exactly as she was told and stepped back into the shadows.

Tomorrow night there would be beautiful lights and robust applause, but she didn't need that today. As cast member after cast member joined her on stage, something foreign took hold of her. This play, the theater, the family of actors—she was part of something bigger than herself.

A fierce protectiveness washed over her. There was no way she was going to let Miss Walker or Mr. Jurgenson ruin this special world. Not while she could do something about it.

Pinching her cheeks, Charlotte took stock of herself in the mirror. Joel would soon arrive, then they'd all leave for Tessa's play.

Hannah and Aunt Sam had fussed over her all morning, insisting she rest. Finally she'd had enough and had enlisted them all in addressing ball invitations. It had been a relief when it came time to get ready for the evening.

After tapping on her door, Hannah entered. "That dress is an excellent choice. Joel is here, but you need to wait a few minutes so you can make a grand entrance."

"Thank you, but I pale compared to you." She took in Hannah's soft green satin gown with a panel of embroidered rosebuds on its front. "Lincoln will be so busy looking at you, he won't see a bit of the play."

Hannah laughed, then grew serious. "Lottie, you pale to no one. You know that, don't you?"

"That's easy for you to say." She chuckled and inserted a pearl-studded comb, wincing when it touched the lump on her head. The decorative comb went well with the ivory satin gown she'd chosen. She loved the empire waist and voile overlay with its elaborate gold thread swirls. She pressed her gloved hand to the pearl necklace lying against her exposed décolletage and turned toward Hannah. "Is anything amiss?"

"You look perfect." Hannah's eyes glittered. "I wish Mother could see you now. She'd be so proud."

Charlotte swallowed the lump in her throat and fanned her face with her hand. "Don't make me cry now. I'll look awful for my grand entrance."

Hannah opened the door. "And we mustn't have that. I'll go down first, and then you can follow in a couple of minutes."

"Why am I so nervous?"

"Because."

"That's your answer?"

"I'm afraid so." She shrugged. "I'm new at being a mother, after all."

"I hope you improve before Ellie needs this talk."

Hannah gave her an impish grin. "By then, you can give it to her."

Every few seconds, Joel looked up the staircase, expecting Charlotte to make an appearance. He tugged at the crisp white collar and the black bow tie at his neck, which felt as if it were cutting off his air.

Then he saw her and his heart raced. Like an angel, she descended the stairs in a halo of ivory and gold. Her reddish-brown curls were pinned up, leaving the creamy skin of her neck exposed.

He stepped forward and held out his hand to help her down the last few steps. "You take my breath away."

Pink tinged her cheeks and a smile bloomed on her face. "That's kind of you to say."

"I wouldn't say it if I didn't mean it."

"Thank you."

A commotion at the top of the stairs drew their attention.

Mrs. Phillips shook Nurse Pierce's hold from her arm. "I said I'll do it myself and I will."

"Excuse me." Joel winked at Charlotte and jogged up the stairs. He offered Aunt Sam his arm. "May I have the honor?"

"You're incorrigible." She slipped her right hand in the crook of his arm, palming her cane with her left.

They began their slow descent. "Actually, my motives are selfish. If you fall, then I'd need to stay here and take care of you. That would keep me from escorting that stunning lady down there to the play."

"She is quite lovely tonight."

"Isn't she always?"

"Dr. Brooks, I do believe you're smitten."

"Did you know this would happen when you set us to planning the ball together?"

"I certainly hoped that would be the case." She smiled up at him. "Feelings can only simmer so long before they boil over."

When they reached the bottom step, she released his arm and greeted Hannah and Lincoln.

Nurse Pierce rolled the wheelchair into the room.

"I am not using that." Aunt Sam gave the floor a firm knock with her cane. "I will be perfectly fine with this."

"Doctor, please reason with her."

Joel looked from the nurse to the older woman. "We'll keep a close eye on her."

"But remember, I'll not have you coddling me." She wagged her finger at Joel. "Henry will escort me to the motorcar, so you escort Charlotte. I wouldn't want her to stumble in that lovely gown."

"Nor would I." He offered Charlotte his arm. "Shall we?"

Wendy, Peter Pan, and Tinker Bell stood calmly in the hallway outside the dressing room ready to take the stage, but Tessa felt as if someone were churning butter inside her stomach.

The captain pushed past her, shouting something about not being able to find his hook. When the stage manager called out, "Places, everyone," a hush fell over the cast. Each actor scurried to his or her place.

The curtains rose and the play began. From her place in the wings, Tessa sucked in her breath. She peeked out and saw the theater filled with patrons. What if she forgot her lines?

Her turn was coming up. She waited for her cue, took a deep breath, and made her entrance. Beneath the glare of the electric lights, excitement replaced her nerves.

She'd done it. She was on the stage!

39

"You were brilliant!" Charlotte wrapped her arms around Tessa and drew her close. They'd waited in the lobby for almost half an hour for her to change and come join them, and now that Tessa was with them, Charlotte felt as if she'd burst with joy on her sister's behalf. "How did it feel to be up there in front of all those people?"

"It was amazing." Tessa clasped her hands beneath her chin. "And I get to do it again tomorrow and then the next two weeks after this. I feel as if I've fallen into a dream."

Hannah captured Tessa's hands. "I'm so proud of you."

Aunt Sam, Lincoln, and Joel all offered their congratulations, and the group headed to Hannah and Lincoln's house. Earlier in the day, Hannah had asked Mrs. Umdahl to prepare homemade ice cream for a celebration in Tessa's honor. Since Aunt Sam wasn't fully recovered, Henry had taken her home, then returned for Tessa, Joel, and Charlotte.

When they arrived at Hannah's, Mrs. Umdahl had the table spread with condiments and toppings for the ice cream. As soon as she had her cup in hand, Charlotte slathered her ice cream with caramel syrup and topped it with chopped pecans while Joel buried his in strawberry preserves. Tessa filled her cup to overflowing as she chatted on and on about the other actors and all of the behind-the-scenes occurrences.

Charlotte slipped the caramel-laden spoon between her lips and let the flavors mingle on her tongue. She closed her eyes. Ah. The perfect way to end a perfect day.

The celebration lasted late into the night. Charlotte laughed so hard at some of Tessa's stories her cheeks hurt. Through it all, Joel fit perfectly into the family. So much so that it seemed as if he'd always been there.

More and more, she hoped he always would.

"I rather fancy the idea of never growing up." Tessa stood and began to gather the empty dishes.

Lincoln draped his arm around Hannah and pulled her close. "But if you don't grow up, you'll never find true love."

Tessa giggled. "Why would I want to fall in love if some man's going to make me into something I'm not and tell me what to do? I have you two for that already."

"You think I tell Hannah what to do?" Lincoln squeezed his wife's shoulder. "Tessa, I think you've got things all wrong. If a man loves you, he won't try to make you into something you're not."

"George sure turned Charlotte into a stranger."

The room grew silent. Charlotte pressed her backbone against her chair and prayed Joel hadn't been listening. If they were to have a future, he needed to know about George, but discussing it right now when things were going so well made her cringe.

"That's no longer a subject we need to discuss." Hannah glared at Tessa, then sent an apologetic look toward Charlotte. "And I believe it's time to call this a night."

After a round of goodbyes at the door, Joel and Charlotte followed Tessa to the waiting motorcar. The drive home was short and awkward. When they reached the house, Charlotte sent Tessa off to bed so she could speak with Joel. To her great relief, Tessa did as she was told.

Charlotte suggested they sit down on the swing on the south side of the porch. The swing squeaked as it began to move to and fro. A light from inside cast gray shadows on the tiled floor and gave enough illumination for her to see Joel's face. He took her hand in his. The gesture, so simple and yet so sweet, almost brought tears to her eyes. What a wonderful evening it had been—the stuff dreams were made of—right until Tessa had to blurt out George's name.

Before she lost her courage, she took a deep breath and found her voice. "I'm sure you want to know about the fellow Tessa brought up—"

"George?"

Charlotte nodded.

"You don't have to tell me if you don't want to."

"No, you need to know. If you'd had a sweetheart who'd influenced you, I'd want to know." She swallowed and plunged in, trying to explain how she'd let this young man dictate her decisions and actions. She left out the kiss he'd stolen but told Joel everything else. "I vowed I'd never let another man try to make me into someone I'm not."

Beside her, Joel's chest rose and fell in labored breaths. When she glanced at him, his jaw was set firmly.

She looked down at her shoes. "I'm sorry that I didn't say anything earlier."

"You"—he kissed the back of her hand—"have nothing to be sorry about. Now, if this George fellow was around, I might have a word or two—or twenty—I'd like to give him." He stood and pulled Charlotte up to face him. "Please listen to me. I've seen men like George in my practice. Men who thought they were tougher or stronger because a woman did their bidding. But that's not a real man, Charlotte. A real man isn't threatened because the woman he loves is smart or beautiful or talented. He wants her to be all God made her to be."

"I was foolish and lovesick. I wanted him to like me, so I let him control me."

"Charlotte." He tipped her chin up to look into her face. "I've seen the courage it takes to stand up to a man like that, and I've seen how you have no trouble standing up for what you believe in today. If you're passionate about something, I don't think anything will stop you. I know you want people to like you, but I don't think that controls you anymore. It sure didn't when you first met me." He chuckled, but then a tear slipped from her eye and he thumbed it away. "Hey, I didn't mean to upset you."

"It's not that." She wiped a salty tear from her lip. "Thinking about that time with George reminds me of losing my parents. After they died, I needed someone. Sometimes I missed them so much I ached, and the more time I spent alone, the worse it was. I hated being alone."

"You're not alone anymore." He trailed his fingers down her bare arm, sending a tremor through her. "You have me."

His hands settled on her waist and he drew her close. They locked gazes as she brushed her hand along his cheek. She didn't resist when he pressed his lips to hers, nor did she protest when he deepened the kiss. How could she? Nearly every inch of her heart was becoming his.

Too bad Charlotte wasn't a songwriter. Some mornings deserved a song all their own, and today was such a day. The birds outside seemed to agree. As she entered the dining room, she heard the trill of a lark through the open windows.

Aunt Sam sat at the head of the table with Nurse Pierce beside her. Charlotte spooned a poached egg onto her plate from the chafing dish on the buffet, took a couple of orange wedges, and added a biscuit. As much as she didn't relish the idea of dining with Nurse Pierce, she recalled her decision to befriend the woman and took the seat across from her. Besides, there was nothing Nurse Pierce could do that would ruin her day.

"Good morning, Aunt Sam, Nurse Pierce." She turned toward her sister. "Good morning, Tessa."

Tessa trailed in and started to fill her own plate. "Morning. Why are you so cheery? I went to bed at least an hour before you, and I'm exhausted."

"Oh, I don't know." Charlotte broke her biscuit in half, buttered it, and drizzled honey over its surface. "It's a beautiful morning."

"Uh-huh." Tessa eyed her skeptically and slid into the seat beside her. "I think you're seeing everything through the eyes of loooove."

"Tessa." Aunt Sam gave her a reproachful scowl and set her coffee cup down. "Charlotte, I'm about to make your day even better. Today we're shopping for ball gowns."

Nurse Pierce frowned. "Mrs. Phillips, I'm not sure you're up to such a rigorous outing."

"Nonsense. What is there to it? My driver takes us to the Golden Rule. We take an elevator upstairs, and I watch while my girls try on lovely gowns." She chuckled. "And you'll be going with us. Of course, you'll have to change out of your uniform."

"I don't have another dress here that I could wear, Mrs. Phillips."

Charlotte set down her fork. "We're about the same size. You can wear one of mine. It will be fun to have you join us."

"Then it's settled. We'll leave in one hour." Aunt Sam smiled at all three of them. "Dresses for all of you—and that means you too, Nurse Pierce. You can't go to the ball in your nurse's uniform."

"I-I couldn't accept that."

Tessa giggled. "Don't even try to resist. It's useless. She's had years of practice at being stubborn, and she always wins."

Nurse Pierce had clearly never shopped for an evening gown before. In truth, Charlotte had only done so a couple of times since she'd met Aunt Sam. Still, she helped the nurse into the dressing room and explained how the clerk would bring her several dresses to try on.

Retiring to the salon, Charlotte sat back and watched Aunt Sam perform like a fairy godmother, selecting five dresses for the nurse to wear. Nurse Pierce modeled each, and they all agreed the bronze satin with the black shadow lace overlay looked the best with the nurse's dark hair.

The nurse blinked back tears. "I've never had anything so beautiful."

Charlotte passed her a handkerchief. "When we get back, would you like me to show you a different way you might wear your hair to the ball?"

As if she were self-conscious, Nurse Pierce touched her hair, pulled back into a bun. "I think I can manage on my own. Mrs. Phillips will need my attention when we return."

"If you change your mind . . ." Charlotte slipped into the dressing room. She adored the first dress she tried on. The deep sapphire silk dress had gathered chiffon sleeves, lots of glimmering beads, heavy raised embroidery, and a short train.

"Dr. Handsome will love that." Tessa sighed dreamily.

Charlotte sneaked a peek at Nurse Pierce for her reaction and was delighted to see that the nurse still had a smile on her face. Maybe this day was the beginning of a friendship for the two of them.

Before they left, they each selected a gown and added the appropriate matching hair ornaments and shoes. Aunt Sam directed the clerk to have their purchases delivered while they enjoyed a light lunch in the store's tearoom.

When they returned home, Nurse Pierce assisted Aunt Sam out of the automobile. "Thank you for allowing me to join you all."

"It was our pleasure." Charlotte flashed her a warm smile, but the nurse didn't reciprocate. Tessa rolled her eyes and heaved a sigh.

As they climbed the steps, Charlotte refused to be disheartened. She and Nurse Pierce had made progress today. Given time, surely the situation between them would improve.

"Good afternoon, ladies." The butler held the door upon their return to the house. "Miss Charlotte, you have a gentleman caller, a Mr. Lewis Mathis, waiting in the drawing room. I told him I wasn't sure when you'd be back, but he insisted on waiting."

She hurried into the drawing room. "Lewis, has something happened to Molly?"

He jumped to his feet. "No, she's fine. The doctor said she can leave on Monday or Tuesday."

"Then why are you here?"

He glanced at the other women standing by the door. "Can we go somewhere private to talk?"

She blinked and followed his line of sight. "Yes, let's go to the garden."

He followed her out the back door and down a path. Charlotte sat at a bench flanked by two special rosebushes. They'd once belonged to her mother, and Tessa had insisted on bringing them from the farm when they lost their house. They'd brought one bush for each sister, so the third bush was now planted at Hannah's.

Lewis remained standing. "The doctor is courting you?"

She nodded. "It hasn't been very long."

"Why didn't you tell me?" Hurt crept into his tone. "You went to the picture show with me the other day. You let me believe there was a chance for us."

"You have a right to be upset with me."

"I'm not upset." He stuffed his hands in his pockets. "I'm disappointed. But I think I already knew you weren't as taken with me as I was with you."

"Your friendship means so much to me."

"If things don't work out with him, would you consider me for a suitor?"

She stood and took Lewis's hands. "You deserve a girl whose face lights up when you walk into a room. You'd always know you weren't my first choice. I don't want that for you, Lewis. It was wrong of me to hold on to you just in case. I know that now, and I want more for you. And if you're honest with yourself, I think you'll see you want that for yourself too."

He looked down at their clasped hands, then back at her face. "It's going to be hard to find someone better than you."

"It won't be as hard as you think, and I know you will." She stood on tiptoe and kissed his cheek. "I'm sorry for any hurt I've caused you. Truly I am."

"Goodbye, Charlotte." He squeezed her hands, then released them. Instead of returning through the house, he followed the path around to the sidewalk.

Charlotte hugged herself, tears spilling as guilt washed over her. Holding on to him had been selfish and had given him false hope. She'd hurt him—all because she was afraid to be alone. Would she never learn?

She ran her fingers beneath her eyes and turned to go into the house. A flash of movement drew her attention upward. Nurse Pierce and Joel stood in Aunt Sam's window. She sucked in her breath. Had they been watching her exchange with Lewis?

40

Joel crossed his arms over his chest and glared at Charlotte in the garden below. Her nervous reactions and Lewis's attentions all made sense now. How had he allowed himself to be duped again?

"I've seen that young man come here more than once," Nurse Pierce whispered. "And I believe he's telephoned as well. What do you think they've been doing on those road trips?"

Grinding his teeth together, he whirled to his right and marched from the room. If Mrs. Phillips hadn't been indisposed when he arrived, he might have missed Charlotte's tawdry display.

"*We're just friends.*" Her words echoed in his head. *Friends, my eye!*

Joel gave no explanation to the butler as he plowed through the house to the garden, anger coursing through his veins. He'd thought she was different.

He swung the door wide and came face-to-face with Charlotte.

She jammed her hands on her hips. "How long were you spying on me?"

"Long enough. How long did you think you could go on seeing both of us? One man in the city and one on the road. Very handy." His tone dripped with venom. "And you told me you two were just friends."

She took a step back. "We *are* just friends. I was making that clear to him."

"If that's true, then quit your job with the gas company." He gave her a solid, unblinking stare. "Walk away from him."

Surprise siphoned the blood from her face, then her back became ramrod stiff. "You're telling me if I want to be with you, I have to give up everything so I won't be near Lewis—a man with whom I have only a friendship?"

"I can't see any other way."

"I can." Fury sparked in her eyes. "Get out."

Joel stared at her for several moments, his chest heaving. Deep down he hadn't wanted to believe it, but he must have been right about her and Lewis. If not, why would she act this way? And now she was choosing Lewis over him. How could this be happening all over again?

Without a goodbye, he marched back through the house. Getting involved with Charlotte had been a mistake from the start. He should have realized he would end up getting burned.

Hot, angry tears threatened to fall from Charlotte's eyes as she pounded the piece of steak with her meat mallet. Seeking solace in the kitchen had done little to quell the ache in her heart.

She gave the meat another whack. She'd like to tenderize Joel Brooks. How dare he tell her what she had to do. *Whack*. And why didn't he believe her? *Whack*. If he'd given her the chance to explain, he'd have found out the truth. *Whack*.

"You do know the steak is already dead?" Hannah asked as she entered the kitchen.

"Did Tessa ring you?"

Hannah nodded, then poured herself a cup of coffee. "I see you chased poor Mrs. Agle out of her kitchen again."

"I told her to enjoy an evening off." She set a heavy crockery bowl on the counter before cubing several slices of bread.

"Will you tell me what happened?"

It took only a few minutes to fill her sister in. She dropped the bread cubes into the bowl and started chopping an onion. At least it gave her an excuse to cry. "I don't know what came over him."

"It's hard to imagine Joel reacting like that. He really told you to quit?"

"He did." Charlotte added garlic and sage to her stuffing. "That's when I told him to leave. I'm not going to have another man telling me what I should do, Hannah."

"You shouldn't have to. I'm proud of you for standing your ground."

"I just wish my ground wasn't so hard." She sniffed. "Hand me that melted butter off the stove." She poured it into the bowl and then wet the bread cubes with beef stock. After a quick stir, she spooned the stuffing atop the pounded flank steaks, rolled each one up, and tied them with string.

"Do you think there's any hope for the two of you?"

"If he thinks he can tell me who I can be with or what I can do whenever he doesn't like how I'm acting, then there is no future for us."

"What if he was simply overreacting? Jealous men do odd things."

Charlotte slammed the oven door with a bang. "I think it's better that it's over. I don't know if I could ever trust him again."

Giving the rope a hard yank, Joel secured the swing to the tree branch. He climbed down the ladder and tested the swing's strength before turning to face the eager orphans. "Okay, who's first?"

Several hands shot up, but one caught Joel's eye. He'd wondered if Jacob would ever return to his jovial self following the death of little Harvey. Even though Joel had tried to spend a little extra time with the boy, this was the first sign of Jacob making an effort to have fun again.

"Jacob, come on up and give it a go." He held the swing until the boy clamored on. "Now, we need you to go high and test it out, understand?"

"Yes, sir."

Joel gave the swing a starter push, but Jacob took it from there, pumping his arms and legs and launching the swing toward the clouds.

A few minutes later, the boy slowed and hopped off. "It's a good swing, Dr. Joel. I was up so high I bet Harvey could hear me laughing."

"I bet he could." Joel ruffled his hair. "Now, go help Alice Ann get on the swing. She'll need someone big and strong like you to push her."

Jacob skipped away and Mattie walked over. "The gas company's installation man is here to put the stove in. Where's Charlotte? I thought you were going to surprise her."

"She won't be coming." The thought added another weight to his heavy heart. It had taken Charlotte awhile to convince him to let the orphanage have the stove, but once she did, he'd wasted no time in arranging to have it installed.

He spotted the gas man carrying in a length of pipe. Mrs. Goodwin planned to keep the children out of his way with a picnic in the backyard. Hanging the swing had been Joel's idea. Every child should have a good swing.

"Why is Charlotte not coming?"

"She just isn't. Okay?"

Mattie eyed him critically. "Joel Brooks, what's going on?"

He should have known Mattie would see right through him. "She and I won't be courting any longer."

"Oh, Joel. What did you do?"

"Me? What about her?"

"Yesterday you were happy as a lark. I can't imagine Charlotte doing anything in that short period of time to make you call an end to your courtship."

Thinking about what he'd witnessed reopened the raw wound, and the last thing he wanted to tell anyone—even his sister—was that once again a woman had played him for a fool.

Mattie laid her hand on his arm. "I'm sorry. I can see something happened. What was it?"

He drew in a long breath. "Charlotte's been living a double life."

"Are we talking about the same Charlotte? I find that hard to believe."

Some of the older girls heard Mattie's raised voice and now seemed intent on listening to the conversation. Joel suggested they walk across the yard to the picnic table to talk. Once they were seated, he rubbed the kink in his neck. "You know Charlotte travels for her work with the gas company. I knew she had a traveling companion named Molly Larkin who accompanied her, helped set up her lectures, and acted as a chaperone of sorts."

"Okay."

"And I knew she traveled with a singer who performed prior to her lectures to draw in a larger crowd." He leaned forward, his elbows resting on his knees. "What Charlotte failed to tell me was this performer was a man close to her age named Lewis Mathis."

Mattie's eyes widened. "So you ended the relationship?"

"No. I was taken aback by Lewis when I went to meet Charlotte in Red Wing, but I didn't say anything. The way he acted toward her irritated me, but I kept my mouth shut."

"For once."

He scowled at her. "Are you going to let me finish?"

"Yes. Go on."

"On the way home, I asked her about him and she assured me they were simply friends."

"And you didn't believe her?"

"I did until this morning. I drove over to pick her up to bring her here, but first I went upstairs to check on Mrs. Phillips. While I was in Mrs. Phillips's bedchamber, Nurse Pierce called me to the window because she wanted to discuss something in private with me. That's when I saw Charlotte—in the garden with Lewis, holding hands."

Mattie paled. "Holding hands?"

He nodded and swallowed hard. "Then she kissed him."

"*She* kissed him? How?"

"With her lips."

"That's not what I mean and you know it." Her brows pulled together. "Was it a passionate kiss? Or was it a friendly kiss on the cheek?"

"What difference does it make? Nurse Pierce told me he's been there before, and he's telephoned Charlotte too. Clearly she's lived a double life. She's had one fellow on the road and one at home."

Mattie stood up and shook out her skirt. "She admitted to that?"

"Of course not. She insisted they were only friends."

"She kissed him on the cheek, didn't she?" She pursed her lips. "You know what? You're a fool, Joel Brooks."

"I know that!" He hit his thigh with his fist. "How could I fall in love with two unfaithful women?"

She shook her head slowly and chuckled. "That's not why I said you were a fool."

"This isn't funny. Charlotte was the most passionate, creative, and warmest woman I've ever met. I was planning a future with her. Do you think I wanted to discover this?"

"No." She took his hand and tugged. "Let's talk about it while we help Mrs. Goodwin set out the food. She looks like she has her hands full trying to keep the children out of the gas man's way. Who's that with her? And why is he smoking around the children?"

"Karl Ottosen. He's a good man and he's the chairman of the orphanage board, but he's never without that cigar."

When they reached the picnic baskets, she opened one of the lids and withdrew two jars of canned peaches. She passed them to Joel before reaching in for another two. "You're a scientist. Take a look at things with Charlotte in a logical way. She may very well have stepped out with this Lewis fellow a few times before she met you. After all, they are on the road together, and they are both young and single. She was free to do so, wasn't she?"

He set the peaches on the table and frowned. "Yes."

"At the very least I'm sure they've become dear friends. Wouldn't you be protective and concerned about your female friend given that nasty situation?" She popped open the jar. "Charlotte isn't Prudence. She's never lied to you. If she says they're friends, then you should believe her."

"But Nurse Pierce said—"

"Let me get this straight. You went to the window because Nurse Pierce needed to talk to you in private. Had she ever done anything like that before?"

He shook his head.

She returned to the basket and took out a plate of sandwiches covered in waxed paper. "So the same woman who's been hoping for months you'd open your eyes and see her as the answer to your prayers told you this Lewis had been to the house and had also telephoned Charlotte on various occasions. But I'm guessing you didn't give Charlotte a chance to explain that."

He took the sandwiches from her. "Perhaps listening to Nurse Pierce might not have been the wisest choice."

"Then I'm guessing you marched down to the garden and accused Charlotte because all those memories of Prudence came flooding back." She handed him a second plate of sandwiches. "Does Charlotte even know about Prudence?"

"No." He set the plates down. "I didn't know how to tell her."

"And you're angry with her for not telling you about Lewis?" Mattie shook her head. "Joel, you were engaged!" She took a deep breath. "Did you even let Charlotte defend herself?"

"I gave her a chance to make things right."

She narrowed her eyes. "How?"

"I wanted her away from him."

"And?"

He forced the air from his lungs. "I told her to quit her position with the gas company."

Mattie rubbed her earlobe. "Good grief. What did she say?"

"Basically, 'Get out.'"

"Frankly, I don't blame her." She opened a second basket and withdrew a large bowl of potato salad.

"I wanted them away from each other. No temptations."

"And what makes you think you should get everything you want? Furthermore, what gives you the right to boss her around?"

Boss her around? Her words struck him hard. When Charlotte had told him about her old beau George, he couldn't believe any man would be so callous, and now he'd been no better. On more than one occasion, he'd told her what to do, when to do it, or how to do it. All because he wanted things his way.

Mattie hit him in the stomach with a handful of napkins. "Set these out."

"Now who's bossy?" He tried to sound cheery, but the words came out hollow. He laid the napkins in place and glanced at Mrs. Goodwin, who was rounding up the children. Mr. Ottosen was headed toward the house, probably to check on the gas man's work.

Turning back to Mattie, he sighed. "You're right about how I've been acting. What's wrong with me?"

She began pouring lemonade into glasses. "Joel, you've got a heart of gold, but you've spent your whole life trying to prove yourself. You hated what people said about Dad, and you're determined to show them you're different." She paused and handed him a glass of lemonade. "You'd do anything for anybody, but you feel like you need to be in control. In the hospital, that works well. In a relationship, you need to be able to give and take."

"Don't you see? When things start spinning, I need order." Joel took a sip from his glass.

"I know. Control is your lifeline, but your lifeline should be the Lord."

As Mrs. Goodwin herded the children toward the table, Joel considered what his sister said. Was control his lifeline? Apparently he had some serious soul-searching to do.

He glanced toward the house and saw the man from the gas company return to his wagon for more supplies. Then he spotted

Mr. Ottosen walk up the stairs to the house. He should probably go invite the man to join them.

"Dr. Brooks, would you offer grace?" Mrs. Goodwin asked once they'd all formed a circle.

He nodded and thanked God for his provisions, for his unexpected gifts, and for blessing them all with one another. The children all joined him when he said, "Amen."

"Okay, you all know what to do." Mrs. Goodwin stepped behind the table. "Make a line. Older kids help the young ones."

Joel picked up a plate to pass to blue-eyed Alice Ann when the whole world suddenly tilted.

41

As the ground shook and children toppled like dominoes, debris raining down around them, Joel covered Alice Ann with his body. When the shock faded, he pulled himself up on the edge of the table and whirled toward the house. What had happened?

The back of the house, where Mr. Ottosen had been standing a few moments before, was gone, but where was the board member?

He spun back to assess those with him. Locating his sister first, he helped her up. Her foot caught in the hem of her skirt and she wobbled. "Mattie?"

"I'm fine."

"Everyone else?" One by one, each child climbed to his or her feet. "Leroy, run to the fire station. Tell them there's been an explosion."

The older boy sped away in that direction.

Joel hastily checked each of the children. Some had a few scratches and bruises, but nothing serious. Mrs. Goodwin, however, would be sore from the tumble she took.

Mattie gathered the upset children. "We're all safe now."

Joel squeezed Mattie's shoulder. "I have to go check on the gas man and Mr. Ottosen."

"I'll come too. You might need my help." She started to pull away from the child clinging to her.

"No, not yet." He touched the child's head. "Get the children as far back from the house as you can."

"You think there might be another—"

He silenced her with a stern look.

"I'll get them to move away." She closed her eyes. "Please, Joel, be careful."

Arriving early to prepare for the evening's production, Tessa entered the theater. She paused to let her eyes adjust from the bright sun outside. She started down the hallway toward the dressing rooms but stopped when she saw Mr. Jurgenson speaking with someone.

Even though she'd finished that letter, it had been well after five o'clock when she'd done so. Since he wasn't around when she'd finished, she'd placed it on his desk and locked the office on her way out. The last thing she wanted was to speak with him now.

She froze. If only the two men would continue on their way, she could as well. While she couldn't discern their muffled words, she could tell the discussion was heated by their fierce expressions and wild gestures.

The man with Mr. Jurgenson looked up and spotted her. She'd never seen him before. Was this Mr. K. O.?

Apparently not wanting their conversation to be public, Mr. Jurgenson led the man down the remainder of the hallway and they stepped into the director's office. Tessa eased her way behind them. Maybe she could surreptitiously listen to their conversation. That's what any good Pinkerton agent would do.

She reached the wall outside the office door and plastered herself against it.

"Listen, this can't go on forever." Mr. Jurgenson's voice sounded tense.

Then the office door closed, and so did her hopes of hearing any more about the mysterious visitor.

Charlotte traced the butterfly template on a sheet of yellow construction paper and then began to cut out the delicate creature. Beside her, Hannah did likewise with pink paper. They both passed their butterflies to Nurse Pierce, who added a wire stem to each one. At the ball, they'd insert the butterflies throughout the floral decorations.

"Thank you for helping me with these." Charlotte laid her butterfly in front of the nurse. "I think these will help tie the decorations together for the ball."

"About the ball . . ." Hannah set down her scissors. "How are you holding up?"

The butterfly blurred beneath Charlotte's gaze. A teardrop splattered on the construction paper and spread in a dark circle. Her heart ached in a way so different than it had at the loss of her parents. Every time she thought of Joel, anger and love mixed in a painful swirl.

If she'd only made things clear to Lewis when she had the chance, then this wouldn't have happened. Still, why had Joel overreacted?

Worst of all, she now knew any future with him was impossible. His telling her to quit her work for the gas company spoke volumes. She'd always known he liked control, but she thought he kept that confined to his work. Now she had no doubt the tendency would always follow him home at night.

The butler stepped into the doorway. "Miss Charlotte, Dr. Brooks would like to speak with you outside."

Hannah cut another butterfly out of the paper. "I'll go talk to him, Charlotte. You don't have to."

Charlotte blotted her eyes and squared her shoulders. "No, I'll go."

Too many things had gone unsaid, and she intended to rectify that.

She stepped onto the front porch and gulped. Instead of the polished man who usually greeted her, Joel had arrived in a dirty, torn shirt. Black smeared his cheek, his face pale and drawn.

Charlotte pressed her hand to her throat. "What's wrong?"

"Let's go to the south porch and sit down."

He sounded so tired she didn't have the heart to argue with him—at least about that. Instead, she walked around to the side and settled in a rattan chair.

After he sat down in the chair facing her, he ran a hand through his hair. "There's been an accident."

"With your motorcar?"

"No, at the orphanage."

She felt the blood drain from her face. "What happened? Is anyone injured?"

"Mrs. Goodwin and the children are all fine, but the gas man was installing the new gas stove and there was an explosion. A visiting board member suffered a broken leg. The man from the gas company received a concussion."

"My stove caused it?" Her stomach roiled. "If I hadn't—"

"Stop right there." He held up his hand. "This isn't your fault. Mr. Ottosen tossed a cigar butt. There must have been a slow leak and that's what ignited it."

"Where are the children?"

"Mattie and Mrs. Goodwin took them to my house."

"But you don't have enough room for twelve children, do you?"

"We'll make do."

Charlotte stood. "Come with me."

She didn't wait for him, but his footsteps told her he was following. Inside the house, she found Aunt Sam sitting at her desk. The nurse set her butterfly aside as soon as she spotted Joel.

"Dr. Brooks, we weren't expecting you again today." Nurse Pierce glanced from him to Charlotte and frowned in disappointment.

Charlotte clenched her fists. She'd been trying so hard to be kind to the nurse. Why did she have to act like this? "Joel, tell Aunt Sam what's happened at the orphanage."

"Yes, please do." Aunt Sam lowered her spectacles.

He quickly relayed the events of the afternoon. "Charlotte

thought you might have an idea for a place the children might temporarily stay?"

"As a matter of fact, I do." She straightened in her chair. "They'll come here. Tessa can share a room with Charlotte. Nurse Pierce can return to her home at night, as I no longer need her twenty-four hours a day. Then there will be a room for Mrs. Goodwin and two others for the girls upstairs. The boys can sleep in the billiards room on cots and pallets. It might be a little crowded, but I think they'll have a grand adventure."

Nurse Pierce paled. "B-b-but Mrs. Phillips, that will be a great inconvenience."

"To you or to me?" She waved her hand dismissively. "We'll all have to bend a little, but I won't have it any other way. Dr. Brooks, have Henry follow you back with the motorcar, and he can begin transporting the children here."

Joel smiled. "They can take a streetcar, Mrs. Phillips."

"They've already lost their parents, and now they've lost their home. I think the least I can do is give them a ride in a motorcar. We'll provide good food and a place to sleep until we can find more suitable accommodations."

"Thank you, ma'am."

She shooed him away. "Go on now and bring those children back."

Charlotte watched him walk away and swallowed the lump in her throat. How was she going to get over him if he was constantly around?

By the time twelve children and one additional woman squeezed into Aunt Sam's home, Charlotte discovered that even a large house on Summit Avenue could begin to feel rather crowded.

"Geoffrey, will you show these lovely ladies to their rooms? I'm sure they'd like to get settled. Maybe show them the gardens too." Aunt Sam turned to Charlotte. "And you take Dr. Brooks down to the billiards room and help him set up those cots."

Scooping up a pile of blankets, Charlotte nodded to Aunt Sam, then hurried out of the drawing room. Joel followed behind with the cots from the attic in hand. When she opened the door to the stuffy room, her gaze fell to their unfinished game on the billiards table, and her heart throbbed. She set the blankets on the table and ran her hand down the green felt along the side rail.

Joel lowered his armload of cots with a clatter. "Where do you want—" He stopped speaking and approached the billiards table. "Charlotte, I think we need to talk."

She ignored him and picked up the top blanket. If she tried to talk now, her feelings would spill out like an upturned sugar bowl. These children were homeless because she'd wanted to be kind. She and Joel were over because she'd wanted to be nice to Lewis. Wanting to be loved was costing her a lot of heartache.

She swallowed the lump in her throat. "I think we could set the cots up over here if we move these chairs to the other side of the room. The three little boys will have to sleep on pallets." Tears gathered in her eyes, but she couldn't let them fall. "I thought maybe we could put them under the billiards table." Her voice broke, so she quickly unfolded the blanket. "It would be like they'd have their own clubhouse."

Joel reached for the blanket, then stilled her hands with his own. "I'm sorry."

"Please, Joel, not now."

"I said things I'm ashamed of. I would never want you to give up something you love. I was angry and I didn't mean it." He hung his head and drew in a deep breath. "And I was prideful. I didn't tell you something I should have." Joel released her hands and reached for the cot's heavy burlap. He began to insert the first long, wood slat along the side. "I was engaged to a woman named Prudence."

A tiny gasp escaped Charlotte's lips.

He jammed the second slat in and leaned against it. "I know I should have told you."

"What happened?"

"I discovered her kissing a friend of mine."

"So when you saw Lewis and me in the garden—"

"It felt like it was happening all over again." He set the cot down and slipped the crisscross support pieces in place. "I should have given you the chance to explain."

"And I should have told you about Lewis earlier." She sat down in a chair and clutched the blanket to her chest. "He'd been asking to see me, and every time he said something, I put off giving him a firm answer—until earlier today when I told him about you."

"Then like a heel I came down and accused you." Joel sat down on the cot he'd constructed. "Can we simply forgive each other and get on with planning the ball? We can get back to normal, and soon we'll have all the money you need to get your new food ideas started at the hospital."

"That can't happen now, Joel."

"You mean you don't want to work with me on the ball?"

"No, I mean we're going to have to change the cause." She set the blanket in the chair, walked over to the pool table, and leaned against it. "With the explosion at the orphanage, the children's needs are more immediate. It won't be hard to get word out that the charity ball has a new cause—a new home for the orphans. We'll probably raise even more money."

"Charlotte, are you sure?"

"I've never been more certain." Absentmindedly, she rolled the white ball on the table toward a striped green one. It sank in the corner pocket, missing the target altogether. Scratched. Like her plans.

"I hate this. You've worked so hard. What about your dreams for the hospital?"

She forced a smile and lifted one shoulder. "I can share some of the ideas with you that don't require more money. In fact, some of them might actually help you cut costs."

"Save us money? Why didn't you share that with me when we first met?"

"You didn't really give me a chance."

He stood and joined her at the table. "Will you give *us* another chance?"

When he reached for her, she stepped back. "Joel, I can't."

"I thought we agreed to forgive and forget."

"I can forgive you." She met his gaze, staring into his green eyes. Her words came out as a whisper. "But I can't forget. I don't dare."

"What are you talking about?"

"I promised myself I'd never be courted by anyone who wanted to control me."

"Is this about me telling you to give up your position?" His voice rose. "For heaven's sake, Charlotte, I said I was sorry. I didn't mean that. I don't want to control you. I want to love you."

Love? The air squeezed from her lungs. This was the second time he'd uttered that word, but she couldn't let it sway her—not now when she knew what she had to do.

"I want to give my heart to you, but I can't. We're like oil and vinegar. We'll never blend. If it isn't one thing, it's another. You have goals and so do I, but they don't mix. That seems to make an exciting but truly combustible pair, and today of all days should be a clear indication of what can happen when sparks fly."

"You know what I think the problem is?" The muscle in his jaw twitched, making the mole on his cheek bob.

"What?"

"You'd rather settle for what's easy than fight for something better." Frustration filled his voice. "You haven't ever given anything your whole heart."

"And you'd like everything to be in a nice, predictable order, even when it comes to your heart. Well, I've got news for you, Joel Brooks. Love is messy."

"You're right, Charlotte. We'll never really mix." His hand sliced through the air. "We'll finish planning the ball."

"And then?"

"We'll say goodbye for good—like you want."

42

Mr. Jurgenson needed to do something with those bushy eyebrows. Tessa bit back a chuckle as she exchanged a cheery "good morning" with her employer and Miss Walker.

After the tumultuous weekend at the house and a festive trip to Saint Paul's Independence Day parade yesterday, coming to work this Tuesday morning was almost a relief. Between twelve grieving children in the house and a lovesick Charlotte, Tessa needed to get away. Even Sunday's church service and the parade had done little to lighten the heaviness that had descended over Aunt Sam's home.

Instead of a polite response to her greeting, Mr. Jurgenson crossed his arms over his chest. "We seem to have a problem, young lady."

"If this is about the letter, I'm sorry it took so long for me to finish." She dutifully averted her eyes and tried to look chastened.

"If only it were that simple." His sharp tone made her bristle. "No, it's about some missing receipts."

Her gaze darted to Miss Walker. "Receipts?"

"A few weeks ago, I began to wonder why our receipts for the weekend didn't seem to match the numbers in attendance, so this week I counted the money before I left the cash box with Miss Walker. She tells me she had you tally and enter the figures. Is that correct?"

"Yes, she told me you wanted me to enter them, but—"

He silenced her with a glare. "The figure you entered is significantly less than what I knew to be in the box." Flipping open the ledger he had tucked under his arm, he pointed to the figure Miss Walker had changed.

"That's not what I entered, Mr. Jurgenson. That's not even my handwriting."

"The only people who had access to this ledger were Miss Walker and yourself. Do you expect me to believe Miss Walker would steal from the theater? That's utterly ridiculous."

"But she has been, long before I came. She admitted it to me." Tessa turned to Miss Walker. "Tell him. You know it's the truth."

Miss Walker met Mr. Jurgenson's momentary scrutiny with a look of wide-eyed innocence. She followed it with a well-timed eye roll in Tessa's direction.

Apparently Tessa wasn't the only one who could act.

"Miss Gregory, you expect me to believe that our proper Miss Walker would stoop to theft? How dare you accuse such a fine lady."

"But—"

"Enough. I intend to visit with your aunt about this directly."

Aunt Sam? Why did he need to speak with her? Oh dear. If she was told, Hannah and Charlotte would soon know too.

"Aunt Sam is still recovering. Are you sure it's necessary to bother her?"

"I think she needs to know she has a thief living in her home. Gather your things, Miss Gregory. You are no longer welcome in the theater."

"I did not steal that money, Mr. Jurgenson." Her heart pounded so hard she feared she might faint.

She took a calming breath. It was going to be all right. Although she hated being blamed for something she didn't do, her sisters would believe her, and not coming to this office was perfectly fine with her as long as she still had the play.

Mr. Jurgenson snapped the ledger shut. "One more thing. Miss Walker told me about your role in the play. I've already spoken to the play's director about your dismissal. He's securing your replacement as we speak."

Her part in the play? Tears flooded her eyes and an ache spread across her chest. This wasn't fair. She'd earned that role.

She glanced at Miss Walker, who merely quirked her lip with a hint of smug satisfaction. She clenched her fists. Miss Walker would not see her cry.

If only she'd spoken to Mr. Jurgenson right away. Would he have believed her then? Now she was trapped. Her sisters would believe her, but what about Aunt Sam? Would she believe the "niece" she'd only known a short time, or her old family friend?

One glance in the mirror told Joel he didn't look any better than he felt. Three agitated nights and another early-morning baby delivery had left him exhausted. He'd slept in this morning with Dr. Ancker's blessing, but he was due for rounds at eight.

He washed his face, squeezed a bit of shaving cream onto his fingers, and spread it over his coarse beard growth. Adding a little water, he rubbed it until he had a foamy lather and then ran his safety razor down his cheek.

He could still feel Charlotte's hand against his cheek from when they'd last kissed. Everywhere he went, she haunted him—in his office, in his Model T, in his dreams. He couldn't even look at an apple without thinking of her. Like a shell pressed into the damp sand, she'd made an imprint. But what would he need to do in order for a sea of forgetfulness to come wash the memories away?

But is that what he truly wanted? To say goodbye to her forever?

At church Sunday, the minister had talked about self-sacrifice, and again Charlotte had taken her place at the forefront of his thoughts. She'd been the perfect example of self-sacrifice, giving up her dream for the hospital because the orphans needed the funds right away.

"What have you sacrificed for the ones you love?" the minister had asked. "What are you willing to give up to secure their happiness?"

Since Sunday, Joel's prayers had become more fervent than ever. For years, his favorite verse had been Psalm 37:4, "Delight thyself also in the LORD: and he shall give thee the desires of thine heart," but for the first time in his life, he wasn't sure what the desire of his heart truly was. Sure, he wanted the assistant superintendent's position at the hospital, but would it fill the gaping hole in his heart?

No, only one person would do that, and she didn't believe they could have a future together.

He tapped the razor on the side of the sink and set it aside before rinsing his face and patting it dry. Back in his bedroom, he slipped his shirt on and began to do up the buttons. His fingers fumbled. What was wrong with him?

Charlotte.

She'd told him love was messy. Did he like things to line up in neat rows so much that he expected it in his relationships? He'd told Mattie that when things started to spin in his life, he reached for control. She'd said he clung to control like a lifeline, but she reminded him the Lord should be his lifeline. When had he stopped turning to the Lord for his answers?

The realization kicked him hard. He sank down on the edge of the bed and lowered his head to his hands. *Lord, I've been trying to do it on my own again, haven't I? I can't believe the mess I've made of things, but I'm clinging to you now—my real lifeline. Show me what I should do about Charlotte. I refuse to control her. I can't push her, and I won't demand anything of her. But I can't stop loving her either.*

He'd never felt more powerless or less in control.

Or more at peace.

I'm putting her in your hands, Lord. Please show me how to love her, even if she won't let me come near.

With a basket of paper butterflies on her arm, Charlotte walked toward Hannah's house with Tessa in tow. Despite Aunt Sam's adamant refusal to believe Mr. Jurgenson's accusations, Tessa had lost her usual zeal.

"Tessa, why didn't you tell anyone about Miss Walker?"

"I did tell someone."

"Lincoln? Then we should telephone him."

"No, I told Joel."

Charlotte stopped on the sidewalk. "Are you certain? He didn't say anything to me."

"I swore him to secrecy. He tried to get me to tell you."

Ooooh, that man. Accusing her of keeping secrets when he hadn't said a word about her sister being in trouble. He probably thought he could handle it all himself.

She took a deep breath and tempered her thoughts. That wasn't fair. With Tessa's imagination, he probably thought she was making most of it up. "Why didn't you have us call Joel yesterday when all this happened?"

She shrugged. "It wouldn't have made a difference. Besides, he was picking up Molly, remember?"

Given all that had transpired between Joel and her, Charlotte was surprised when he'd telephoned the house on Monday and left a message that he would be picking up Molly as planned. He said he would take Molly to her sister's home to convalesce, and Charlotte should give her a couple of days before visiting.

"I still can't believe he made me quit the play." Tessa heaved a sigh.

Shaken from her thoughts, Charlotte touched her sister's arm. "I know you loved acting in the play. I'm sorry you lost your part."

"I guess it's time for me to return from Neverland. Everyone has to grow up some time."

Charlotte wrapped her arm around Tessa's shoulders. "Not you, Tessa. You're going to be my little sister forever."

She dropped her chin to her chest. "That's what I'm afraid of."

Charlotte chuckled as she climbed the steps to Hannah's house. She knocked on the door and Mrs. Umdahl answered. "Mrs. Cole is in the parlor with the baby."

"Thank you." A few seconds later, Charlotte set the basket on a marble-topped table and glanced at Hannah, who had Ellie with her on the divan. Hannah bent over and smiled at the baby. Ellie cooed and blew spit bubbles in response.

"My turn." Tessa knelt by the divan and took over playing with Ellie, so Hannah joined Charlotte at the table.

"How's my favorite niece?" Charlotte asked.

"Magical." She glanced back at her daughter. "You need more butterflies?"

"I'm afraid so. Can you make some when she naps?"

"Sure." She studied her sister's face. "How are you—honestly?"

Moisture formed in Charlotte's eyes. "Do you think I'll ever get over him?"

Tessa moaned. "Lottie, if love was a virus, you'd be on your deathbed."

Charlotte scowled at her, but Hannah laughed. "Okay, wise one, what's our sister's cure?"

She hiked a shoulder. "You need to ask the doctor."

"That's not funny and you know it." Charlotte sat down in a rose-colored parlor chair and traced a carved hand rest with her finger.

Ellie's giggles turned to fussing, so Hannah swaddled her, lifted her to her shoulder, and swayed back and forth. "Are you sure you can't make things work?"

Charlotte dabbed her eyes. "I truly don't see how two people who are so different can have a good relationship."

"Nothing's impossible with God, Lottie." Hannah patted Ellie's back. "Joel should never have spoken to you like that, but why did you let things with Lewis continue in the first place?"

"I guess part of me didn't want him to hate me, and part of me wanted to have him on the back burner in case things didn't work out with Joel."

"Would you rather be with someone you don't love than be alone?" Tessa sounded incredulous.

Charlotte swallowed. "No, now that I've felt the real thing, I know how silly that was."

Ellie nestled into Hannah's shoulder, sleep finally claiming her. Hannah laid her in a cradle she kept in the corner and then sat in the chair beside Charlotte. "Before you can be happy, you've got to get over that other ailment you have."

"More medical stuff? You too, Hannah? Do you both enjoy making me cry?"

"Sorry, but you also have a bad case of people pleasing. You want people to like you."

"Doesn't everyone?" Charlotte picked up one of the butterflies and began to wrap a wire around it.

"I don't care if people like me. I'm going to be myself no matter what." Tessa leaned her back against the divan, raised her knees, and wrapped her arms around them. "Unless it was a movie director or Allan Pinkerton. I'd want a director to like me, and I'd love to be a Pinkerton agent."

"So you'd want them to like you because you want something from them." Charlotte gave her a disapproving frown.

"So?"

"Ladies." Hannah sighed. "I suppose most people do want to be liked, but you have to realize you can't make everyone happy. The only one you should want to please is the Lord."

Hannah's words stung. "And now? You think I'm trying to make Joel happy?"

"No, that's why I think you need to give this relationship a second thought. For the first time in your life, you're willing to not make him happy, which means you feel safe enough with him to risk disappointing him. You would never have done that with George. I think you believe deep down that Joel will love you even if you don't give him what he wants. Charlotte, I think you trust him."

Charlotte rubbed her temples. Was Hannah right? Had she

settled all those times in order to keep others happy? She hadn't considered what God would have her do in any of those situations.

And did she believe Joel loved her enough to free her to be herself? Even if that were true, how could two people so prone to disagreeing ever agree on anything as important as a future together?

All they had was a dab of love in the bottom of a jar. How did she know if it was time to gather some empty vessels?

43

Up at four in the morning, Charlotte gathered the ingredients for the desserts she planned to make for the ball tonight. Although the hotel's kitchen would be providing a lovely iced white cake, Charlotte was adding some different specialty cakes of her own. She'd make three batches each of Lady Baltimore, lemon jelly, and coconut cream cakes. Yesterday she'd made the Lady Baltimore cake, so this morning she could fill it with raisins, dates, and nuts while the other cakes were baking.

The house was blissfully quiet. By eight o'clock, it would most likely be bustling with activity. With twelve children present, chaos had become the norm, but with the ball imminent, today would become rather exciting.

She hummed while she worked. It was nice to have the kitchen to herself too. Mrs. Agle would arrive by six to start breakfast. By then, Charlotte hoped to be nearly finished with her preparations.

Once the gas oven was lit, she mixed up the lemon jelly cake batter, poured it into the prepared round pans, and slid the pans into the oven. She'd mix the lemon filling for those and then get things ready for the Lady Baltimore cake.

Hearing the front door open, she sighed. Mrs. Agle must have decided to come early. She didn't fault the cook for her early arrival. After all, she was preparing for more folks than usual. But so much for Charlotte's solitude.

She slipped into the pantry to find the six lemons she'd set aside for the lemon filling. Where were they? They'd been on the second shelf the other day. Finally she noticed the yellow orbs in a colander set on an upper shelf. Mounting the step stool, she reached for the colander.

Just as her fingers found the rim, the pantry door slammed shut.

Charlotte jumped, dropping the colander on the cupboard. The lemons rolled onto the floor with a thunk. She bolted for the door and tried the knob, but it didn't give. How had it locked? Charlotte yelled for several minutes, but her shouting brought no one. That didn't surprise her. The kitchen was a long way from the bedrooms.

If Mrs. Agle had been the person who arrived a few minutes ago, wouldn't she be in the kitchen by now? But what if it wasn't Mrs. Agle? Maybe it was Nurse Pierce. She had a key and often came early. Would she ignore Charlotte's cries?

A whiff of browning lemon cake drifted in. If she didn't get them out soon, the cakes would be a charred mess.

Glancing upward, she noticed the transom window. It opened toward the kitchen, away from the pantry. Could she climb out that way?

Charlotte looked around the pantry. Opposite the built-in cupboards, a small table was pressed against the wall. She pushed it over to the door, but even if she stood on it, she'd not be able to reach the transom.

Ah, but if she put the stool on the table, she could make it.

She set the stool on the table's surface, then hoisted herself onto the table and stood. So far so good.

She nudged the stool in place, then carefully climbed onto it. It wobbled and she caught herself on the window frame. With the added height, she could stick her head and shoulders through the opening, but it wasn't enough to get out.

Thickening smoke made her choke and sputter. If she didn't get to those cakes in the next few minutes, the smell would surely wake everyone in the house. That wouldn't be a good way for the orphans, whose experience was all too recent, to start their day.

She yelled again through the open window. *Please, God, send me some help.* After several minutes, she stopped shouting. Since no one had come, she had no choice but to attempt to climb out.

Hoisting herself as far into the transom as possible, she pushed off the stool with her toes. She felt the stool teeter, then it tumbled over and rolled onto the floor with a bang. She wiggled a little farther until she was halfway out. Just a little more . . .

She stopped. What was she going to do if she went any farther? Fall on her head? This had been a horrible idea. If she backed out now, hopefully she could drop safely to the table.

Her eyes watered and burned from the smoke. At least the air was clearer down below. Bracing herself, she tried to inch back into the pantry, but her body didn't budge. She squirmed but remained fast. What was she caught on?

She released an exasperated breath. This day was not starting out well.

The Model T rumbled up Summit Avenue. Once again Joel couldn't sleep, so he'd decided to give Charlotte a hand in transporting her cakes.

Who was he kidding? He wanted to see her. Since the other day, he'd done some serious soul-searching, and he had something important to talk to her about.

He parked the motorcar, hurried up the walk, and went around to the kitchen door in the back. That way he wouldn't wake anyone.

He rapped on the back door. No answer. That was odd. Charlotte had to be up by now.

Concern mounting, he tried the knob and found the door locked. He cupped his hands to one of the panes and peered inside. Darkness greeted him.

No! The room was filled with dense smoke.

"Charlotte! Open up!" He pounded on the door again. Where was she?

He heard a faint response. Was she hurt? Overcome by the smoke?

He seized a rock from the herb garden and broke one of the windowpanes on the door. The glass chinked onto the kitchen floor, and he cleared the remaining shards with his gloved hand before reaching to unlock the door and swing it wide.

"Charlotte?" He coughed on the smoke.

"Up here!"

He followed the sound of her voice until he spotted her. Good grief. How did she get up there?

Charlotte trembled with relief at the sight of Joel. But how would she explain her predicament?

Before reaching her, he threw open the sashes on two windows. The air began to clear. He rushed over to her. "What are you doing up there?"

Even though her ribs ached from the pressure on them, she had to take care of first things first. "I'll tell you after you get the cakes out of the oven."

He yanked open the oven door and black smoke billowed out. Using a dish towel, he pulled the first pan from the oven and tossed it out the back door. He repeated the process with the rest of the cake rounds.

Charlotte cringed at the damage he was doing to her pans, but she'd probably be doing the same thing if she wasn't dangling from the ceiling. "Can you get me down now?"

He hurried over and looked up at her. With a chuckle, he shook his head in disbelief and pulled off his gloves. "I can't wait to hear about this."

"Just get me down. I think the key is still in the lock."

He jiggled the key and she heard a click. He started to turn the handle, but at that moment she realized what he would see when he opened the door—her feet hanging in the air over the table, ankles and undergarments in plain view. "Wait!"

"What's wrong? Does it hurt you when I move the door?"

"No, but you need to close your eyes."

"How am I going to get you down with my eyes shut?"

"It's not proper to see me this way."

He sighed. "Charlotte, I promise not to look anywhere I shouldn't, okay?"

"It's not like I actually have a choice."

Joel eased the door open but had to push the table out of the way to squeeze inside. He chuckled again. "Let me climb up on this table, and then I'll help you out."

"What would help me the most is for you to stop laughing at me."

Two solid thumps and the sound of his voice told her he was now standing on the table behind her.

"Why are you just standing there?"

"Enjoying the view."

"Joel!"

"Easy, Charlotte. I'm only teasing." She heard him move on the table and felt his hands press onto her hips. "Can you wiggle out now?"

She squirmed in the window frame and he pulled. Her face flushed hot as he wrapped his arm around her upper thighs. As long as she lived she'd not forget this.

"That's it. Come on down. I've got you."

With a final twist, she freed her upper body. With her flush against him, he lowered her down until her shoes touched the table. But instead of releasing her, the hand now around her waist tightened. She could feel the rapid rise and fall of his chest against her back.

They were standing on a table inside a pantry, but the moment that passed between them stole her breath.

Then she coughed and the spell was broken.

"Let's get you out of here." He released her and hopped off the table.

She placed her hands on his shoulders and let him lift her down. Again, he held her longer than necessary and a current raced through her. If they were still courting, she'd have wished he would steal a kiss.

Truthfully, even though they weren't courting, she still wished it. Was he thinking the same thing?

"I, uh, uh . . . better move the table," Joel said.

"Probably."

He removed his hands and tugged the table out of the way. Finally Charlotte could step into freedom.

Mrs. Agle entered the kitchen and stopped when she saw the two of them exiting the tiny room. "Charlotte Gregory, what were you and the doctor doing in my pantry?"

44

"But I don't understand why Nurse Pierce didn't come to your aid." Joel plowed his hand through his hair. "Mrs. Agle, are you sure you saw her when you came in?"

"Yes, sir. She was sitting in the drawing room."

"Then she had to hear me yelling and smell the smoke," Charlotte said.

"Why would she do such a thing?"

"Oh, I don't know." She dramatically batted her eyelashes at him. "You're so wonderful, Dr. Brooks. Maybe you can figure it out."

"That's not funny, Charlotte. She's always flirted with me, but by not helping you, she's gone too far." Mouth rigid, jaw flexing, Joel gripped the back of a kitchen chair until his knuckles whitened. "Whatever her reason, I'll release her from her work here today. I won't have her mistreating you anymore. I'll have Mattie come to do any further rehabilitation your aunt requires."

"No, Joel. Don't release her. She's good for Aunt Sam." Charlotte drew in a long breath. "Besides, I got myself locked in the pantry."

"Then I'll at least make the situation clear."

"Well, what are we going to do about these?" Mrs. Agle carried in a stack of burnt cakes. She set them on the kitchen table, and like uneven bricks they tumbled over in a charred heap.

"I'll never get the cakes done now." Charlotte's voice cracked.

"I'll help you." Mrs. Agle struck the first pan against the trash bin and then pried out the remaining bits with a knife. "After I make breakfast, I'm all yours. What do you have left?"

"I need to assemble the Lady Baltimore cake, remake those lemon rounds, and then bake and ice the coconut cream."

"Well, I can make the cakes for you if you'll mix up the icing you want me to use."

Joel took the empty pan from Mrs. Agle, then turned to Charlotte. "And I can help after I find Nurse Pierce and set her straight. I'll scrub these so you can get started on making the cakes again. I'll do whatever you need, and you can boss me around for a change."

Everything was perfect. Charlotte surveyed the ballroom and her lips curled in a broad smile. In one corner of the room, the Saint Paul Orchestra was setting up. On the far wall, one of the hotel's staff was filling the pedestaled cut-glass punch bowl with lemonade. She prayed that in less than an hour, the room would come alive with wealthy patrons, all giving to the orphans.

It was hard to believe it had all come together. When she'd arrived an hour and a half behind schedule this morning, she'd been shocked to find everything well in hand. The nurses were garnishing the garden arches with flowers, and Tessa was adding the whimsical paper butterflies. The lemonade table had been set up, as had the banquet room.

She recalled Molly telling her about Elisha and the widow and how he'd told the widow to collect all the empty jars she could. This ball was Charlotte's empty jars. She was setting out the whole affair in hopes that God would turn her little effort into a grand success.

And she hadn't made a mess of anything. A smile curled her lips again. She shouldn't feel so proud of Joel for the way he'd reprimanded Nurse Pierce, but she was. She'd heard his roar all the way in the kitchen. His defense of Charlotte had been touching, and his anger on her behalf was heartwarming. Still, she'd felt a bit sorry for the love-struck nurse.

Charlotte walked down the hall into the banquet room, located her cakes, and set the first ones out on the footed cake stands she'd brought. Joel had proven an able assistant, whipping frosting for the coconut cream cakes for nearly twenty minutes without complaint. Then he'd helped her transport the finished cakes and later returned for the ones Mrs. Agle had prepared. She'd thanked him before he left to get ready for the ball, but he'd said nothing to indicate his generosity was meant for anything other than supporting the orphans. He hadn't even asked her to save him a dance.

She shook her head. It was just as well. She had too much to oversee without Joel invading her thoughts at every turn. But he'd seemed so different today. Oh, he was the same strong, caring, meticulous man, but he was also abundantly supportive. She could almost convince herself he believed in her like she'd always wanted.

Almost.

It didn't matter anyway, because after tonight, they'd agreed to go their separate ways. If only her heart didn't ache so much at the thought.

When Joel arrived, he found Charlotte standing by Lewis in the foyer. The sight kicked him in the stomach. Why hadn't he thought of this? Of course Lewis would escort her now. The young man probably leaped at the chance, and he couldn't blame him one bit.

Charlotte stole his breath. Her deep sapphire dress had lots of glimmering beads that caught the light in her hazel eyes. No necklace graced her creamy neck, but her hair was done up and was decorated with a matching beaded hair ornament of some sort.

Truly a vision.

But he'd promised himself not to push her. He'd show her his love and wait for God to show him when he should make his feelings known. He'd been prepared to this morning, but God had closed that door, with Charlotte dangling from a transom. He chuckled to himself. Maybe he should have spoken to her when she was trapped and couldn't get away. She would have at least had to listen.

He spotted Terrence Ruckman sitting at the ticket table, and his chest constricted. He still had no answer about the missing charity funds at the hospital.

Knute Ostberg flanked him. Good. He simply couldn't trust Terrence.

Dr. and Mrs. Ancker would be arriving soon, and Joel would need to help get the reception committee in place. He couldn't avoid Charlotte all night. It was time. Taking a deep breath, he squared his shoulders and walked over to speak to her.

If Joel looked good with his shirtsleeves rolled up, he was toe-curling handsome in a black tailcoat. The satin-faced lapels on the jacket accented the white waistcoat and bow tie. White gloves, a top hat, and his ever-present stunning smile completed his ensemble.

"Hello, Lewis." He nodded to the man, then turned to Charlotte. He gave her an appreciative smile. "Charlotte, you look stunning."

Her cheeks warmed. "Thank you."

He dipped his head. "Now, if you'll both excuse me, I see Dr. Ancker and his wife arriving."

A few minutes later, Joel brought the hospital's superintendent and his wife over to meet Charlotte. "It's a pleasure to meet you, Miss Gregory," Dr. Ancker said. "Dr. Brooks has been singing your praises. Thank you for organizing this event."

"Thank you, Doctor." She self-consciously touched the base of her throat with her gloved hand. "I only wish we could have given the funds to the hospital. I know there are many needs."

"Terrence found some money for Dr. Brooks's microscope." Dr. Ancker smiled. "God always provides."

Soon the guests arrived. When Charlotte caught sight of Kathleen O'Grady, she flinched. What kind of trouble would she cause?

Kathleen waved to her. "Hello, Charlotte. I'd like you to meet my brother Kelly."

"Mr. O'Grady, you brought Kathleen to one of my cooking demonstrations, didn't you?"

"Yes, I did. I'm glad we could come tonight. Kathleen made it sound like all the bigwigs would be here."

"There are a lot of people who want to support the children." Charlotte turned to Kathleen. "How did you hear about the ball?"

"Actually, Kelly heard about it from a client."

"I see." She gave them a solicitous smile. "I need to go greet some other guests. Thank you for coming. I hope you have a lovely time."

By the time the clock chimed eight, the ballroom was abuzz. Charlotte had never seen so many lovely dresses in one place.

Hannah wrapped her arm around Charlotte's waist. "I'm so proud of you. This is truly an accomplishment. Thank you for all your hard work."

She smiled and glanced around the roomful of guests. "Thank God for filling the jars."

Aunt Sam nudged Charlotte's arm. "Dear, why isn't the music starting? Isn't Joel the chairman of the floor?"

Charlotte sucked in her breath. Although they'd talked about it, they'd never decided who would fill that role. If someone didn't start things off soon, this ball would be over before it began.

Joel glanced from Lewis to his watch to the orchestra. Why wasn't Lewis taking Charlotte out on the dance floor to begin the ball?

Joel knew the program by heart. The first dance would be the grand march to "The Millionaires" by Henninger. Once the chairman of the floor and the woman he escorted took the floor, the others would follow.

He made a beeline through the crowd to Lewis. "It's time to start. Why are you still standing here?"

"I'm not the chairman of the floor. You are."

"But this is Charlotte's event and you're with her."

Lewis looked perplexed. "No I'm not. The only one she has eyes for is you, and you're an idiot if you let her go."

Joel blinked. He already knew that to be true. Was this the moment he'd been praying about?

"You're right, Lewis. Thanks." Looking across the ballroom, he found Charlotte standing with her sister and aunt. Inquisitive gazes pierced him as he crossed the dance floor, but his eyes locked only with Charlotte's.

He stopped in front of her and held out his hand. "I believe it's time we led the grand march, Miss Gregory."

She hesitated and Hannah elbowed her side. "Go."

Charlotte licked her lips, then placed her hand into his. He nodded to the orchestra and the fanfare began.

Quick, quick, slow, slow. With flutes twittering a lively beat, Charlotte recalled the movements to the two-step march. Joel released his hold on her back, slid his hand down her arm, and turned her until they were both facing forward in a sweetheart wrap. My, but he was a wonderful dancer.

Alone on the dance floor for the first full spin, she should have felt self-conscious. Instead, in his arms, she felt an explosion of joy from deep inside her, refusing to be stifled. If this was to be the last time he ever held her, she'd relish every moment.

The floor around them began to fill with other couples. Joel's strong hands did not pressure her into following his lead but directed her in subtle ways. Had she been wrong about him? Was Joel trying to lead her in their relationship, or was he controlling her?

Her father had been a strong man. He'd tried to protect her mother and all three of his girls from every danger and heartache. Why had she not seen that as controlling?

There was only one reason. Just as Joel had come into their

relationship with a Prudence-filled fear, she'd carried a George-filled fear.

A strong man like Joel never had a chance.

He drew her into another sweetheart wrap. As they danced side by side, he leaned his mouth close to her ear. "I still love you, Charlotte."

Her heart skipped a beat. The last strains of the music died away and there they stood. Words wouldn't come. There was too much to say.

Then the theme song of the evening began, a waltz called "Butterflies," and without hesitation he swept her into his arms again.

45

Being relegated to Aunt Sam's side was seriously hurting Tessa's ability to enjoy the ball. Hannah and Lincoln, enamored with one another like always, made googly eyes on the dance floor. Didn't they realize there were other people in the room?

Charlotte, who'd finally let a few other women have a chance to dance with Joel, had gone off to check the refreshments.

"Aunt Sam," Tessa said, "I'm going to go see if Charlotte needs some help, okay?"

"That's fine, but if I see you out on that floor dancing with some gentleman, I'll hobble out there and pull you off myself. You're too young to participate. Understand?"

She sighed. "Yes, ma'am."

Well, at least she got to wear a new gown.

Tessa wandered down a back hall that led to the room where the buffet was being served. When she heard Mr. Jurgenson's voice, she stopped and listened—as any good Pinkerton agent would do. He and another man were arguing in a room to the side. Despite their raised voices, she could only catch a few words and phrases. Mr. Jurgenson's words were easier to decipher. What did he mean by "You can't take that from them," "I'm done," and "I refuse to pay it anymore"?

He refused to pay what? And who was he talking to?

She walked by the door, and with a quick glance she got a peek at the other man. He was the same man she'd seen Mr. Jurgenson speaking to backstage at the theater the other day, but why was he here?

Neither man noticed her, so she continued on to the banquet room. Charlotte was nowhere in sight, but she found Joel sitting at a table with another woman. Anger surged through her. How dare he find someone else that fast.

She marched up to him. "Dr. Brooks, who is this lady?"

Joel laughed. "Tessa, may I introduce my sister, Mathilda Brooks. Mattie, this is Tessa Gregory, Charlotte's little sister." He motioned to the empty chair. "Tessa, why don't you have a seat?"

She sat down and turned to him. "I'm glad I found you. I need your help."

"With what?"

"Remember when I told you about Mr. Jurgenson paying money to a Mr. K. O.? Since then, I saw Mr. Jurgenson acting suspiciously with a man at the theater, and then I saw that same man here, fighting with Mr. Jurgenson in a back room."

Joel's eyebrows scrunched together. "Fighting? Where?"

"Down that hall." She pointed to the far end of the room. "I heard Mr. Jurgenson say he refused to pay him anymore and something about taking something. Why would he say that?"

Mattie laid her hand on Joel's arm. "Maybe you should go see what's going on, Joel. It does sound suspicious."

"All right. Come on, Tessa. Show me where they were."

After warning Tessa to walk by and point to the room but not go inside, he followed her down the hall. Instead of passing as they'd planned, she stopped in the doorway and turned to him. "They're gone, but I know they were here a few minutes ago."

"I believe you. Let's take a look in the foyer, and if you see him, you can point him out to me."

They found Charlotte speaking with Terrence Ruckman in the foyer. "Joel, Mr. Ruckman was telling me we exceeded our goal. Isn't that wonderful?"

"So where's the money?" Joel's voice was cool.

Terrence shrugged. "Dr. Ostberg is off counting it one more time."

Tessa gasped and clutched Joel's arm. "That's him."

Joel stared at the man coming from the direction Tessa indicated. Why would Knute be involved with Mr. Jurgenson, and why would the theater manager say he refused to pay him anymore? Was Mr. Jurgenson ill?

"Hey, Joel, come to check up on us?" Knute set the money box down on the table. "I've got good news and bad news."

"What's that?" Joel glanced at Charlotte.

"Well, we must've counted wrong the first time. We met the goal, but barely. Our first count was off by about five hundred dollars."

"Five hundred?" Terrence scowled. "That's hard to believe."

"Yes, it is." Joel's stomach fisted. He didn't want to believe the things racing through his mind, but the pieces of the puzzle seemed to be falling into place. The money Terrence claimed was never there—a gift from the charity group headed by Knute's mother. Money that Knute himself had delivered. Then there was the Mr. K. O. listing in the theater's ledger, and now missing funds from tonight's ticket receipts.

All along he'd suspected Terrence of dishonesty, when he should have been thinking of his best friend.

Betrayed. Again.

"Joel, don't look at me that way." Knute held out his hands, palms upward. "Okay, I admit I left the money in the office for a minute with the theater manager and his friend. I figured he was trustworthy, but maybe one of them stole from the box. I don't know. All I know is there are five hundred dollars less than we thought."

Joel's gaze never left Knute's. "Charlotte, take Tessa back into the ballroom, please."

Tessa stomped her foot. "But—"

Charlotte touched her sister's arm. "If Joel thinks you should go, then you should listen to him."

"But I didn't mean this man. I meant *him*." Tessa pointed to the man a couple of yards to the right who stood with that annoying young lady from Charlotte's cooking contest.

"Kelly O'Grady?" Charlotte's voice rose.

Upon hearing his name, the man turned in their direction. He took one look at Tessa's extended finger, grabbed his sister's hand, and bolted down the hotel's hall.

A gasp escaped Charlotte's lips.

"Stay here!" Joel barked as he took off after the man, coattails flapping. Knute and Terrence followed.

Charlotte's gaze swerved to Tessa.

Tessa grinned. "What was that you were saying about listening to him?"

"Oh, come on."

Charlotte covered the hallway in record time. But instead of seeing Joel with Kelly and Kathleen O'Grady in hand, she found him and the other men at the end of the hallway staring back at her. Why weren't they chasing them? Had the O'Gradys gotten away?

The men started silently, methodically searching each of the rooms and closets off the hallway.

"Tessa, go find Lincoln," Charlotte whispered. "Now." She silenced any further protests with a glare. If things continued as she feared, someone was bound to need an attorney. At the least, Lincoln could contact the authorities without making a scene.

Once Tessa was gone, Charlotte stood perfectly still, unable to move, unable to breathe.

"Go," Joel mouthed.

She wanted to, but her legs weren't moving.

One of the doors burst open. With his arm around his sister's neck, Kelly stepped into the hallway. "Back off or I'll hurt her."

"Your own sister?" Charlotte couldn't believe she'd spoken.

He risked a glance at her. She could almost see him considering his options. In one swift motion, he shoved Kathleen at Joel and barreled toward Charlotte's end of the hall.

She plastered herself against the wall. All he wanted was to get out, so she'd not get in his way.

Wait. This man had taken money from the orphans. How could she stand there and let him pass?

In a split second, she made a decision to stop him once and for all.

46

Heart racing, Joel righted the O'Grady girl and passed her to Knute. He had to get to Charlotte.

He rushed toward her. Thank goodness she had the sense to get out of O'Grady's way. Then, without a second thought, she stuck her foot out and tripped the man. Kelly sprawled on the hallway floor.

Charlotte drew her foot back and met Joel's gaze. He'd never been more proud of her—or more frustrated. Hefting Kelly O'Grady to his feet, he yanked one of the man's arms behind his back.

He turned to Charlotte. "Life is always going to be messy with you around, isn't it?"

She bit her lip. "I did warn you."

When Charlotte returned to the ballroom with Joel, Hannah and Tessa hurried to join them.

"Is everything all right?" Hannah asked.

Charlotte smiled and glanced at Joel. "It is now. Lincoln will be back in a few minutes."

Thankfully, Knute and Terrence offered to secure Kelly O'Grady in one of the rooms while Lincoln contacted the authorities. Besides them finding the missing five hundred dollars on Kelly, Mr. Jurgenson admitted that Kelly had been extorting money from him in order to secure "protection" for the theater. In light of the events, he also offered to take a second look at Miss Walker and the missing box office receipts. He told Tessa he would need some office help if it all turned out to be true, so she could have her old job back. He even said he'd put in a good word for Tessa for a role in future plays.

"Joel." Charlotte slipped her arm into the crook of Joel's arm. "What about the money you said was missing from the hospital?"

"Ironically, Terrence said he found it. It had been allocated to the wrong department. An honest bookkeeping error. He apologized, but it didn't look easy for him to do." Joel narrowed his eyes. "Is that my sister dancing with Lewis?"

"Yes, I introduced them."

"You could have introduced him to Cora Pierce."

Charlotte touched his cheek. "Don't scowl so. Lewis is a very sweet man."

Hannah smiled at the two of them. "And he's stepped up to chair the floor admirably in your absence."

"Then I guess I'm not needed at the moment." He turned to Tessa, then Hannah. "If I promise to have your sister back before the last waltz, may I have your permission to steal her away for a while?"

Hannah beamed. "By all means."

Charlotte stiffened. "Don't I get a say?"

"No," Tessa and Hannah answered in unison.

He held out his arm. "Shall we?"

She hesitated for a moment. Tonight they were supposed to be saying goodbye forever, but instead it felt like a beginning. Could she let him take the lead? Was it all a matter of trust—not making backup plans for God, not settling for the easy road, and not refusing Joel's request?

Who knew losing control would be harder for her than for him?

The brass revolving door swished as Charlotte stepped out of the Saint Paul Hotel on the arm of Dr. Joel Brooks. Across from the hotel, the lights in Rice Park twinkled, as if Tessa's Tinker Bell had sprinkled the evening with fairy dust. How different this night was than the day she'd first approached the hotel and the doorman had barred her access.

Joel gave the valet parking operator his number, and in a few minutes his Model T was brought up.

When they reached the Model T, Joel helped her inside, then pulled a dark scarf off the seat. "I know you think I'm controlling, and sometimes I am, but one more time I want you to let me be in control. I promise there's a reason for it. I want to surprise you. Will you let me put this blindfold on you?"

A blindfold? Was he kidding? She met his gaze, and even in the dim light she could see he was sincere. *Lord, please help me make the right decision. I have a feeling this is about a lot more than he's saying.*

She drew in a deep breath and nodded. Once she'd turned her back to him, he carefully covered her eyes with the silk scarf, then knotted it behind her head. "You can't see, right?"

"No, nothing."

"Good." He eased the motorcar onto the street, explaining what was going on every step of the way but refusing to give any details about their destination.

He drove a short distance, parked the Model T, and helped her out. With her hand nestled in the crook of his arm, he led her up a set of stairs and inside a building.

"I smell rubbing alcohol." Her voice echoed in what seemed like a hallway. "Are we in the hospital? Are you going to let me mess up your office again?"

Joel chuckled. "Be patient. You'll know soon enough."

She heard a few snickers as they walked down some sort of corridor. She must look quite odd in a blindfold. Joel stopped and explained he was going to push open a door and hold it for her until she entered. Once they were both inside, he pulled a chain. Even through the blindfold she knew he'd illuminated the area.

He laid his hands on her shoulders. "Okay, are you ready?"

"Yes."

He tugged the blindfold free, and she blinked as her eyes adjusted to the light. Then he stepped back, giving her a good view of the room.

A wall of gas stoves, shelves of dishes and pots and pans, and a long row of tables graced the room. At one end, large windows warmed the otherwise sterile kitchen.

"It's a lovely kitchen, but why are we here?"

The corners of his lips curled. "How would you like to be in charge of the largest kitchen in the city?"

"Here? But Joel, I can't let you talk to Dr. Ancker about me. It could cost you your position."

"Too late. I took a chance and already did." He swept his arm around the room. "And he agreed with me. The hospital's food service needs someone with your expertise. You won't be able to make all of your proposed changes at once, but bit by bit you'll get everything in order. And you can teach nutrition in the nursing school. You'd have a staff of twenty to manage, and you'd be serving nearly six hundred meals a day."

Walking down the row, she ran her hand along the surface of the tables. She could hardly breathe. All this could be her kitchen? "I don't know what to say."

"This is your choice. I won't tell you what to do." He winked at her and moved close enough to take her hands. "And Charlotte, you can say yes to this position and still say no to me."

What now, Lord? What would you have me do? "We're so different, Joel. As I told you before, we're like oil and vinegar."

"I know, but don't oil and vinegar work well on some things?"

She smiled. "They do."

"Listen, Charlotte, I'll admit that you and I can have words in a heartbeat, but I like the way you stir up my life." He cupped her cheek with one hand. "Your warmth, your passion, your intelligence—I love all those things, but most of all I love *you*. I'm sorry about what I did the other day, and I'm sorry I kept things from you and got jealous. I know we have things to work on, but—"

She pressed a finger to his lips. "Yes."

"Yes to the kitchen or to me?"

"To both." Her heart soared as she saw the love in his eyes. God had taken the little oil in her jar and multiplied it tenfold.

Nothing existed in the next few minutes except the two of them. Joel placed his hand on her bare shoulder, then brushed her lips with his. He let the love between them simmer before he deepened the kiss.

She shivered at his touch, marveling at how they'd found everything they'd ever wanted in each other.

At last, Charlotte placed her hand on his chest. Breath ragged, he stilled and pulled back.

She gave him a teasing grin. "You know, we'll still argue."

"I know." Joel drew his hand down the length of her arm and squeezed her hand. "And I'm counting on the pleasure of making up each time we disagree."

Author's Note

While I'm researching, I am often struck by the influential people of the past we know so little about. This book was born after reading about one of those people—American culinary expert and cookbook author Fannie Merritt Farmer. Fannie, who suffered a paralytic stroke or possibly polio, some researchers believe, at the age of sixteen, took up cooking during her recuperative period.

Fannie never lost her limp or finished formal education, but she did enroll in the Boston Cooking School at the height of the domestic science movement. Fannie excelled and eventually became principal of the school in 1891. It was during her time there that she wrote *The Boston Cooking-School Cook Book*, which is still in print today. Her cookbook included very specific, standardized measurements. Before this, cookbooks gave estimates of how much to add—a dash of salt, a pinch of pepper, a teacup of flour, a piece of butter the size of an egg. She was the first to treat cooking and baking as a science.

In 1902 she left the Boston Cooking School to start Miss Farmer's School of Cookery. Besides teaching and lecturing across the United States, she began to focus more on the nutrition and care of the ill. She wrote *Food and Cookery for the Sick and Convalescent*, and her expertise on the subject led her to be one of the first women invited to lecture at Harvard Medical School to prospective doctors and nurses.

What about the chocolate company bearing her name? She had nothing to do with it. They were simply using her well-known name.

Acknowledgments

Special thanks to . . .

My reader friends. With so many things in life vying for your attention and time, I want to thank you for choosing to read *While Love Stirs*. I hope you were blessed while you read as much as I was while I wrote Charlotte's story.

My editors, Andrea Doering and Jessica English. Your excellent eye for detail and your kind encouragement make writing for Revell a joy.

The entire Revell publishing team. From the art department to marketing to sales, you fight for readers like warriors.

Brenda Anderson, Judy Miller, and Shannon Vannatter, for your honest critiques.

Dawn Ford and Sandra Dollen. Thank you for listening and giving me ideas. Life is never boring with you two around.

My family—David, Parker, Caroline, and Emma. You are my greatest blessings.

My Lord and God. Thank you for putting a story in my heart. I pray I can glorify you in all I do.

A history buff, antique collector, and freelance graphic designer, **Lorna Seilstad** is the author of the Lake Manawa Summers series and *When Love Calls*. She draws her setting from her home state of Iowa. A former high school English and journalism teacher, she has won several online writing awards and is a member of American Christian Fiction Writers. Contact her and find out more at www.lornaseilstad.com.